BLOOD PACT

A WARHAMMER 40,000 NOVEL

Gaunt's Ghosts

BLOOD PACT

Dan Abnett

For Dave Taylor

A BLACK LIBRARY PUBLICATION
First published in Great Britain in 2009 by
BL Publishing,
Games Workshop Ltd.,
Willow Road,
Nottingham,
NG7 2WS, UK

10 9 8 7 6 5 4 3 2 1

Cover by David Palumbo.

A CIP record for this book
is available from the British Library.

US ISBN 13: 978 1 84416 692 3

Distributed in the US by Simon & Schuster
1230 Avenue of the Americas, New York, NY 10020, US.

Printed and bound in the US.

See the Black Library on the Internet at
www.blacklibrary.com

Find out more about Games Workshop
and the world of Warhammer 40,000 at
www.games-workshop.com

IT IS THE 41st millennium. For more than a hundred
centuries the Emperor has sat immobile on the Golden
Throne of Earth. He is the master of mankind by the will
of the gods, and master of a million worlds by the might of
his inexhaustible armies. He is a rotting carcass writhing
invisibly with power from the Dark Age of Technology. He
is the Carrion Lord of the Imperium for whom a thousand
souls are sacrificed every day, so that he may never truly die.

YET EVEN IN his deathless state, the Emperor continues his
eternal vigilance. Mighty battlefleets cross the daemon-infested
miasma of the warp, the only route between distant stars,
their way lit by the Astronomican, the psychic
manifestation of the Emperor's will. Vast armies give battle in
his name on uncounted worlds. Greatest amongst his
soldiers are the Adeptus Astartes, the Space Marines,
bio-engineered super-warriors. Their comrades in arms are
legion: the Imperial Guard and countless planetary defence
forces, the ever-vigilant Inquisition and the tech-priests of the
Adeptus Mechanicus to name only a few.
But for all their multitudes, they are barely enough to hold
off the ever-present threat from aliens, heretics,
mutants – and worse.

TO BE A man in such times is to be one amongst untold
billions. It is to live in the cruellest and most bloody regime
imaginable. These are the tales of those times. Forget the
power of technology and science, for so much has been forgotten, never to be re-learned. Forget the promise of progress
and understanding, for in the grim dark future there is only
war. There is no peace amongst the stars, only an eternity of
carnage and slaughter, and the laughter
of thirsting gods.

At length, the beast fell upon a hunter
and devoured him too. But the hunter had
an open knife in his pocket, and
the knife slit the beast's belly
open from inside, and all
of the villagers were spilled out and saved.

*– from the Nihtgane legend of the
hunter and the beast*

*'*A*fter a promising period of advance, Warmaster Macaroth's main battle groups were brought to an unexpected and complete standstill at the frontiers of the Erinyes Group.*

Archon Gaur, the Archenemy overlord, managed to withdraw his forces from the Carcaradon Cluster with sufficient alacrity to construct a robust position of resistance along the Erinyes border.

For the Warmaster, no help was to be had from the Crusade's secondary front. Comprising as it now did the Fifth, Seventh, Ninth and Twelfth Armies, the second battle group was operating trailwards of Macaroth's principal strengths. Despite years of grinding struggle, the second battle group remained unable to dislodge the legions of Magister Anakwanar Sek, Gaur's most capable lieutenant, from the Cabal Systems.

Between them, the Archon and his magister had created a line of defiance that was entirely frustrating both prongs of Macaroth's crusade. An attempt to break the deadlock through the establishment of a third front ended in miserable disaster with the loss of the Second Army, under Marshal Aldo, at Helice.

However, far behind the front line, on Sabbat Worlds long pacified by the Imperial crusade, events were taking place that would have, though few recognised it at the time, fundamental consequences for the future of the campaign.

It was 780.M41, the twenty-fifth year of the Sabbat Worlds Crusade.'

– from *A History of the Later Imperial Crusades*

ONE

The Solace

THE DEAD SEEMED to have a knack of finding their way back to Balhaut.

Such had been the opinion of E. F. Montvelt's uncle, soon after the Famous Victory, and such was the opinion of E. F. Montvelt himself, some fifteen years later. E. F. Montvelt had inherited the opinion from his late uncle, just as he had inherited his uncle's post as wharfinger of Pier Thirty-One, a large and florid nose, and a carton of personal effects which included a medal from the days of the Khulan Wars, a pot of hair tincture and a pornographic chapbook featuring the celebrated musical theatre performer Adele Coro.

The dead found their way back, in almost unimaginable numbers. It was as if the blood that had soaked into Balhaut's soil during the accomplishment of the Famous Victory had, by some alchemical reaction, become a lure for the dead: a temptation, a siren song that called them back across space from the far-flung places where they had fallen. E. F. Montvelt had once read, in one of the cyclopedias packed into the bottom of his uncle's carton of effects, of predatory fish with nostrils so acute that they could detect a drop of blood in an ocean of water, and seek it out. So it was with Balhaut and the dead. Balhaut was the drop of blood, and space the ocean. The dead could smell the place, and the smell drew them back. They had made a pact in blood, after all.

11

Balhaut, so steeped in blood, had become the place of pilgrimage for the dead, and for many, many living souls too; souls whose lives were tied to the fallen. Balhaut was where people came to be buried, if they were dead, or to mourn, if they were not. This was because of the Famous Victory.

Even after fifteen years, one was obliged to pronounce the words with emphatic capital letters, or else refer to it as Slaydo's Glory or the Intrepid Action or the Turning Point, or some equally leatherbound phrase. Balhaut was still counted as the most considerable victory of the crusade so far, and was therefore a touchstone of success, emblematic of all Imperial aspirations and, by extension, a place where the dead could be interred and mourned in the uplifting glow of triumph. The caskets of the officer classes were carried back to Balhaut to be shut in the mausoleums and crypts of the new regimental chapels. The tagged bones of common soldiers were shipped back to fill the ever-increasing plots in the endlessly expanding cemetery fields. The ashes of the nameless dead, the faceless and unidentified, were freighted in kegs like gunpowder to be scattered into the wind at the mass public services held five times a day, every day.

The bereaved came too. Some brought their dead with them, in honour or agony, to see them laid to rest in Balhaut's groaning soil. Others came to pay their respects to the tombs and marble markers of loved ones that had already found their way to Balhaut.

Others, the greatest number of all, came to Balhaut because they did not know the fate or final resting place of the sons and fathers, and brothers and husbands they'd lost, and thus chose Balhaut, with its symbolic value, as a site of memorial. In a decade and a half, Balhaut's chief imports had become corpses and mourners, and its chief businesses, sericulture and monumental masonry.

E. F. Montvelt's business was import and export, and the supervision thereof. He oversaw Pier Thirty-One, a radial spar of the giant orbital platform called Highstation, with a diligence and precision that he hoped would have made his uncle proud.

From his glass-floored office, he could look down on the ships moored in the pier's slipways, and keep track of their comings and goings on a vast hololithic display, projected above him like a canopy of light. His rubricators, at their separate cogitators around the rim of the office, managed the inventories and duties, while vittaling clerks negotiated supply contracts, and fuelling burdens and laytimes were calculated.

All data was routed to him through plugs, but, like his uncle before him, he liked to use his eyes. He liked to watch a vessel in berth, and fret that it was taking too long to unload and clear so that another could take its position and pay a tariff of its own, just as he liked to complain when a slipway remained vacant for more than a day or two. He knew the tugs and lighters by sight, and the flitting cargo-servitors by their paint jobs and codes, and he could identify a pilot boat simply by the style and accomplishment of its attitude manoeuvres.

Above all, he enjoyed the view: from the office, straight down through the glass floor, through the thicket of girderwork and fuelling lines, through the scudding dots that were tugs and handlers, through the open structures and hard shadows of the giant slipways, and the radiation-scorched hulls of the vast ships that sat in them, down through it all into the brilliance of sunlight on slowly-tracking clouds, and the pinsharp clarity of the bright air, and the one hundred and forty-kilometre drop to the blue and grey and brown of Balhaut turning slowly below.

That particular day, the *Gemminger Beroff Wakeshift* was occupying the fourth slip, the *Superluminal Grandee Ulysses* the fifth, and the *Pride of Tarnagua* was beginning its pilot sequence to enter the eighth. The *Relativistic Iterations of Hans Feingolt*, line-lashed into slip seven, had developed an ignition fault that E. F. Montvelt had been told would delay its departure for a minimum of a week. He had already calculated the penalty tariff. The *Eleksander Great Soljor* was due to make shift in less than an hour, provided the charter agents could agree on the demurrage. In slip two, the *Solace*, just arrived, was beginning to discharge its cargo.

E. F. Montvelt hadn't seen the *Solace* for two years. It was Plackett's boat, and Plackett was known for long trailward runs down through Khulan and the Bethan Halo. However, the docket passed to him by the assistant rubricator told E. F. Montvelt that the *Solace* was eight months out of San Velabo, and had come to them from spinward. Plackett had changed his habits. E. F. Montvelt decided he would ask the shipmaster about it when he came on shore. E. F. Montvelt made a point of greeting each master in person. It was an old-fashioned courtesy that his uncle had taught him.

He already suspected the answer Plackett would give him. War changes fortunes and the contours of trade. The crusade had reopened much of the Khan Group and other spinward territories. Plackett had gone where the business was.

Except it wasn't Plackett. E. F. Montvelt looked at the docket again. The *Solace* had changed hands. The name of her new owner was written up as Jonas.

'Jonas,' he read. Several of his clerks raised their heads from their work.

'You spoke, sir?' one called out.

E. F. Montvelt looked up at the junior man.

'Jonas,' he repeated. 'Docket gives the name of the *Solace's* master as Jonas.'

'Which matters because?'

'Jonas!' snapped E. F. Montvelt. 'You know? As in Jonas?'

'I don't catch the significance, sir,' admitted the clerk.

They were all young idiots these days, E. F. Montvelt often reminded himself, too young. None of them knew the traditions. In his uncle's day, everybody had known the name Jonas. It was a joke name, a makeweight. You wrote it on the docket as a placeholder when you didn't know the master's actual name. Sometimes rogue traders would even run under the name to conceal their identity or divert attention away from an affreightment scam.

'Jonas!' E. F. Montvelt repeated. 'As in, Devil Jonas!'

'Oh,' nodded the junior, 'like in the children's story? What was it he had again? A box, was it?'

'A locker,' E. F. Montvelt sighed.

'That's it, a locker,' the junior laughed, 'far away in the depths of space, where he kept the souls of poor, shipwrecked wayfarers.'

The junior chuckled at the notion, and shook his head.

E. F. Montvelt went down to slipway two himself.

He made his way through the crowds thronging the quay. Crew and passengers were flooding off the ship, and all kinds of humanity had come to greet it. There were the slipway crews, the excise men in their bicorn hats, the inspectors from the Interior Guard, vittalers, itinerant peddlers, porters, hucksters; grifters offering guided tours of the battle-fields, luxurious accommodations or surface transfers; scalpers selling permits and ask-no-questions paperwork; and commercial men and private citizens, who had come up to Highstation to greet the ship. E. F. Montvelt shoved his way through the bustle. He could smell armpits and foul breath, the garlic sweat of meat patties on a stove cart, the burnt sugar of a candy vendor, the ozone coming in off the pier's atmospheric pressure fields and, behind all other odours, the oddly soapy, rancid fug that hung upon a slipway when a ship exhaled the recycled air that had been wheezing through its oxygen scrubbers for eight months.

Servitors chugged past him, hauling trains of crates. A tug boat whickered by overhead, its running lights flashing. The *Solace*, a juggernaut of pitted rust and seared void plating, sat up tall in the slip. Service crews were already at work, scaling her carbonised flanks like mountaineers on a rockface. E. F. Montvelt heard the *tunk-tunk* of magnetised footsteps as servitors crossed the hull perpendicular to him. He leaned over the rail, down into the shadow of the slipway drop. He saw the airgates extended and connected, and the firework sputter of welding teams. Below the gloom of the slip's shadow, the dazzling white clouds of Balhaut crawled past.

E. F. Montvelt opened his data-slate and took another look at the ship's paperwork. The *Solace*, it came as no surprise, was bearing the dead. Amongst the goods on its bill of lading were 'Fifty mortuary containers, fully certificated, transported for the purpose of internment at Balhaut'. Further fine print revealed that each container held twenty human cadavers or partial cadavers, individually secured in closed caskets. They were men of the 250th Boruna Rifles, a native Balhaut regiment, and casualties of Aldo's tragic failure on Helice. They were Balhaut lads, coming home.

Accompanying parties of mourners from San Velabo were listed on the passenger manifest. High-borns, some of them, by the look of the titles and honorifics, making the grand tour to Balhaut in a formal display of duty and respect. E. F. Montvelt straightened his collar, and brushed the sleeves of his coat. Courtesy, always courtesy.

The great hold jaws of the *Solace* were beginning to gape. Cantilevered metal tongues, cargo ramps and hinged bridgeways were extending to link the lamp-lit caverns of the hold spaces with the slipway dock. Bulk servitors were hoisting down the first of the containers. E. F. Montvelt saw more passengers and members of the crew coming down the nearest gangway bridge.

He saw two widows, arm-in-arm, with a single, twin-shafted mourning parasol held above their veiled heads. Behind them came three liveried servants bearing a rosewood chest, and a crewman in oily pressure gear draped with a roll of heavy cable. After them, a tired-looking colonel with an empty sleeve limped down the gangway beside his attentive adjutant, followed by a tall, athletic man in a long coat of beige leather. The man's shaved head was sculptural and sharp-featured, as if it had been ergonomically designed. The balance of the skull seemed rather off: a cunning, clean-enough face, but a compact and streamlined cranium that seemed a little too small to match it. The man carried himself with a straight neck and a raised head that spoke of military formality.

Then E. F. Montvelt saw the other widow. She was dressed in long weeds of black silk, and carried a sable fan and a purple handkerchief. The skirts of her dress, silk and crepe layered, rustled as she moved. Her hair, white gold, was pinned up, and from it draped a veil of black gauze so fine it hung like smoke. He could not see her face, but he could see the pale, slender rise of her neck. The nape seemed indecent, like wilful nudity.

E. F. Montvelt walked towards the passengers discharging onto the dockside.

'Master Jonas?' he inquired. 'Master Jonas?'

No one seemed bothered to acknowledge him.

'Where's your master?' he asked the crewman with the cable. The man shrugged indifferently. Annoyed at his manner, E. F. Montvelt tapped the badges and buttons of guild, of rank and of Munitorum service that he wore on the left breast of his juniper coat.

'You're on my shore now!' he told the listless fellow.

'And glad of it,' the man answered, shifting the heavy coil to his other shoulder.

'Where is the master of this vessel?' E. F. Montvelt asked.

'The lady there, she asked him to check upon her cargoes personal,' the man replied, nodding towards the widow with the scandalous nape.

'Mamzel?' E. F. Montvelt called as he approached her. 'Begging your pardon, but would you know where the shipmaster is to be found?'

'Oh dear, he is dead,' the lady answered. Her voice was small, but perfectly clear, and rounded with a distant accent. There was a wobble to it too, as if she was fighting to contain her emotions.

'He is dead?'

'Indeed, most terribly,' she agreed, with another catch in her voice.

'But how?' E. F. Montvelt asked.

'Why, we were obliged to murder him when he would not cooperate with us,' she said. E. F. Montvelt could not see her face through the fine mesh of the veil, but he felt her eyes fix upon him, registering his expression of disquiet.

'What did you say, mamzel?' he asked.

'I cannot lie,' said the veil. 'I am sorry for it.'

'Mamzel,' said E. F. Montvelt, concerned by the rising strength of the catch in her voice, 'are you quite well?'

'No, no,' she said. 'I cannot speak a lie. Upon my soul, it is my great burden. I am compelled to tell each and every truth, even the dirty ones.'

'Perhaps you should sit down?' E. F. Montvelt suggested.

'My dear sister, have you over-wrought yourself again?'

The tall man in the long, beige coat appeared at the widow's side, and was placing a solicitous hand on her sleeve. His hands were gloved.

'This gentleman asked me about the shipmaster,' the lady said.

The man looked at E. F. Montvelt. Like the widow, his voice was spiced by a distant accent.

'My apologies,' he said. 'My sister is rather troubled, and you must excuse her. Grief has terribly affected her mind.'

'I am sorry to hear it,' E. F. Montvelt responded earnestly. 'It was not my intention to distress her.'

'I did not for a moment presume it was, sir,' the man said. He was holding his sister's arm quite tightly, as if she might otherwise slip her lines and fly away.

'It is true, though,' the lady said. 'I cannot tell any lies. Not ever, anymore. It is quite beyond me to do so. This is the price I must pay. If I desire the truth, I must have all truths, so that only truth can spill out of my mouth and—'

'Hush now, sister,' the man said, 'you will make yourself ill. Let me take you to a quiet place where you can gather your wits.' He glanced at E. F. Montvelt. 'Sir?'

'There is a lounge in the disembarkation hall, there at the end of the slipway,' said E. F. Montvelt, pointing.

'You're most kind,' the man said. 'The Lady Eyl appreciates your understanding. She does not know what she says.'

'Well, that is apparent,' said E. F. Montvelt. 'I asked the whereabouts of the shipmaster, and she told me plainly that she had murdered him.' He laughed. The man did not.

'It is because I am witched!' the widow protested.

'The shipmaster went to hold sixteen aft, to attend to our baggage,' the man said. 'I believe you will find him there.'

'I'm obliged to you,' said Montvelt.

The man took his sister away. Montvelt went up the gangway and entered the ship. He cued the manifest list back onto the screen of his data-slate and scrolled down it. Lady Eyl. There she was, Lady Ulrike Serepa fon Eyl, of San Velabo, travelling with her brother Baltasar Eyl and a household party.

Still rather discomfited by his encounter with the damaged Lady Eyl, E. F. Montvelt descended into the bowels of the ancient packet ship. He wondered who she had lost. A husband, he felt. Perhaps another brother. Such things she had said. For a mind to be that torn and frayed by grief, well, it did not bear thinking about. The dead came back to Balhaut, and brought their ghosts with them, but the truly frightening apparitions were the souls destroyed by loss.

The underdecks of the *Solace* were quiet: dark halls, dark companion-ways, a current of heat against his face, dissipating from the drive vents, the bad odour of air breathed too many times, the sounds of hull fabric creaking and settling as commonplace orbital gravity replaced the distorting insanity of the Empyrean.

Caged lamps glowed soft yellow, their once-white shades stained brown by age. Oily condensation dripped from the pipes of the climate systems running along the ceiling. The *Solace* was clicking and settling and easing her bones, like the arthritic grand dame she was. E. F. Montvelt enjoyed the smells and sounds of a thoroughbred packet ship. He'd crewed one, the *Ganymede Eleison*, in his youth, serving three years as junior purser before his uncle's influence secured him a shore-job at Highstation. The hollow echoes of footsteps on deck grilles, the low stoops of the bulkhead hatches, the scents of priming paint and grease and scrubbed air brought it all back.

Without needing to check the doorframe code markers, for the *Solace's* layout matched the deck plan of all ships of her class, E. F. Montvelt found hold sixteen aft.

The air inside was full of vapour. The hold's jaws were open, so that sunlight shone in, and a magnificent open drop down to ferociously white and snowy clouds was revealed through the cage floor of the stowage space. He stepped out onto the cage floor, Balhaut turning below him, and called out the shipmaster's name.

No one answered.

Bulk containers were lashed along the cage, ready to be discharged by the servitor-handlers. Their certificates had been pasted to them, and their seals were intact. E. F. Montvelt called the shipmaster's name again.

He took out his scanning wand, and flashed the nearest container to check that its certificate code matched the number on his dockets.

It did, but there was something odd. The wand had registered a temperature blip.

He put his hand against the container's side, and then drew it away again sharply.

'Something wrong?' asked the man in the beige coat. He came down through the steam onto the cage floor, and approached the wharfinger.

'These containers,' E. F. Montvelt replied. 'They are not what they seem, sir.'

'How so?'

'Trace heat,' the wharfinger replied. 'There is a mechanism here. These are not containers.' He showed Baltasar Eyl the dial of his wand. 'You see?'

'I do.'

'Test for yourself.'

The man pressed his gloved hand against the container's side.

'No, sir, take off your glove and do it,' said E. F. Montvelt.

Baltasar Eyl peeled off his right glove. The hand that was revealed was so terribly marked by old scars that the sight of it made E. F. Montvelt baulk. Eyl saw his reaction.

'I keep them covered, for the most part,' he explained. 'I know how they look. They proclaim the pact I have made with my master.' The wharfinger stared at him, wide-eyed. Eyl smiled.

'I don't expect you to understand. Listen to me, I gab like my sister. The isolation of the voyage has made me talkative. I am betraying secrets.'

E. F. Montvelt took a step or two back.

'I have seen nothing,' he said. 'Truly, sir, I have heard nothing.'

'Why do you say that to me?' asked Eyl.

'Because I fear that otherwise you are going to be obliged to kill me,' said E. F. Montvelt.

'I think I might,' said Eyl. 'Sincerely, I mean nothing by it.'

'Please, sir,' said the wharfinger, backing away.

'A MOST DREADFUL thing!' cried Lady Eyl, running along the slipway quay. 'A most terrible accident! He fell. He just fell! Please come! There has been the most awful occurrence!'

E. F. MONTVELT dropped away from the open hold jaws of the *Solace*. Arms spread wide, he descended into air and bright cloud. It was a long way down.

He was approaching terminal velocity, already dead. The atmosphere began to ablate him, until a tail of fire was racing out behind him, the sort of shooting star upon which one might make a wish.

He fell towards the planet. He and his late uncle had been quite correct.

The dead did seem to have a knack of finding their way back to Balhaut.

TWO

Back to Balhaut

'Do you remember Vergule?' asked Blenner, over lunch at the Mithredates Club.

'Vergil?' Gaunt replied. 'Auguste Vergil? The Oudinot staffer?'

'No, old man,' Blenner laughed. 'Ver-*gule*. Salman Vergule. Urdeshi fellow, served with the 42nd. We were in the field alongside him at Serpsika.'

'You maybe,' said Gaunt. 'I was never at Serpsika. You're thinking of somebody else.'

'Am I?' asked Blenner, with a touch of concern.

Across the table, Zettsman chuckled at them.

'You're like an old married couple, you pair,' he said. He finished clipping the end of a fine, Khulan-leaf cigar, and lit it with a long, black match.

'Are we indeed?' replied Blenner.

'I'm not sure which one of us should be more offended,' said Gaunt.

'Neither am I,' Blenner agreed.

'You witter on so,' remarked Hargiter, sipping caffeine from a little, heavy-bottomed glass.

'I've never wittered in my life,' said Gaunt.

Hargiter caught the look, and shrugged.

'Well, maybe not. But he does,' he said, gesturing at Blenner.

'I resemble that remark!' returned Blenner.

'So what were you saying about this Vergule fellow?' asked Edur.

Blenner tapped the top sheet of the broadside gazette he had been reading. 'It turns out he's been here all this while. Arrived a year ago, about the same time you did, 'Bram.'

'Wait,' said Gaunt, putting down the sugar tongs. 'This Vergule, was he a tall fellow with a hangdog expression?'

'That's the one,' said Blenner.

'Yes, I do remember him. He was at Phantine, I believe. Anyway, if he's here, I haven't seen him around.'

'You wouldn't have done,' replied Blenner. 'It says here he's entirely dead. His body's been in the Urdesh regimental chapel for twelve months.'

'What did he die of?' asked Zettsman.

'Oh, you know, war,' said Blenner.

'Where?' asked Gaunt.

'It doesn't say,' said Blenner, peering at the broadside. 'Oh, wait, it does. Morlond.'

'Not the only good soul lost there,' remarked Edur grimly.

Blenner looked at Gaunt. 'I was thinking, we should go and pay our respects. This afternoon, perhaps?'

'I've got things to do, Vay.'

Vaynom Blenner sighed. 'Tomorrow morning then? Come on, old man, we ought to toddle over there and apologise to him for not dropping by sooner. It's the decent thing.'

'I suppose,' said Gaunt.

The majordomo, in crimson, black and gold, hovered beside the table where the five Imperial commissars were sitting.

'Will there be anything else, sirs?' he asked.

Gaunt shook his head. 'Just bring me the tab to sign, would you?'

The major domo nodded. Blenner looked crestfallen.

'I was considering another helping of fruit tart,' he announced plaintively.

'You'll end up *looking* like a fruit tart,' said Edur.

'Steady, old man!' Blenner replied. He looked hurt. He patted the orange Commissariat sash that was stretched around his ample stomach. 'Solid muscle, that. Solid.'

'Edur's right,' said Gaunt, taking a stylus from the majordomo to sign the bill. 'When I came back from Gereon the first time, my duty breeches hung off me like a tent. The other morning – and they're the same pair, mind – I realised I had begun to fasten them on the third button. I used to have a washboard stomach.'

'Some of us still do, old man,' said Blenner.

'Wash-*house*, more like,' muttered Hargiter.

'Oi!' snorted Blenner. The others laughed.

'It's the passage of time,' said Blenner. 'That's what I'm saying. You came back from Gereon in '76, Ibram. That's knocking on five years ago. Face facts. We're all getting old.'

'Speak for yourself!' the other four men chorused. There was more laughter.

Gaunt told the majordomo to have his car brought around. He waited for Blenner in the atrium, out of courtesy. His oldest friend had disappeared into the club's cloakroom, complaining about a missing glove.

The atrium's marble columns had been draped in swathes of mourning crepe, and white lilies had been set in the onyx jardinières. At the far end of the hall, under the dished window that looked out across the street and north towards the Oligarchy Gate, two craftsmen in overalls were working on the last phase of restoration to the inlaid murals. The night manager of the Mithredates had told Gaunt the work was expected to be finished in another eighteen months. It had taken fifteen years to get that far. The club had been hit by a tank round in the final hours of the war, and the intricate murals had been badly damaged.

Gaunt wondered if there might not be better things to spend fifteen years rebuilding.

'So what's on your plate for the rest of the day?' asked Zettsman, buttoning up his stormcoat as he walked over.

'I might spend a few hours with the Kapaj,' Gaunt replied.

'You rate them?'

'They're decent enough,' Gaunt answered. 'I'd rather spend time with my own mob, but the Kapaj need to be whipped into shape, and Section is very keen on this mentoring role.'

'Tell me about it,' Zettsman replied. 'I've been given a group of cadets and I'm expected to get them through their SP31s. They're appalling. Throne help me, they manage to make Blenner look like he operates at an acceptable level of competence.'

Gaunt laughed, but it rankled. Lately, Blenner had been taking too many jibes below the waterline.

'I don't know why you put up with him,' said Zettsman.

'Who?'

'Blenner, of course.'

Gaunt paused.

'We were at schola progenium together,' he said. 'Vaynom has survived longer than anyone else I've known. I have to give him some credit for that.'

'I suppose,' replied Zettsman. 'And he was right, of course, about time rolling on. None of us are getting any younger. It must be strange for you especially.'

'What must?' Gaunt asked.

'Well, we've all done our bit over the years, and we've all had our moments, but your track record puts most of us to shame. If I'd done half the things you've done, I'd have taken a marshal's baton and a seat at high command years ago.'

'Not my style.'

'Oh, and this is? Like I said, it must be very strange for you, this easy life, these leisurely meals, the evenings at the club. It must be odd to accept that your active service is done, and this is the end of it, mentoring new-founds and growing a paunch while you fly a desk towards semi-retirement.'

'WHAT'S THE MATTER?' Blenner asked, catching up with Gaunt. He had found the elusive glove.

'Nothing.'

'Don't give me that, Ibram. There's a look on your face. Zettsman was here, just a moment ago. I saw him walking away. What did he say to you?'

'Nothing,' said Gaunt, again.

'I'll wrestle you to the ground, don't think I won't.'

Gaunt looked at Blenner. Blenner still hadn't quite got used to the flash in his old friend's new eyes.

'Zettsman just said something,' Gaunt replied. 'He didn't mean anything by it. It was just something I hadn't really thought of before.'

'Well, what?' asked Blenner. 'That you owe your entire career to my inspirational example?'

'That part obviously came as a shock,' said Gaunt. He smiled, but there was frost on it. 'No, he just assumed that I was done. Didn't give it a second thought. There was no malice meant. He just took for granted the idea that I'd done my part, and that my front-line career was over.'

'Ah,' said Blenner.

'I have always assumed that, in due course, the routing order will come through, and I'll take the First and Only back to the line. Crusade main front, secondary front, I don't care. It never occurred to me it would be any other way.'

'You worry too much,' said Blenner.

'I will get posted again, won't I?'

'You worry too much.'

'But–'

'Look, old man,' said Blenner, patting Gaunt on the sleeve, 'you were on the line a bloody long time. You and the Ghosts, how long was it?'

'From the Founding? Twelve years.'

'Twelve bloody years, old man! Twelve bloody years without rotation out of the line! Most regimental commanders would have been sending formal complaints to the top of the chain!'

'I'd thought about it.'

'And thank goodness they rotated you out before you had to.'

'It's been two years since Jago, Vay.'

'You needed that long to recover, you old devil. The bastards nearly murdered you.'

Gaunt shrugged.

'We're rested now,' he said. 'We've come all this way back to Balhaut, to a world I never expected to see again, and we've sat around for a year, getting fat and bored and out of shape, and none of those things have filled me with anxiety, because I've been expecting the routing order any day.'

'It'll come,' said Blenner.

'Will it?'

'Yes.'

'They'll send me back?'

'Throne's sake, Ibram, you're the bloody poster boy for ridiculous Imperial heroism. They won't be able to do without you at the front line for much longer.'

Gaunt nodded.

'If you ask me,' said Blenner, heading for the door, 'I don't know why you're in such a bloody rush.'

OUTSIDE, THERE WAS a winter chill as hard as Gaunt's mood. There was a touch of pink in the sky, and the light had turned the cityscape a pale, floury white. They stood on the steps and pulled on their gloves, their breath fuming.

'I'm sorry for the delay, sirs,' said the doorman. Gaunt's staff car had yet to appear. Hargiter was down on the pavement, waiting for his own limousine to arrive from the parking garage. They joined him.

Hargiter was studying the skyline. So many of the spires and domes were still clad in scaffolding and canvas lids. Like a gap-toothed smile, there were pieces missing.

'You were here, weren't you?' Hargiter asked.

'Oh, it was all very different then,' said Blenner. 'I remember the Tower of the Plutocrat–'

'You weren't here, Vay,' said Gaunt. 'You and the Greygorians were on Hisk.'

'Fair play,' pouted Blenner. 'If you had let me finish, I was going to say "I remember the Tower of the Plutocrat from the many mezzotints and engravings I have seen". Yes, Ibram was here. In fact, I believe he's the principal reason there isn't a Tower of the Plutocrat any more.'

'I doubt you recognise the place,' said Hargiter. 'It took such a pounding, there can't be much left that was standing when you were here.'

'No,' Gaunt agreed. 'Time passes and things change. You tend to see things with different eyes.'

'Of course, in his case,' said Blenner, 'he means that literally.'

THREE

Captain Daur and the Jack of Cups

HE WALKED TO the end of Selwire Street and then, on a drafty corner, checked the directions that had been written on the scrap of paper. Daylight was bleeding away fast, and it felt as if it was taking the heat with it. He wondered if there was going to be snow. He wondered if it was going to be as heavy as the trouble he was getting into.

Left at the corner, the instructions read, along an underwalk, and then across a small court hidden behind a merchant's townhouse and a busy garmentfab loft. Follow the six steps down from street level, the ones with a black iron handrail ending in a gryphon's beak. There'll be a red door, the colour of a victory medal's ribbon.

Also, he thought, the colour that tended to edge the pages of a Commissariat charge-sheet.

There was no point thinking like that. He'd come too far to turn back. He went down the steps, and pressed the ivory button of the bell. He waited. The court above was lit by the lights of the garmentfab loft. They were working late. He could hear the clatter of stitching machines and thread-runners, like distant stub-fire.

The door opened, and a handsome woman in a green dress looked out at him. She seemed faintly amused, as if someone he couldn't see had told her something funny just before she'd opened the door.

'Captain,' she said.

'Hello,' he replied.

'I take it you haven't rung the wrong bell by mistake?'

'Not if this is Zolunder's,' he said.

'It doesn't say so above the door,' she replied, 'but it is. You'll need two things to get in.'

He showed her the fat roll of bills that had been sitting like a hot coal in his trouser pocket.

'That's one,' she said. 'The other's a name.'

'Daur,' said Ban Daur.

THE HOSTESS TOOK him along a chilly corridor and downstairs into the main area of the parlour. The air smelled of quality spice from the burners, and music was provided by the cantor-finches fluttering and trilling in their delicate, suspended cages. Zolunder's was several levels removed from the common gaming dens and rowdy-houses where enlisted men lost their pay. It was demure and exclusive, catering for officers and aristocrats.

Three games were in progress around the broad, lacquer-work tables arranged in bays around the room. Attentive girls in long gowns drifted about with trays of drinks.

'Why did you need my name?' Daur asked the hostess, but he knew why. Zolunder's had an illegal hardwire link to the Munitorum database, which they used to check identities. To get past the red door and the hostess in green, you had to be who you said you were. Deception did not go down at all well.

'Security,' she replied.

She took him to the bar. He was amused to see that it was made of a single, polished section of nalwood. Now was that a good omen or a bad one?

'What's amusing you?' she asked.

'Nothing.'

'You haven't done this before, have you?' she asked.

'No, it's not really my speed,' he said.

'Then why?' she asked

Daur shrugged. 'I need to make a little money.'

'You've got a little money in your pocket.'

'A little more.'

'You're in trouble?'

'Isn't everyone?' he asked.

The hostess frowned. It was a decent answer. Pretty much everyone she saw through the red door was in trouble, even if that trouble was just an over-fondness for cards. She always felt sorry for the punters who came along with desperate dreams of turning a little into a lot. It never happened.

She always felt especially sorry for the men, like the nice-looking captain before her, who seemed honest and good-hearted, but who were about to ruin their good character forever.

'I'll send someone over,' she said.

'Why?' he asked.

'To keep you company until a space opens at a table,' she replied.

'I thought you were keeping me company?' he said.

She laughed.

'You can't afford me, captain,' she said.

He blushed immediately.

'I didn't mean–' he began.

She was genuinely surprised by the offence he imagined had been taken.

'I'll send someone over,' she said.

THE HOSTESS LEFT Daur at the bar and went away through a curtain into the private rooms. Urbano was watching the bar area on a monitor. He seemed in a particularly foul mood.

'What's up with this one, Elodie?' he asked, gesturing at the screen image of Daur. 'He's got a fidget I don't like.'

'Well, he's got a stake in his pocket that you will,' she replied. 'He's a proper gentleman, and as pure as the driven. You can take him for everything. I'm sure you'll enjoy that.'

'How much has he got?' Urbano asked. He was daintily cleaning his teeth with a stainless steel pick. Elodie had worked for Cyrus Urbano for eight years, and she still could not reconcile his gentile mannerisms with the frenzied brutality she knew he was capable of.

'I didn't take it and count it,' she replied snidely, 'but I'd say a thousand at least.'

Urbano whistled. 'Where did a man like that get a thousand?'

'Maybe he borrowed it from Guard payroll. That might explain his nerves.'

'The wirelink says he's an officer in the Tanith First,' said Urbano, reading off the data-log.

'He's obviously got problems on his shoulders,' said Elodie. 'That makes him desperate, which makes him careless.' She looked around at the girls waiting on the couches.

'I need someone to charm him,' she said. Two or three of her regulars were about to raise their hands.

'Did you say he was Tanith?' asked the new girl.

'That's right,' said Elodie.

The girl got up.

'I'll take this one,' she said.

'That's right, you're from the dead world too, aren't you?' asked Elodie.

The girl nodded. She was good-looking, with the dark hair and pale skin of the Tanith. She'd only been with them two nights, on probation still, and she hadn't yet hosted a customer.

'Send someone with a bit more experience,' Urbano told Elodie.

'No, let's give her a chance. The Tanith connection's too good to miss out on. This Captain Daur needs careful handling if he's going to owe the house.'

Urbano shrugged his heavy shoulders. He looked over at the new girl and nodded.

'Off you go then,' Elodie told her. The new girl smiled, checked her reflection in the mirror, straightened her red silk gown, and headed for the exit.

'Just remember,' Elodie called after her. The new girl stopped and looked back.

'Try not to screw it up, Banda,' Elodie said.

The new girl smiled.

'I'll do my best,' she said.

'WE SHOULD GET a drink,' she said.

Daur looked up. He'd been watching the cantor-finches in the nearest cage.

'I wanted to keep my head straight,' he said.

'You here to play?' she asked, sitting down next to him, and draping the skirts of her red silk dress over her legs elegantly.

'Yes,' he said.

'Then you're here to have a good time,' she said. 'We'll have a drink, and then perhaps another.' She made a two-fingered gesture at the drinks servitor. 'Sacra,' she said.

'That's hard stuff,' said Daur.

'You don't drink sacra?'

She leaned close to him, and sniffed him.

'You're not Tanith at all, are you?' she asked.

'Verghast,' he said. 'The regiments amalgamated after the siege of Vervunhive, and it was restructured–'

The girl in the red dress made her hand mimic a chattering mouth.

'Lots of words, none of them interesting,' she said. 'What's your name, Verghast?'

'Ban. Ban Daur.'

'Ban, eh? Well, I'm Ban-da.'

'Really? Do you know, there's a Tanith girl in the First called Jessi Banda. She looks just like you.'

'Does she?' asked Banda. 'And I thought I was a one-off.'

'Well,' said Daur, 'she's quite beautiful too.'

Banda smiled. 'There, you see. Mouth moving, better words coming out. That was almost charming.'

'Oh, I can be,' said Daur.

'When?' she asked.

The servitor put two small glasses of sacra in front of them.

'I'll warn you when it's going to happen again,' he said.

They clinked glasses.

'You're nervous,' she said quietly.

'This is all very new to me,' he said.

'Then why come here?'

'I didn't have much choice.'

'Under pressure to perform are we?' she asked.

'Something like that.'

'Let me guess,' she said. 'There's an evil superior officer, and you're horribly beholden to him, in debt somehow. He's sent you here tonight to raise funds to get him off your back, because you're such a butter-wouldn't-melt innocent that you'll take the house. You're his secret weapon.'

Daur turned pale.

'Don't,' he shuddered.

'What's the matter?'

'Why did you say that?'

'I was just joking. Throne, did I hit a little too close to home?'

Daur took another sip of his drink.

'What's his name?' she asked.

'Rawne,' he replied.

'Are you his secret weapon?'

'How can I be if you've already seen through me?'

She shrugged. She saw Elodie signal from the curtain.

'There's a seat opening,' she told Daur. 'Are you feeling lucky?'

* * *

URBANO WATCHED THE monitor as the Tanith captain took his place at one of the lacquer-work tables. The girl in the red dress stood at his side, draping an over-familiar arm across his shoulder.

'This is going to be painful,' he smiled. 'The ninker's terrified. Way out of his comfort zone. Easy meat.'

'Either that,' said Elodie, 'or the best hustler you've ever seen. He's almost too good to be true.'

'He's the genuine article,' Urbano scoffed. 'It's right there on the data-log. We need to make him reckless. Let him play a couple of hands, and then take twenty thousand out of the safe and move it to the dealer's drawer. Make sure he sees it. Make sure his mouth waters. I want his safety catches to flip all the way off.'

THE CARDS WERE tall and hand-coloured. They flowed from the dealer's hands like punch-tokens from a cogitator. There was a charged atmosphere around the table.

Rawne had taught Daur the rudiments of the game, a trick-and-trade variety called Suicide Kings, but he was hardly an expert. With each hand, it was a constant struggle to remember the basic combination hierarchy and the correct moments to discard, let alone the tips he'd been given. Three of a kind sweeps two pairs, and quads sweep everything except the dynasties. The odds of a straight or regal dynasty are 649,739 to 1, so a lousy player always chases hands that are statistically unlikely. The deuce of swords reverses the march, the sequence of play, and allows for out-of-turn wagers. The king of cups, Blue Sejanus as he is called, is wild when the march is clockwise, and the ace of swords, its single pip bloated and enlarged to incorporate the tax-paid duty stamp, is wild counter-clock. Base your wagers on a calculation of your available outs. Certain court cards are magic kickers that could break tied hands.

So much to remember. Daur focused on the two chief rules. Limp, to stay in as long as possible, but make them aware of just how much you have in your pocket.

He played the minimal bets on every hand, but between deals, or when the march switched, he took out his roll of bills and pretended to count them under the edge of the table. He played through four hands, won nothing, and lost the minimum.

'For Throne's sake, have a real bid, why don't you?' the Tanith girl whispered into his ear.

Just before the fifth hand was dealt, the hostess in green came over to the table with a flat leather case. She unlocked the wooden drawer under the tabletop where the dealer was standing, and slid it out. There was cash in its wooden tray already, about fifteen hundred in mixed bills. She opened the case and loaded the tray with twenty thousand in crisp bricks of currency. Daur watched the whole process, his blink-rate rising.

'Could I get a drink?' he asked the Tanith girl. 'My mouth's a little dry.'

'Of course,' she said, and left the table.

The hostess closed the drawer and went away with the case. The fifth hand came out. Daur had a pair of sevens. He began to bid with a little more vigour.

The Tanith girl came back, and put his drink on the table beside his wrist.

'All done,' she whispered in his ear. She looked at the table. 'Getting a little bolder?' she teased. The bidding went around the table again. It came down to Daur and another player, a sour-looking Navy officer, who called him.

They each had a pair sevens. The Navy man sniffed and turned his kicker. It was a ten of swords.

Daur flipped his own kicker.

The jack of cups.

The dealer swept the pot across to Daur. He'd just taken over a hundred on a single hand.

'I'm beginning to like you,' chuckled the Tanith girl, stroking his ear.

There was a sudden crash. It was the sort of crash that a door the colour of a victory medal's ribbon would make if it got kicked in. There was a commotion, and some shouting. Players jumped up from the tables, cards knocked askew. Four men in battledress burst into the parlour aiming service pistols. Some of the players and girls tried to leave, but the soldiers had all the exits blocked.

'What the hell is this?' Urbano demanded, storming out from the private areas. Elodie shrank back. She hoped her boss would have the sense not to kick off.

'Looks like an illegal game to me,' replied the Imperial commissar who wandered into the room through the soldiers aiming the pistols.

'Oh, come on!' said Urbano. 'You know this is a waste of your time.'

The commissar looked around. 'Huh. This is the famous Zolunder's, eh? You've no idea how long the Commissariat has been trying to close you down.'

He looked at Urbano. 'Nice place. I mean, tasteful. You've got a pattern on your carpet that's not the consequence of vomit. That's rare, by gambling parlour standards.'

'You're making a mistake, commissar…'

'Hark,' replied the commissar.

'Well, Commissar Hark,' said Urbano, 'you should know that the Commissariat has tried this before, to no avail.'

'Oh, I know how you cover yourself,' said the commissar. 'The oh-so-expensive lawyers you keep on retainer throw out any raid as an illegal search, and you keep your considerable cash supplies locked up in a safe, knowing that we can only confiscate monies in game circulation. So we take a few hundred off your tables, stick you with a nuisance fine for unlicensed gaming, and go away with our tails between our legs.'

The commissar smiled at Urbano. 'The thing is, pal, we're not here to mount another pointless raid on Zolunder's tonight. But you're going to wish we were.'

'What are you talking about?' growled Urbano. 'Just give me the fine notice and get out.'

The commissar placed his hand on Daur's shoulder. Daur kept staring at the cards on the table, but he shivered.

'Hello, Daur.'

'Sir,' Daur whispered.

The commissar looked at Urbano. 'We're here for Captain Daur.'

'What's he done?' asked Urbano.

'Not your business, but it wasn't pretty,' said the commissar. 'And it was enough to send him here tonight in a desperate attempt to raise enough cash for a ticket off-world. Let's have him, boys.'

The soldiers closed in around Daur and got him to his feet. One of them cuffed him and began to lead him away.

'Let him be!' the Tanith girl snapped.

'Bring her too,' the commissar told his men. 'Let's see what she knows about his activities.'

The Tanith girl began to scream and shout as another of the soldiers manhandled her off the premises.

The commissar looked back at Urbano.

'One last piece of bad news for you,' he said. 'We've just apprehended a deserter in flight. That'll make felony two, and it means we can seize all assets involved in said commission.'

'You've got to be kidding me,' Urbano breathed, his eyes wide with rage.

The commissar shook his head sweetly. His two remaining men cleared the table of all cash, emptied the pockets of the other players, and then opened the table drawer and removed the fat, crisp bricks of notes that Elodie had put in the tray. They dumped the takings into three canvas evidence bags.

'Do you want a receipt?' asked the commissar.

'Get out,' said Urbano.

OUTSIDE, IT HAD begun to snow. The garmentfab had closed for the night and its windows were dark. The night sky over the ancient city was a threatening maroon haze. The men bundled Daur and the Tanith girl into the back of a cargo-8 and clambered aboard. The truck started up, and rolled down out of the court onto the empty street.

In the back of the truck, the commissar sat down on the bench facing Daur and the girl. He weighed the evidence sacks in his hands.

'About twenty-two, twenty-three thousand,' he said.

Daur stared back at him.

'Commissar Hark' he smiled. 'Nice work, captain.'

'Thanks,' replied Daur. 'You look a complete gimp in that commissar suit, by the way.'

Rawne took off the commissar's cap.

'Well, it did the trick,' he said.

'I'll say,' chuckled Meryn, sitting back and unbuttoning the collar of his battledress.

'Can I hold the stash?' Banda asked Rawne. 'Just hold it, for a moment?'

Rawne laughed and tossed her the evidence sacks.

She opened the canvas pouches and sniffed.

'We'll make a career criminal out of you yet, Daur,' said Meryn.

'This was strictly a one-time thing, Meryn,' Daur replied.

'Oh, they all say that,' said Varl. 'They absolutely all say that.'

The truck began to slow down. Rawne leaned over and rapped his fist against the partition.

'Leyr? Cant? Why are we slowing down?' he called.

'Looks like the road's shut, boss,' Leyr's voice came back from the cab. 'We're going to go left instead.'

The truck swung around.

'As I was saying,' said Varl, waggling a cheeky finger at Daur. 'You have the poise of a master conman.'

Daur was about to respond when the truck slammed to a halt.

'What the feth?' asked Varl. 'What the feth's the matter, Cant?' he shouted through the partition into the cab.

'Roadblock!' Trooper Cant's voice answered.

'What?'

'It's only the fething Commissariat!' they heard Cant yell. 'The real one, I mean!'

Rawne looked at Meryn, Varl, Banda and Daur.

'Oh, not good,' said Varl.

'Yeah,' said Rawne, 'this is absolutely what not good feels like.'

FOUR

Aarlem Fortress

It was dark by the time the limousine brought him back to Aarlem Fortress. As they raced down the hill road, he looked out at the sodium lights flashing past, the perimeter line, and the blur of chain-link and razorwire. Snowflakes caught the light, and turned the air into white noise.

Beyond the ditch and double fence, like a theatre's stage brilliantly lime-lit for a performance, he could see the main exercise quad fringed with lights, and the strings of pole-lamps radiating off the quad, lighting the rows of modular sheds. Aarlem Fortress was so named because a fortress called Aarlem had once stood on the spot. It had been razed during the Famous Victory, and the garrison erected on its rendered foundations.

It had been their home for a year.

Gaunt had never expected to go back to Balhaut, and he certainly hadn't expected to be stationed there for any length of time. He divided, arbitrarily, he supposed, his life into three parts: his cadet-ship, his service with the Hyrkans, and his command of the Ghosts. Balhaut was the end-stop of the Hyrkan period, before the Tanith watershed. It was like revisiting a past life.

Then again, everything had been like revisiting a past life since Jago.

They'd given him skin-grafts, significant skin-grafts, and somehow patched his brutalised organs back together. It was the organ damage that had come closest to ending him in the weeks after his rescue from the hands of the Archenemy torturers, and it had come fething close half a dozen times.

The eyes, oddly, were the most superficial injuries. Augmetics could be easily fitted into emptied sockets. General Van Voytz, perhaps nagged by guilt, had authorised particularly sophisticated implants of ceramic and stainless steel. In terms of performance, they were better than Gaunt's original eyes. He had greater range and depth perception, and appreciably enhanced cold-light and latent-heat vision. And they sat in his face well enough. They looked like... eyes. A little like the porcelain eyes of an expensive doll, he often thought when he saw them in a mirror, but at least they were alive, not dull like a doll's. When you caught them right, there was a flash of green fire in them.

It was the eyes, though, that bothered him most, more than the months of itching grafts, and more than the regime of drugs and procedures to heal his sutured innards. The eyes didn't hurt, they worked perfectly, and they didn't scare children; they just weren't his.

And every now and then, he saw...

It wasn't entirely clear what it was he saw. It was too fast, too subliminal. Doc Dorden said the phenomenon wasn't anything to do with his new eyes at all. It was a memory of the trauma of losing his old eyes. The memory was haunting his optic nerves.

This seemed likely. Gaunt couldn't remember much about what the Blood Pact had done to him, and the glimpses conveyed more of a feeling than anything visual, but he could taste pain in them. He was convinced that the intermittent glimpses were flashes of the very last thing his old eyes had seen.

The limousine's tyres drummed over the ribbed decking of the ditch bridge, and they swung up to the main gate. The headlamps picked up the black-and-yellow chevrons of the barrier as they rose like the jaws of a beast.

THE TANITH BARRACKS were on the west side of the quad, facing the drab blockhouses used by the 52nd Bremenen. It was still snowing lightly, though nothing had settled. The fat snowflakes looked yellow as they milled down into the amber glow of the sodium lamps. The air was full of a raw, metal cold that you could taste in the back of your lungs.

Gaunt got out of the limousine beside the steps of the command post. The Munitorum driver held the door for him.

'What time tomorrow, sir?' the driver asked.

'Don't bother,' Gaunt replied. He looked at the man, who stiffened suddenly. 'I'll be requesting another driver.'

'Sir?' the man mumbled. 'I don't understand.'

'You kept me waiting,' said Gaunt.

'I… I have apologised about that, sir,' the man said, standing rigidly to attention and trying not to catch Gaunt's ceramic eyes. 'There was a delay at the parking garage, and–'

'There was a card school at the parking garage. You and the other drivers. A good hand you didn't want to toss in, so you kept me waiting.'

The man opened his mouth, but then shut it quickly. It was bad enough to get a notice of reprimand from a commissar, far worse to be caught by a commissar in a lie.

'That'll be all,' said Gaunt.

The man saluted, got back into the motor, and drove away.

Gaunt walked up the steps into the post. The card school had been a lucky guess. Where had that come from? Were these idiots getting so predictable in their malingering and incompetence, or was he just getting too old and cynical? He'd seen it all before. He'd made an educated guess.

Except, it felt as if he'd somehow witnessed the man's crime: the drivers, hunched around an upturned crate beside a brazier in the chilly garage, the cards going down, a steward from the club coming in, calling out the numbers for the staff cars requested, a dismissive wave of the hand and the words, 'Let the bastard wait a minute.'

Clear as day.

He laughed. Too many years a discipline officer: he knew all the tricks and dodges. He'd seen them all a thousand times.

CAPTAIN OBEL HAD the watch. He got up from his desk beside the clerical pool, which was empty for the night, and saluted. The troopers stationed at the doors snapped to attention.

Gaunt waved an 'at ease' in their direction as he came in, pulling off his gloves.

'What's on the scope tonight, Obel?' he asked.

Obel shrugged.

'Square root of feth all, sir,' he said.

'Can I see the log?'

Obel reached towards his desk, and passed Gaunt the data-slate holding the regiment's day-book and activity log. Gaunt sped through it.

'Major Rawne off-base?'

'Three-day pass, sir.'

Gaunt nodded. 'Yes, I remember signing it. You got the whole night?'

'I'm on till two; Gol Kolea has lates. Did your adjutant find you, by the way?'

Gaunt looked up at Obel. 'Beltayn? He was looking for me?'

'Yes, sir. Earlier on.'

'Know what it was about?' Gaunt asked.

Obel shook his head. 'He didn't say, sir. Sorry.'

Gaunt handed the log back to Obel. 'Anything I should know about?'

'There was some rowdy business this afternoon on the quad between some of ours and some of the Bremenen boys. Lot of hot air. Commissar Ludd put a lid on it.'

Gaunt made a mental note to have words with the Bremenen CO. Base-bound boredom was beginning to sour the once-friendly rivalry between the neighbouring regiments.

'Anything else?'

'Commissar Hark got called out to the city about an hour ago, sir,' said Obel.

'Official?'

'It sounded like it, sir.'

Gaunt sighed. There were at least three hundred Ghosts off-base on passes at any one time. That meant drinking, betting, whoring, and a list of other, less savoury activities. One of the regiment's commissars was getting dragged up to the hive every couple of days.

We're getting fat, Gaunt thought. We're getting fat and idle, and our patience is wearing thin, but it's the thin that's going to cause the worst trouble.

GAUNT WANDERED ALONG the blockhouse hall towards his quarters, and saw a man sitting on one of the chairs outside his office. He was a civilian: a young, slightly scruffy fellow in a black, buttoned suit and cravat. Several leather carrying boxes and instrument cases sat on the floor beside him. When Gaunt appeared, he rose to his feet.

'Colonel-Commissar Gaunt?' he began.

Gaunt held up an index finger.

'Just a moment,' he said. He walked past the man and entered his office.

'Where the hell have you been?' asked Beltayn.

Gaunt raised his eyebrows, looked at his adjutant, and calmly closed the office door behind him.

Beltayn blinked and composed himself. He put the sheaf of papers he had been sorting on Gaunt's desk and executed a trim salute.

'My apologies, sir, that was out of line. Good evening.'

'Good evening, adjutant,' Gaunt replied, taking off his coat.

'So where the… where have you been, sir?' asked Beltayn.

'I spent the afternoon with the Kapaj. Is that all right?'

'It would have b…' Beltayn began. He changed his mind. 'It's unfortunate we weren't able to speak during the course of the day, sir. You did have several commitments.'

'Did I?'

'A three o'clock meeting of the joint review board,' said Beltayn.

'Well, it's probably a mercy I was spared, then, isn't it?'

'And you were due here at five for Mr Jaume.'

'Who's Mr Jaume?' Gaunt asked.

His adjutant raised his arm in a swan-neck and pointed towards the office door.

'The civilian outside?'

'Yes, sir.'

'What the feth is his business?'

'He's a portraitist,' replied Beltayn. 'He's been commissioned to make portraits of officers who served during the Balhaut War.'

'I'm not sitting for a painting.'

'He makes photographic exposures, sir. There was a letter of introduction. I showed it to you. You authorised the appointment.'

'I don't remember.'

'The portrait's for a memorial chapel, or something.'

'I'm not dead,' said Gaunt.

'Clearly,' replied Beltayn. 'Mr Jaume presented himself at the appointed time, and you weren't here. He's been waiting ever since.'

Gaunt sat down at his desk. 'Just send him home with my apologies, and reschedule. Tell him I didn't know anything about an appointment.'

'You did, though,' said Beltayn.

'What?'

'I pinned a note of your schedule to your copybook first thing this morning and left it on your blotter.'

Gaunt looked down at his desk. He shifted the pile of documents to one side. His brown leather copybook, a sheet of yellow notepaper attached to the cover, lay on the tabletop.

'You didn't take it with you,' said Beltayn.

'It would appear not,' replied Gaunt.

Beltayn sighed.

'I'll go and rearrange the meeting,' he said. Gaunt looked at him. He could see Beltayn's exasperation. He could see him saying, *You've got to be more focused! There's work to be done, and you treat everything like a game! There's no rigour in you anymore! You'd rather duck out and go off gallivanting! That drunken idiot friend of yours, Blenner, he's the ruin of you!*

Of course, Dughan Beltayn would never say anything like that to him, but, just for a moment, Gaunt could see him saying it, standing there beside the desk. Gaunt could see the adjutant blowing his whole career in one infuriated outburst.

Beltayn said nothing. Nevertheless, with a slightly queasy feeling, Gaunt realised that was exactly what the adjutant was thinking.

'How about tomorrow morning?' Beltayn asked.

'Nine o'clock sharp, Bel, that'll be fine.'

'Thank you, sir.'

Beltayn headed for the door. Before he got there, it opened, and Dorden walked in.

'I heard you were back.'

'Come in,' said Gaunt, with a careless wave of his hand.

Beltayn went out into the hall to speak to the portraitist, and closed the door. Dorden sat down in the chair facing Gaunt's desk. With one exception, Chief Medicae Dorden was the oldest person in the regimental company. Gaunt realised just how old the doctor was beginning to look. Out in the field, Dorden had been grizzled and haggard, but two years off the line had put a little meat back on his bones and ruddied his complexion. He'd gone from being a prematurely aged whipcord of a man to a soft, slightly plump country doctor. The tarnish of grey in his wiry hair had turned as white as the Saint's gown.

'I've been looking for you all day,' Dorden began.

'Don't you start,' replied Gaunt.

'I will, actually,' Dorden said. 'Medicae and Section are breathing down my neck. Quarterly certification was due two days ago, and it can't be completed until all regimental medicals are done and submitted.'

'So do them,' said Gaunt.

'Ha ha,' replied Dorden. 'It's all right for you. If the certification is late, you might get a slap on the hand from Section. As the delay is medical-related, I get fined or worse. Can you please get this sorted out?'

'And the root of the problem is?'

Dorden shrugged as if he barely needed to say it. 'The regimental medicals can't be completed because one member of this company is refusing the examination.'

'Is it who I think it is?'

Dorden nodded.

'Is he refusing the medical on religious grounds?'

'I believe he's refusing it on the basis of being a cantankerous old bastard.'

'I'll speak to him.'

'Tonight?'

'I'll go now,' replied Gaunt.

THE TEMPLE HOUSE adjoined the command post on its east side, just another modular blockhouse like all the other structures in the camp. It could easily have been put to use as a dorm or a storage barn, but they'd taken out the internal floor, so that the square chamber was two storeys deep, filled it with benches, and had a shrine consecrated on the north wall facing the seating. It was a typical Imperial Guard conversion.

Father Zweil, the old ayatani, had attached himself like a barnacle to the Tanith First during the tour on Hagia, and he had never let go. Nor had they ever had the heart to scrape him off their hull. By default, by habit, and by convenience, he had become the company chaplain. He was inconsistent, unpredictable, ill-tempered and belligerent. His age and experience had invested him with a degree of wisdom, but it was generally a challenge to mine that wisdom out of him. On paper, in regimental reports, it was often hard to justify his continued association with the unit.

On the other hand, Zweil had a certain quality that Gaunt found as difficult to deny as it was to identify. Apart from anything else, Zweil had been with them, steadfast, all the way since Hagia. He had been through every fight, every brawl, every set-piece; he'd survived the knife-edge of Herodor, the compartment war of Sparshad Mons, the liberation of Gereon, and the siege of Hinzerhaus. Every step of the way, he had ministered to the needs of the dying and the dead. His blood had become tied to Tanith blood in a way that could not be unworked.

Zweil ran daily services in the temple house, and other notable observances when they cropped up on the calendar. Every morning, without regard to the weather, he walked from Aarlem Fortress to the Templum Ministoria at Aarlem-Sachsen, four kilometres away, and spent an hour there in private worship. This daily, eight kilometre pilgrimage was, he

declared, his way of justifying the *imhava* or 'roving' part of his title as
imhava ayatani. Years before (how many years Gaunt did not know),
Zweil had taken up a life of wandering devotion to travel through the
Sabbat Worlds in the footsteps of the Saint, and repeat the epic circuit
she had made. When they'd met him on Hagia, he'd claimed that his
great journey was nearly finished. He'd walked with them and followed
their route ever since, but he had always insisted that, eventually, he
would have to finish his devotion. 'One day, you know,' he'd said, 'we'll
part company. Oh yes. You'll be going your way, and your way won't suit
me any more. So, we'll say our goodbyes, and I'll take off on the way I
need to go. I've spent too much time as it is, following after you. You'll
miss me when I'm gone. I know you will. You'll all be heartbroken and
rudderless. I can't help that. I've got devotions, devotions I must attend
to. The Saint expects it of me. In fact, now I come to think of it, I may
start tomorrow, or the day after. Is it dumplings tomorrow? It is, isn't it?
Right, I'll start the day after.'

EVERY NIGHT SINCE they'd taken up post at Aarlem Fortress and con-
verted the temple house, Father Zweil had offered what he described as
'occasions of enlightenment'. After supper, any member of the regiment without duties, and any member of the regimental train, was
welcome to come to the temple house for a couple of hours and listen
to him discourse on whatever subject had piqued his interest that day.
Sometimes, the occasions were out-and-out sermons, full of piss and
vinegar if Zweil's dander was up. Sometimes, they were more like lec-
tures, methodical and instructive, and delivered with reference to the
teetering stack of texts he'd dragged over from the library of the
Templum Ministoria. Sometimes, he simply read aloud, covering top-
ics from history to poetics and philosophy or even basic ethics.
Sometimes, he handed books out so that everyone present could read
privately for an hour. Sometimes, he went amongst them, and used the
occasion to help a few of the less-well educated to brush up on their
literacy.
    In the course of any week, his homilies would veer from the sacred to
the profane and back. He would talk about the Saint, or other saints, or
the tradition of the ayatani. He would digress at length on the history
and customs of the Sabbat Worlds. He would seize enthusiastically on a
news story of the day, and use it to ignite animated discussion and
debate amongst his congregation. He would teach, directly or indirectly,
grammar and numeracy, history and politics, music and poetry. He

would air, almost at random, one of the many attics of his mind, and lay out the contents for all to examine.

Gaunt went along whenever he got the chance. Whenever, apropos of nothing, Zweil came out with a fact or detail that he hadn't previously encountered, Gaunt would make a brief note of it in his copybook. In a year on Balhaut, Gaunt had been obliged to request three copybooks from stores.

That evening, when Gaunt entered the temple house, the chosen subject appeared to be either the history of poetry or the poetry of history. There were about forty Ghosts present, and Zweil, perching at the lectern like a roosting vulture, was getting them to read verses aloud from faded, green-bound schola copies of the *Early Sabbatists*.

It was Shoggy Domor's turn. He was on his feet, carefully reading short cantos that Gaunt reckoned were either Ahmud or some middle period Feyaytan. Gaunt waited a while. When Domor had done enough, Zweil gestured for him to sit down, and then picked on Chiria, Domor's adjutant. She got up, wiped her palm across her scarred cheek uncertainly, and started up where Domor had left off.

Gaunt found a seat near the back, and listened. When Chiria, halting and clumsy, had done, Costin got up and embarked on an over-hasty run at one of the Odes of Sarpedon. After Costin, Sergeant Raglon read a Niciezian sonnet, and after Raglon, Wheln, who offered up a surprisingly fluid and spirited recital of Kongress's *Intimations*. After Wheln, it was Eszrah's turn.

The Nihtgane rose to his feet, a tall and considerable presence, and read one of Locaster's *Parables*. It was peculiar to hear his Untill vowel-sounds rounding out Low Gothic. In the two years since Jago, and especially in that last year on Balhaut, Zweil and Gaunt between them had taught Eszrah ap Niht his letters. The Nihtgane virtually never missed one of the ayatani's 'occasions of enlightenment'. He read well. He even removed his battered old sunshades when required to read from a book indoors. When he wrote out his name, he spelled it *Ezra Night*.

If a year on Balhaut has civilised Eszrah, Gaunt thought, what has it done to the rest of us? How soft have we become? How much of our bite have we lost? Is there an edge left on us at all?

When the meeting broke up, Gaunt went down the front to speak to Zweil. The old ayatani looked up from a discussion he was having with Bool, and saw Gaunt approaching.

'This can't be good,' he said.

'It's nothing,' said Gaunt.

'If it's about that amasec in Baskevyl's quarters, somebody had already drunk most of it.'

'It isn't about that,' said Gaunt.

'Well, if this is about the Oudinot mascot, I didn't roast it, nor did I suggest to anybody that it should be roasted, and I certainly didn't supply any recipe for ploin and forcemeat stuffing.'

'This isn't about the Oudinot mascot,' said Gaunt. He paused. 'What Oudinot mascot?'

'Oh, they don't have one,' said Zweil hurriedly.

'They don't?'

'Not since someone roasted it,' Zweil added.

Gaunt shook his head. 'It's not about any of that. I just need a little help, father.'

'Help?'

'That's right. The benefit of your great experience.'

'And my wisdom?'

'And that. There's a problem with one of the men, and I'd like your advice.'

Zweil furrowed his brow, concentrating. 'Oh, certainly. No problem. Hit me.'

'There's a member of the regimental company–'

'Do I know him?' asked Zweil.

'Yes, father.'

'All right, go on.'

'This member of the regimental company, he's causing a big bureaucratic problem.'

'Oh, the little fether!' Zweil hissed, nodding conspiratorially. 'Are you going to have him flogged?'

'Flogged?'

'Flogging's too good for him. I know, have him tied to a rocket and fired into the heart of the local star,' said Zweil.

'Well, that's certainly on my list of possibilities.'

'Is it? Good.'

'The problem,' said Gaunt, 'is that the man is refusing to take his medical.'

'Refusing?'

'Everyone needs to be certified fit, and he's refusing to submit himself for the exam.'

'There's always one, isn't there?' said Zweil. He frowned more deeply and tapped his finger against his chin. 'I'd make an example of him, if I were you.'

'You would?'

'You can't have insubordination like that, Gaunt. You're meant to have some authority. Don't stand for it. Have the man drummed up and down the quad, and then maybe tied to something heavy while the rest of us throw blunt objects at him.'

'So, in your opinion, this man's definitely out of line?' asked Gaunt.

'Absolutely, categorically, inexcusably out of line. He needs to be certified fit, and he knows it. It's just pure bloody-mindedness, is what it is. He has to be made to follow the rules down to the letter of the– Waitaminute. It's me, isn't it?'

'It is,' said Gaunt.

'Hmm,' said Zweil. 'That was very sly of you.'

'I know. Will you go and see Dorden?'

'I suppose.'

'What's the problem?'

Zweil rocked his head from side to side and shrugged. 'I've never liked doctors. Yurk. Poking their noses in places where noses weren't supposed to fit. I won't have it.'

'You'll have this.'

Zweil stuck his tongue out at Gaunt.

'What are you afraid they'll find?' Gaunt asked.

'I'm old. I'm very, very old. What *aren't* they going to find?'

Gaunt smiled. 'Tomorrow morning, please. Don't make me have this conversation with you again.'

Zweil scowled.

'Now bless me.'

Zweil waved some half-hearted business with his hands. 'Bless you, in the name of the God-thingumy, blah blah.'

'Thank you.'

Zweil returned to the conversation he had been having with Bool. Haller was waiting to ask a question of his own. Gaunt wandered over to the seat where Eszrah was working. The Nihtgane was patiently writing in a copybook. He was concentrating, threading the pen across the paper in a slow, exact hand.

'Histye, soule,' Gaunt said.

Eszrah looked up. 'Histye.'

Gaunt sat down beside him. 'Busy?'

Eszrah nodded. He carefully blotted out the paragraph he had already written, using a square of tan blotting paper.

'The father, he asked of me to written down stories that have belonged to my regiment,' he said.

'Zweil asked you?'

Eszrah nodded. By *regiment*, Eszrah meant his people, the Nihtgane of the Gereon Untill. His vocabulary was expanding every day, often with nuanced meanings, but he understood the word regiment in a very particular way. He could not be encouraged to use 'tribe' or 'people' or even 'community' in relation to the Nihtgane, nor could he be persuaded of the specific military definition of regiment. The Tanith First was a regiment and, to Eszrah, it exhibited precisely the same dynamics of loyalty and collective reliance as a tribe or a family.

'He's asked you to record Nihtgane stories? Do you mean histories?'

Eszrah shook his head. 'Not of things that were done, but of older than things.'

'You mean like folklore?' Gaunt asked.

Eszrah shrugged. 'Soule not know word.'

'I mean legends. Myths,' Gaunt said.

Eszrah smiled. 'Aye. That is word how the father says it.'

'Do the Nihtgane have many myths?' Gaunt asked.

Eszrah puffed out his lips and turned his eyes up to indicate the level of Gaunt's understatement.

'They have belong many, many,' he said. 'There is the story of the sleeping walker, which I have writ here, and the story of the moth and the jar, and the story of the snake and the branch, which I have writ here and writ here both. Also there is the story of the walking sleeper, and the story of the old sun, and the story of the hunter and the beast–'

'How many have you written?'

'Four and ten,' said Eszrah. He looked at the open copybook. 'This I am written, it is the story of the hunter and the pool. It will make five and ten. The hunter, he walks in many of my regiment their stories.'

'Can I read them?'

Eszrah nodded willingly, and then hesitated. 'But I must need the book to written down more of them.'

'Here's what,' said Gaunt. 'Why don't I get you a second copybook. You write a story down in one book while I'm reading another, then we'll swap. How's that?'

Eszrah seemed quite satisfied by this compromise. Abruptly, he touched Gaunt on the sleeve and nodded towards the door of the temple house.

Beltayn had just entered, followed by Nahum Ludd, the regiment's junior commissar. Ludd was in full uniform, and thawing snowflakes speckled his stormcoat.

'There he is,' said Beltayn.

Gaunt got up. 'Something awry, Bel?'

Beltayn gestured to Ludd. The junior commissar drew an envelope from his coat. Gaunt could see that it was trimmed with a blue stripe, indicating an order despatch from the Commissariat.

'A courier just brought this in, sir,' said Ludd. 'It's come direct from Section, for your eyes only.'

Gaunt slit the envelope open quickly, took out the tissue-thin sheet inside and opened it to read it.

'You're going to have to reschedule Mr Jaume, Bel,' he said.

'How come, sir?'

'Because I've got to report to Section at daybreak tomorrow.'

'Does it say why?' asked Ludd.

'No,' said Gaunt, 'it doesn't say anything else at all.'

FIVE

Ennisker's Perishables

LONG AFTER THE last of the clock towers in the Oligarchy, and away down the hill below in the sprawl of Balopolis, had finished chiming midnight, the men in Ennisker's Perishables began to die.

The night was as cold and hard as quenched iron, and flurries of snow came and went under the yellow street lighting. Traffic on the New Polis Bridge and the Old Crossing lit up the skeletal girderwork with their headlights, and caught the snowflakes like dust in sunlight. Light rippled across the oil slick river.

Ennisker's Perishables was a meat-packing plant on the north bank, a large outcrop of ouslite and travertine that dominated the city wall in the shadow of the New Polis Bridge. There was ground access to the place through the warren of streets threading the land-side of the city wall, and water access via pulleys and cage-lifts on the river side.

The plant was grim, and smelled of dank stone. The ooze-breath of the river pushed up into it through its deep basements, and through the vent holes that dotted its stained facade above the waterline like arrow slits in the curtain wall of a donjon. It had been essentially derelict since the war. The Henotic League, a beneficial order founded for the relief of veterans and unhabs, had used it as a hostel for a few years until they had secured larger and less miasmal accommodations up near Arkwround Square. The phantom remnants of a notice announcing this shift of venue, and inviting lost and needy souls to come looking for the 'hall with the yellow doors' on Arkwround, still lingered on one of the plant's paint-scabbed loading doors. A subsequent attempt to revive the plant's fortunes as a meat-packing site had foundered badly in '81, but the power, waterlines and heating systems installed at the time had never been disconnected, a fact that Valdyke had noticed with satisfaction while sourcing the venue for his employer.

Nado Valdyke had come recommended by a man who knew a man who knew a man. His reputation was as a fixer, an arranger. A lack of scruples, and a willingness to get on with a job no matter how sound its legality, rounded out his resumé nicely. Though he had enjoyed correspondence with his employer, a series of letters that set out the employer's requirements in some detail, Valdyke had not met his employer personally.

His employer was from off-world.

When Valdyke received notice that, after a long and arduous voyage, his employer had finally arrived at Balhaut Highstation, Valdyke left his apartment in the Polis stacks and set out to make sure all the arrangements were in place.

He took four men with him, four thugs from the stacks that he'd paid very well to mind him. Valdyke did not intend to leave himself vulnerable to some off-worlder he'd never met.

The employer turned up at Ennisker's Perishables late, riding in a car leased from the city landing grounds. A few minutes behind the car came two hired tractors, towing cargo trailers that barely fitted down the narrow, riverside streets.

Two of Valdyke's thugs obediently trundled open the loading doors at the first hint of approaching lights. Valdyke already had the power running in the plant, and had brought in, as instructed, two bulk servitors for lifting work, and a medicae, a man called Arbus, who asked no questions and took what work he could get, due to the small matter of him having been struck off the community registry for malpractice.

The three vehicles drove into the plant's vast loading dock, a musty cavern lit by sputtering naphtha flares. The bay's floor had been stained brick-red by decades of blood-letting. At a sign from Valdyke, the thugs rumbled the doors shut.

'I'm Valdyke,' said Valdyke, walking up to the man getting out of the leased car. 'Are you Master Eyl?'

The man brushed off his beige leather coat, and looked Valdyke up and down.

'Yes,' he said.

'Pleasure to meet you at last,' said Valdyke. He thought about proffering his hand, but the man didn't seem like the sort. Not the sort at all.

'So, you want these shipments unloaded,' Valdyke began, 'and th–'

'Did you receive my instructions?' Eyl asked him, in an accented voice.

'Yes, I got them.'

'Were they clear in all particulars?'

'Oh, absolutely,' said Valdyke

'And the remuneration that I wired across, that was received correctly?'

'It's the down payment we agreed,' Valdyke noted with a nod.

'Then I'm not entirely sure why any further conversation is required,' said Baltasar Eyl.

Valdyke hesitated for a second. The man had come in with his attitude set to 'arsehole', and Valdyke had diced men for less, for a lot less. Valdyke decided, however, to respond with an agreeable smile and a courteous nod. The smile-and-nod combo was inspired by two things. For one, the balance payment promised for the job was considerable, and Valdyke knew the only way to guarantee getting it was to finish the job properly.

For afters, the man, this off-worlder, had an air about him, something that said he was more than just dangerous. Dangerous was too small a word. He was still and contained, and his gestures were small and restrained, but Valdyke felt that was because an effort of sheer willpower was going on. Eyl's flesh and behaviour were tightly controlled so that they could hold something in check, the way a straitjacket pinned a man's arms. They were keeping a tight grip on something that smoked with feral cruelty, something that none of them, not even Eyl, wanted to see get out.

So Valdyke did his smile-and-nod, and clapped his hands. The thugs dragged open the dock's inner shutters, exposing a second cavern-space, wreathed in steam, and filled with oily black machinery. Arbus the medicae readied his kit, and the servitors plodded forwards, bright orange and pincered like tusker crabs, to unload the containers.

As the work got underway (and Valdyke congratulated himself on his choice of venue, because it was a noisy business of clanks and thumps and piston-whines and vapour-hisses and, anywhere except the half-derelict piles of the riverside, it would have woken the neighbourhood and attracted the attention of the Magistratum), Valdyke assessed his employer a little further. There were three others in Eyl's party, two men and a woman. The men were whip-cord, dog-eyed men like their master, and Valdyke presumed they were purchased muscle, though they were close with Eyl, their conversations tight and intimate. They were wearing leather bodygloves, boots, gloves and patched, Guard surplus jackets, but then so was every other thug in the sub. The two men had driven the tractors. Eyl had driven the leased car. Given the respect he apparently commanded, it seemed odd that he didn't have a driver.

The fourth member of his party was a woman, a widow, weeded in a veil and black silks. She'd been riding in the back of Eyl's motor, as if he was her chauffeur. There was something off about her too. When Valdyke looked at her – and widow or no widow, she was a handsome woman who deserved being looked at – it was as if she kept popping in and out of focus, like a film image distorting slightly as it was exposed to heat. It made Valdyke feel pretty sick to watch, so after a while he stopped.

The servitors detached the containers from the tractor flatbeds, and rolled them back up the dock into the adjoining chamber. Valdyke personally connected them up to the plant's power source, just as if they were crates of meat, cold-stored, switching their refrigeration supply from mobile to static. Ducting systems inside the containers began to chatter and hum. Display lights lit up on the control panels.

Valdyke checked the lights. It was looking good.

'Ambient's coming up, and I've got clean green on the vital boost.'

He looked over at Eyl.

'They look just like shipping pods,' he said.

'Of course,' replied Eyl.

'But they're hibernaculums.'

Eyl stared back at him.

'What?' asked Valdyke. 'Come on, I've been around. Even if I was so stupid that I couldn't add together the resources you needed and the medical expertise you wanted on hand, you're not the first person to smuggle live bodies onto Balhaut inside mortuary boxes.'

'Am I not?' asked Eyl lightly. His face, half-lit by the fluttering naphtha flares, was unreadable.

Valdyke shrugged. 'Deserters, illegal immigrants, people who'd prefer to avoid the light of the Throne, it happens a lot.' He grinned. 'Sometimes the poor stiffs inside actually survive the process.'

Valdyke picked up a locking bar and wandered around to the hatch of the first container.

'Shall we?' he asked.

Eyl nodded. Valdyke beckoned the medicae over, and then unscrewed the lid of a little pot of commiphora and wiped a smear of the gum resin across his philtrum. The astringent scent filled his nose. Eyl certainly wasn't the first person to smuggle living contraband onto Balhaut as part of the mortuary trade, and Valdyke had assisted several of his predecessors. The low-berth survival rate was worse than Valdyke had joked. Most of the time, you really didn't want to smell what was thawing out in the box.

He broke the shipping seal, slid the locking bar into the slot, and rotated it. It took a push and a grunt of exertion, but the teeth of the lock popped, and the main drum of the lock swung away on its hinges. Valdyke pulled it wide, uncoupled the bar, inserted it into the inner socket, and heaved on it again.

The hatch seals released. There was a deep and nasty groan of bad air, an exhalation like the long, lingering and last breath a man ever took, one final lung-emptying exhalation for the ages, after which no more breaths would ever be drawn. Valdyke pulled the hatch open.

'Oh, Throne,' the medicae said, coughing, and fanning the air in front of his face.

'Yeah, that's ripe,' said Valdyke, who could smell it despite the commiphora. It was a warm, gorge-raising stink of off-meat, of dirty blood, of gangrene. Stained meltwater ran out over the lip of the hatch and spattered on the dock. It was viscous, and filled, like broth, with lumps of organic matter.

'Mind your shoes, doc,' Valdyke said. Arbus muttered a caustic reply, and took a snifter of something medicinal from a hip-flask. Valdyke dropped the locking bar, and pulled out a hooked packing knife, a bent spar of blade forty centimetres long with the edge on the inside of the curve. He *chokked* the tip in through the polymer sheeting wrapping the pod's contents, and cut down in a half-sawing, half-slicing motion. The smell got worse. Valdyke could see the first of the packets inside. Glad of his gloves, he reached in and slid it out on its telescoping rail. It came out like a side of meat, wrapped in a polymer shroud, clamped to the suspension rail by heavy-weight metal runners.

The corpse inside the bag was human. The hair had been burned off, and it was uniformly the colour of rare steak, except for the cinder-pits of its eyes and the pearl wince of its teeth. Its arms were crossed over its shrunken breast.

'Do you think you can save him?' Valdyke asked.

'Don't be an idiot,' Arbus replied.

Valdyke laughed and clattered out the second packet. This one was even more mutilated. Both corpses had dog-tags threaded around their ankles and secured through the seals of their shrouds.

Valdyke turned and looked at Eyl. Eyl was standing a way back, at the edge of the dock, with the widow and the two men, watching the work.

'You got dead meat here, sir,' said Valdyke. 'Just dead meat. In fact, it looks like a regular shipment of cannon fodder back from the front line.'

'No,' said Eyl. 'Look harder.'

Valdyke frowned, and then a smile spread across his face and became a leer.

'Did you pack the front end with stiffs?' he asked, jerking his thumb at the pod. 'Is that what you did? You packed the front end with genuine stiffs, in case the container got inspected?'

'No,' the widow replied suddenly, speaking for the first time. 'The bodies and blood, they are for the sealing ritual, or the casket won't be–'

'Hush, sister,' said Eyl gently, patting her arm.

'What did she say?' asked Valdyke.

'She said you're right,' said Eyl.

'Sneaky,' said Valdyke, nodding appreciatively. 'Very sneaky, my friend.'

'I'm not your friend,' said Eyl.

Valdyke brushed that off with a shrug of his shoulders. He had no great desire to be the off-worlder's pal either. He reached back into the container, and rattled out the third sack of meat.

'Ah, damn,' he said.

'What?' asked Eyl, taking a step closer.

'This one's gone too. Sorry, you must have had a pretty serious failure in the hiber systems. Face looks like it's been gnawed off.'

'Valdyke?' Arbus whispered at his side.

'What?'

'This one's alive.'

'What?' Valdyke turned and looked down at the body hanging in the stained sack. There was blood pooling in the slack parts of the polymer sheaf, and the poor bastard's face and shoulders looked like someone had taken a razor blade to them.

'That's nonsense,' Valdyke said.

Arbus shook his head. He was using a receptor wand to scan the body for trace levels.

'The vitals are low, but they're what I would associate with coming out of hibernetic suspension.' He looked at Valdyke, and Valdyke saw something akin to terror lighting the wretched old quack's eyes.

'You're reading it wrong, you old fool,' Valdyke told him.

'I'm not, I swear!' Arbus replied. Then he let out an exclamation of horror, and recoiled from the hanging sack.

'What?' Valdyke cried.

'The eyes! The eyes!' the medicae stammered.

Valdyke looked back down at the body. Its eyes were open, slots of yellowed irises and small, black pupils staring filmily out of the bloody mask. They were staring right at him.

'Holy Throne of Terra,' Valdyke said, and stepped back. 'What is this?' he asked. He looked at Eyl. 'What the hell is this?'

'It is what it is,' said Eyl. 'The scars are ritual marks of allegiance. I don't expect you to understand.'

Behind him, Valdyke could hear short, muffled gasps of breath, and the wet crackle of polymer sheathing as slippery weight moved around inside it. He heard scrabbling noises and the occasional hiss or thump from inside the pod.

'I think I'll be going now,' Valdyke said.

Eyl shook his head. The widow started to shudder. Valdyke thought for a moment that she had burst into tears behind her veil, but then he realised she was sniggering.

Nado Valdyke yelled for his thugs. No one answered. When he turned to look, all four of his men were lying on the ground. They were lying in curiously slack, unnatural poses. Eyl's two men were standing over them, hands limp by their sides, staring at Valdyke with their dog-eyes narrowed.

Valdyke spat an oath at them, and one of the men smiled back at him, baring his teeth. The teeth were pink. Blood flowed out over his lip.

Valdyke yelped and turned to run. He slammed into something solid, as solid as a wall. It was Eyl.

Valdyke scrambled at him, but Eyl felt like stone, cold and unrelenting. Eyl shoved him, a light shove that nevertheless felt like the impact of a wrecking ball.

Valdyke staggered backwards, breathlessly sure that some of his ribs had just parted. He felt entirely disorientated. Eyl suddenly had the packing knife that Valdyke had been using.

He put it through Valdyke's throat, splitting the adam's apple and driving the blade so deep that the tip poked out through the back of the neck under Valdyke's hairline. Valdyke hung for a moment like a fish on a hook. His hands clenched and unclenched. His mouth gagged open as if he was gasping for air. Blood welled out over his chin. His eyes were shock-wide as he tried to cope with the massive pain, and tried to deal with the comprehension that he hadn't just been hurt, he'd suffered a catastrophic injury that had destroyed his life, and which could not be repaired.

Eyl let him fall.

The medicae, Arbus, was cowering and sobbing beside the open container. He looked up as Eyl approached.

'Please,' he said, 'please, are you going to kill me too?'

'I need you to successfully revive my men,' said Eyl, frankly.

'A-and after that?' Arbus sniffed.

Eyl did not reply.

'What in the name of Terra are you?' Arbus wailed.

Eyl looked down at him.

'We are nothing in the name of Terra,' he said. 'We are Blood Pact.'

SIX

An Interview at Section

THE GREY BRICK mansion known as Section stood near the heart of the Oligarchy, and dominated both Avenue Regnum Khulan, which it peeped into over high walls and black railings on its western side, and the gardens of Viceroy Square, which it faced. Its official names were Viceroy House, or the Ministrative Officio of the Commissariat, Balopolis (Balhaut), but it was referred to by everyone as Section, which was shorthand for the highest local stratum of Commissariat authority.

It was not an inviting place. Second only to the Manse of the ordos on Melkanor Street, it was the most dreaded building on Balhaut. It was part administrative hub, with whole floors devoted to bureaucratic activity, part courthouse, and part gaol. Though there were several penitentiary facilities in north-hemisphere Balhaut for the detention of military offenders, a lower level of Section contained a maximum security cell-block where the most sensitive prisoners were held.

Gaunt arrived before first light.

Though the chronometer on his wrist put the sun at less than five minutes away, there was no trace of dawn in the sky. Daybreak, the order despatch had said. He'd never been late for anything, and he was not going to start now.

He got out of the car. Over to the west, above the lights of the city, another lit city passed over head. It was like a brown thunderhead cloud moving against the night sky, speckled with lights, like a mirage, as if the sky was a still lake that was reflecting Balopolis beneath. It was one of the orbital docks, Highstation probably, gliding past on its cyclical turn, catching the sun earlier than the land below it.

Behind the wheel of the car, Scout Trooper Wes Maggs yawned. Gaunt bent down and looked at him.

'Too early for you?'

Maggs straightened up fast. 'Sorry, sir.'

'You're going to have to wait,' Gaunt said. 'There's a gate around the side where you can show your pass and park. I'll send for you when I need you.'

Maggs nodded.

The previous evening, frustrated by the poor service provided by the local drivers, Gaunt had told Beltayn to detail one of the Tanith instead. He had suggested making it someone who had punishment duties to work off. As a consequence, he'd got up that morning to find himself with Wes Maggs as a chauffeur.

Maggs was a Belladon trooper, one of the first Belladon to make it into the Tanith scout cadre. He had a mouth on him, and certain unruly ways that reminded Gaunt of Varl, but he was a damn fine soldier, and an excellent stealth fighter.

'What did you do?' Gaunt had asked him.

Maggs had murmured something in reply.

'I can't hear you, Maggs.'

'Commissar Hark put me on a charge for disreputable behaviour, sir. I've got to do sixty hours of punishment duty.'

'Looks like you'll be doing them with me, Maggs. You know how to drive a staff car?'

GAUNT ENTERED THE main lobby of Viceroy House. The lights were down, just glow-globes fixed over the reception desks. A man was up a long ladder, changing filaments in one of the massive but unilluminated chandeliers. Three Commissariat cadets were on their hands and knees, scrubbing the marble floor with bristle brushes.

Whhshrrk, whhshrrk, whhshrrk! went the brushes as Gaunt walked past. None of them dared to look up.

Been there, done that, Gaunt thought.

The duty officer at the desk had been alerted to Gaunt's arrival by the outer gate, and was waiting, on his feet.

He saluted. 'Good morning, sir.'

'Good morning.' Gaunt handed him the slip, and the man read it quickly, as if he already knew what it said.

'Thank you, sir. I've called through and announced you. Someone will come for you in a moment, if you'd just wait.'

Gaunt nodded, and stepped away from the desk, removing his gloves and unbuttoning his stormcoat. The duty officer resumed his seat and got back to work. A minute passed. The brushes continued to go *Whhshrrk, whhshrrk, whhshrrk!* A courier ran down the hall and out through the main doors. The man fixing the chandelier climbed down off his ladder, folded it up, and carried it away.

Gaunt heard more footsteps, and turned.

It was Viktor Hark.

'Where did you come from?' Gaunt asked.

'I've been here all night,' replied Hark. Gaunt could see how much sleep Hark hadn't had. Hark was the only man in the regiment whose workload and responsibilities seemed to have increased since they'd moved off the line. War gave men something to do, and when you took that away...

'It must be bad.'

'You don't want to know,' said Hark. 'Sometimes I think we're in charge of a penal unit.'

'Who is it?'

Hark sighed. 'It's a little team this time. A little team of hustlers that includes two captains and a major.'

'Not Rawne?'

'I'm afraid so.'

It was Gaunt's turn to sigh. In the two idle years since Hinzerhaus, Major Rawne seemed to have slowly regressed back to the venomous and untrust-worthy malcontent that Gaunt had first encountered in Tanith Magna.

'And Meryn too, if Rawne's involved?'

Hark nodded.

'Who's the other captain?'

'You're not going to believe this,' Hark replied. 'Ban Daur.'

'Well, that's got to be a mistake. Not Daur. He'd only be involved by accident.'

Hark shrugged.

'So it's bad?'

Hark nodded again. 'It's a genuine mess, and the charges are going to be severe. I'm not sure how we're going to pull their arses out of this little conflagration.'

'So why was I only called in this morning if you've been here since last night?' asked Gaunt.

Hark paused. 'Well, I was handling it. I was going to go back to Aarlem about an hour ago, but someone told me you had been summoned, so I waited.'

'You didn't send for me?'

'No,' said Hark.

Gaunt showed him the slip. 'They sent me this last night.'

Hark looked it over. 'Damn, Ibram. This isn't anything to do with Rawne's latest disgrace. This is something else entirely.'

Somehow, Gaunt already knew that. He'd known it the moment he'd seen Hark coming across the lobby to meet him.

GAUNT SENT HARK back to Aarlem to get some sleep, and waited to be seen. It was another twenty minutes before anyone appeared.

'Sorry to keep you waiting, Gaunt,' Commissar Edur offered as he approached. Gaunt shrugged a *no-matter*, and decided against asking, right away at least, why he was being received by an officer he'd lunched with just the day before.

The truth was, he hadn't known Usain Edur long, and he didn't know him well. Hargiter and Zettsman had been regulars at the club for seven or eight months, and Gaunt knew them and the regiments they were attached to. He counted them as decent acquaintances, two of the semi-regular faces that frequented the Mithredates for lunch or supper. Edur had only been in the city for a week or two. He'd gravitated into their company easily enough; Gaunt had a feeling that Zettsman had introduced him. Edur was affable, a reasonable conversationalist, and expressed an attitude towards duty that Gaunt found appealing, but he had no idea of Edur's background, service or attachment, and as he followed Edur along the hall, he realised that was unusual. That kind of talk always came out. Men talked about their service, and looked for points of shared experience. They noted the places, people and battles they had in common.

Over the two or three times Gaunt had been in Edur's company, Edur had not volunteered anything of the sort, which meant that he was either a remarkably private individual, or he was concealing something.

Gaunt could see that now, too.

Edur led him into a side office. There was a stenographic servitor, and a desk with a chair on either side of it. Edur gestured to one of the chairs.

'Has anybody offered you caffeine?' he asked as he took the other seat.

'No one's even offered me an explanation,' replied Gaunt.

Edur looked up from the closed dossier on the desk in front of him and held Gaunt's gaze. Edur was a few years younger than Gaunt and a few centimetres shorter, and he was good-looking in a clean-cut but bloodless way, like a classical statue. His skin was regally black, and he reminded Gaunt of the Vitrians he'd served alongside. Edur smiled, and the smile was relaxed and genuine.

'Let's just ease our way into this,' he said. 'I've only just been put on this one, so I'm coming up to speed. I know it's a little awkward that you and I have encountered each other socially in the last week or so, but I think that's why I was put on the matter. I'm known to you, and so this brief can be a little less formal before–'

'Before what?' asked Gaunt.

'We'll get to that,' said Edur.

You're not really known to me at all, Gaunt thought. Where is this going? How much of a chance was it that you suddenly started coming to the club and moving in my circle of comrades? I can almost see through you.

Edur nodded to the servitor, which whirred into life. Delicate cogs chattered the drum of transcript paper around, and the blocks of letter keys lowered into place on their servos.

'Preliminary interview, Ibram Gaunt,' Edur began, and followed that with the date and time. The servitor started to chatter, the little keys tapping the paper, the paper advancing under the platen with a soft ratchet sound. Edur opened the dossier, creased the first page flat with a slide of his hand and read out Gaunt's service summary, which was also duly recorded by the servitor.

'Can you confirm those details?' he asked.

'I confirm them,' Gaunt replied.

Edur nodded. 'You're the CO of the Tanith First?'

'That's correct.'

'A position you've held for twelve years?'

'Correct, aside from a hiatus period about five years ago.'

Edur turned a couple of pages. 'That would have been during the… ah… insert mission to Gereon?'

'Yes.'

'And that mission was?'

'A security mission.'

Edur looked up at Gaunt and smiled as if expecting more.

'And classified,' said Gaunt.

Edur pursed his lips and raised his eyebrows. 'Your command was restored on your return?'

'It wasn't quite as clear-cut as that, but yes.'

'You're a colonel-commissar?'

'Yes.'

'Split rank. That's unusual.'

'It is what it is.'

Edur fixed Gaunt with an amused look again. 'Did you take the Commissariat's "Advanced Interview Techniques and Methodology" class?'

'Is that one of your questions?' asked Gaunt.

Edur shook his head, still amused by something. 'No, I just thought I'd ask. I've seen less deflection in a sword fight.' He looked back at the dossier, and turned another page.

'The Tanith First was retired from the front line two years ago?'

'Yes.'

'And you transitted here to Balhaut for resupply and retraining?'

'Yes.'

'You've been here a year?'

'Yes.'

'How are you finding it?'

'Dull,' said Gaunt.

'Why?'

'People keep telling me things I already know.'

Edur laughed. 'I'm just asking what they've told me to ask, Gaunt. It's a pain in the arse, I know.'

'Well, let's get to the part where you tell me why they've told you to ask me these questions.'

Edur nodded. 'We will. You've been here a year? Yes, we established that. Anything odd to report in that time?'

Gaunt sat back. 'What sort of odd?'

Edur shrugged. 'Odd approaches? Odd contacts? Anybody shadowing you or hanging around Aarlem?'

Gaunt shook his head.

'Note head-shake,' Edur told the steno. 'Nothing strange at all, then? In the last month especially?'

'No,' said Gaunt. 'One way or another, there's a whole bundle of odd in the Tanith First, but nothing I'm not familiar with.'

Edur pursed his lips again and nodded. 'All right, Gaunt, here's what it is. We've got a prisoner here. A significant capture, very sensitive. There's some talk he should have just been executed, but Section believes there's a potential high value to his intelligence, so they've kept him alive. He's downstairs.'

'What's this got to do with me?'

'We need to get inside his head, and find out what he's got.'

'I understand that,' said Gaunt, 'but again, what's this got to do with me?'

'The prisoner clearly appreciates that the remaining duration of his life, and the comparative quality of that life, will rather depend on how he gives up his secrets. He knows that he will be disposed of the moment we feel he's exhausted his usefulness.'

'So he's not talking?'

'No, he's not,' said Edur.

'Did you bring me down here just so I could suggest you employ methods of persuasion?'

'No,' Edur replied. 'We'd already thought of that, funnily enough. He's quite resistant to pain. Our thinking was, we'd try a different approach. Offer him something he wants in return for his submission.'

'I see. At the risk of sounding like a vox stuck on auto-send, what's this got to do with me?'

'Everything, Gaunt,' said Edur. 'He wants *you*.'

SEVEN

Prisoner B

AN ARMOURED ELEVATOR took them down into the detention level. The cell-block area, heavily guarded, was tiled in white stone, and felt more like the surgical zone of a medicae facility than a prison. Edur took Gaunt to an observation room that looked into a simple tank cell through a murky one-way mirror.

When the sanctioned torturers, their sackcloth hoods tucked into their belts for the time being, led the prisoner into the cell, caged phosphor lights flickered on, and bathed the cell in a sick, green glare. The torturers, burly men with bitter faces, strapped the prisoner onto the single cage chair screwed to the deck in the centre of the cell floor.

'I don't know him,' said Gaunt.

The prisoner was a soldier. Gaunt could tell that from a glance. It wasn't so much the size of him, which was considerable and heavily muscled, it was his bearing. He was straight-backed and upright. He was somehow noble. He was underweight, and he had evidently suffered physical abuse, but he was not cowed. He held himself the way a soldier holds himself.

The prisoner was dressed in a simple prison-issue tunic and breeches, and he had been given hessian slippers to cover his feet.

'Are you sure?' asked Edur.

'I don't know him,' Gaunt repeated.

'Please, make certain.'

'Edur, don't be an idiot. I'd remember a face like that.'

The prisoner's face and head were not noble. The scalp was shaved, and the flesh was covered with deep ritual scars, old scars, scars that signified the most mortal and bloody pact.

'He asked for you by name,' said Edur. 'He has made it clear that he will speak only to you.'

'How does he know me?' asked Gaunt. 'How does he know I'm here, on this world?'

Edur shrugged. Gaunt could see that Edur was watching him for tell-tale body language, any little slip or give-away. He also knew that just as they were watching the prisoner in the cell, they were in turn being watched.

'You're desperate to unlock him,' Gaunt observed to Edur, 'and I'm the best hope you've got, but you don't trust me either.'

'This is a complicated matter,' Edur replied, his genial tone unable to mask his tension. 'It's very sensitive. Objections were raised at the idea of bringing anyone else in. Your clearance is not as high as they would have liked.'

'My clearance levels have been pitiful since I came back from the Gereon mission,' replied Gaunt. 'I imagine your colleagues have reviewed that, and they'll have read the dossiers compiled on me by Commissar-General Balshin, Commissar Faragut, and a number of other individuals, including a servant of the holy ordos.'

'I think they probably have,' agreed Edur.

'I imagine they don't present me as an attractive participant in this business, which is why you've spent the last week or two vetting me, and why they're watching us now.'

Gaunt looked up at the ceiling, and ran his gaze along the walls.

'But, for all that, the Gereon mission is precisely why I'm here, isn't it?' he asked.

Edur nodded.

'This man is connected to Gereon?'

'Specifically, your mission there,' said Edur.

Gaunt paused and looked back at the prisoner in the cell. The man wasn't moving. He was just staring blankly at the mirror wall.

'He has told us that his name is Mabbon Etogaur,' said Edur.

'Well, that's not strictly accurate,' said Gaunt.

'What do you mean?'

'Mabbon may be his name, though I doubt it's his given one. It's probably a saint name he adopted when he took his pact.'

'A saint name?' asked Edur.

'They have saints too, Edur,' replied Gaunt. He looked at the prisoner again. 'Etogaur isn't a name. It's his rank. He gave you his name and rank. An etogaur is roughly the equivalent of a general.'

'I see.'

'It's a senior rank in the army of the Blood Pact.'

'Anything else?' asked Edur.

Gaunt nodded. 'Yes. For all that, he's not Blood Pact.'

'He isn't?'

'The ritual scarring on the face and the scalp, those are pact-marks, definitely, but look at his hands.'

They looked through the mirror wall. The prisoner's forearms were buckled to the arms of the cage chair. His hands were resting, limp and open, against the ends of the chair-arms.

'I don't see anything,' said Edur.

'Exactly.'

Edur glanced sideways at Gaunt. 'If you know something, say it.'

'There are no scars on his hands,' said Gaunt, still staring at the silent prisoner. 'None on the backs, none on the palms. Of all the pact-marks, the hand scars are the most significant. When a warrior of the Blood Pact makes his oath, he slices the palms of his hand against the sharpened edges of his heathen master's armour. That solemnises the pact. That *is* the pact. This man has no scars.'

'No, he doesn't,' said Edur.

Gaunt narrowed his eyes to peer harder. 'It's hard to tell in this light, but the flesh of his hands looks new. It's unblemished. A little smooth. I can't be sure, but I'd wager he's had grafting done to conceal or remove the rite scars. The chances are, this man was Blood Pact, but he isn't any more.'

'So you suppose he has renounced his pact?'

'Quite possibly. He's a man of significance in their world, and he's gone to a lot of trouble and expense to have those grafts to erase his scars. It's quite a statement.'

'Could he not just be concealing what he really is?'

Gaunt shook his head. 'This isn't about concealment. He'd have had the rite scars on his head done, otherwise. They show his connection to the Sanguinary Worlds clearly enough. No, the hands are telling. He's not hiding his scars, he's deleting them. He's actively rejecting the pact.'

'What does that make him?'

'It could make him any number of things, Edur, but at the very least it makes him a traitor. A traitor general.'

'Interesting,' said Edur.

'Not really. You know all of this already,' Gaunt replied.

Edur raised his eyebrows. 'What makes you say that?'

'Oh, come on, commissar,' Gaunt sighed. 'The idea that you, and our invisible handlers, and the whole of Section's intelligence division hadn't already worked all of that out is frankly insulting. We've been studying the Pact for years. This was all about you finding out how much I know.'

Edur smiled and raised his hands submissively. 'Fair play, Gaunt. You can't blame us.'

'So how did I do?' asked Gaunt.

'Not bad at all. What else can you tell me?'

Gaunt took a deep breath and looked back at the prisoner. 'The key thing, I suppose, is that he's changed sides. That's a huge psychological marker. He is capable of being sworn to something, to be absolutely committed to it, and then to switch away and renounce it. If he's done it once, he can do it again. It's like infidelity.'

Edur chuckled. 'What sort of switch are we talking about, do you think?'

Gaunt shrugged. 'An awful lot of Blood Pact start out as Imperial Guard or PDF. Most of the time, it's a "join us or die" dynamic, but sometimes the choice is rather more personal. Like all converts, willing or not, they can often be the most radical, the most zealous. This man may have been Imperial once. Then he took the blood pact. Then he renounced that too. For some reason, he's serially unfaithful.'

'What do you suppose he is now?' Edur asked.

'It's just a hunch,' Gaunt replied, 'but I think he's one of the Sons of Sek.'

'Explain your logic,' said Edur.

'The Blood Pact is a warrior cadre sworn to the personal service of the Archon. Magister Sek, called by some the Anarch, is Archon Gaur's fore-most lieutenant. It's a king and prince dynamic, a father and son thing. Sek is ambitious, and envies the Gaur's Blood Pact shamelessly. When I was on Gereon, we heard that Sek's agents had set out to build a Blood Pact of their own, the Sons of Sek. Just as the Blood Pact have stolen bod-ies from the Imperial Guard over the years, so the Sons have begun to pilfer from the Pact. Officers, particularly, men with experience to help them shape the Sons quickly and robustly. This man says he's an etogaur, and the Sons have pretty much the same rank system. It's the best reason I can think of to explain why he still holds the rank, but has erased the scars from his palms.'

Edur smiled and nodded.

'Yes,' he said, 'that's exactly what we thought.'

'Two questions stand, then,' said Gaunt. 'What does our etogaur know, and why does he want to talk to me about it?'

'Indeed,' Edur replied.

'So, do you want me to talk to him?' asked Gaunt. 'Or am I too great a liability?'

Edur hesitated.

The vox-plate mounted on the tiled wall beside the mirror jangled suddenly. Edur lifted the handset before it could complete its first ring.

'Yes?' he said. Gaunt waited. He could just hear a whisper of voices talking on the other end of the line.

'Very well. Thank you.'

Edur hooked the handset back on its cradle. He looked at Gaunt.

'You can go in,' he said.

EIGHT

Etogaur

'I'M GAUNT.'

The prisoner, clamped into his seat, turned his head to look. He stared at Gaunt for a long while, expressionless. The tank door closed behind Gaunt with an anvil clang. It was airless in the cell.

The prisoner began to speak. His voice sounded dry, almost dusty, as if it had been left neglected and unused for years.

'I never met you,' he said. 'On Gereon. I never met you in person. I will need some… verification.'

Prisoner B's command of Low Gothic was excellent, but he had an accent, an out-worlds accent that put a burr on the words, and made each syllable sound as though it was draped in razor-wire.

Gaunt walked around the cage chair once, and came to a halt facing the prisoner. The prisoner made direct and immediate eye contact without flinching. His eyes seemed to loom at Gaunt in the phosphor-green glow of the tank. Gaunt could see–

Nothing. There was nothing there to see!

Gaunt cleared his throat.

'My unit eliminated the traitor general Noches Sturm at Lectica Bastion,' he said, skidding matter-of-factly through the account as if it was a summary of how he'd spent an idle morning off-duty. 'The head-shot that ended him was self-inflicted, a last moment of honour in an otherwise despicable life. Out of respect for that, I covered his face with a cloth from his bed chamber before I left the body. The cloth was green silk.'

The prisoner nodded.

'Now how do you know me?' asked Gaunt. It was still and airless in the tank cell. Gaunt wanted to rap on his side of the one-way mirror and urge Edur to crank up the air-cycling.

'I was a senior officer in the occupation forces of Gereon,' the prisoner replied in that voice of dust and barbed wire. 'My remit was to examine Sturm and, by means of interrogation and interview, extract as much useful intelligence from him as I could. After his death, a great effort was made to identify, locate and execute his killers.'

'I remember. I was there,' said Gaunt.

'You were active on Gereon for quite some time after the assassination. You worked with the resistance. You effectively built the resistance from the ground up. Though we never caught you, your name was known to us. The name Gaunt, the names of your elite team... They were notorious.'

'That almost sounds like you're paying me a compliment,' said Gaunt.

The prisoner shrugged as much as the restraints would allow. '"Any soldier who does not respect another soldier's achievements is a fool".'

'You're going to quote Slaydo at me now, are you?'

'I'd quote the Archon Gaur, but your ears would bleed.'

Gaunt walked over to the tank door.

'Where are you going?' asked the prisoner.

'I don't think we've got much to talk about,' Gaunt replied.

'We've only just begun,' the prisoner said.

Gaunt looked back at him. 'The Imperium wastes very little time capturing or interrogating soldiers of the Archenemy. Their corruption is considered too pernicious. No intelligence obtained from them can be considered reliable, and there is always the risk of contamination to the interrogators. You should have been executed before now, not preserved in detention.'

'I have managed to convince my captors to allow me to remain alive this long. You are my last chance.'

'Why should I care?'

'For the sake of the Imperium,' said the prisoner.

'Is that something you care about?' Gaunt asked, making no effort to disguise his sarcastic tone.

'I have pretty much ceased to care about anything,' said the prisoner. 'But I know you care, and that's enough. I can help the Imperium, Gaunt, but in order to do that, the Imperium has got to learn to trust me.'

'I don't think that's going to happen.'

'I believe you are the one person who can convince them to listen to me.'

'Why?' asked Gaunt.

'You were on Gereon for a year,' said the prisoner. 'An occupied world, Gaunt. A tainted world. It doesn't matter what you did or how bravely you served the Golden Throne, you ought to have been executed on your return. No one lasts that long without falling prey to the taint of Chaos. But you're alive, and still in service. Somehow, you convinced your masters that you were clean.'

'By the skin of my teeth,' said Gaunt, 'and there is still dissent.'

'But you did it. There is no one better equipped to judge me, to estimate how genuine I am, and then convince the powers that be to listen.'

Gaunt shook his head. 'I'm not sure I want to do that. I'd be damning myself.'

'If you refuse me, I'll be dead before the day's out,' said the prisoner. 'I'm an asset, Gaunt, and only you can see it, if you look.'

Gaunt had walked back to the cell door, and was reaching out his hand to bang on it. He hesitated.

'When you say you can help the Imperium, what do you mean?' he asked.

'I mean,' the prisoner replied, 'that I can help the Imperium win the war for the Sabbat Worlds.'

NINE
Sweet Tooth

THAT MORNING, COLD and overcast in the west, the enemy was a slice of *almonotte*. It had a layer of cream, and another of rotchka, and the soft cake was scented with popoi nuts, and capped with a caul of blue sugar icing.

She ran north, along the Wharfblade, her usual route, keeping the river to her right and the glower of the Oligarchy to her left. She crossed the wide rockcrete paddocks where the old markets and commercias had met before the war, and paused overlooking the reservoirs to sip a little rehyde from her flask and flex out her calf muscles.

Overnight, it had snowed. The vast, mesh-covered filtration tanks that processed river water for municipal needs looked like winter-issue camonets. In the outhab streets, black lines in the street snow described the routes of early vehicles. When she ran on, her own trail began again.

An outhabber market was assembling on the concourse behind the Polis power mills. She could smell the brazier smoke as she approached. Hundreds of sink-dwellers and stack-rats had gathered, draped in shawls and weatherproofs, to erect the plastic tent roofs for the stalls and lay out their wares. It was a community barter moot, nothing more.

She'd been running the route so regularly, many of them waved to her as she went by. She was the girl who ran past, every morning, sun or snow. She was the girl who sometimes waved back. She was the lean, off-world girl with the cropped blonde hair and the shabby, Guard-issue exercise kit and the long legs.

From the market, she jinked left along Sloman's Concourse, and then crossed the empty cisterns of the tidal docks on the pedestrian footbridge, enjoying the spring of the metal pans shivering under her running steps. Then she was back on the northern tip of the Wharfblade and heading for the Limecut Bridge.

The slice of *almonotte* lurked at the back of her mind.

She could see vermin birds mobbing the garbage barges moored out in the middle of the river. Their rasping calls floated to her on the cold air, hard and shrill, like the distant squeal of las-fire.

How far today? Across the bridge and into the Oligarchy proper? That would make the round-and-back to Aarlem more than sixteen kilometres. No one ran that far, except her. The enemy forced her to do it.

Two figures were coming towards her along the tow path, in step, a good rhythm going. It was Vadim and Haller, the only two Ghosts she knew who had a running regime even slightly as rigorous as her own. She saw them on this route every few days. The Limecut Bridge was as far as they ever went.

'Hey, Tona,' Haller called out as they came up to her. All three of them jogged on the spot as they stopped to talk.

'Cold today,' said Vadim.

'Yeah, cold and getting colder,' Criid agreed.

'How far are you going?' Haller asked.

She shrugged.

'Maybe up as far as Tournament Square,' she said.

Vadim whistled. He and Haller took their training seriously, and the running had kept them in shape on Balhaut, especially Haller, who was a big guy and prone to a little flab. By regular regimental standards, they were super-fit. By their standards, she was a fanatic.

'You going to swing by Section and wave to Rawne?' asked Haller with a snort.

'I don't get it,' Criid replied.

'Didn't you hear?' Vadim asked her. 'Last night?'

She shook her head.

'Rawne got busted real bad,' Haller told her, with some glee. 'That's what I heard anyway. Hark got called in. It's going to go to sanctions.'

'What did he do?' Criid asked.

'We don't know,' said Vadim, 'but he wasn't the only one in it. Meryn. Leyr. Varl.'

'Gak! You're kidding?'

'No, and Daur too.'

'Daur? Now I know you're kidding!'

'Seriously, Tona,' said Haller. 'It was some kind of big scam and they got busted hard, and Daur was in it too.'

'I can't believe that.'

'It's off the leash,' Vadim agreed.

'It really is,' Haller said. Haller was ex-Vervun Primary, and he'd known Ban Daur and his clean-cut ways for a long time. If Haller considered the story genuine, that was good enough for Criid.

'They took them all up to Section,' said Haller.

'I heard they were sent to the Stockade at Braunhem,' Vadim put in.

'Section,' Haller insisted. He looked at Tona and smiled. 'On the bright side, there may be some promotion slots to fill soon, eh, "Captain" Criid?'

'Yeah, shut up,' she replied.

Tona Criid had started running about a month after they'd arrived on Balhaut. It was all down to her past, and the years she'd spent growing up on the bad side of Vervunhive. It was all down to her sweet tooth.

As a sink-kid on Verghast, she'd been raised as much by her peers in the stacks as by her parents. Her parents had been penniless. In fact, they'd been short on a lot of things, including parental instinct, a work ethic, a desire to abide by Imperial Law, an interest in their offspring, or a reliable method of birth control.

She'd learned to fend for herself early on. She'd run with others who'd taught her some life-skills. She'd spent a lot of early years as a sink-kid and a ganger, doing things that she wasn't especially proud of. War, the ruin of Verghast and Balhaut, had been the making of her.

She could remember the old days, days spent with empty pockets and an emptier belly, when she and some of the others would venture up-hive to try to score a little food or readies. They'd lift a few bill-folds, or bait and switch at a food stall, even menace if the back street was private enough and someone had bothered to bring a blade.

Up-hive was a wonderland. It was big and sparkly, and bustling with people in good clothes with expensive augmetics, people who owned more than her family's collective wealth in the outfits they were standing up in, people whose conversations, when she overheard them, were about culture and politics and art, and the financial systems, and all sorts of other ridiculous issues that seemed to her a waste of breath. The up-hive commercias were glittering pavilions of luxury merchandise: silks, laces, jewellery, body-augs, xeno-pets, carpets, servitors, crystal ware, spices, gee-gaws, so much stuff, it made her laugh in disbelief. What would make anybody dream of wanting this stuff? And if they did dream, how did they possibly afford those dreams?

She would spend hours pressed against the glass of display windows, gazing at extravagance, until irate shopkeepers chased her away.

She was about nine or ten years old when she first saw the pastry maker's in the Main Spine Commercia. She never knew its name, because it was written in such ornate golden script on the shop-board that she couldn't tease out the individual letters. She'd seen luxury food stores before, many times, but the pastry maker's was something else. Under its candy-stripe canopy display, behind the panes of its window, there were cakes, slices, puffs, timbales, tarts, éclairs, strudels, rosettes, buns, pin-wheels, gems, and a thousand other confections of sugar and art that were every bit as exquisite as the displays in the jewellers' quarter. The colours, the structures, the decorations, all of these things made her marvel. So did the exotic names handwritten on the cards beside each work of art. And the *prices*...

If they cost so much, what in the name of the Golden Throne did they *taste* like?

At the age of nine or ten, Tona Criid could cheerfully scoff at almost all the luxury trappings of up-hive life, but in the pastry maker's she'd discovered her own dream. To her young mind, the cakes and ices were the epitome of wealthy living, not just their cost or their beauty, but the fact that if you bought one it would not last forever like a bracelet. It would vanish in the time it took you to wolf it down. *That* was luxury. *That* was high living.

It became her habit, every week or so, to find one of the up-hive pastry shops or bakers, and spend a few, wet-mouthed moments admiring the unobtainable things in their windows, and wondering what they tasted of.

When the Ghosts came back to Balhaut, Tona Criid was confronted by a life she'd never known before. Before the Guard and the war, she'd been a sink-kid, and then she'd been a Ghost, rattling wearily from one gak-hole zone to another.

Suddenly she was a grown woman, an officer, with responsibilities, and a pretty comfortable billet, and the best part of ten years' back-pay stagnating in her service account. There was nothing to do except wait and drill, and prep, and sit around and find something to spend your pay on. There was no immediate sign of active deployment in the offing.

Any line veteran can tell you that adjusting to retired life is a hard slog, like kicking a stimm habit. Your body is too used to living on an adrenaline high for months at a time. You grow detached. You get jumpy, antsy, restless. You suffer migraines, dizziness, anxiety. Your sleep suffers. Your hands sweat. If you're really unlucky, you get phobic or develop anti-social habits. You experience memory flashes cued by something innocent, like the sound of shouting or the smell of a bonfire, and wind up on a medicae scrip taking lithium or some anti-stress pharm cocktail, or in the cage on a formal statement.

Criid had taken to running to burn off the withdrawal.

She'd been on Balhaut about a week and a half when she'd found the bakery, during an exercise loop around the Old Side of Balopolis. The window display had stopped her, and made her jog backwards to peer in. The work of a high-class pastry maker was spread out before her, a memory flash to her childhood in the Vervunhive commercias.

This time, she had enough money to just walk right in and buy a slice.

The counter-staff had regarded the lean, tough-looking woman in sweat-damp gear with a great deal of suspicion.

It was a treat she repeated three or four times in the following weeks. Running was mindless, but a bakery gave her a destination, a point. She began to scout out others, increase her range, vary her routes. She noticed, to her disgust, that she was putting on a little weight, so she started adding distance to counteract the calories she was ingesting. Long, hard runs became obsessively long, hard runs. A strict, controlling part of her mind, an unhealthy part, she was pretty fething certain, required her to run until she was almost lost in fatigue and muscle pain every time she gobbled down another intricate sugar creation. It was a penance. It was punishment for her sweet tooth. Robbed of a conventional foe to fight, the confections had become her nemesis.

Tona Criid was not a stupid woman. She was well aware that the pathology was pretty twisted, which is why she hadn't shared its details with anybody. She counselled herself that it was a reward system, that it kept her fit, and that it beat descending into the hell of stimm abuse, or drink, or much, much worse.

SHE UPPED HER pace and went across the Limecut Bridge, smelling the cold metal scent of the river beneath her. The sky was the colour and texture of a jammed pict-feed. Once on the Oligarchy side of the river, she

turned east along the causeways and industrial paths that followed the
north bank all the way through the old wharf area to the New Polis
Bridge. A greater part of the area was derelict: old warehouses and fab-
shops fallen into decay and disuse, invaded by vermin and
wind-gathered refuse, their windows dimmed with cataracts of dirt, their
roofs patched and punctured, their breath sour with mildew, rot and
stagnant rainwater. That morning, the sills and eaves and rooflines were
all crowned with snow, like ermine trim, like a dusting of icing sugar.

The area could be a little rough, but Criid kept her straight silver
strapped under her vest. She wanted to head east, and then turn up into
the centre of the Oligarchy. Her original plan had been to run to
Tournament Square, and eat a slice of *almonotte* at Zinvan's on the parade
behind the Ministorum College.

She'd ditched that idea. She was going to head to Section, like Haller
had suggested. She was going to take a look: just a look. There was a
place a few streets from Section where she could get a passable lime
soforso.

The box skeleton of the Old Crossing and, behind it, the New Polis
Bridge, loomed up ahead.

Any line veteran can tell you that adjusting to retired life is a hard slog.
That morning, Criid felt particularly twitchy. It could have been the news
about Rawne, but her palms were damp, and there was a coppery taste
in her mouth. It felt like adrenaline, combat adrenaline, the feeling you
got in the zone, the feeling of being on all the time. She hadn't had it this
bad in weeks, and it seemed to be getting worse and worse as she jogged
in under the shadow of the bridge.

She came to a halt, pulse thumping, and looked around. For an over-
whelming few seconds, it felt as if she was back on the line, advancing
through some hab burb, knowing the enemy was behind every wall and
window. She had to fight back a desire to duck for cover.

What was doing it? What had set her off? She looked around, turning
a full circle, but there was nothing to see and no one around. She was
hyper-aware of the distant hum of traffic, the iron shadow of the bridge,
the sky like arctic camo, the crusts of snow, hard and bright in the morning sun, the languid lap of a river running glossy with ice mush, the drab
black of the dank stone walls, the ouslite and travertine, the smells of
river-rot and sewage outfall and gnawed stone, the fume of her breath in
the air, the beat of her heart, a golden aquila on a steeple across the river
catching the light, and the flaked and faded paint of the name *Ennisker's
Perishables* on a nearby building.

Nothing.

She sniffed a breath, and took off again, running east.

BALTASAR EYL RELAXED his grip on the handle of the packing knife. There had been someone right outside, and he had braced himself to deal with an intruder.

Whoever it was, whatever it was, it had gone now. Eyl climbed up into one of the crumbling arches that overlooked the riverside walk. There was no one down there. He kept watch for another minute, and then went back down to the loading dock.

In the dock space, both containers were open, and all those who would ever wake had been woken. One of Eyl's two headmen, his sir-dar Karhunen, was supervising the revival of the philia in the fluttering naphtha light. Some of the company, the most recently roused, were just sitting and shivering, too numb to do anything except rock and stare blankly. Others had become more mobile, flex-ing their sore limbs to get the circulation going, or prostrating themselves in prayer and offering fierce words of thanks to the Kings of the Warp.

A few were injecting stimm shots from what remained of the medicae's pack. Valdyke's medicae had done everything in his power to bring the men out of their hibernation torpor. Karhunen had eventually decided that the medicae's blood was more useful to them than his skills, and had found a packing knife of his own.

The most alert members of the philia had begun their duties. Ritual marks of gratitude to the High Powers were finger-drawn on their cheeks and foreheads with the blood of the medicae, Valdyke and his minders. The men greeted Eyl with deep bows and firm embraces as he walked amongst them. Shorb was renewing the pact-marks on his left hand with a rite knife. He made a firm incision in Eyl's honour and held the hand up, palm out, to his damogaur.

Eyl kissed the bloody palm.

'We should remake all the vows upon our souls as we step on this earth, damogaur,' Shorb said. 'The old rites must be performed.'

'They must, they should,' Eyl agreed, 'but time is bleeding away. Duty comes first. The philia must hit the ground and move.'

'Do we know the location of the pheguth?' Imrie asked.

'Soon,' Eyl assured him.

Imrie nodded. He was binding his foot. Freezerbite had reduced most of the toes to blackened pegs.

Malstrom, Gnesh and Naeme were seeing to the weapons. Eyl had listed his exact requirements in the messages he had sent ahead, and Valdyke seemed to have supplied everything that had been asked for. The materiel was all Guard issue, packed in khaki munition boxes that Valdyke had brought in and unloaded long before dawn. There were assorted lasguns, autorifles, pistols, a few heavier pieces and a fair quantity of ammunition.

'What's the quality like?' Eyl asked.

Malstrom shrugged, checking the action of a carbine he had picked from the crates.

'Beggars can't be choosers, Eyl Damogaur,' he said. 'It's old. Surplus, most of it. Sourced through illegal markets and decommission plants.' He tilted his head back and held the weapon up to examine it better by the light of the naphtha flares. His teeth were pink with blood.

'Good enough, though?'

'Mostly. I'll need to clean and bless a few pieces.'

'Do it quickly.'

Malstrom nodded.

'Upon my soul, magir,' he replied.

Naeme was pulling laspistols from another crate, checking them deftly, and snapping power cells into their receivers. As ever, he was muttering his list of names.

'Utaleth, then it is Sharhoek, next it is Muulm...'

He looked up as Eyl approached, and offered him one of the loaded pistols. Eyl took it.

'How goes the pedigree?' he asked.

The old soldier smiled.

'I wake today in this strange place and find, upon my soul, I'm nearer the end,' he said. He paused, and looked away, as if hearing a distant voice. He began to mutter again. 'Next it is Hjeve, then it is Umeth...'

It was Naeme's chosen rite, one he had taken as a burden upon his soul as a young man first pacted. He would attempt to utter, in his lifetime, every single one of the uncounted names of Death, and having said them all, would become Death. The Pedigree of Death was a popular rite amongst the philias of the Blood Pact, though Eyl had never met a soldier who had progressed so far through the holy catalogue.

Malstrom uttered a quiet curse, and Eyl looked back at him.

'There's no explosive, damogaur,' Malstrom said.

'Have you checked?'

'All the boxes. There are a few grenades, but no charges.'

Eyl thought for a moment. Valdyke hadn't been so reliable after all. It was a setback.

'We'll have to use a blood wolf,' said Gnesh.

Eyl nodded.

'Yes,' he said, 'we will.'

IN THE CHAMBER beside the loading dock, Barc and Samus were stripping down the corpses that had been used to pack and ritually seal the containers. The mission profile had relied on there being weapons available at the target area, because a munition payload of any decent size would have been too visible to Imperial sensors. Nevertheless, it had been vital to bring certain items, and these had been packed inside the spare carcasses to minimise their traces.

The company's rite knives – saw-toothed, single-edged blades about the length of a man's hand, with grips turned from human bone – had been sutured in under the meat and muscle, against the long bones of the arms and legs. Barc and his companion had gouged the first two out, and then used them for the remainder of the fleshwork. Body cavities had been used to stow the company's iron grotesks.

When Eyl entered the chamber, Barc was using the tip of his rite knife to strip sheets of yellow fat and translucent tissue away from a ribcage so that he could open it. Eyl offered him the larger, cleaver-like packing knife, and Barc took it eagerly. He began to strike the ribs away like a butcher preparing a crown rack. He reached into the cavity he had opened, and lifted out one of the grotesks.

Eyl took the heavy iron mask and turned it over in his hands. From the particular design of the scowling eyes and howling mouth, he recognised that it belonged to Johnas, but Johnas Katogaur was one of the men who hadn't survived the hibernaculums. The mask would go unused. It would need to be ritually disposed of to appease Johnas and his patron spirits.

'Find mine,' Eyl said.

Samus had already found it. With blood-speckled hands, he offered up the damogaur's silver mask. Samus's eyes were filmed blank, and he wore an idiot expression. For many years, Eyl had known Samus by his flesh name, Bezov. Samus was the name of his patron spirit, a particularly noisy thing that had gradually taken up residence in Bezov's soul. Since then, Bezov had insisted on being known by his spirit name, and the person that Eyl had known had faded behind milk-dull eyes, palsied tics and animal sounds.

Eyl rejoiced that his comrade had been singled out for such a blessing by the High Powers.

He took his silver mask. He had missed its cold weight.

THE WITCH HAD been taken to a dank chamber in the attic levels of the building. Kaylb Sirdar, Eyl's other headman, had been set to watch her.

'How many?' he asked Eyl when the damogaur reached the upper floor.

'Six didn't make it,' replied Eyl quietly.

'God's corpse!'

'Johnas was one.'

Kaylb shook his head and cursed again.

'That leaves thirty-four. We can do the job with thirty-four.'

'Of course. But six. Six!'

'They were the tithe,' Eyl told his old friend. 'They were the blood-price to get us into the enemy's heart unseen.'

'There's truth in that. When do we move?'

'As soon as we can. As soon as she tells us. Is she ready?'

Kaylb looked through the doorway behind him. In the darkened room beyond, they could see Lady Ulrike Serepa fon Eyl pacing up and down beneath the tattered and faded inspirational posters of the Henotic League. She was still wearing her veil and her mourning dress. She was talking to herself.

'I'll deal with her,' Eyl told his sirdar. 'Go down, arm yourself, help Karhunan with the rites.'

Kaylb nodded, embraced his commander, and then disappeared down the rotting, treacherous staircase.

Eyl entered the attic.

'Sister?'

Ulrike stopped pacing and looked at him. Eyl could feel her eyes behind her veil.

'I do not like this place,' she said.

'We knew we would not like it, sister,' he replied.

'We will all die here,' she declared.

Eyl nodded. She was never wrong, and as for dying on Balhaut, he had never expected anything else. That really wasn't what mattered.

'Will the Anarch die?' he asked.

'You know that's the one thing I can't see,' she replied. She fidgeted with her hands under the long lace cuffs of her weeds.

'Then tell me what you can see,' he said.

She sighed. 'I am tired. I do not want to. I am hungry. It's going to snow again. I don't like this place.'

'The snow can be damned, and there'll be time to eat and rest later,' he replied. 'You know what I want to see.'

'I am tired!' she repeated, petulantly. 'The truth is making my head hurt. Prognostication is tiresome. Don't make me do it.'

Eyl was suddenly in front of her, his hands, like spring traps, pinning her wrists. She uttered a noise of surprise and pain.

'Do not make me hurt you,' he said quietly, looking directly into the veil. 'Do not make me hurt my own blood. This is your purpose. This is why the gore mages of our Consanguinity made you. This is why they bred you and witched you.'

'Upon my soul,' she replied, 'I wish they had not.'

'I know.'

'I really wish they had not.'

'Hush,' he said, letting go of her wrists.

'You want to know where the pheguth is?' she asked.

'You know I do.'

'Have you brought any props for me?'

Eyl nodded. He reached into the pocket of his coat, and brought out a neatly-folded paper chart of Inner Balopolis and the Oligarchy. It was another of Valdyke's procurements. It had been sitting in an envelope on the top of the munition crates.

Eyl slit the seal on the chart, opened it, and spread it like a cloth on a soot-blackened old side table under the gloomy roof beams. He smoothed it out.

She came over, looked down at it, and ran her fingertips across the paper, tracing the lines of streets and thoroughfares with jerky, rapid gestures.

A cold wind gusted in through the attic's paneless window, and flapped the overhanging edges of the map.

She shuddered, and made a low moaning sound in her throat, the sound of a feline, mauled and cornered. Eyl held her shoulders, gently but firmly. He could feel the chill of her through his gloves. Her panting breath was showing through her veil as vapour. His own breath was starting to smoke too.

Without warning, she tore free of him, and ran towards the attic window, a black shape against the dull white sky.

Eyl cried out, thinking that she was going to jump, and moved to block her as fast as his enhanced metabolism could carry him.

He caught her in the window, grabbing her by the black silk of her long skirts, but she hadn't intended to jump at all.

He let go. She stood up on the sill in the window space, and looked out over the Imperial city. It was bone-pale in the winter light, and the sky was the colour of a frozen lake.

He heard her sigh. She reached up and lifted the veil away from her face so that she could look upon the world without any barriers. Eyl didn't look up. He didn't wish to see her face. He just wanted to know what she was seeing. He stared out across the towers and stacks, the rooftops. The city was vast, perhaps the biggest he'd ever seen. Its complexity filled the world up from horizon to horizon. In this place, less than a lifetime before, a great strand of fate had been decided. It had seemed like a loss to the Consanguinity at the time, but it had simply been a necessary cost, the birthing pains of a new age. It had allowed the Gaur to rise and take the crown of Archon. It had set a new course for destiny.

Now a second great strand of fate was going to be decided on Balhaut, a strand of fate he clutched in his hands, though it slithered and slipped still. It made the first look insignificant by comparison.

Ulrike laughed. Silent, heavy flakes of snow were floating down out of the gleaming sky.

'I told you it would snow,' she said.

'And I believed you,' he replied, though he was not sure that she hadn't *made* it snow.

'Can you see him?' he asked.

'I can,' she said. 'Lift me down.'

He put his arms around her thighs and lifted her down off the sill. She had lowered her veil and there were snowflakes melting in the mesh.

'Kaylb's going to die first. You need to know that.'

'All right,' he said, nodding. He swallowed.

'I mean, Kaylb's going to die soon. Today, probably.'

'All right,' he said, again.

'Won't you miss him?'

'Forever.'

She shrugged and went back to the chart. She traced the streets with her fingertips again.

'So?' Eyl asked. 'Where will I find the pheguth?'

'Here,' said the witch, tapping a point on the map with her finger. 'He is in this building on Viceroy Square. The building is known as… Section.'

TEN

Snow on Snow

THE SKY ABOVE the city had turned a sick yellow, and snow had begun to fall again. The flakes made soft, ticking noises as they struck the glass of the tall windows that overlooked the courtyard, and the ticking became a counterpoint to the heavy, funereal beat of the ornate timepiece on the corner stand.

Gaunt sat for a while, and the began to pace in the anteroom. He stared down into the courtyard where the snowflakes were softly beginning to accumulate. He watched the imperceptible crawl of the hands across the brass dial of the timepiece. He went to the door of the anteroom, and looked out into the cold hallway. People were busy elsewhere. He heard the echo of raised voices in the distance. He went back, sat down in the armchair, and sipped at the cup of now-cold caffeine the duty officer had brought. He took out Eszrah's copybook, and tried to read another of the Nihtgane folk tales, but his mind wasn't on it.

Commissar Edur reappeared, and shut the anteroom door behind him.

'What's going on, Edur?' Gaunt asked, rising to his feet. 'When can I resume the interview?'

'In a short while, I trust,' Edur replied.

'You heard what he said to me, Edur,' Gaunt snapped. 'It's vital I keep talking to him. Why in the name of the God-Emperor did you pull me out of there?'

'There are complications,' said Edur, evasively.

'What kind of complications?'

Edur looked particularly awkward.

'I want to talk to him,' Gaunt said.

'We want you to talk to him,' Edur assured him.

'Then why aren't I doing that right now?' asked Gaunt.

'You're going to have to wait a little longer,' said Edur. He flexed his chin, as if there was much more he wanted to say that he simply couldn't.

Gaunt stared at him, and then slowly sat down again.

'In the meantime, is there anything I can arrange to have brought to you?' asked Edur. 'Some refreshment? Or perhaps you'd like to see your men?'

'My men?'

Edur hesitated, and took a copybook out of his jacket pocket. He flicked through the pages and consulted a memo.

'Uhm, a Major Rawne, is it? Him and six others were brought in last night. They're downstairs in detention. I thought, as you had time to kill, you might–'

'Major Rawne has been a pain in my arse for twelve years,' said Gaunt. 'I don't know what sort of trouble he's got himself into now. I hardly care. He can stay downstairs in detention, and rot until I feel like being bothered. It might teach him not to get into trouble in the first place, though I doubt it.'

Edur cleared his throat and put the notebook away. 'It was merely a suggestion,' he said.

He turned to leave, but the door opened. A duty officer stepped in and whispered something to Edur, who nodded and turned back to Gaunt.

'Come with me,' he said.

Gaunt followed Edur out into the hallway. He had to stride purposefully to keep up with Edur's brisk pace.

'Listen carefully,' Edur said to Gaunt, quietly and urgently, as they strode along. 'Late last night, the ordos got wind of what was happening here. They're insisting we hand Prisoner B over to them. Section is protesting our jurisdictional claim to hold and interrogate the prisoner, but the Inquisition is getting rather heavy-handed about it.'

'I can imagine,' replied Gaunt.

'They're talking about a legal challenge to the Commissariat's authority, and a ground-up investigation by the Ordo Hereticus. Mercure is trying to head them off. He's arguing that this is entirely within our remit.'

'Mercure? You mean Isiah Mercure, head of the Intelligence Division?'
'Yes.'

Gaunt whistled. They turned a corner together, and, maintaining their pace, started down another hallway. Several armed guards flanked a pair of imposing doors at the far end.

'He's called you in,' said Edur. 'Answer all the questions put to you simply and clearly. Don't play games with these people. This is not a moment for showboating.'

'Understood,' replied Gaunt.

'I hope so,' said Edur. The guards snapped to attention as the two commissars strode up.

'How did they find out?' asked Gaunt.

'What?'

'How did the ordos find out about Prisoner B?'

Edur stopped in his tracks, and glanced at Gaunt.

'I don't know,' he said. 'It didn't come up.'

'You ought to find out,' said Gaunt. 'If the ordos can find out, the information is not secure.'

Edur stepped past the guards, knocked emphatically on the doors, and then opened one of them. He held it open to usher Gaunt inside.

'Colonel-Commissar Gaunt,' he announced.

Gaunt stepped into the room and made the sign of the aquila. There were about twenty Commissariat officers and clerks in front of him, along with several representatives of the Imperial Inquisition. They were arranged on either side of a large table, lit by the wan snow-light coming through the large windows. The way everyone turned to glare at him when he entered made Gaunt feel as if he had walked in at an especially delicate point in the conversation.

'Right, Gaunt,' said the senior Commissariat officer. 'Don't just stand there, man. Approach please.'

Gaunt did as he was told. No one had returned his salute. No one had stood back or vacated a seat for his benefit. A couple of Section officers shuffled their chairs aside so that Gaunt could stand next to the table beside the senior officer.

It was Isiah Mercure. Gaunt recognised him well enough from dozens of high-level briefings, though the two of them had never spoken. Gaunt was ordinarily far beneath Mercure's notice. Mercure dealt with Crusade business at sector level, and kept the company of system governors, lord generals, and the Warmaster. There was very little room for advancement left to him within the Commissariat. Gaunt had heard it suggested that

Mercure's future might include a lord militancy, or even the mastery of some significant theatre.

Mercure was a robust man with greying dark hair, and his strong features managed to be both craggy and fleshy. He was not a handsome man at all. His skin was a bad colour and pock-marked, and the bulk of his torso spoke of excessive high living, but he had exceptional presence. His voice was deep and his manner somehow reassuringly coarse and unaffected.

'You've interviewed Prisoner B, right?' Mercure asked Gaunt without really looking at him.

'Briefly, sir.'

'First impressions?'

'We shouldn't execute him, not until we've got everything we can from him.'

Mercure nodded. He still wasn't bothering to look at Gaunt. Half of his attention seemed to be caught up in leafing through the paperwork spread on the table in front of him. The other half seemed to be considering the being seated opposite him.

This individual was, without doubt, a servant of the ordos. He wore dark body armour, and a mantle with a trim of white fur. His physique was long-limbed and lithe. He occupied the chair like a dancer at rest, or a mannequin that had been artfully posed as an artist's model. He had a striking, leonine mane of hair swept back from his forehead, and his features were almost perfect in their refined construction: his eyes, for instance. It occurred to Gaunt that he'd seen eyes like that before. He'd seen them in his own face. The inquisitor's eyes were extravagantly machined replicas, and it wasn't just the eyes. The aesthetics of his face, the lines of the jaw and cheek and nose, were all too noble, too magnificently handsome to be true. At some point, the inquisitor had had his entire face rebuilt by the Imperium's finest augmeticists.

'What exactly do you think we can get from him?' the inquisitor asked, staring at Gaunt.

'Information vital to the prosecution of this crusade,' Gaunt replied.

'What qualifies you as an expert on the analysis of such information?'

Gaunt hesitated. 'I'm sorry,' he said. 'Who am I addressing?'

There were half a dozen men in black bodygloves standing behind the inquisitor's chair. His agents, Gaunt presumed, his team, his henchmen. Like their master, they were lean and lithe, and stood like a troupe of dancers, limbered up and ready to perform. Even unarmed, none of them looked like the sort of man you'd choose to tangle with. There was something curious about them that Gaunt couldn't quite identify. They bristled at Gaunt's question.

'Watch your tone,' one of them began.

The inquisitor raised his hand.

'That'll do, Sirkle,' he said.

The henchman, Sirkle, backed down slightly, but his hard gaze didn't leave Gaunt's face. Studying Sirkle and his cronies, Gaunt realised what was so disconcerting about them.

They all wore their master's face.

Hair colour, eye colour and even details of complexion were different from face to face, but the basic elements of the physiognomy were identical and unmistakable. The faces of the inquisitor's agents had all been augmetically remodelled to echo the heroic perfection of his own.

An odd piece of vanity in the first place, Gaunt thought, but doubly odd when the face you're immortalising is an artifice to begin with.

'I am Handro Rime,' the inquisitor said. 'I am here today in the service of the Ordo Hereticus. My question was, what qualifies you as an expert?'

'Gaunt's expertise isn't up for debate, Rime,' Mercure cut in. 'He's got extensive experience of the Gereon Campaign, and that's where we dredged up Prisoner B. If Gaunt says there's something in this, I trust him. He's my man on this. Aren't you, Gaunt?'

Gaunt found that Mercure was looking at him directly for the first time. It was a look that said: *Don't make me look stupid now, you little shit.*

'Absolutely, sir,' said Gaunt.

Rime leaned forwards. He smiled, but the smile was not warm. It was a perfect facsimile of a smile, executed by hundreds of synthi-muscle tensors and subcutaneous micro-motors. He fixed Mercure with his augmetic stare.

'I think the real issue, sir,' he said, 'is that the Commissariat Intelligence Division, without reference to, or permission from, any other department or agency, including the holy ordos, has detained a toxic Archenemy prisoner in the heart of one of Balhaut's cities. It's an extraordinary risk to take, not to mention fundamentally contrary to the express determination of operational procedure, as set down by the Inquisition and the High Lords of Terra. The Imperium doesn't do this, Mercure. You don't do this. The only body qualified and authorised to handle prisoners of this type is the Inquisition.'

'This is too important to waste time on a jurisdictional squabble, Rime,' said Mercure.

'Oh, if only that's all this was,' the inquisitor replied. 'You will hand Prisoner B over to us, and we will evaluate him and dispose of him.'

'But he doesn't want to talk to you,' said Gaunt.

'What did you just say?' demanded another one of the henchmen.

'Enough, Sirkle!' Rime declared.

Are they *all* called Sirkle, Gaunt wondered?

'I said he doesn't want to talk to you,' said Gaunt, gesturing generally at the ordo team. 'And he doesn't want to talk to them either,' he added, with a nod at Mercure and the Section officers. 'He wants to talk to me.'

'Is this true?' asked Rime.

'Prisoner B made it known that he would only speak to Colonel-Commissar Gaunt,' said Edur, who was waiting patiently by the door.

'Why?' asked Rime.

'That's one of the things I intend to find out,' said Gaunt, 'if I'm given the chance.'

MERCURE DISMISSED GAUNT, and Edur took him back to the anteroom. The timepiece was still ticking out its deep, regular beat, and snowflakes were still prickling the glass.

'You did well,' said Edur.

'Did I?'

'I think you impressed Mercure.'

'I couldn't tell,' said Gaunt.

Edur smiled and said, 'You never can with him. But I think your bluntness piqued the inquisitor's interest enough for us to broker some cooperation. Perhaps we can persuade them to let you interview the prisoner with them as observers. At least that way we share anything you find out.'

'The ordos should damn well respect our need for concrete intelligence,' Gaunt growled.

Edur was still smiling.

'You've been at the front line a long time, haven't you Gaunt?' he said. 'You've forgotten just how total their authority is. We're lucky they're even asking us politely. They could have just burst in here and taken him by force. You wouldn't believe the number of promising subjects the Inquisition has snatched away from us before we've been able to get to work.'

'So I've just got to wait?' Gaunt asked.

'I'm afraid so,' replied Edur.

* * *

THE SNOW WAS falling more heavily than before, in the yard beside Viceroy House. Wes Maggs started the engine of the staff car again, in the hope of squeezing some warm air out of the heaters. He knew that if he ran the engine for too long, some pen-pusher would garnish the fuel costs from his pay.

Huddled in his jacket, his hands stuffed deep inside the armpits of his vest, Maggs sat in the front passenger seat of the car, and reflected on the suckiness of the duty he'd pulled.

He was cold to the bone, and the waiting was killing him. How many hours had Gaunt been inside? The sky had gone the colour of a bad bruise, and it felt too cold for snow. He wondered about getting out and sweeping away the snow that was accumulating on the car, but he couldn't face it. He wondered about approaching one of the guards for a chat and a lho-stick to warm his hands, but they were up at the gate or in the guard towers, and looked pretty unapproachable.

Even the mechanics, who had been working on some of the other transports parked in the yard's garage area nearby, had given up their efforts and had gone to huddle around a pathetic brazier. Maggs wondered if they'd make room for him, but he doubted it. They didn't look very friendly. In fact, the whole place seemed like the coldest and least-friendly location he'd ever had to spend any time in, and that included some warzones.

He gazed across the yard through the windscreen and the fluttering snow, and finally worked out the purpose of the odd architecture he'd been staring at for half a day. The side of the main building had a sort of loading dock built into it, overhanging the main yard area. There were no windows.

Maggs realised that he'd parked facing the execution block. The trap-door in the underside of the dock overlooking the yard was the drop where men's bodies thumped down when they were hanged. This yard, otherwise used for parking and light maintenance, was where the official witnesses and observers stood.

He shuddered. The place was getting unfriendlier by the moment.

GAUNT HAD STOOD up out of the armchair and put Eszrah's copybook away before it occurred to him to wonder why he'd done either of those things.

Something had prompted his decisive movements, something very clear, but he couldn't identify what. He stood there, with the timepiece ticking solemnly behind him, and heard the feathery brush of snowflakes against the anteroom's windowpanes.

He'd seen something. He'd seen something he couldn't have seen, *shouldn't* have seen.

Just for a second, with his attention focused on the pages of Eszrah's next story, there had been a flash, a little flash behind his eyes, like an electrical flare, like the tremor of aurora lights.

Stupid. It was stupid, really. Just another twinge of his old, traumatised optic nerves. Just another function-glitch of his new, gleaming eyes.

But there was a taste in his mouth. The metallic taste of blood.

He went to the door.

'Do you THINK they're deliberately turning the heating down to piss us off?' asked Varl of no one in particular. No one in particular answered him.

The Tanith offenders occupied seven adjacent cages on the fifth bay of Detention Four. The only other prisoners on the bay were a pair of Oudinot drunks, who were still sleeping off the night before, and an ugly fether from one of the Varshide regiments, who occupied the cage next to Rawne's. The Varshide had volunteered a long and graphic commentary on exactly how pleased he was to see Jessi Banda, and precisely how much more pleased he'd be if they weren't separated by ceramite bars, until Rawne had leaned close and gently whispered something to him, as a direct result of which the Varshide had shut up and gone to hide in the corner of his cage.

Since the seven Tanith had been brought in the night before, the bay temperature had been fairly constant, but in the last hour it had begun to drop, noticeably. Varl could see his breath in the air in front of him.

No one had talked for a long time. In the first couple of hours of detention there'd been a fair amount of chat and a lot of recriminations, especially from Ban Daur, who was sitting forlornly in his cell with a look on his face that announced that his world had ended. Young Cant, dragged into the scam by peer pressure and the notion that maybe if he grew some, Varl might stop ragging on him, looked dispirited and scared. Meryn, true to form, had started to whine and blame, which had oiled the wheels of an argument between him and Banda that had gone on until the guards told them all to shut up.

Then Hark had shown up from Aarlem in the small hours with a face like murder. He'd reviewed the situation, told them they were all fething idiots, and added that he had no idea how he was going to sort 'Rawne's latest shit' out this time. He told them he'd be back later in the day.

None of them had spoken much after that.

'Yeah, what's with this?' Leyr asked, sitting up on his cot and sniffing the air. 'Varl's right. It's getting really cold.'

'Do you want me to ask the concierge if he can tweak the heating?' Meryn asked.

Banda snorted and showed Meryn a very specific number of raised fingers through the cage bars.

'It *is* getting colder,' said Cant. 'That can't be right.'

The young trooper shut up the moment he realised what he'd said, but it was too late.

'No, it can't, can it, Cant?' sneered Varl.

'Everybody give it a rest,' said Rawne, and they fell silent. Rawne got up and stood very still, as if he were listening.

'What's up?' Varl asked him.

'You hear that?' Rawne asked.

GAUNT STEPPED OUT of the armoured elevator into the white-tiled cell-block. The combination of artificial lighting and tiles made the air in the block seem sickly and fulminous, like the snow-light outside.

'You shouldn't be here, sir,' said a detention officer, hurrying up to him. 'It's not permitted.'

'I just need to look at the prisoner for a moment,' Gaunt said.

'Why, sir?'

'I just need to look at him,' Gaunt insisted.

'On whose authority?'

Gaunt turned to glare at the officer. The man recoiled from the flash of electric green in the colonel-commissar's eyes.

'Talk to Edur. Clear it for me.'

'Yes, sir.'

The man hurried away. Gaunt walked to the door of the observation chamber. He just wanted to look. He didn't want to talk. He just wanted his eyes to see.

He let himself into the observation room, and looked into a tank cell through a murky one-way mirror.

The sanctioned torturers had left Prisoner B sitting in the cage chair, his face and head uncovered. The prisoner was staring straight ahead, apparently oblivious to his discomfort and prolonged confinement. He seemed to be staring directly at Gaunt, as if the mirror wasn't one-way at all. In their wire cages, the phosphor lights filled the tank with a bilious green glow.

'What the hell are you?' Gaunt murmured, staring into the mirror. He jumped back with a start. The prisoner's mouth had moved, as if in reply.

Gaunt reached over and threw the switch on the tank intercom.

'What did you say?' he demanded. 'What did you just say?'

In the tank, the prisoner turned his head in several directions, surprised by the voice suddenly coming through the speakers. Then he looked back at the mirror.

'I said it's too late,' he replied. 'They're here.'

'Who's here?' asked Gaunt.

The prisoner didn't reply. Gaunt looked up.

From somewhere in the huge mansion above them came the unmistakable sound of gunfire.

ELEVEN

The Assault

SECTION'S MAIN GATEHOUSE faced Viceroy Square. The watch had just changed, and the guards taking up their stations in and around the gate had been on duty for less than five minutes. Those men who were obliged to work outside, in the lea of the arch, performing stop-and-searches and vehicle checks, were still doing up their stormcoats and foul weather capes, and looking sourly at the snowfall.

One trooper, out by the barrier and stamping his feet to warm up, saw it coming, but he was dead before he could raise a cry. In the final few seconds of his life, he saw dark figures, indistinct and ominous, coming towards him through the silence of the square's gardens, like phantoms conjured by the snow-light. The falling snow that veiled their menacing, steady approach seemed, to the young soldier, to be falling ever more slowly, like a pict-feed set on increasing increments of slow-motion until the feed, and the descending flakes, came to an unnatural, vibrating halt.

He was opening his mouth to remark upon both of these oddities when the blood wolf killed him.

It killed him in passing, with a gesture of its hand. It killed him on its way in through the gatehouse, throwing him aside with such force that the impact of his hurled body against the wall of the gatehouse pulverised most of his bones and left declarative pressure sprays of blood stippled across the snow.

The blood wolf was moving too fast for any human eye to properly follow it. The warp-wash that surrounded it distorted reality, making time run out of step, and the snow hesitate in mid-air. It flew in through the gatehouse, exploding both barrier beams like tinder. It made a keening noise like the bogies of a runaway train drawing sparks from steel rails. The keening caused the windows, even those specially strengthened to resist weapons fire, to shatter explosively. These blizzards of toughened glass, which moved far faster than the blizzards of snow in the gardens outside, shredded all the troopers caught in their blast zones. Two more guards were decapitated beside the inner barrier, and another by the door. Another, who was unfortunate enough to be standing directly in the blood wolf's path, disintegrated on impact in a spray of gore like a jar of fruit conserve hit by a shotgun round.

A blood wolf is like a missile. You aim it and you fire. In the absence of the explosives that Valdyke had promised to procure, Eyl had been obliged to get his witch to conjure a blood wolf as the focus of the raid.

A sacrifice had therefore been required. Every single man in the philia had volunteered for the combat-honour. Eyl had eventually chosen Shorb, a choice his sirdars had approved. One by one, the men had gathered to say farewell to Shorb's soul, and then they'd let the witch have him, to cut.

Eyl didn't understand the process. He generally left such matters to the gore mages, but he understood enough to know that the conjurations that produced a blood wolf were not all that different from the conjurations that wove wirewolves, which were commonly used to police and protect the worlds of the Consanguinity. Those rites put a daemon-spirit into a conductor-body of metal, allowing it to walk abroad. The blood wolf rites put a daemon-spirit into a man's body.

It was a less precise art. Teams of philia metallurgists and wiresmiths might take months or even years to properly machine the metal chassis of a wirewolf to perfection, inscribing it with the most precise runes and sigils, forging it just-so, so that it could best house the spirit it was designed to capture and harness.

Even with a sharp rite knife, a human body could not be modified so cleanly, especially not at short notice. As a vessel for the burning light of the High Powers, flesh was far too perishable compared to metal, even when the flesh was as devoted as Shorb's. A wirewolf might last forty or perhaps even fifty minutes before burning out. Eyl had never seen a blood wolf last longer than sixteen.

The blood wolf was a one-use weapon, a flash-bang. It would burn Eyl's beloved Shorb out and leave him nothing more than charred meat. The trick with a weapon like a blood wolf was to use it fast, and to use it well.

The trick was to use it for *maximum effect*.

Shorb had become a keening ghost. He was an energised, trembling shape, a shape that had once been a man, leaping and bounding, laughing and surging, like voltage freed from a shorting cable.

As Eyl hefted up his weapon and followed Shorb and the philia in through the gate, he knew that the blood wolf had little more than a few minutes left in it.

They would have to count.

An Imperial Guardsman ran towards Eyl through the hesitating snow, bewildered, his rifle half-raised.

'What the hell's going on?' he demanded.

Eyl lifted his autorifle, and evacuated the Guardsman's braincase in a brief, but considerable, pink shower.

'We've come for the traitor,' Eyl told the corpse steaming on the snow as he stepped over it.

THE MEN OF the philia spread out into the courtyards as they came through the gate. They moved firmly, with a purpose, passing over the bodies and bloodstains of the Imperials. They were wearing their grotesks, so their iron faces were frozen in silent howls and malign sneers. Their shooting was sporadic: a crackle of gunfire here or there whenever a target presented itself. Munitions were not unlimited. Imperial soldiers were mown from the wall tops and smashed off access staircases. Imrie, brandishing a heavy autorifle that was older than all the men of the philia put together, shot one of their few rifle grenades up through the slot of the guard tower behind the gate. The blast jolted the tower and squirted smoke out through its seams and gaps.

A siren started to wail. A few of the Imperials gathered their wits enough to begin returning fire. Las-bolts cracked and whined across the snowy yards. Three Imperials armed with carbines had grouped inside the entrance of the administration wing, and were shooting towards the gatehouse. Gnesh moved past Eyl, striding with insouciant ease like a man on a recreational stroll. He was the biggest man in the philia, tall and broad-backed, with a lumberhand's shoulders, and a neck as wide as the skull that sat on it. He had taken the bipod off a heavy lasgun, and cinched the weapon over his right shoulder on a long strap so that he could shoot it from the hip. The chest-pumping pop of each discharge threw a javelin of light out through the smoke and the snow. Gnesh casually aimed at the administration wing. His shots punched a series of deep holes along the facing wall until they found the entrance and wrought catastrophic damage on the three Imperials. Then he aimed a couple more shots into the architrave, and collapsed the entrance onto their smouldering bodies.

Led by Kaylb Sirdar, the first element of the philia had reached the lobby of the main building. The blood wolf had already come through, and the wide marble floor was covered with a crust of glass from the doors, the chandeliers and the hoods of the glow-globes. Kaylb swung his element to the left, and headed towards where the witch had said the secure stairwells were located. An Imperial trooper and a man in a commissar's long coat tried to fend them off, firing from the cover of some broken furniture. Kaylb killed them both. There was no time to waste, but Kaylb paused for long enough to read the marks their blood had made on the floor and walls. The prognostications were good.

Karhunan brought the second element into the main building through a large, side entrance that Imperial staff called the catering door. It had once given vittallers and suppliers access to the kitchens, in the days when Section had been a private residence. The old kitchens and larders had become a despatch office, a vox station, and a workroom for intelligencers, with access to the principal briefing chambers and the map room. Karhunan's force met fierce resistance from a group of company officers and commissars who had been meeting in the workroom. Shouting for support, the Imperial men held the main hallway, armed only with the pistols and dress weapons they had been carrying that day. Behind them, groups of unarmed or non-combatant staff fled deeper into the building, away from the assault.

Malstrom took a light wound, the first injury suffered by the philia, but righted himself quickly. He ducked into the hastily abandoned despatch room to evade the determined small arms fire. Las-shots and hard rounds from the Imperial officers pinged and cracked off the inside of the catering door archway.

Karhunan heard Malstrom laugh.

'What?' he shouted. 'What's so amusing?'

Malstrom reappeared in the doorway of the despatch room. As one of the building's watch points, the room had been supplied with an emergency weapons locker. Malstrom had smashed the lock with the butt of his carbine.

'It's as if the enemy is on our side,' he told his sirdar. 'They leave toys for us to play with.'

Malstrom had swung his carbine over his shoulder so that he could slap a shell into the clean, polished grenade launcher that he'd taken from the box.

'Brace!' Karhunan bellowed to the other men.

Malstrom leaned out of the doorway and fired the launcher. The fat grenade spat up the hallway, arcing high, smashed off a ceiling light, and began to tumble on its downward path before detonating. The blast sent a scratchy, concussive clap of smoke and hard air up the hall.

'Again?' Malstrom growled. He had a satchel full of shells.

'Do it again,' Karhunan agreed.

Malstrom broke the fuming launcher on its hinge, and slapped a second grenade home. He clacked the stocky weapon shut with a snap of his wrist, and fired again.

Again, hard, hot air rasped back down the space. There was grit in it, pieces of glass and chips of stone, and it rattled down like hail.

The Imperials were broken. As the element advanced through the smoke, they found most of them dead, blackened and raw from the blasts. A few, deaf and blind, were convulsing or struggling feebly on their hands and knees. Karhunan and his men put a shot through the head of anyone still moving.

One of the commissars had got clear, dragging an injured colleague with him. When he saw Karhunan emerging through the smoke, he started to spit curses at him. He was yelling like an animal, fuelled by fear and hate. He let the colleague he was dragging flop to the floor, and brought up his pistol.

The gun barked twice. Karhunen felt the double impact, one hit right after the other, striking his right shoulder and the right-hand side of his mask. The collision turned him, twisting his body. Pain seared through his shoulder. His head was wrenched violently to the right. One round had gone through the meat of his shoulder, the other had glanced off the brow-ridge of his iron grotesk. The mask had smashed back into his face, breaking his cheek bone and tearing his lip across his upper teeth. Hot blood filled his mouth.

Karhunan smiled. He lifted his carbine and fired a burst on auto. The commissar jerked backwards, as if he'd been snatched off his feet by a sharp yank on a rope. He bounced off the wall behind him, and landed on his face.

The sirdar moved forward to finish the man's injured colleague, but the limp body was already dead. Karhunan raised his hand and made some quick pact signs to direct his men.

The element rushed on. Several of the men were wielding clean, new Imperial Guard weapons they had taken from the dead.

ALARMS WERE RINGING furiously, and the air was filling with sounds of gunfire and shouting, and the increasingly acrid smell of smoke.

'What in the name of the Throne is this about?' Mercure roared as he burst out of the conference room with his agitated aides in tow. There was panic outside. Staff members were fleeing down the corridor without any discipline or composure. Troopers were clattering in the opposite direction, trying to marshal the fleeing personnel, and trying to fathom, like Isiah Mercure, what the hell was happening in the middle of an afternoon at the heart of an Imperial stronghold.

It wasn't a drill. Mercure knew that immediately. You could ring the alarm bells and raise a hue and cry, and even stand out in the yard and fire a gun into the air to generate an atmosphere of urgency for a shake-down drill, but no one would ever go to the bother of putting that subtle flavour of burning into the wind, and the best drill coordinator couldn't manufacture the tight look of real fear and bewilderment that Mercure could see on the faces around him.

Besides, a shake-down this big couldn't be staged without his approval and knowledge, and nobody on the staff was gun-eatingly mad enough to have set something up on an afternoon when Mercure was head-to-head in the main meeting room with grox-loving sons of bitches from the ordos.

Everyone was shouting and gabbling. A squad of soldiers almost knocked Mercure down in their urgency to reach the front of the building.

'Shut up. Shut up!' Mercure yelled. 'I asked a question. Shut up, listen to me, and answer it! What's going on?'

'Section is under attack, sir!' a junior commissar replied in a voice squeaky with anxiety. Mercure punched him in the mouth hard enough to knock him off his feet.

'I didn't ask for the bloody obvious!' Mercure shouted. 'Give me plain facts. Give me something I can use!'

'Protocol 258,' said Commissar Edur, suddenly appearing at Mercure's side. Edur had a squad of S Company storm-troopers with him, and a look of true and solemn concern in his dark, handsome eyes.

Mercure looked at Edur in disbelief. 'No. That bad? Edur, tell me!'

'Protocol 258 is in effect, sir,' replied Edur. 'Sergeant Daimer and his men will escort you to the safe area, and evac you if necessary.'

The storm-troopers closed in, shoving the aides aside to get at Mercure. They were big men, armoured in black and green, their shoulder guards bearing the silver flash insignia of S Company, the Commissariat's close protection detail assigned to guard the most senior personnel. When Protocol 258 was put into effect, you didn't argue with S Company, not even if you were Isiah Mercure.

'How bad?' Mercure demanded as Daimer and his men moved in around him.

'A significant assault,' Edur called back. 'Many casualties. As far as we know, a squad of some size, perhaps as many as twenty or thirty men, hit the main gate four minutes ago. Some are already in the building.'

'Who the hell are they?' one of the senior aides demanded. 'I mean, who the hell attacks Section HQ on Balhaut?'

Hemmed in by the S Company men, Mercure looked at Edur. Their eyes met. Neither of them knew the precise answer to the aide's frantic question, but they knew enough to realise that the answer wasn't going to be pleasant.

'Oh God-Emperor,' Mercure murmured. 'Someone's come for him.'

'I think so, sir,' Edur replied.

'We've got to move you now, sir, I'm sorry,' Sergeant Daimer insisted, and the protection detail started to manhandle Mercure away.

'They can't have him, Edur!' Mercure yelled. 'You hear me? They can't have him. You know what to do. No mistakes.'

'Yes, sir!' Edur shouted back over the general pandemonium. He was about to add something else when he heard the weird, keening noise. It was coming from somewhere behind him. It sounded like a night wind shrieking down the stack of an old chimney.

The blood wolf burst into the long hallway. Edur turned, and saw it, yet did not see it. He knew something was coming, something that wailed like an old flue, something that bubbled reality around itself, like a cloak of un-being. Edur gagged. He felt bile rise in his throat. He pulled out his bolt pistol. His hand was shaking.

The blood wolf entered the hallway at the far end, and though it was essentially invisible, its passage down the hall towards them was vividly narrated by the carnage it wrought. The wooden doors splintered in an explosive blizzard of pulp and fragments. The carpet scorched and shrivelled. Section personnel, ranged along the hallway, began to die, as if some murderous wave was sweeping through them. Bodies were suddenly severed and collapsed in fountains of blood, as if snipped in two or three or even four by giant, invisible shears. Others burst like blood blisters, or were smashed aside into the walls and ceiling by unseen, demented hands.

The tide of destruction bore down on them. Edur raised his weapon. The S Company storm-troopers opened fire with their hellguns. Droplets of blood from the wolf's killing spree had filled the air like raindrops, and now hesitated in their descent like the snowflakes outside.

There was a loud bang that jarred Edur's teeth and hurt his eyes. A beam of force had hit the bubble of tortured light that hid the blood wolf from the side.

The blood wolf was blasted sideways into the hallway wall, leaving a ghastly skidmark of blood smeared across the wallpaper. It fell, scrabbling, wounded, winded, and Edur realised that he could see something properly, for the first time. A human shape was making frenzied animal motions inside the blue of warp-wash, something flayed and bloody that screamed and thrashed its limbs with inhuman violence. Edur saw the white enamel of bared teeth against the bloody mass of the whole. He saw reality blotching and distorting around its clotted, skinned form, and it made him vomit.

A second beam of force hit it, and made it writhe backwards. The keening increased in pitch.

Handro Rime, the inquisitor, had emerged from the meeting room. His mane of hair was lifting in a wind that seemed to be affecting only him. He was brandishing a sceptre, an ornate metal rod the length of a walking cane that looked as though it had been fashioned from chromium steel. It fizzled with power, as if a charge was running through it. The top end was shaped like a winged human skull.

There was a third, painful bang. Another beam of force, like a needle of light, spat from the skull-top of the sceptre that Rime was holding and struck the baying blood wolf. This time, the beam was continuous, pinning the thing to the ground. Rime's henchmen spread out around him and drew their weapons. Edur could see the strain on Rime's face. Several ripples of warp-vapour crackled out of the gibbering thing, and then all the blood droplets hanging in the air fell at once, in real time, and covered the floor with a million tiny splashes like the first few seconds of a monsoon.

'I believe I have it contained,' Rime yelled through gritted teeth. 'Get Senior Commissar Mercure to a place of safety!'

Edur shook himself and turned to obey. He fell in with the storm-troopers, and they began to hurry Mercure away. Mercure was staring in ashen disgust at the thing the inquisitor was attempting to ensnare, and at the bloody horror that it had left in its wake.

'Get downstairs!' Mercure stammered at Edur. 'Get downstairs and see to it!'

Edur shoved Mercure and his escort onwards with one hand, and turned to make for the nearest staircase. He saw a drop of blood, a single drop of blood, hovering and wobbling in the air, its gleaming surface tension undulating. He realised it was hanging there, in virtual freeze frame, and that his own limbs and movements had run slow, and that time was disjointed again.

The blood wolf ripped free from the spear of energy with which Inquisitor Rime had staked it to the floor. The sceptre was wrenched from his grip and whirled away across the blood-soaked floor. Rime was slammed back into the wall and pinned there, his legs kicking. His mantle of white fur caught fire, and then his hair did too. In a second, his entire head was engulfed in raging flames. He was screaming. The blood wolf let him go. He slid down the wall, found his feet somehow, and then staggered forwards, ablaze from the shoulders up.

His henchmen tried to close with the beast. Edur saw one disembowelled and another flung away like a broken doll. Rime fell to his knees, and then collapsed on his face, his head and shoulders still engulfed. The keening grew loud again.

Edur ran.

GAUNT STARED AT the ceiling, listening. He could hear gunfire. It was distant, but there was a lot of it. He'd heard at least two significant explosions, and a great deal of commotion. A lot of voices were echoing down to him, muffled through the floors.

He glanced at the prisoner, who was as still and silent as before, and then headed to the door. There was no one in the corridor outside. He could still hear the shouting and the shooting from above.

A detention officer suddenly ran into view, red-faced and out of breath.

'What's going on?' Gaunt asked.

The man didn't stop.

'Get this area secure!' he yelled as he ran past.

'Don't give me orders!' Gaunt shouted after him. 'What's going on? Hey!'

The officer ran out of sight.

'Hey!'

Gaunt wondered why he was asking the question. He knew what was happening. He knew in his bones and in his heart. He'd *seen* it. He'd seen what was coming.

He knew how fast and how bad things were going to get, and it scared him to think how he might know that.

He knew what he had to do.

He drew his bolt pistol and walked to the door of the holding cell.

THE CARBINE IN Kaylb Sirdar's hands retched twice and spat ugly blades of red light. They punched into the Imperial trooper coming up the staircase towards him, hurling him backwards with a strangled cry. The trooper crunched and cartwheeled down the stairs, and ended up face down on the landing below.

Kaylb barked commands to his element, and they clattered on down the stairwell. Emergency lights had come on, and the smell of smoke was getting stronger. Behind the plaintive wail of the sirens, they could all hear the keening.

There were two exits on the landing.

'Which way?' asked Barc. Weapons ready, the men waited for instructions, covering the staircase access, up and down.

There were signs. Kaylb traced his finger across the letters and tried to make the unfamiliar words in his mouth. It was hard to know. He dragged up his left sleeve and consulted the blood map that the witch had put in his forearm. She'd given one to both sirdars and to Eyl too, a little schematic plan of the target building mapped from her divination, and formed by raised veins and swollen capillaries under the skin. As the element advanced through the area, the blood map on the patch of skin moved with them. Kaylb ran his filthy fingertips over the bumps and ridges.

'That way,' he pointed. 'The left-hand hatch.'

'HOLY THRONE,' MERYN whispered. 'Holy fething Throne!'

He was right up against the bars of his cell in Detention Four, his hands clamped around them.

'Rawne?' he hissed.

'What?'

Rawne cast a look at Meryn with hooded eyes. The fear they were all feeling was most obviously etched on Captain Meryn's face. It wasn't a fear of fighting, because they'd all done more than their share of that in their lives, nor was it a fear of death.

It was a fear of being trapped. It was a fear of helplessness.

'This is definitely not good,' said Leyr.

'The building's under attack,' stammered Meryn. 'I mean, it's under assault. You can hear it. You can smell it.'

'You can shut up,' said Rawne.

Meryn was right. For several minutes, they'd been able to hear the muffled scream of alarms from somewhere above them. The alarms had begun just after it had got really cold. Then, straining, they'd begun to hear the other sounds, coming very faintly through the reinforced walls and floors of the detention level: cries, shots, detonations.

'We've got to get out of these cages,' said Meryn.

Rawne looked at him, looked at the ceramite bars, and then looked back again.

'I mean it,' Meryn barked.

'He means it,' said Varl.

'Yeah, well unless you've got a key made out of solid wishes,' said Rawne.

Meryn got on his knees and started to examine the lock mechanism of his cage door again.

Ban Daur was still sitting back on his cot, his arms folded, a sour look on his face.

'That's a good idea, Meryn,' he said. 'Brilliant. The locks in the detention blocks of Commissariat sections are famously easy to pick, especially if you're only using fingernails and nostril hair.'

'Shut the feth up, you superior son of a bitch!' Meryn yelled, turning on Daur. 'You do something. You think of something! We're stuck in here, and something bad's coming. We're stuck in here and, when it comes, we will be helpless, and we'll die like fething rats!'

Daur swung to his feet and faced Meryn through the bars. He was taller than Meryn. He looked down on him in almost every way.

'We're stuck in here because we were stupid,' Daur said. A twitch of his head showed that he meant that to include everyone. 'We were stupid, and this is what happens to stupid people.'

'Oh, you feth-head,' said Meryn. 'This is your philosophy, is it, Mr Goody-fething-two-shoes? Be a man and face your punishment?'

'Pretty much,' replied Daur.

'You're fething unbelievable!' retorted Meryn.

'And you're an idiot,' said Daur. 'You're crapping yourself over nothing. This is a drill.'

'A drill?' asked Meryn in disbelief.

'Yes, of course it is!' said Daur. 'Come on, they're blasting the sirens and shooting off some dummy ammo. It's a shake-down. It'll be over in another five minutes.'

He looked around at the other Ghosts. Everyone was looking at him.

'What? Come on, it's got to be, right?'

Daur looked at Leyr, and the big scout looked uncomfortable. Daur looked at Varl, but Varl sniffed and looked at the floor. He looked at Cant. The young trooper just looked scared.

'This is Balhaut!' Daur declared. 'This is gakking Balhaut, for Throne's sake. We're so far from the front line it's not even worth joking about. Who the gak's going to attack Commissariat Section in the middle of Balopolis...'

His voice trailed off. He looked at Banda. She looked back at him, smiled a little sad smile, and shook her head.

He looked at Rawne.

'Major? Come on, help me out here,' said Daur.

Rawne looked at him.

'It's not a drill,' Rawne said.

Daur opened his mouth, and then closed it again.

'Feth,' he said, eventually.

The cell bay door clanged opened. A detention officer burst in and stared at them all for a moment, his eyes flicking from one cage to the next: the seven Ghosts, the slumbering Oudinot, and the lone Varshide in the cell next to Rawne's.

The detention officer looked scared and bewildered. His hair was messed up and his jacket was buttoned up wrong. He looked like someone who had just woken from a bad dream.

Through the open bay door behind him, they could all hear the sirens much more clearly.

The detention officer took a last look at them, as if he wasn't sure what he was supposed to be doing.

'Stay here,' he told them, and ran back out, pulling the hatch shut behind him.

Varl looked through the bars at Rawne.

'You know,' he said, 'sometimes people say the stupidest things.'

The shots outside made them start and tense: two shots, just on the other side of the hatch. Instinctively, all of the Ghosts backed away from the fronts of their cages.

'What the hell's happening?' the Varshide trooper mumbled.

The cell bay hatch opened again. From outside, they could hear shouting, clattering footsteps and repeated gunfire.

KAYLB SIRDAR SWUNG in through the detention block hatchway, his carbine raised.

Prisoners. The sirdar saw prisoners, just prisoners in cages, all staring at him in pathetic terror. Check them. Find the pheguth. Kill the pheguth. Kill anyone who wasn't the pheguth. The men of his element were spreading out through the bays of the cellblock doing just that. He could hear the shots.

The sirdar stepped forward. He saw the eyes staring back at him, wild, animal eyes; caged men who recognised death when it approached.

RAWNE WATCHED THE man approach. He took in the ragged, dirty combat gear, second- or third-hand at least, the purposeful pose, the confident, well-trained advance. Only one detail mattered. The scowling iron mask that the man was wearing over his face identified him very clearly. It was the fighting grotesk of a Blood Pacted warrior.

He heard Cant whisper, 'Holy Throne.'

The sirdar reached the first cage. He had the carbine's stock tucked up against his shoulder, aimed down and wary. He stared at the blinking Varshide trooper through the bars.

'Who are you supposed to be?' the Varshide slurred.

Kaylb fired between the bars of the cage. The two shots hit the Varshide in the chest, and threw him against the back wall of the cage. His corpse overturned the cot and the covered chamber pot beside it as it crumpled onto the cell floor. The sour smell of stale urine filled the cell bay, and mingled with the acrid reek of scorched flesh and cooked blood.

The next cage in line was Rawne's. Rawne didn't move as the killer advanced towards him. He kept his eyes locked on the grotesk.

Kaylb looked the next prisoner up and down quickly, and then raised the carbine to execute him.

'Voi shet, magir!' Rawne said.

Kaylb froze.

'Ched qua?' he replied.

'Voi shet, magir,' Rawne repeated, stepping closer to the bars, his hands open and visible. 'Eswer shet edereta kyh shet.'

Kaylb came closer, the gun still aimed at Rawne's chest.

'Shet atraga gorae haspa?' he demanded. 'Voi gorae haspa?'

Rawne smiled, and said, 'Fuad gahesh drowk, magir.'

'Ched?' the sirdar queried.

'Abso-fething-lutely,' said Rawne and shot his arms out through the cage. His left hand grabbed the carbine's barrel and yanked it in between the bars. The weapon fired, but the shot struck the back wall of the cell, harmlessly. Rawne's right hand had seized the sirdar by the collar. Taken by surprise, the sirdar found himself being dragged headfirst into the cage door. Rawne slammed him into the cage so they were face to face with only the bars between them. Though the sirdar still had his right hand clamped to the carbine, most of the weapon was pulled through the bars and wedged against them by Rawne's vicing left-hand grip. The weapon fired again. Two more futile las-bolts left scorch marks on the back wall.

It was all happening too fast for the sirdar. Kaylb started to cry out, to fight back. He clawed at Rawne through the bars with his left hand.

Teeth bared, Rawne began to slam the sirdar's face against the bars with his right hand. His grip on the collar was so tight that he was already choking off the man's air. In a furious, steady, almost mesmeric motion, Rawne began to pump his right arm in and out, smashing the iron-masked face of the pinned man off the bars over and over again. It was like the action of an industrial stamping press. Rawne didn't have the time, space, opportunity or means for a single clean killing blow, so he compensated with frenetic quantity.

By the eighth blow, the sirdar had begun to struggle with real fury, and the carbine fired again. By the tenth, his teeth were broken, and there was blood spattering out of his shuttling head. By the twelfth, there was blood and nicks on the bars. By the fifteenth, the grotesk had cracked, and the sirdar's head had become a limp, lolling punch bag, snapping to and fro.

Kaylb Sirdar finally tore free, somewhere around the seventeenth blow. He staggered backwards, drunken and swaying, howled a curse to the Kings of the Warp, and shot Rawne.

Except he was no longer holding his carbine. Rawne still had it in his hand.

Rawne swept the weapon in between the bars, rotated it end-over like a piece of show-off parade ground drill, aimed, and fired out of the cage without hesitation.

The las-bolt hit Kaylb Sirdar in the forehead, and hammered him back into the bay wall. The grotesk split in half, and the two pieces flew off his face and bounced away across the deck in opposite directions.

The sirdar slid down the wall, and finished up, dead, in a sitting position, his head tilted to one side. He had left a long streak of blood down the wall above him. If he had been alive to see it, Kaylb Sirdar would have recognised that the prognostications of the blood mark were not good.

Rawne lowered the carbine.

'Holy shit,' breathed Meryn.

'Wh-where did you learn to talk that language?' Cant whispered.

'Yeah, Cant, this is really the time for *that* conversation,' said Banda.

Rawne poked the snout of the carbine into the cage lock and pulled the trigger twice, enough to blow the mechanism. He swung his cage door open and headed for the exit.

'Hey. Hey!' Meryn yelled. 'Where the feth are you going? What about us?'

'He's going to check we're secure, and then he's going to get the keys,' said Varl calmly. 'Feth, Meryn, what are you, a child?'

Rawne reached the bay hatch and peered out, the carbine ready. There was a lot of shooting going on outside, quite close by. The smell of burning was intense. He could see smoke in the air now. He could hear screams. In the neighbouring cell bays, prisoners were being slaughtered.

He pushed the hatch to, and opened the wall box where the detention officers kept the cage keys. They jingled as he shook them out in his hand and hurried back to the cage row.

'Unlock and get out, fast,' he said passing the keys to Varl, the first in line. 'We're getting out of here.'

'But what about–' Daur began.

'If we stay here, we die,' Rawne said, cutting Daur off. 'We get out, and find out what the feth's going on. Then we worry about the consequences.'

PRISONER B TURNED his head to look at Gaunt as he entered the sick green light of the tank cell. He looked at the bolt pistol in Gaunt's hand without a blink or the sign of an expression.

Then he turned his head again and sat looking straight ahead.

'There's no time for a conversation,' Gaunt said.

'I know,' said the etogaur.

'We have an understanding?' asked Gaunt.

'Just do it,' the prisoner replied.

With his free hand, Gaunt began to unbuckle the shackle cuff pinning Prisoner B's left arm to the chair. Prisoner B looked around at him, startled.

'What?' asked Gaunt.

'I thought–'

'What?'

'I thought you were going to execute me.'

'I will. Give me the slightest excuse, and I will,' Gaunt said, working at the next set of buckles. He kept glancing over his shoulder at the door.

'I will give you no reason to–'

'You wanted us to trust you,' Gaunt snapped. 'You wanted me to trust you. I don't and I probably won't. But you wanted my help to stay alive because you swore you could help us. One chance. Do not test me.'

'I will not, Gaunt.'

'Don't use my name either.'

'Of course,' said Prisoner B.

Gaunt unclasped the body straps and shook them off the etogaur's shoulders.

'Are your hands numb? Your fingers?'

'No,' said Prisoner B.

'Then get the buckles on the leg straps undone,' said Gaunt.

Prisoner B leaned over in the restraint chair and diligently began to undo the heavy iron buckles on the leather straps binding his legs. Gaunt crossed back to the heavy tank door and peered around it. The hallway outside was empty, but he heard a loud burst of full auto-fire, close by. Somewhere else, someone was screaming.

He could smell smoke, and he could hear some kind of... *keening* sound.

He ducked back into the tank cell, and looked over at Prisoner B. The prisoner had managed to free one leg.

'Hurry up!' Gaunt yelled.

There was a noise outside. He went back to the door. Looking around its rim, he was in time to see a detention officer and a sanctioned tor-turer fly in through the door at the far end of the interrogation unit. The detention officer was backing up, frantically blasting a lasrifle from the hip at unseen targets beyond the door. The torturer was simply running for his life, hurtling along the white-tiled hallway towards the heavy door half-concealing Gaunt.

Answering fire hammered in through the doorway, and cut down the detention officer, who simply crumpled and collapsed. Two or three more stray shots whined in, and then an armed man burst through the door, bounding over the dead detention officer. He was armed with an old lasrifle and dressed in shabby combat gear. A man dressed just like him appeared on his heels.

Both were wearing black-iron grotesks.

The first of them raised his rifle and pinked off a shot that hit the fleeing torturer in the spine, bringing him down hard. Belly down in a pool of blood that looked glossy, like spilled enamel paint against the polished white of the corridor's tiling, the torturer tried to drag himself forward. His legs were useless.

He saw Gaunt behind the heavy, open cell door ahead of him.

'Help me!' he gurgled.

A las-round took the top of his head off.

Gaunt swung out from behind the door and fired his bolt pistol. The shot hit the first of the Pacted raiders square in the sternum, and exploded his torso. Blood and meat suddenly decorated a considerable section of the corridor's white-tiled surfaces.

The other Pacter yelled something and began firing.

Gaunt ducked back behind the tank cell door as the auto fire ripped past. He felt it spank hard against the other side of the hefty door, driving it back against his body. He tried to keep it wedged open. If it slammed shut, the lock might engage, and if the lock engaged, he and Prisoner B would be trapped, and that would be the endgame.

More wild shots whacked against the door shielding him. The impacts were beginning to drive the door into him with enough force to bruise his shoulder and arm. Gaunt could hear shouting from the far end of the hall. Someone was shouting words in a hard, ugly language that he, thankfully, hadn't heard much since Gereon.

With a curse, Gaunt kicked the door wide open and opened fire again, his bolt pistol braced in a two-handed grip. Three wailing bolt-rounds seared down the hallway, and detonated against the tiled walls, blowing clouds of tile fragments and plaster in all directions. The masked raiders, and there were three of them in sight, ducked frantically, and pulled back into the cover of the end door.

Gaunt fired another two shots with his great cannon of a pistol to keep them ducking, and turned back into the tank cell.

Prisoner B was standing right behind him.

Gaunt leapt back and brought his gun up, but Prisoner B just stood there.

'Don't sneak up on me!' he ordered.

'I didn't mean–' the etogaur said.

A flock of las-rounds cracked past. Gaunt winced and turned back, firing two more bolts that scattered the raiders sniping at them from the far hatchway.

'Move!' Gaunt yelled. He took off down the corridor with Prisoner B behind him. He could hear the raiders behind them shouting. What was that word?

Pheguth.

'Come on!' Gaunt yelled. Two las-bolts clipped the wall beside him, chipping the tiles.

Four metres more. A hatch on the left.

Gaunt skidded up in front of it, grabbed Prisoner B by the shoulder, and physically shoved him through the doorway out of the line of fire. He turned to fire one more hefty round at the raiders advancing along the corridor towards them, and then dived through the hatchway before he'd had time to see if he'd hit anything.

On the other side of the hatch, in the small access way adjacent to the main corridor of the interrogation unit, Prisoner B had come to a halt.

The Blood Pact soldier facing him had hesitated in surprise for a second. Now, his rifle was coming up to fire.

Gaunt fired past the etogaur's shoulder and blew the raider's head apart. Gore spattered across Prisoner B's face. He didn't flinch. He wiped it away with the back of his hand.

Gaunt slammed the hatch behind them shut, and wound the locking ring.

'Move,' he said to Prisoner B.

'Which way?'

'This way,' said Gaunt.

'Where are we going?'

'I'll find a way out,' said Gaunt.

The raiders started beating on the other side of the locked hatch. Gaunt ejected his smoking bolt pistol's clip. It was spent. Ten rounds. He was only carrying three spares in the pouches of his uniform belt.

'They won't let you go,' said Prisoner B.

'Pheguth,' Gaunt replied.

'What?'

'They called you pheguth.'

'What other word would they have for me?' asked Prisoner B.

'It's what you people called Sturm,' said Gaunt slamming a fresh load home and racking the mechanism.

'What other word would they have for either of us?' Prisoner B asked.

Gaunt shrugged.

'This way,' he said. Above the sound of the sirens, and the clamour of hammering and shouting from the other side of the hatch, he could still make out the curious keening noise. He looked back at Prisoner B.

The etogaur was looking down at the blood-soaked corpse of the raider at his feet. Specifically, he was staring at the fallen rifle.

Without any attempt at misdirection, he bent down to pick it up.

'What are you doing?' asked Gaunt.

'What?' asked the etogaur, his pink, scarless hand about to close on the rifle's grip.

'What are you doing?'

'Getting a weapon. Two weapons are better than one.'

'Forget it,' said Gaunt.

'We have to fight our way out.'

'I said forget it.'

'But–' Prisoner B began.

'I'm not arming you. You can forget it. I am not arming you,' said Gaunt.

The etogaur straightened up. He nodded.

'I understand,' he said.

THEY SET OFF down the access way. There were sounds of fighting all around them, from the floors above them and below, and from areas nearby. They crossed over a cell bay where all the cages had gunshot-riddled corpses sprawling in them. Pistol raised, braced, Gaunt led the way.

Another hatchway took them into another long, white-tiled corridor, the trademark style of the detention levels, it seemed. There were no doors and no windows, just a long, gleaming white tunnel.

'Which way?' asked Prisoner B.

Raiders appeared down the tunnel to their right, and made the decision for them.

They started to run. As shots began to streak their way, Gaunt turned and fired, bundling Prisoner B ahead of him. He hit someone, and made the others duck back.

'Move!' Gaunt yelled.

BALTASAR EYL STEPPED over the bloody mess that had once been one of his men.

'Where?' he asked.

'This way, upon my soul!' Naeme declared, pointing down the hallway.

'You sure it's him?'

'I saw him,' said Imrie.

Eyl pushed past them and started to run. He had trodden in the blood of his dead comrade, and he left bloody footprints on the white tiles.

THEY WERE COMING after them. Gaunt could see them every time he looked back. They were giving chase. One of them, a big man in a beige leather coat, was leading the way, a carbine in his hands. His grotesk was silver.

The officer, Gaunt thought, the mission leader.

Shoving Prisoner B on, Gaunt turned again and fired. The screaming bolt-round barely missed the Blood Pact officer on their heels, but the man in the silver mask didn't even flinch.

He's sworn to this deed, Gaunt thought. He doesn't care about his own life. He is resolute.

Gaunt fired. He missed the leader in the silver mask again, but the round explosively eviscerated the Pacted warrior running at his side. Still running, the silver-masked leader raised his carbine, and fired from the shoulder like a huntsman. A las-bolt hit the floor. Another went through Gaunt's coat tail. A third stabbed into Prisoner B's left shoulder blade.

Prisoner B didn't fall, but he grunted and stumbled. Gaunt grabbed him to keep him upright, and tried to hustle him on. Shots smacked into the walls around them.

The white-tiled corridor was getting narrower. They struggled past a point where it was actually stepped in on both sides, losing about a quarter of its width. Five metres further, and the corridor stepped in again. The tall, white-tiled corridor had been designed progressively narrower in width.

It had been specifically designed to place increasing restrictions on anyone moving along it: to stop a man from turning or breaking free from the guards flanking him in escort.

Gaunt suddenly realised there wasn't going to be an exit ahead of them. They had unwittingly run into a dead end, a literal dead end. The narrowing corridor was the long, deliberately confined approach to the execution chamber, the last walk that all capital prisoners of the Commissariat took, the last walk from which there was no turning back.

Baltasar Eyl extended his long stride. His beige coat flew out behind him. The corridor's overhead lights strobe-flashed off his silver grotesk.

He raised his carbine.

TWELVE

A Place of Execution

Like the narrowing throat of the hallway that had brought them to it, the execution chamber was entirely lined with glossy white tiles. They were easier to wash, easier to hose down. There were small brass drain covers in the floor under the stout gibbet beam set in the ceiling.

Gaunt bundled Prisoner B through the doorway into the hopeless little box of a room. Despite his wound, Prisoner B made no show of pain. Two las-bolts shrieked past their ears and struck the far wall of the chamber. Gaunt turned. The Archenemy leader in the silver grotesk was right on them.

Gaunt fired.

The blast threw their pursuer's body backwards along the distressingly tight gullet of the execution walk. It crashed into two of the men behind it and brought them all down. The narrow space filled with the stink of charred skin and fyceline.

Gaunt moved to the door, a heavy hatch, and began to swing it shut, hoping to bar or lock it in place. It didn't seem to want to move.

'Help me!' he snarled, struggling.

Prisoner B was leaning against the wall nearby, breathing hard. The left-hand side of his coat was soaked in blood.

Gaunt ignored him and heaved at the door again. He holstered his bolt pistol to get a good grip on its frame with both hands. It began to budge, very slightly. Gaunt exclaimed in frustration. The wretched thing felt like it was made of stone. Several more las-bolts zipped in through the open doorway and creased off the far wall.

The door moved another couple of reluctant centimetres.

Something crashed into Gaunt and carried him across the execution chamber into the facing wall. The impact squashed the air out of him.

He was grappling with the man in the silver grotesk. The enemy leader's face and chest were scorched and burned, and his gloved hands were torn and bloody, but he was far from dead. Gaunt's bolt-round, intended as a hasty body-shot, had struck the carbine in Eyl's hands and blown it up in his face. The force of the detonation had tossed him backwards into his men, but the round had not killed him.

Eyl forced Gaunt into the wall, and hooked a hand around his throat. Wide-eyed in surprise, his arms too pinned for a proper blow, Gaunt jabbed with an elbow, following it up with a clumsy kick that rocked his attacker back a step.

Gaunt broke the constricting grip around his arms, and smashed Eyl's hands away. Eyl threw a clawing punch that was supposed to seize Gaunt's face and twist his head around, but Gaunt deflected it, caught the extended firearm under his armpit, and violently levered Eyl into the chamber wall by way of his straightened arm.

Eyl grunted at the impact. Gaunt tried to slam him into the wall a second time, but Eyl's left fist came around, catching Gaunt across the jaw. He reeled backwards, losing his grip on Eyl's right arm.

Eyl immediately went on the offensive again. There was no hesitation. The intense, blow-upon-blow speed of the fight was manic and frantic. Eyl aimed a kick at Gaunt's ribs, which didn't properly connect, but, as Gaunt tried to shield himself, Eyl aimed another kick with the other foot.

Gaunt deflected it with his forearm, but wasn't fast enough to catch the heel or ankle. Changing step, Eyl tried a third kick, from the original angle that had grazed Gaunt's ribs. Warding off the successive kicks was driving Gaunt across the small chamber towards the doorway.

This time, Gaunt caught the raider's heel. It smacked into his palm with a satisfying slap. He yanked and dragged the foot upwards, kicking Eyl's other leg out from under him.

Eyl slammed over onto his back on the white tiles, but broke free and executed an alarmingly agile flick of his body that whipped him back onto his feet. He was upright in time to meet Gaunt's fist coming the other way.

Gaunt was aiming for the throat, but he misjudged, and caught his knuckles across the edge of the silver grotesk. Eyl's misdirected response drove a fist into Gaunt's left collar bone. As Gaunt recoiled, Eyl went for his throat. Eyl was tall, with a long reach, and he was astonishingly strong, but it wasn't his strength so much as his solidity that was a problem for Gaunt. He was an unyielding force, like a weight or a gravitic wave. It was as if he was made of some substance far denser than human matter. Gaunt had never tackled a man so implacable or so hard to unseat.

Eyl's iron-hard hands brushed Gaunt's fists aside and closed around his neck. As he felt his windpipe shut, and the tendons of his throat throttle and grind, Gaunt responded with instinct rather than any coherent plan. His gut verified that the only remaining thing he could use against his attacker was his attacker.

Gaunt let himself be carried over by the surging impetus of Eyl's attack. He let himself fall onto his back, onto the hard white tiles. He let momentum carry the feverishly determined man in the silver grotesk clean over his head.

Eyl hit the floor with one shoulder just inside the chamber doorway, half-cartwheeled, and landed on the other side of the doorframe.

Gaunt swung up onto one knee and drew his boltgun to finish the contest.

The execution chamber hatch slammed shut in his face, putting ten centimetres of steel between him and the man in the silver grotesk. Their entire battle had lasted less than thirty seconds.

Gaunt looked up.

'You needed to pull this,' said Prisoner B. There was a heavy brass lever beside the door. Gaunt had missed it entirely. Engage the lever, and the hatch trundled shut on a geared mechanism. Small wonder the hatch had been impossible to budge with his shoulder. Prisoner B was leaning against the lever, and he was still breathing hard.

Fists, and possibly shots, began to bang against the other side of the hatch.

Gaunt rose to his feet.

'I had him,' he said. 'You spoiled my shot.'

'Yes, that's right,' replied the etogaur. 'You had him.'

'Is that sarcasm?'

'Another ten seconds, and the damogaur would have been wearing your windpipe as a necklace.'

Gaunt sniffed, and spat pink saliva onto the white tiles. 'He would have tried.'

'He would have succeeded,' Prisoner B replied.

'You called him damogaur. You know him?' asked Gaunt.

Prisoner B shook his head. 'His mask told me his rank. I don't know the man personally. They would have sent one of their best.'

'To silence you?' asked Gaunt.

'To silence me.'

Gaunt looked around the execution chamber. Shutting the hatch had simply prolonged the inevitable. Once the Pacted warriors blew it, or broke it off its seal, death would be inescapable.

Gaunt cursed. At the same moment, a blow struck the hatch with such inhuman ferocity that the metal sill began to buckle.

Gaunt looked up. He eyed the ominous black gibbet beam that traversed the ceiling. Generations of ropes had been expertly looped around it by the Section house executioners. He could see the wear marks.

'You should be glad this has happened,' he said to Prisoner B.

'What? This attack?'

'Yes,' said Gaunt.

'Why?' asked the etogaur.

Gaunt looked at him.

'Because all of a sudden I'm taking you *very* seriously,' he said.

Another blow buckled the hatch frame more significantly.

'I think it's time we left,' said Gaunt.

'How? There's only one door.'

Gaunt nodded.

'Yes, there is,' he said, 'but there are two levers.'

Gaunt walked to the other side of the grim chamber, to a second brass lever that matched the door control. The gallows drop, a trapdoor built seamlessly into the white-tiled floor, slammed open. Cold air blew up out of the black void.

THEY DROPPED. THEY dropped where, on a normal day, only the dead dropped, the dead or the split-second-from-dead.

The chute below the execution chamber was too gloomy for them to see or judge the bottom from the trapdoor, and too deep for them to land securely. Both of them fell and rolled, and jarred their bones. Gaunt prayed that neither of them had turned an ankle or broken something significant.

It was cold and dank, and smelled of hard stone. The trapdoor was a dull square of light and white tiles in the shadows above them. They were outside, in the pale snow-light of the yard. They heard the inner hatch of the execution chamber break at last and crash onto the tiles above them. They heard the snarling voices and the clattering feet of the would-be killers.

A tiny part of Gaunt wished they could have closed the trap, and left nothing but a vacant, white-tiled mystery behind them to delay and frustrate the Blood Pact.

There were no convenient brass handles on the dead side of the trapdoor, just a chilly chute in the open air where the bodies of the condemned were cut down and disposed of.

Gaunt hauled Prisoner B to his feet, and dragged him away from the chute's bottom. Scant seconds later, gunfire blasted down through the trapdoor and sparked off the snow-blown cobbles.

They staggered out into the yard, into the open. The light was sickly yellow, and snow was swirling thickly. Gaunt tasted it on his lips and tongue, and felt it prickle on his face. Their boots crunched on the gathering snow. Somewhere in the building behind them there was a considerable explosion, which blew grit and debris down across the yard. Thick black smoke was pluming the winter sky, and Gaunt could hear flames. The end of Section's administration wing was on fire. Shrill sirens continued to scratch the glass-cold air like diamonds. Gunfire chattered back and forth, like conversations between machines.

'Head for the gate!' Gaunt yelled.

The etogaur nodded, but he was slowing down. He was leaving a little trail of pattered blood across the crusted snow. It felt like a dream out in the yard, a delirious dream where everything was too slow and too bright, and too cold.

Behind them, Eyl and his men began to drop down through the execution trapdoor. They saw the fleeing figures through the billowing snow. Eyl roared a command and ran forwards. A couple of his men took aim.

The black staff car came out of the garage to their left without warning. Its engine was wildly over-revving, and its fat tyres squirmed on the snowy cobbles. Two or three of the Blood Pact's shots punched into its bodywork. It fishtailed across the yard in an undignified skid, and wrenched to a halt, blocking Gaunt and the etogaur from the direct wrath of their attackers.

'Get in,' Wes Maggs yelled. 'Get in the fething car, sir!'

Gaunt turned, baffled for a second. He saw the staff car, and Maggs leaning out from behind the wheel, shouting, his face red.

Gaunt bundled Prisoner B towards the car, and manhandled him into the back seat. Shots whined close. One destroyed a wing mirror, and another took out a door window in a shower of glass. Gaunt fired his bolt pistol in reply, blasting over the bonnet, and then threw himself in after the etogaur.

'Go!' he bellowed.

Maggs let out the clutch, and the big limousine lurched forwards, wheels slipping frantically.

It stalled.

'For feth's sake, Maggs!' Gaunt howled. Las-rounds thumped into the body panels. Two passed clean through the passenger section, leaving neat little dots of daylight in the doors. The rear window shattered.

Maggs turned the engine over once, twice, and then it caught. He found the gear with an ugly grind of metal, and they sped forward as more shots, both las and hard, smacked into them, punching holes. The car's engine tone protested, and rose and fell unsteadily. The limousine juddered, and slewed across the inner yard, its wipers beating away the whirling snowflakes. It clipped one of the mechanics' braziers, and spilled hot coals across the snow. Sparks flew up into the falling snow like luminous flakes.

'The gate. Head for the gate,' Gaunt yelled.

Shots were hitting the back of the car with such force that it felt like someone was repeatedly kicking the bodywork. Three hard rounds tore through the back of the canopy, and travelled through the car's interior before burying themselves in the dashboard. One of them creased Maggs's skull and sliced the top off his right ear. He howled in pain, and his ear bled with alarming vigour. The other side mirror exploded. The car lurched and wallowed. There was no grip.

The man in the silver grotesk landed on the rear of the car with a thump. With his feet braced on the fender and the rear mudguard, and one hand clinging to the roof edge beading, he struggled to get the back door open.

'Sacred feth!' Maggs wailed, wrenching on the wheel. The limousine slewed wildly, but Eyl stayed on. Maggs aimed the car's nose at the narrow gateway linking the side yard to the main gate yard in the front of the house. Eyl succeeded in pulling the rear door open and leaned in, stabbing at them with his ugly rite knife.

The car ran the narrow gate. The open door mashed against the gate post and slammed on Eyl's arm. Once they were clear of the gateway, the dented door flapped open again, but Eyl withdrew his arm. He was trying to manoeuvre to get his body in through the door, and attack them face to face.

Maggs raced the car across the gatehouse yard. Men from Eyl's murderous philia ran after it, rifles and carbines raised, but not risking a shot for fear of hitting their damogaur. The yard was littered with Imperial dead, the men cut down and butchered during the first minutes of the assault. They lay tangled and twisted under thin shrouds of snow. Greasy smoke as dark as gunpowder boiled out of the administration wing, and foamed across the yard in thick, oily ropes. The folds of it, fat and black, swirled up snowflakes like stars in the deep range void. Part of Section's roof was ablaze. Tongues of vivid yellow flames leapt triumphantly at the snow-blurred sky.

As the car roared towards the main gatehouse, Eyl made one final attempt to get inside. Lurching on the backseat, Gaunt had drawn his pistol. He aimed it up through the canopy at Eyl's head.

The man in the silver grotesk saw Gaunt's weapon at the last second and threw himself off the car. The bolt-round punched through the canopy and split the light metal fabric open in great tattered petals like a cycad. Eyl hit the cobbles behind the speeding car in a roll that took several tumbles to arrest. He was getting to his feet as his men ran up to him. Imrie steadied his arm.

The staff car hurtled under the arch of the main gate and out of sight.

Eyl turned to his philia, congregating from all sides through the heavy snow. He noted that there were several missing, and knew that he'd never see them again.

He signalled. They were leaving. They were finished with the place. Their target was moving, and they had to pursue.

THE STAFF CAR belted along the snow-quiet road, outside the stricken headquarters.

'Which way?' Maggs yelled, a note of panic in his voice. He was steering with one hand and pinching his wounded ear with the other. His hand and sleeve were wet with blood.

'Just keep going,' Gaunt instructed.

'But–'

'Just keep going,' Gaunt repeated firmly. 'Any way you like, so long as you keep them squarely behind us.'

'They looked like Blood Pact!' Maggs blurted.

'They *were* Blood Pact,' Gaunt replied. 'Weren't they?'

He looked at Prisoner B. The etogaur was sagging in the corner of the back seat. His eyes were glazing. When Gaunt moved to him, he found that where his hands touched the dark chestnut leather upholstery, they came away sticky with blood.

'Throne!' Gaunt snarled.

'What is it?' Maggs shouted over his shoulder.

'He's hit,' Gaunt replied. 'He's losing blood.'

'Who is he?'

'It doesn't matter. It's complicated. All you need to know is that we need him alive. Keep driving.'

Gaunt propped the etogaur up. His eyes fluttered open.

'You have to stay awake.'

The etogaur nodded.

'I mean it. You have to stay awake. Do you understand?' asked Gaunt.

Prisoner B began to close his eyes slowly.

Gaunt slapped him across the face. 'Stay awake, Throne damn you. You need to stay awake. You need to live!'

The etogaur opened his eyes. There was a little more spark in them.

'I will,' he coughed.

The streets were mostly empty, as the snow had driven most people inside. Even so, Maggs's reckless driving took them straight across a couple of junctions at speed, and traffic had to brake sharply to avoid him. One delivery van veered, mounted the pavement, and clipped a pollarded tree.

Gaunt peered out of the window, watching the old streets whip by. His mind was racing. Where were the security forces? The city-wide alarms? Where were the emergency cordons and the fast deploy reaction teams of the PDF? By now, the whole central area of the Oligarchy ought to have been locked down, the bridges closed, gunships overhead, troop carriers on the streets...

Unless warpcraft had sealed Section in a cone of deceit, and masked the brutal attack, so that the true infamy of the strike was only just seeping out into the world.

Warpcraft, witchcraft: he could smell it and taste it, and he'd had the scent of it ever since he'd been waiting in that anteroom. It explained a lot. It explained how an elite Archenemy strike team had been able to get so close to such a sensitive target so far behind Imperial lines. The man in the silver grotesk and his heathen killers weren't alone on Balhaut. They had the most infernal support mechanisms guiding them, cloaking them and protecting them. From now on, nothing, not a single stone or snowflake in the world around them, could be properly trusted. The Blood Pact's unholy shamans were warping a trap shut around them.

'Get off the road.'

Gaunt snapped around. The etogaur was sitting up, much more alert and bright eyed than he had been.

'Get off the road. It isn't spent. It isn't spent.'

'What in the God-Emperor's name are you talking about?' Gaunt demanded.

Prisoner B didn't reply. Gaunt realised that the etogaur had fallen into some kind of trance, perhaps brought on by wound-shock. He was trembling, his joints stiff and rigid.

Then Gaunt heard the keening sound, the sound he'd last heard in the depths of Section. Something was coming after them.

'Get off the road!' he shouted at Maggs.

'What? Where?'

'Anywhere. A side street!'

Maggs hauled on the steering wheel and swung the heavy car around into a narrow side street between old, age-blackened tenement offices. In the light of the streetlamps, permanently lit in this shadowy thoroughfare, the snow was falling in huge, downy clouds.

Turning had done no good. The keening grew louder.

The blood wolf had their scent.

The thing that had been Shorb wasn't done. A great deal of energy had burned out of it, and a great deal of its strength had ebbed away, but a hot ingot of determination still glowed in the small part of its mind that remained sentient. It wanted to serve its damogaur. It wanted to serve its philia. It wanted to serve the Consanguinity. It was not going to give up. It was not going to fail them.

The pheguth had fled. He had escaped from under their noses, and was beyond the range of the philia moving on foot, but the blood wolf had the power and speed to catch up. A blood wolf could easily catch a car. It howled around the street corners of the snow-blasted city. It moved like an arctic wind or a leaping electrical arc. It made windows shake in their frames, and streetlamps pop and explode. Reality buckled and twisted in its warp-wash.

Gaunt could hear it coming closer.

He opened the dented back door of the idling staff car and stepped out into the snow. He looked up into the dim sky beyond the buildings that overhung him like silhouetted cliffs, and saw nothing but the billowing flakes.

He could hear it.

'Hide,' said Prisoner B in a small, hoarse voice from the back of the car. 'Hide, run. Save yourself.'

With a shriek of tortured air, the blood wolf flew around the corner into the side street. It was two or three storeys up, above the line of the streetlamps, sailing like a bird through the static pattern of the snow. It wasn't so much there as *un*-there: a moving blotch of corrupted air, like a stain in water or an imaging flaw in a pict-feed. Reality ulcerated and wept around it, as if the world was trying to reject it, and throw it back into the un-world of the warp from whence it had come.

It swept down at them, keening.

Gaunt raised his bolt pistol and fired. He couldn't see a target, but he could see its absence. He could see the moving shadow of the warp besmirching the air.

As the blood wolf raced down at them, every streetlamp it passed shattered and darkened. The snow stopped falling and hung, suspended, in the yellow gloom. Gaunt's shots seemed to hit nothing. He threw himself flat.

The blood wolf swept over them, shaking the staff car violently on its shocks. Several more side windows cracked or blew out. The headlamps exploded. The blood wolf was turning, banking in the air, coming around again.

It came right at Gaunt. He tried to shoot it, and then threw himself desperately out of its path, colliding with the car on his way down. The running board smacked into his wrist, and his bolt pistol spun out of sight. He felt the rush of the blood wolf pass over him, shaking the car again.

The keening was right in his ears.

He rose, looking for a weapon. The blood wolf was circling for a final pass.

The back door of the staff car hung open. On the back seat, pale with blood loss, Prisoner B sat in an almost catatonic state. Maggs was shouting. Gaunt saw something, just a flash.

Damogaur Eyl's rite knife was embedded in the rear footwell carpet where he had dropped it.

Gaunt leaned in and grabbed the ugly blade. He turned, raising its dirty, jagged length to meet the blood wolf's warp.

His eyes really saw it. He could see past the warp-wash and the buckled, blistered distortion of reality. He could see the thing inside, the screaming, flaying-raw thing, its energies almost gone, its once-arms outstretched into wing-claws, its once-mouth wide open in a scream. He could see the blood pumping furiously in its exposed veins and arteries. He could see the gristle and tendons of its joints, and the remaining shreds of its skin, shrivelling and blackening like paper as they burned away.

Its mouth opened impossibly wide to bite through Gaunt's skull. Teeth the size of fingers sprouted like tusks from its receded gums for the purpose.

Gaunt rammed the rite knife into its heart.

The blood wolf screamed, and perished in a clap of un-thunder. There was a fierce pressure drop and a burst of freezing air, as if a cryo-bay hatch had opened and then slammed again. The blast threw Gaunt back into the car with enough force to dent the side panels. Charred gristle, sticky brown meat and bone fragments rained down, littering an area with a five-metre radius.

Gaunt sat up and blinked. The rite knife was cooked black with soot, as if it had been left in a grate.

Its pause suspended, the snow calmly and silently began to fall again.

THIRTEEN

Awry

THERE WAS A word for the CO of the Bremenen 52nd, but it wasn't one Viktor Hark would ever use around ladies.

As he stomped back towards the Tanith barracks in the blowing snow, there were no ladies present, so he used it freely and often.

During the lull triggered by the day's heavy snowfall, he had trudged across the exercise quad for a quiet word with the commander of the neighbouring regiment, in the hope of patching up some of the bad feeling that had begun to eclipse inter-regimental relations, thanks to months of boredom and escalating practical jokes. Unfortunately, the Bremenen CO had chosen that morning to breakfast on iron filings, have his sense of humour amputated at the neck, and sit down very suddenly on a broom handle, as a consequence of which he was as rigid and unyielding as a sheet of flakboard. His response to Hark's off-the-record nice-making had been dismissive, and he'd essentially blamed the catalogue of infractions and write-ups entirely on the Tanith 'tricksters'. Then he'd given Hark a curt, 'Good day to you' to take home with him.

The Bremenen had done their share in the months they'd been stationed side by side. Of course they had. It had been tit for tat every step of the way, and some of the earliest run-ins had been playful and forgivable. Hark knew that, and he knew that the Bremenen CO knew it too, but it had stopped being funny some time before, and Hark understood

that the Bremenen CO had simply had a gut-full. He wasn't going to tolerate it any more, and part of his not tolerating it was to dump the whole
thing on the Tanith.

The wind was bringing the snow in across the quad in huge, smoking
clouds like flour caught in a mill's through-draught. There was a good
hand's depth on just about every surface, and the ice-flakes were stinging
his nose and lips, and catching in his eyelashes. Hark had his collar
turned up and his hands stuffed into his stormcoat pockets. The snow
cover was so heavy that the sodium lights around the Aarlem compound
had come on in response to the gloom. Snowflakes batted dizzily
around the hooded glow of the lights like moths.

It was all turning to crap, and Hark had had a gut-full too. In the years
that Hark had been with the Tanith, he'd seen them on the verge of
defeat and almost destroyed, but he'd never seen them so close to disin-
tegration. They'd been inert too long. They had become bored and
fractious, and spiteful. They'd been without an enemy for so long, they'd
invented one, and it was themselves. Their idleness and frustration had
turned them into wasters and idlers, and worse.

Every day, there was a list of fresh fethery. Hark was running out of
options. Some men had crossed the line so often he was hard-pressed to
know how to punish them, and just when he thought it couldn't get any
worse, some new monster raised its head, and took his breath away. This
thing with Rawne and the others, with Daur for feth's sake! That was a
whole new league of crap.

Daur was a yardstick. There wasn't a straighter man in the regiment.
That was how far they'd slipped. Every night when he went to his bed,
and every morning when he woke, Viktor Hark offered up a little prayer
to the God-Emperor of Mankind. It went:

For feth's sake, post us. Post us today or tomorrow. We need a war.

Peacetime had been remarkably revealing about the Tanith character.
Kilo for kilo, they were the best infantry troops Hark had ever seen or
had the pleasure of serving with. In the field, they had an abundance of
skills and an abundance of courage, and they were, in the strangest way,
extraordinarily principled. They took pride in a sort of moral code that
entirely forgave any lapses in discipline of conduct. They flourished in
adversity.

They were not a garrison force. They were not a regiment you could put
into reserve or turnaround, and expect them to sit tight and behave
themselves in a safe little barracks compound. They would not spend
their time polishing their buttons and practising their parade drill and

reading their primers. Well, they would, but it wouldn't be enough. They would get crazy.

The Tanith (and this quality had spread to the non-Tanith in the First) were a wild force. In the field, you didn't notice their rough edges. Retire them to Balhaut for a year or two, and they were like caged animals. They wanted to get out, and if they couldn't get out, they wanted to bite the hand off the next idiot who tried to feed them.

The Bremenen were a garrison force. There was nothing wrong with them; they were a decent, unexceptional, well-drilled infantry outfit. To them, two years turnaround on Balhaut was a sweet deal, the posting they'd been hoping for their entire service. For the Tanith, it was a prison sentence.

Hark stopped in the middle of the quad, tipped his head back, and cursed. He cursed the Bremenen CO, though it wasn't personal. The Bremenen CO had simply become a hobbyhorse for Hark to take out his frustration on. When he'd finished cursing, he checked to see if he felt any better, and found that he didn't very much, actually.

He looked at his watch. If he called up a car from the pool, he could be at Section by nightfall. Despite the snow, the roads were still clear enough for a decent run into the city. He could go to Section, and quietly call in a few favours. He could find out how the land lay, and get the inside track on the likelihood of an imminent posting, maybe even seed the idea and get some gears moving. The Munitorum moved at its own pace, but sometimes it didn't hurt to give it a little shove. He should have done it months ago. Yes, he'd go on up to Section, stick a finger in the air to see which way the wind was blowing, and maybe bend the ear of a couple of senior commissars he knew.

He turned and looked towards the fence in the direction of the city. Even in the snow-light gloom, he could see the immense spread of lights through the chainlink, like a fallen constellation, with the crown of the Oligarchy rising behind it. He was resolved. Doing something, anything, was better than this backbreaking damage control.

Hark sniffed. He realised he might have to revise his travel plans. It looked like worse weather was on the way. From where he was standing, the storm clouds over the Oligarchy looked especially black and menacing, like smoke.

He heard a voice calling his name, and turned to see Ludd thumping across the quad towards him. *Now* what?

'Excuse the interruption, sir,' Ludd declared as he reached Hark. 'Something's going on.'

'Ludd,' said Hark, brushing snow off his nose, 'you realise your sole use to me is to supply meaningful and intelligible nouns and adverbs in place of the word *something* in sentences like that?'

'Yes,' Ludd shrugged, 'but sometimes they don't issue me with enough nouns from stores.'

'Was that a joke, Ludd?'

'Like a joke, but smaller, sir,' Ludd replied, and handed Hark a message slip. 'The vox office sent this through ten minutes ago. Your eyes only.'

A discipline matter. Hark groaned. It had to be a discipline matter, or it would have gone straight to Kolea, or whoever was officer of the watch. What *now*? What *now*?

Hark tore the slip open, and sniffed as he unfolded and read it. Snowflakes made little *tick* noises as they struck the sheet of paper in his gloved hands.

'Summon the senior staff,' he said to Ludd.

'Sir?'

'Summon the senior staff. Five minutes.'

'Well, Rawne's in jail, and the colonel's off-site. Do we have any senior staff left?' Ludd asked.

'This isn't even slightly the time for jokes, Ludd,' said Hark.

Ludd saw the look on Hark's face, and his grin quickly vanished.

'Right, sir. At once,' he said, and ran off through the snow towards the Tanith blockhouses.

'And take us to Active Pending, please!' Hark yelled after him.

Ludd stopped and looked back.

'Active Pending?' he asked.

'You heard me, Ludd.'

'Yes, sir!'

Ludd turned back and started running again.

Hark looked back down at the paper. Where the snowflakes had hit it, they had turned into drops of water and run, smudging the crude black ink of the printout. They looked like tears from a woman's eyes, causing her make-up to streak. They looked like blood leaking from bullet holes.

'Feth!' he cried. 'Feth! *Feth!*'

Just when he thought morale and behaviour were at their lowest, a whole new universe of bad had opened up.

ACTIVE PENDING. THE regiment woke up fast. It shook and galvanised itself to stand to, the pre-transit or pre-combat prepped status. Activity boiled through the Tanith barracks. Everything was suddenly bustling. Beltayn hurried along the main link corridor carrying the day-book and the other logs. Ghosts ran past him in both directions, scrambling for their assigned stations.

'Is this a drill?' Dalin Criid asked Beltayn as he went past.

'What?' Beltayn replied, looking up from the logs that he was reading as he walked.

'It's a drill, right?' asked Dalin. He was with several young troopers from his company.

'Just get on with it, trooper,' Beltayn said.

Dalin shrugged and hurried away with his comrades.

Beltayn tutted and resumed his reading. A thought struck him.

'Wait! Criid!' he shouted after the departing soldiers.

Dalin turned and ran back to him.

'Yes?'

'You need to attend senior staff.'

'Why? Did I get a promotion?'

'Don't be a feth-head, Criid,' said Beltayn wearily. 'You're E Company adjutant.'

'For my sins,' Dalin agreed.

'Well, Captain Meryn is off-site.'

'Captain Meryn's banged up in jail, that's what I heard,' Dalin said. The look on his face suggested that he didn't think it could have happened to a more deserving soul.

'Captain Meryn's status is not your business, trooper,' Beltayn said, 'so let's ditch the lip. His *absence* is your business. As his adjutant, you have to attend and gather all the relevants for him, or for whoever ends up in charge of your fething shower.'

'Really?'

'Two minutes, please, in the temple house.'

Dalin let out an oath and ran off.

Beltayn turned and resumed his course. As he swept past medicae, he stopped, rapped on the door, and stuck his head in.

'Senior staff, two minutes, doctor,' he called.

Dorden looked up from his desk.

'Thank you, adjutant,' he said.

Beltayn nodded and went out, closing the door behind him.

'It seems I'm called away,' said Dorden.

'Well, that's a gigantic shame,' replied Father Zweil. The ayatani was sitting across the desk from the chief medic.

'It really is,' Dorden agreed. 'I finally get you to show up here for your examination, and I'm called out.'

'We can finish at a later date,' said Zweil.

'We're almost done as it is,' said Dorden. He was busily writing up the notes that would accompany the little phials of blood and tissue samples he'd collected. 'Can you be patient for a moment longer?'

'Patient or patient?' asked Zweil.

Dorden smiled, and got up. He walked through to the adjoining room, where Ana Curth was loading stainless steel instruments into the autoclave.

'Can you finish up for me?' he asked.

'With Zweil?'

'Yes. Just finish writing up the notes, ask him the green slip questions, and bag the samples and documents with his signature.'

She nodded, and said, 'I can take them over to the pharmacon if you like.'

'Thanks. Some kind of staff meeting's been called.'

'I know,' she smiled. 'I think it's a drill. We've gone to Active Pending.'

'Have we indeed?' asked Dorden. He turned to leave.

'How did you get him to show up?' Curth asked.

'The ayatani? I sicced Gaunt on him,' Dorden replied.

'And how did you get him to sit still for the samples? Zweil hates needles.'

Dorden showed her his left arm. His sleeve was rolled up and there was a small swab dressing taped in the crook of the elbow. 'I did everything I was going to do to him to myself first to show it wasn't going to hurt.'

'Very clever.'

'I learned that dealing with children years ago. It's a technique that works on the old and cranky too.'

Curth laughed. 'And Zweil's *ancient*. He's got all of… what, five years on you?'

'Age is a state of mind, Ana,' Dorden replied with pretend hauteur. 'Anyway, thank you. I have to go.'

She followed him back into the examination room.

'Doctor Curth is going to finish up for me,' Dorden told the old priest.

'Is she?' asked Zweil suspiciously. 'She's not a real medicae, you know. She hasn't got any qualifications. Gaunt just lets her hang around because she's pretty.'

'I'm sure that's exactly right, father,' said Curth, sitting down at the desk.

'Your hands better not be cold,' Zweil warned her.

'Why?' asked Curth. 'All I'm doing is making notes.'

'Damn!' said Zweil.

Sniggering and shaking his head, Dorden let himself out of the room and joined the human traffic in the hallway. His amusement was superficial. An ugly mood had settled on him that was as cold and sudden as the snowstorm outside.

As he approached the entrance to the temple house, he saw Gol Kolea in the crowd. The big Verghastite major was smiling.

'Afternoon, doctor.'

'Gol.'

'Active Pending, eh?'

'You look delighted.'

Kolea nodded.

'Could be the posting we've been waiting for,' he said.

'You think so?'

'Orders had to come through sooner or later.'

Dorden nodded.

'To be frank, major, if it is our orders coming through, and we're being posted back to the front, that hardly fills me with delight.'

'We're going gak-happy here, Doc. The Ghosts need a tour. It's overdue,' said Kolea.

'You seem to forget, major, that when we go to war, people die. That's hardly something to look forward to.'

They went into the temple house. The snow beat against the tall, narrow windows. The senior staff were finding places to sit. All the company commanders had assembled, or were represented by adjutants or juniors. Dorden saw Kolosim, Obel, Raglon, Sloman, Arcuda, Domor, Theiss and Baskevyl, as well as Elam and Seley, who had been promoted to the commands of H and L companies respectively to replace men lost at Hinzerhaus. He could also see Mkoll, the master of scouts. Bonin was the representative for B Company in Rawne's absence, Daur's adjutant Mohr for G Company, and a very nervous-looking Dalin Criid for Meryn's Company E.

'Take your seats. Let's have you!' Commissar Ludd called out, climbing onto the stage. 'That's enough, come on!'

'A little order and attention, please, gentlemen!' Baskevyl called, backing the young commissar up. The noise level dropped appreciably.

'Thank you,' said Baskevyl. 'Door, please, Shoggy.'

Shoggy Domor got out of his seat to close the temple door, but Hark walked in and shut the door behind him. Hark marched to the front, all eyes following him. Dorden noticed that at some point during the assembly, Eszrah ap Niht had slipped into the temple and was standing at the back in the shadows.

'What's going on, Hark?' Baskevyl asked.

'Have we got marching orders?' Kolosim added. 'We've got marching orders, haven't we?'

There was a general murmur.

Hark cleared his throat. Dorden realised that he didn't like the look on Hark's face, and it wasn't for the reasons he had expected.

'As of twenty-seven minutes ago,' Hark began, 'Aarlem Fortress is on security lockdown.'

Everybody started talking.

'Shut up and listen!' Hark shouted. 'Security condition two has been imposed on this station, and on Balopolis and the Oligarchy. The PDF is locking all orbital links, and transit is forbidden. An advisory has been issued.'

'What the feth?' Kolea grumbled.

'There was a serious incident this afternoon in the Oligarchy. All I know is that Section was attacked by forces unknown.'

'An attack?' echoed Obel. 'Are you kidding? Who attacks Balhaut?'

'Somebody,' said Hark. 'This is serious. We are to remain on base until further notice. Nobody goes off-site.'

'On whose orders?' Baskevyl asked.

'Section's, and it's been ratified by Guard Command. Beltayn?'

'Yes, commissar?'

'Consult the day-book and check with the other adjutants. I want a list of all personnel off-site as of right now.'

'Yes, sir,' Beltayn nodded.

Hark gestured to Kolea, who had quietly raised a hand.

'Yes, major?'

Kolea breathed a sort of sigh, and then said, 'What's the scale of this? Has the Archenemy mounted a counter-offensive? Have they punched right through?'

'We'd know about it,' said Mkoll.

Kolea looked over at the chief scout.

'However optimistically you want to place the Crusade front line on the star-maps,' Mkoll said, 'Balhaut is over a sector's distance from the fight zone. If an enemy counter-offensive had pushed through, we'd have heard about it months ago.'

'But a long, deep-warp jump? A bounding strike into our heartland?'

'Doesn't feel like that, Gol,' said Mkoll.

'I agree with the chief,' said Hark, 'but that's not important. It isn't our business to figure this out. Orders are simple. We confine ourselves to base and lock down. No one leaves. No one is unaccounted for. All Guard strengths on the surface are to secure their base facilities and stand ready for deployment.'

Bonin looked up at the ceiling.

'I hear incoming,' he said. 'Engines.'

THE STEADILY INCREASING throb of turbofan motors drew them out into the snow. Six flying machines, running nose to tail in a line, were hacking in from the city, through the snowstorm, their running lights blinking. They came in low, and circled Aarlem Fortress. The lead bird banked and began to settle towards the open expanse of the lamp-lit quad.

The six machines were Valkyrie gunships. They blew up mini blizzards with their jetwash as they settled side by side across the quad.

'Oh feth,' murmured Hark. 'Would somebody like to tell me what they're doing here?'

Baskevyl looked at Hark, and the commissar pointed.

On the side of each Valkyrie, plainly visible despite the snow, was the rosette crest of the Inquisition.

FOURTEEN

The House of Doctor Death

In the early evening, when his day's work was done, and he was in the scrub room washing the instruments of his trade, Doctor Kolding thought he heard a vehicle pass by on the street outside.

This seemed unlikely, for many reasons. It was snowing heavily, and that kept the traffic light, particularly in the hilly streets of Old Side. More specifically, no one ever drove up or down Kepeler Place unless they were lost, which was infrequent to say the least, or they were the ambulance men from the Civic Office, who brought him his work, and they made their deliveries before ten each morning.

Nevertheless, he'd heard the sound of a motor vehicle passing by. It had been a bronchial chuckle, rounded out by the acoustic muffle of the snow lining the otherwise empty street: the ugly engine-cough of a badly maintained truck or van ailing in the freezing conditions.

Doctor Kolding put the last of the stainless steel tools back on the cart's red cloth, covered them, and dried his hands. He let the tap run to rinse away the last of the brown stains in the enamel sink, and his mind returned to the sound. Perhaps it was the ambulance men. Sometimes, rarely, the Civic Office sent rush-jobs up at unsocial hours, outside the timetable of his usual casework deliveries. That would be it, he decided. It was the ambulance men, bringing him an urgent piece of work.

He was poised for the doorbell, but the doorbell did not ring. There was no sound of rear doors thumping open, or of the gurney's legs unfolding with a clatter as it slid off the carrier. He went to the window, and pulled the blind aside. Outside, the street was empty and snow-silent. Fat snowflakes drifted like ancient, amber stars through the light-cones of the streetlamps.

He had been mistaken.

He returned to the theatre, turned the wall tap on, and began to play the hose across the tiled floor. The room smelled of damp stone and disinfectant. He'd been mistaken. It hadn't been an urgent job coming his way after all. As the hose in his hand spattered out onto the floor, he looked up at the steel drawers and smiled. None of his work was ever truly urgent, not, at any rate, to the people it most intimately concerned.

He was just turning the hose off when the doorbell rang. He froze for a moment, listening to the last of the water gurgling away down the floor drains. Had he imagined the bell?

He had not. After a long period of silence, it rang again. This time it did not sound as though someone had pressed the white stud on the brass plate beside his street door; it sounded as though someone had leant on it. The drawn-out blare of the electric bell rattled through his chilly, empty house.

Doctor Kolding took his hand off the wall tap and let the empty coils of the hose slap onto the floor. He wiped his hands on his apron. This was unseemly. This was a *strange turn of events*, and it disturbed him. It disturbed the very ordered pattern of his life. He attempted to manufacture scenarios in his head to explain things. The Civic Office had sent him some urgent work, but the crew driver was a relief fill-in, unfamiliar with Doctor Kolding's location. He'd overshot. He'd driven past, perhaps as far as to the junction where Kepeler Place met Flamestead Street. In this weather, that was not surprising. He'd been obliged to turn around, to turn around in the snow and make his way back. This accounted for the interval between the sound of his vehicle, passing by, and the ringing of the bell.

It rang again, a third time. The finger stayed on the bell-press for a full, indignant, insistent ten seconds.

Doctor Kolding stiffened, and hurried from the theatre. He went up the stone steps into the long hall. The floor was polished dark wood, and it fuzzily reflected the white light of the glass shades overhead in circular splashes like pools of sunlight. He searched for his glasses, which were, of course, in his apron pocket, and put them on. Blue twilight took the edge off the hard, white lamplight.

He reached the door. There was someone on the other side. He could hear them shuffling.

'Wh-who is it?' he called through the heavy door.

'Are you a doctor?' a voice called back. It was a male voice, heavy, impatient or distracted.

'Wh-who is there?' Doctor Kolding called. 'Please t-tell me who you are.'

'Are you a doctor?' the voice repeated. 'I need a doctor.'

'Y-you've come to the wrong place,' Doctor Kolding called out.

'You have the medicae sign on a pole outside. I can see it.'

The voice sounded irritated. Doctor Kolding hesitated. He did have the medicae sign above the door of his old townhouse, because that was his profession. It had been his father's profession, and his father's uncle before that. Nine generations of Koldings had worked as surgeons at this address on Kepeler Place, and that was why the serpent-staff of Asklepios hung proudly from the brass rail above his door. That couldn't be denied. It was as plain as day, even with a crust of snow on it.

But, of course, it was more complicated than that, and it had been more complicated ever since the Famous Victory. Doctor Kolding felt very tense and unwell. This was a *strange turn of events*, and it disturbed him.

'Hello?' the voice outside called.

'Hello?' Doctor Kolding answered.

'Are you going to open this door?' the voice demanded.

'A-are you from the Civic Office?' Doctor Kolding asked, his cheek almost touching the cold black paint of the front door so that he could hear clearly.

'The what?'

'The Civic Office.'

'No.'

'Then I feel sure you have, as I said, come to the wrong place.'

'But you've got the sign up.'

'Please,' Doctor Kolding began.

'This is an emergency!' the voice said, angrier than before. 'It's cold out here.'

Please go away, please go away, this is a strange turn of events and–

Knuckles banged against the door so sharply that Doctor Kolding jumped back.

Sometimes this happened. He'd heard of it happening to others who plied the same trade. The serpent-staff could attract visitors of other types to your door, undesirable types. They had problems of their own. They had needs. They had habits to feed. To them, the sign suggested a source of pharms, a medicae to be pleaded with or threatened, a medicine bag to be shaken out for stimms, a drug cabinet to be raided.

Doctor Kolding felt quite flustered. He opened the door of the long-case clock that stood at the foot of the stairs. The clock hadn't worked for fifteen years, but Doctor Kolding had been unwilling to get rid of it because it had belonged to his father's uncle and it had always stood there. It didn't serve as anything more than a cupboard now. He opened the case door and reached inside. The pistol was there, on a dusty little shelf behind the impotent pendulum. It was the pistol that had been left behind. He snapped the safety off and held the gun against his palm in his apron pocket.

The knuckles banged on the door again.

'Hello?'

Doctor Kolding reached up and tugged open the brass latch with his free hand. As he did so, he saw that his hand was shaking.

His hand was shaking, and there was a tiny spot of someone else's blood on the back of it just under the knuckle of the middle finger.

Doctor Kolding opened the door.

'What do you want, please?' he asked.

A man was standing on his doorstep. He was a rough-looking man, a military man. He was wearing a black combat uniform. He seemed quite threatening. The people who came after pharms were often military or ex-military types with habits that were the legacy of combat tours. The man was standing on the doorstep with the snow coming down around him, lit by the single lamp above him in the roof of the stone porch. To Doctor Kolding, the dark street behind him was a blue void.

'Are you the doctor?' the visitor asked.

'I... Yes.'

'What's the matter with you, keeping us standing out here? It's freezing, and this is an emergency. Why did it take you so long to open the door?'

'I was surprised to have a visitor this late,' said Doctor Kolding. 'It is a strange turn of events, and it disturbed me.'

'Yeah, well, sorry to knock for you after hours, but emergencies choose their own moments to happen, you know what I mean?'

'Not really,' replied Doctor Kolding.

The visitor peered at him, puzzled.

'What's with the dark glasses?' he asked.

'Please tell me what you want,' said Doctor Kolding.

'I want to come inside.'

'Explain your business first, please.'

'It's an emergency,' said the visitor.

'And the nature of the emergency?'

'Well, up to a few minutes ago, it was something else, but now it's that bits of my anatomy are about to freeze off!'

Doctor Kolding gazed at him. This was a *strange turn of events*, and it disturbed him.

It disturbed him even more when the visitor simply pushed past him into the hall.

'You can't just walk in!' Doctor Kolding cried.

'Actually, I can. This is an emergency, and I'm tired of trying to do this nicely.'

'You can't just walk in!'

The visitor looked back at him.

'Are you the doctor?' he asked.

'I said I was. I told you that.'

'You're not an assistant or something? I wondered if you were the manservant or something.'

'No, I'm not.'

'So you're in charge?' the visitor asked.

'I'm the only one here.'

The visitor nodded and looked around again. He went a few steps down the hall, and peered up the stairs to the first floor. Then he bent over the rail and looked down the stone steps into the basement theatre. As the visitor turned his head, Doctor Kolding saw that there was dried blood on the right-hand side of his face and his right ear.

'You've been hurt,' said Doctor Kolding.

'What?'

Doctor Kolding pointed to the visitor's head with his free hand. 'You've been hurt. Is this the emergency?'

The visitor touched his ear as if he'd forgotten all about it. His right hand was also, now Doctor Kolding came to notice it, covered in dried blood.

'No,' he said. 'No, it's not.'

At that moment, Doctor Kolding realised that the visitor had said something that had disturbed him more than anything else. In the confusion and tension, it had been passed over. Only now, with his mind painstakingly running back over the conversation again, did Doctor Kolding see it.

It was a single word, and the word was 'us'.

What's the matter with you, keeping us standing out here?

'I'd like you to go, please,' said Doctor Kolding.

'What?' the visitor asked.

'I'd like you to go. Leave. Please leave.'

'Haven't you been listening to me? I need a doctor. It's an emergency.'

'I'd like you to leave these premises, now,' said Doctor Kolding.

'What's that in your pocket?' the visitor asked.

'Nothing.'

'What have you got in your pocket? There, in your apron pocket. You're holding something.'

Doctor Kolding pulled the pistol out. His visitor blinked and said something like, 'Oh, you've got to be kidding me.' Doctor Kolding wasn't precisely sure what his visitor said because he was too busy falling over to listen. His visitor had somehow bumped into him and the impact, though gentle, had deposited Doctor Kolding on his back in the open doorway. He no longer held the pistol. This was a *strange turn of events*, and it disturbed him.

Doctor Kolding lay on his back and looked up. Two more men were standing on the doorstep above him, framed in the porch light and the falling snow. They were upside down to Doctor Kolding. One of them seemed to be holding the other one up.

'Is this the doctor?' asked the man doing the supporting. He was tall, with a slender face and disturbing eyes. Doctor Kolding couldn't tell much about the man he was holding up.

'I think it's the doctor, sir,' the original visitor replied. 'He's not being very cooperative.'

'Is that why he's lying on his back?' asked the man with the slender face.

'He had this pistol, sir–' said the original visitor.

'Help him to his feet, please,' said the man with the slender face.

'I'll cooperate!' exclaimed Doctor Kolding as he was helped up. He was feeling trapped. He wanted to scream. 'I'll cooperate, but I don't understand what's going on. The men usually only come in the mornings. The mornings, you see? Not at this time of night. Never at this time.'

'Calm yourself,' said the man with the slender face and the disturbing eyes. The other man had called him 'sir'. He certainly exuded a sort of authority. 'Please, calm yourself. We're very sorry to have disturbed you, and we don't mean to put you to any trouble, but this is a rather critical situation. What's your name?'

'Auden Kolding.'

'Are you a doctor, sir?'

'Yes.'

'Then I need your help urgently,' said the man with the slender face. 'This man's been shot and he's dying.'

HE LED THEM downstairs to the theatre, once he'd made sure the street door was closed. They left snow-melt footprints on the hall floor and the steps, and that bothered him immensely, of course, but he reassured himself that he could take the mop to it just as soon as the wounded man was comfortable. A man's life took precedence, of course it did. A man's life was more important than dirty wet marks on a dark hardwood floor.

They got the man into the theatre. He wasn't really conscious, and Doctor Kolding could smell blood. Doctor Kolding told them to get the man onto the examination table, to lay him back on the clean, red sheet he'd hung across the table at the end of his day's work. The blood would stain, of course, despite the colour of the sheet. He would have to boil it later. He washed his hands in the counterseptic bath, and dried them diligently before pulling on a pair of surgical gloves. His hands were shaking.

When Doctor Kolding came over to the table, they had laid the patient back, and Doctor Kolding saw his face for the first time, starkly illuminated by the exam lamp.

'What is the meaning of this?' Doctor Kolding asked in a small voice.

The man with the slender face looked at him. 'What do you mean, doctor?' he asked.

Doctor Kolding indicated the knotted scar-tissue that covered the patient's head.

'You come in here,' he said, 'you come in here and ask my help, and you're bringing me some kind of animal. This isn't a man, it's an animal.'

'I don't have a whole lot of time to debate this with you, doctor,' the man with the slender face said. 'I need you to get to work on him. I need you to do everything in your power to save his life.'

'He's an animal! An inhuman thing!'

The man with the slender face leaned close to Doctor Kolding, and he shrank back because he didn't like to smell another person's breath, or feel it on his face.

'We don't have time to debate this,' said the man with the slender face, 'but if we did, it would run like this. I would tell you that I was an officer of the Commissariat, and that I had the authority, on pain of death, to compel you to carry out my wishes. I would tell you that it was vital to Imperial security that this man remained alive, and would instruct you to carry out your function without further issue or demurral. I might even produce a weapon, just for show, to emphasise my seriousness.'

Doctor Kolding stared back at him.

'But I'm not going to do any of that,' said the man with the slender face, 'because we really don't have the time.'

'I see,' said Doctor Kolding.

'Do you?'

'Yes,' said Doctor Kolding, and reached for his tray of instruments.

SOMETHING WAS GOING on, and Tona Criid didn't need to be told that it was bad. Capital *B A D*.

She'd looped around to take a look at Section, but there had been nothing to see, so she'd gone to find the slice of lime *soforso* she'd promised herself. Then she'd wasted an hour or more sitting in the comforting silence of Saint Theodor's sacristy, until her legs got jittery and told her it was time to run again.

She'd had a simple circuit of Engineer's Mall in mind, just up as far as the memorial, and then the long, steady run home to Aarlem, but some force, like a magnetic impule, had pulled her back towards Section. This time, she thought, she might ask at the guardhouse, and see if there was a procedure that would allow her to visit a prisoner. Whatever this feth-storm was all about, if she could get Rawne's side of things, or Varl's, maybe, she could put in a good word and ease things along. Left to itself, the system would most likely chew them up. She'd seen that happen. She didn't care who shouted her down, the First could not go around losing officers like Rawne, Daur or Varl. Meryn, *obviously*. No one cared about that rat-stool.

So, she'd let the impulse bring her back towards Section. It had begun to snow by then. The snow was heavy, the sky was a sick colour, and there was a funny feeling to the afternoon. It wasn't even that cold. Snow was settling in her hair and on her nose, but she was sweating like a grox in her exercise kit.

She was coming up Viceroy Square when she first realised that things weren't right. What she'd taken to be heavy snow clouds turned out to be smoke. She could smell it. The building was on fire. There were sirens.

There was gunfire, full-on gunfire from inside the walls. She came up into the tree-line of the gardens in the square, and saw bodies in the road beside the gatehouse.

She got down into the cover of the trees, her eyes wide in disbelief, her pulse banging in her ear for the first time in months. It was the old adrenaline high, the combat rush, conquering her with such fury that she couldn't resist it. Every bit of conditioning she'd kept suppressed or contained since the Tanith had retired sprang back into place. She red-lined. All the old habits, all the old crazy tics, reasserted themselves, larger than life, as if they'd never gone. She could taste the sour saliva in her mouth. The lime tang of the *soforso* was long gone. She could smell the smoke, and it smelled like Hinzerhaus. She wanted, more than anything else, for there to be a weapon to hand, a rifle that she could arm and sight. Her hands felt ridiculously useless and empty, like numb paddles, miming the act of holding a rifle.

She tried to control her breathing. She tried to back away a little, without disturbing the snow on the bushes and shrubs around her. She tried to decide on the best course of action.

Raise the alarm: that was all she could think. Something this big, the whole city had to be aware of it, but there was no sign of people rushing in, of reinforcements, of support or relief.

It was as if the whole city had become snow-blind and was ignoring the drama unfolding at Section.

Criid began to crawl her way back through the gardens. The far side of the square would put her back on a main thoroughfare. She could run then. At full stretch, it was about ten minutes to the guardhouse at Zannen Street, and she was sure there was a PDF defence shelter closer than that. Failing either of those things, she'd find a Magistratum station or somewhere with a working vox.

She'd just risen in a crouch, about to risk a run across the snow-covered lawns to the gate of the gardens, when she realised there was someone under the trees nearby.

She turned to look. It was another bystander, she thought, someone who, like her, had come upon this scene of bloodshed by accident.

It was a woman. She was wearing a long mourning dress of black silk and crepe. Her face was covered by a veil of black gauze. She was standing under the trees, the boughs above her head weighed down by the increasing freight of snow upon them. She seemed to be staring at the main building of Section. Criid wondered if she ought to go to her, and offer to escort her to a safe distance away from the gunfire.

Something made her hesitate. It might have been her increasing awareness of a soft, high-pitched sound, like a drawn-out wail, that seemed to be emanating from the woman. It may have been a preternatural sense of self-preservation triggered by the abrupt return of her old adrenaline high.

Something simply made her hesitate. Something told her that taking another step towards the woman in the black silk dress was a Very Bad Idea.

The woman turned to look at Tona Criid. Her veil obscured her face, and Tona was instantly glad of that, because she instinctively knew that she didn't want to see the woman's face, *ever*.

The shrill sound was coming from the woman. It was just rushing out of her with no allowance for breath.

The snow had stopped falling. Tona realised it had stopped falling in mid-air. Snowflakes hung around her in a constellation, suspended in the act of descent.

She began to back away. The woman in the black dress stared at her. Tona took a step forwards.

The shrill sound continued to come out of the woman. She raised her right hand to lift the corner of the veil.

Criid let out an anguished cry, and turned. She started to run. The world was slow, like glue, like treacle. The shrill sound was in her ears. Suspended snowflakes puffed into powder as her flailing arms collided with them. Her feet churned the snowy grass underfoot, and she went down, falling hard.

The shrill sound was in her ears. It was louder. Criid knew it was louder because the woman was getting closer. She also knew it was louder because the woman had lifted the veil. She thrashed, trying to rise. Her legs kicked at the snow. She felt something close around her pumping frantic heart, and grip it, like a ghostly fist. It began to squeeze, constricting the muscles. She knew that unless she got up and started running, that unless she ran and ran until she was out of its reach, it would keep squeezing until her heart burst like a blister.

Her limbs thrashed, sending snow flying. She got up. Her chest was so tight, and the shrill sound in her ears was so loud. She didn't look back. She didn't want to look back.

She didn't dare look back.

She started to run. She started to run more seriously than she had ever run in her life.

* * *

MAGGS TOOK A battered old tin out of one of the cupboards, took off the lid, sniffed inside, and then tilted the tin towards Gaunt.

'Caffeine,' he said.

'Make some,' said Gaunt. 'Enough for three cups.'

Maggs nodded, and began to look around the small kitchen for a suitable pan. Gaunt sat down at the kitchen table. The table top was lined and worn. It had been, Gaunt felt, the location of many solitary suppers.

The kitchen stood off the landing over the steps down to the theatre. There had been no sound from below for a long time.

'So, this is pretty fething insane, then, isn't it?' said Maggs, by way of striking up a conversation. They hadn't said much to one another since their panicked flight from Section.

Gaunt nodded.

'That was Blood Pact?'

'Yes.'

'Really? Here?'

'Yes, Maggs.'

Maggs whistled. He ignited one of the sooty old stove's burners and set a pan of water on it.

'Pardon me for asking, sir,' he said, in a tone that suggested he was delicately skirting a thorny issue, 'shouldn't we contact someone? I mean, summon help, alert the authorities?'

Gaunt looked at him.

'Who do we contact, Maggs? Who should we trust, do you suppose?' he asked.

Maggs opened his mouth to answer, and then closed it again.

'The Blood Pact have infiltrated an ostensibly secure crown world,' said Gaunt. 'They've done so with enough confidence and ability to stage a frontal assault on the Commissariat's headquarters. They've got warpcraft on their side. We have absolutely no idea how far their reach and influence extends. Let's say we were to head back to Aarlem, or to company command, or say we take him to the Imperial hospital for treatment. We could be walking into a trap. Until I know what's going on, I'm not going to trust anyone.'

Maggs shrugged. He was spooning out the ground caffeine powder into a cup.

'You're trusting this doctor chap.'

'Necessity. That's all. We had no choice. Better a backstreet clinic like this than a big, central facility.'

'He's a freak.'

'He's got eccentric qualities, certainly,' Gaunt agreed.

Maggs snorted.

'He's obsessive compulsive,' he said, 'and what's with the shades?'

'The doctor is an albino, Maggs,' said Gaunt. 'Didn't you see? The dark glasses are to protect his eyes.'

'He's still a freak.'

The caffeine was brewing. Maggs took out the gun he'd taken from the doctor and examined it.

'I wonder where he got this? It's ex-Guard issue.'

'Is it loaded?' Gaunt asked.

'Yeah. Ten rounds.'

'So we've got that, your laspistol, and my bolt pistol with one clip left.'

It didn't seem to be much to work with. Both of them had put on a sidearm that morning, Gaunt because it was a uniform requirement, and Maggs because service regulations stated that an appointed driver should bear a pistol, or similar, fit for defensive purposes. Neither of them had even buckled on their Tanith warknives.

'We're deep in the stinky, aren't we, sir?' asked Maggs.

Gaunt nodded.

'I'm afraid so, Maggs.'

'The Blood Pact,' said Maggs, searching the kitchen cupboards in the vain hope of locating some sugar, 'they're after this man? The one with the fethed-up face.'

'Yes.'

'He's key to this whole thing, then?'

'Yes.'

'Can I ask who he is?' Maggs said, looking sidelong at Gaunt from the open cupboards.

'It's probably better if you don't know,' Gaunt replied.

Maggs shrugged.

'Well, you know,' he said, 'I don't see it like that. Right now – and I say this with the enormous deference that a specialist like me owes to his commanding officer – right now it seems to me that I'm the only person you can count on, and vice versa, may the Emperor help us both. So, I think maybe you need to tell me more than you'd usually tell me.'

Gaunt thought about it.

'You're probably right,' he said.

'Don't worry,' said Maggs with a laugh, 'we're not going to become friends or anything.'

'That's a relief.'

Gaunt rubbed the bridge of his nose with his fingers. Then he said, 'His name is Mabbon. He holds the rank of etogaur, and he was an officer in the Blood Pact before switching allegiance to the Sons of Sek. He was on Gereon when I was on Gereon.'

'Old scores?'

'I never met him. The thing is, he's carrying vital intelligence. Serious high-grade stuff. That's why the Blood Pact wants him dead. That's why we've got to keep him alive.'

'Shit,' said Maggs.

'Exactly.'

Maggs wiped three chipped enamel cups with a damp cloth from the sink, and set them in a row to receive the caffeine. They heard footsteps on the stairs. Maggs looked at Gaunt.

Doctor Kolding appeared in the kitchen doorway. His scrubs were badged with blood. He was still wearing his blue-tinted glasses.

'I've done all I can,' he said.

'Will he survive, doctor?' Gaunt asked.

'I don't know,' Kolding replied.

'Well, feth load of good you are!' Maggs exploded. 'What kind of fething doctor are you, anyway?'

'I only work on the dead,' said Kolding softly.

'What?' Maggs exploded.

'I perform autopsies for the Health Department. I don't usually work on the living.'

'Now you tell us! You've got the fething sign outside!' Maggs yelled.

'Maggs,' Gaunt said sharply.

'The sign's always been there,' Kolding said, 'for generations. This was my father's practice. Right up to the war.'

'And now you're a meat carver? A corpse butcher? Feth!'

'That's enough, Maggs,' said Gaunt, scraping back his chair and rising to his feet.

'Oh, tell that to Doctor Death here!'

'Maggs!'

'Have you any idea how fething important that patient is?' Maggs shouted into Kolding's face.

Kolding flinched.

'That's really enough, Maggs,' said Gaunt in a voice that had a rod of steel running through it. 'Why don't you go out and check on the car?'

'The car's fine,' said Maggs.

'The car's shot to pieces and they'll be looking for it,' Gaunt corrected. 'Go and check it. Make sure it's secure. Make sure we're secure. All right?'

Maggs, simmering, sighed and nodded. He handed the doctor's old pistol to Gaunt, took a swig of caffeine from one of the enamel cups and left without another word.

'I apologise,' said Gaunt. He gestured for Kolding to sit at the table, and set a cup of caffeine in front of him.

'There's no need.'

'Will the patient survive?'

'I have worked on the living,' said Kolding. 'For many years, as a junior in my father's practice. I am qualified for human work. But these days, the city is empty. The streets are dark and quiet. The population has never really returned. I need to supplement my workload with autopsy work for the Health Department, or this place would have to close.'

'The war ended your father's business?'

'The war ended my father,' said Kolding. 'He died. So did his assistants and nurses. I was the only one who lived.'

'Will the patient survive?'

'I have stabilised him, and repaired the blood vessel damage. We need to wait for another half an hour to see how the coagulant healing meshes take. His blood pressure concerns me. If he is still alive in a hour, I think he'll be alive in fifty years.'

Gaunt sipped his caffeine. It seemed awful. The truth was, it was simply battlefield quality. Maggs had thrown it together according to trench conditions. Gaunt realised that he'd been spoiled by too many months of fancy quality caffeine. This, this dark murk that Maggs had concocted, was caffeine like the Guard drank it, the bitter taste of the zone and the dug-out.

It was dire, and it was the best drink he'd had in a year.

'Where did you get the pistol?' Gaunt asked.

Kolding looked down at the old weapon. It was lying on the worn top of the kitchen table.

'It's the pistol that was left behind.'

'Left behind?'

Kolding hesitated. It wasn't so much as if he was trying to find the right words, it was more as if he wasn't sure he'd be able to say them.

'It was left behind. Afterwards. The night my father died. My father and his assistants.'

'Doctor, did they die here?'

Kolding took off his tinted glasses and carefully cleaned one lens.

'My father had set up a triage station. Injured men were pouring in from everywhere. There was fighting in the streets all round here.'

'I know. I was here.'

'Then you'll know what it was like. Mayhem. The streets filled with smoke. Noise. Some soldiers came. They were enemy soldiers. They broke in while we were treating the injured.'

'How old were you, doctor?' Gaunt asked.

'I was sixteen,' Kolding replied.

IN THE STREET outside, the snow was silently obliterating all lines and angles. The whiteness of the flakes caught the streetlamp light like blobs of molten metal spurting from ruptured armour. Wes Maggs pulled his jacket close and rubbed his arms. His breath wreathed out of his mouth like gun smoke.

He trudged up the street through the thickening snow cover, wet flakes pelting his face. The night was as black as Rawne's soul, but there was a phantom radiance coming up off all the surfaces on which the snow had settled. It had rounded kerbs, softened walls and blunted iron railings. It had deformed windowsills and gutter lines, and it had upholstered all the vehicles parked up the hill.

They'd left the staff car near the top of the street, tucked in beside some railings. Maggs hoped it would start all right. There hadn't been time or light enough to check if anything vital had been punctured. In the time it had been sitting there, tanks could have drained or hydraulic fluids leaked away.

The hill was steep, and he slithered a little in the snow. He cursed the weather. The car was in sight.

Three men stood beside it.

Maggs stopped walking and gently allowed himself to melt into the shadows of the street wall. He stayed very still. He could see the men clearly. They were shadows, shapes caught in the downlight of a street-lamp, wraiths as silent as the night snow. They were studying the car, moving around it slowly and silently. Maggs couldn't tell if they were armed, and he couldn't make out any details of their clothing or uniforms.

But as one of them turned, Maggs caught the glint of lamplight catching the edge of a metal mask.

Maggs turned and began to make his way back down the hill to the doctor's house as quickly, but invisibly, as he could.

FIFTEEN

The Hunters

'Is THIS ALL of it?' asked Edur. He gave a nod of his head that indicated the barrack's clerical pool in general, and the files and volumes gathered on the central desk in particular.

'Yes, commissar,' said Kolea.

Several Commissariat officials had already begun working through the regimental files, especially the day-book and the company logs. Two agents of the ordos had also begun what looked to Viktor Hark like a forensic examination of the Tanith First's central records.

'Are you going to tell us anything?' asked Hark.

'No,' said one of the ordo agents.

Edur looked at the officer of the Inquisition with some distaste. The Inquisition was already taking over, and that wasn't the only reason Edur had an unpleasant taste in his mouth. He tilted his head to suggest that Hark and the Tanith's acting commander, Kolea, might like to step aside with him.

It had all been, by necessity, hasty, but Edur had been briefed by Mercure before riding the Valkyries out to Aarlem with the Inquisition. Mercure had been emphatic: while Mercure took the matter to Command-level authority in the hope that Command might apply some pressure to the ordos, Edur was to do all he could to make sure the Inquisition didn't trample everything flat on the ground.

'I want us to hold on to some control in this, Edur,' Mercure had said, 'for as long as we can, or until we know there's nothing worth holding on to.'

'Both the Inquisition and the Commissariat are keen to discover the whereabouts of Colonel-Commissar Gaunt,' Edur told Hark and Kolea.

'Wasn't he at Section when this happened?' asked Hark.

'Yes,' said Edur.

'Isn't he still there?' asked Kolea.

'We don't know,' said Edur.

'What does that mean?' asked Hark.

'It means that part of the building has burned out, another part is still ablaze, and there are a fair number of corpses still to be recovered and identified.'

'Gak!' Kolea whispered.

'The thing is, if Gaunt's alive, we can't find him,' said Edur.

'And that's why you've locked us down, and come in to take us apart bit by bit?' asked Hark.

'That's the key reason.'

'Because?' asked Hark. 'I'm sorry, Edur, but you've missed something out. Some key component.'

'A second individual is missing,' said Edur. 'A high-value prisoner. The prisoner may even have been the target of the raid. Gaunt was last seen in the vicinity of the prisoner's cell, and he was aware of the prisoner's significance.'

'And if they're both missing, they could have got out together,' said Kolea.

'Gaunt may have got this prisoner to safety and gone to ground?' asked Hark.

'That's one possibility,' said Edur.

'And the other?' asked Hark.

'Gaunt may have been working with the raiders to extract the prisoner. I hasten to add this is not my theory. However, the Inquisition is understood to be entertaining it.'

'I don't believe this,' said Hark, shaking his head. 'This is all about fething Gereon again.'

'In so many ways,' agreed Edur.

'They're never going to let it go,' said Hark.

'Is there any evidence to back up this slur?' Kolea asked.

'There are some unfortunate details,' said Edur. 'Your Major Rawne and the others were on the premises.'

'On charges, in lock-up,' said Hark.

'Noted. However, they are also now missing or dead. If one was of a suspicious inclination, one might see evidence of a plan. People on the inside, ready to move.'

'Shall I tell you what I think?' asked Hark.

'I think you should all tell me what the hell you think you're doing, discussing these sensitive details,' said Rime.

They hadn't seen the inquisitor approach. He was flanked by two of his henchmen.

'I could have you all executed,' said Rime. 'This is confidential information pertinent to an ongoing situation.'

'I felt, inquisitor,' said Edur, 'that the senior Tanith officers might be very much more helpful to us if they were granted a better overview.' Edur decided not to mention what else he felt, as it concerned the inquisitor rather more directly.

'I don't think it's your place to make that decision,' said Rime.

'Then I will consider myself chastised, sir,' said Edur.

'Gaunt has no part in this,' Hark told Rime.

'Why?' asked one of the henchmen.

'Because I know him,' said Hark.

'Oh, that's all right then,' said Rime.

'Our commanding officer is not a traitor,' said Kolea. 'There is no conspiracy. If he's involved, it will be an improvised involvement. He is utterly loyal.'

'We'll know that when we find him,' said Rime.

'We want to help you do that,' said Kolea, 'in any way we can. We want to clear his name, and the reputation of this regiment. You can inspect us for any information.'

'We are,' said Rime with a smile.

'You can intercept all on- and off-base communications to see if he attempts to contact us.'

'We are,' said Rime.

Kolea stopped. He breathed hard and asked, 'With respect, sir, what else can we tell you? What else can we do to help?'

'You can remain here, and answer any questions we pose,' said Rime. 'Other than that, you shouldn't be involved in any way.'

'The Tanith have an excellent reputation for scouting and tracking,' said Edur.

'That's simply fabulous for them,' said Rime. He turned away.

'Can I have a word, sir?' Edur asked. 'Alone?'

Rime turned, thought about it, and then stepped towards the corridor. His henchmen followed.

'I meant properly alone,' said Edur.

Rime sent a curt signal to his agents, and they stepped back.

Edur followed Rime into the empty hallway and closed the door behind him.

'Speak,' said Rime with a shrug of impatience.

'I think you should use the Tanith, sir,' said Edur. 'They are first-class trackers and scouts. If Gaunt and the prisoner are on the run in the Oligarchy, they will find him. They are motivated. It's a rescue, a matter of honour. And if it turns out that Gaunt's involvement is anything less than proper, it will also present them with an opportunity to restore their reputation.'

'Edur, I'm not going to entertain that for a moment,' said Rime. 'The ordo has first-class agents of its own at its disposal. I don't need a bunch of thick-necked grunts running around–'

'I suggest you read the regiment profile,' said Edur. 'I suggest you properly appreciate the skill and achievements of these *thick-necked grunts*. Forget Gaunt. If the prisoner's alive to be found, the Tanith will find him.'

Rime shook his head and stepped past Edur to return to his men.

'Then consider this, sir,' said Edur. 'Bring the Tanith in on this hunt, and I won't have to mention to anybody what I saw today.'

'What are you talking about?' asked Rime.

'That thing… in the hallway… it burned your face off. It cremated your skull. You shouldn't be here, you shouldn't be alive. You shouldn't be talking to me.'

'You don't know what you're talking about,' said Rime.

'No, I don't,' said Edur, 'but I've got a nasty feeling it's got something to do with the fact that you and your lackeys all look alike.'

'If that's the case, it was evidently one of them you saw burn,' said Rime.

'I know what I saw,' said Edur, 'and it speaks of darkness and warpcraft, and heresy. It speaks of things the Inquisition doesn't want exposed during a situation this sensitive.'

Rime glared at him for a second. Then he turned and strode back into the company office.

'You, soldier,' he said, pointing at Kolea.

'Major Kolea,' Kolea replied.

'Whoever you are,' said Rime. 'I want you to assemble, quickly and efficiently, your finest huntsmen.'

SIXTEEN

The Other Hunters

KARHUNAN SIRDAR STOLE down the silent street, following the trail of little black discs where drops of blood had marked the snow. The street was steep, and the buildings on either side were dark and shuttered against the night and the snowstorm, as if they were hiding with their eyes tight shut. He watched the gusting snow billowing like sparks in the light cones of the streetlamps. Not every lamp in the old quarter street worked.

The beloved magir had put a duty upon his soul, but Karhunan was content. The duty was almost done. They had followed, and they had closed. The vehicle they'd found abandoned up the street behind him was definitely the same one that had outrun them at Section. The blood drops on the snow completed the death warrant.

Some of the philia had moved up with him to reconnoitre the street. Samus was standing outside one of the buildings just ahead, staring up the steps at the front door. The building was dark, and betrayed no sign of life. A sign, some kind of pole device that Karhunan half-recognised from the depths of his scarred memory, hung above the door on a brass rail. Samus was shivering and gnawing at his tongue. As the sirdar approached, he made a soft mewling noise and inclined his head towards the door.

Karhunan patted the misshapen man gently on the shoulder. There were little spots of blood leading up the entrance steps, not yet covered by the softly falling snow.

Imrie appeared to Karhunan's left, and Naeme to his right. They looked eager.

'Melthorael,' Naeme muttered, 'then it is Aroklur, then it is Ultheum.'

'Quiet,' Karhunan whispered.

At the sirdar's nod, Imrie took out the door with a kick, and they swept into the dark wood hallway. The snow came in with them. Flakes settled on a long-case clock standing in the hallway.

Imrie led the way, his weapon level, shoulder-height, hunting. He was the sharpest of them. A long time ago, in what was almost literally another life, Imrie had been, like Karhunan, a Throne soldier. He was a convert, an incomer. The sept word was *elterdwelt*, which meant 'other life' or, more loosely, 'traded item'. He had sloughed off most of his other life, shed it gladly like a snake sheds an old, tight skin, but some parts of it had remained stubborn. Damogaur Eyl, no *elterdwelt*, but rather Consanguinity-born, cherished such old traits in the men of his philia. Imrie had been a scout, a hunter. He saw details almost anyone else would miss.

Imrie swept down the hall. He noticed that one of the six bulbs in the hall lamps had blown, and blown a long time before, because its dull glass was coated in dust. He noticed that the long-case clock was not working. He noticed the dried residue of snow-melt footprints on the dark wood floor, all but invisible.

A small kitchen. Three mugs, all half-full, all cold. A stove-top burner where the wrought iron ring still held some heat.

Imrie nodded Samus on. Samus checked a side room, caving the door in with a crash. Naeme was on the stairs, his weapon aimed upwards, peering.

Imrie went down the stone steps into the basement. Karhunan followed him. The basement areas were quite extensive, stone vaults built beneath pavement level. There was a surgical theatre, a storeroom and a cold room for cadavers.

'There's nobody here,' said Karhunan.

'But there was,' Imrie replied.

'You sure?'

'Sure as blood speckles in the snow,' Imrie replied. 'Sure as a stove still warm. Sure as this.'

They were in the theatre. It was clean and tidy, and empty, but Imrie had lifted the lid of the medical waste bin. Karhunan Sirdar peered in. He saw dirty swabs and blood dressings, along with some disposable medicae materials.

Imrie walked over to the tool counter. He unscrewed the lid of one of the glass sterilising baths, and withdrew a scalpel. He sniffed it.

'Blood,' he said.

Even after a time in the chemical soak, the smell lingered enough for a man like Imrie.

'So, where?' asked Karhunan.

Imrie tilted his head and thought. He could smell something else, something dirty and metallic. He strode out of the theatre into the lower landing. The wood panelled back wall wasn't a wall at all. It was a screen. He found the recessed brass handle and drew it aside.

A service elevator. Cold, damp mustiness drifted up from below.

Imrie rode the rattling carriage down with his sirdar and Naeme. On arrival, after just a short drop, they swung out, weapons raised.

Snowflakes blew into their faces. The front of the house faced one steep street, but the rear let out three floors down onto another street-level of the escarpment. In Old Side, the buildings and streets were stacked in tiers.

The doors of the small basement garage were open onto the back lane. There were oil marks on the rockcrete floor, and a scent of exhaust in the air.

Imrie hurried to the garage doors and looked out.

Nothing had been left behind, except the ghost of squirming tyre tracks.

'It's just an idea, but could you try going faster?' asked Maggs.

'Quiet,' Gaunt warned him. Maggs sighed, and sat back in the rear of the little private ambulance. It was a rickety thing that patently hadn't been used in years. Gaunt was in the cab with Kolding. Maggs was in the back with the unconscious prisoner. The ambulance was creeping through the night at what felt like a mollusc's crawl, except that it was also managing to slide and wheel-spin too.

'Gently,' Gaunt said to Kolding, who was hunched low, glaring over the top of the wheel.

'I'm trying my best,' Kolding replied.

'When was the last time you took this vehicle out?' Gaunt asked.

'A while.'

'At night?'

'A while.'

'Who drove then, doctor?'

Kolding shrugged and found another gear. 'My father.'

Gaunt shook his head.

'Sir,' he said, 'have we forced you to leave your home for the first time in fifteen years?'

Kolding shrugged again, and said, 'It's all right. I keep myself to myself. It's just a strange turn of events, that's all.'

'You've been in that house for fifteen years?' Maggs asked incredulously.

'Enough, Maggs,' said Gaunt.

'No wonder he's such a fethwaste,' Maggs muttered.

'Doctor Kolding,' Gaunt began, 'I think that I should drive.'

'Why?'

'You're evidently having problems with the snowy conditions. It's taxing you. I have recent training in cold weather driving.'

'Do you?' asked Kolding.

The doctor brought the ambulance to a long, lingering halt, and he and Gaunt got out and crossed sides.

Behind the wheel, Gaunt tested the controls, let out the clutch, and raced them forward.

'That was a lie, wasn't it?' asked Kolding.

'What?'

'Your recent training in cold weather driving?'

Gaunt nodded.

'The lamps hurt your eyes, don't they?' he asked. 'That's why you are driving at night in dark glasses.'

Kolding didn't reply.

'I have a slight advantage,' said Gaunt. He double-blinked and switched his focal field to high-gain, low light. Streetlamps or no streetlamps, the way ahead lit up for him.

KARHUNAN RETRACED HIS steps up the street, though his steps were almost gone. His boots *chuffed* in the ever-thickening snow cover.

The damogaur was examining the car their quarry had used. Six members of the philia, under Malstrom's leadership, stood watch in the street around him.

Eyl looked at Karhunan.

'They were in the building nearby, magir,' said the sirdar, 'but they have gone. Another vehicle. Imrie and Naeme are already following its tracks. If we deploy fast, we will catch up and–'

'We'll catch up anyway,' Eyl replied. 'No need to go chasing through this weather.'

'What do you mean?' asked Karhunan.

'Look what we've got,' Eyl answered. He stroked his fingertips along the back of the car's driving seat. They came away tacky and dark.

'Bring my sister here,' he said. 'We've got their blood.'

WHEN SHE COULDN'T run any more, Tona Criid hid instead. Her muscles were burning as if someone was spiking hot wires into them, and she was close to throwing up.

The shrill sound had gone away at some point, and the constriction had faded. A few streets away from Section, a few streets from Viceroy Square where that veiled *thing* had been standing under the snow-dusted trees, she forced her way into an empty building.

Though the Oligarchy and Balopolis had been the epicentre of the most brutal fighting during the war for Balhaut, much of the so-called Old Side seemed to have been miraculously spared. Closer inspection put the lie to that. Many of the buildings were shells: gutted structures that had stood empty for a decade and a half with litter collecting in their wind-blown floors. A few had begun to be included in Balhaut's trudging programme of renewal. In places, old buildings were being demolished and lots cleared to make room for new construction. In others, labour gangs had moved in to renovate and restore the buildings still sound enough to be worth saving.

Criid holed herself up in one of the latter. The windows had been recently covered with whitewashed boards, and there was a strong smell of creosote and young, sawn timber. Dust sheets and protective curtains had been strung between rooms, or erected to close sections where dividing walls had been taken down. The work curtains, heavy and dirty from re-use, stiff with old paint and varnish, swung in the night air, moved by the breath of the snowstorm outside. The day crew had left paint drums, long-handled mop-brushes, sawhorses and stacks of cheap fibreboard behind. An upper floor had been taken away, leaving a space like the interior of an artisan's church, the vault bridged by a half-skeleton of new joists and crossbeams in clean, yellow wood.

Her heart rate was all over the place, and her breathing was ragged. Her hands were quaking so much that she struggled to use them. She snapped the head off one of the long mop-brushes, and used baler twine to lash her warknife to the end as an improvised spear. No gun, but a little more range than a knife, at least. Then she sat down in a corner behind some stacked fibreboard and rested the spear across her lap.

Her body was in turmoil. She knew that. The chronic tension of life in a warzone bent a person's biology out of shape, and left it fit for nothing else. It built shortcut response pathways, and bred bad habits. It altered hormone values and metabolic functions to tolerate prolonged and elevated stress. It modified you to get you through, whatever it took, and then left the modifications in you when you returned to what was laughingly referred to as normal life. It left them with corrosive physiological and psychological damage that took a thousand times longer to erase than it had taken to inflict.

The worst part, as she was now discovering, wasn't coping with the post-combat fall out; it was getting your old, bad self, your *combat self*, switched back on without warning. She'd gone from nothing to superluminal in a second. The toxic flood of hormones and responses had left her almost stupefied. There was a sheen of sweat on her skin, and she knew that she stank of fear. Her mind was numb except for a little tiny nugget at the heart of it, like the dense metal heart of a neutron star that was screaming with radioactive rage.

She tried to control her breathing. She tried to employ some of the focus techniques that Mkoll had taught her for stealth work. It was futile. It was like trying to grasp water. In the end, she gave up and, with a brittle laugh, decided that she might be better off just surrendering to the tide.

After an hour or more, during which she sank into a fugue state, she roused herself, and felt a little more clarity. The old mindset, the one that allowed you to function in the zone, was back so concretely it was as if it had never gone away. She started to be able to think instead of just react.

In her opinion, the biggest problem was the world outside. She simply couldn't understand how the debacle at Section could have happened without all hell resulting. Where were the suppression teams? The counter-forces? The security squads with their armoured cars and fear-gas canisters? Where was the PDF and the fething Guard? The city should have been screeching with raid sirens by now. The skies should have been dense with gunships.

It was quiet out there. It was as if the city had gone into traumatic shock, struck dumb and paralysed. It was as if the snowfall had some kind of anaesthetic property. She couldn't shake the notion that the silent streets were crawling with unchallenged Archenemy soldiers.

She decided she had no choice but to make her way back to Aarlem Fortress. She hadn't got anything like enough left in her to run the route, but she was confident that if she took it steadily, she could make it back before dawn.

She hadn't gone far when she heard a vehicle approaching, its engine tone labouring as it coped with the snow. It stood out a mile. There was nothing else around. Criid stopped and listened. Perhaps it was PDF moving in at long last. Perhaps it was the transport component of a relief column advancing into the city's heart.

Instinct told her it wasn't. It was just one engine, one machine, and a small one at that. It was someone mysteriously active in the mysteriously empty streets.

She decided to take a look, and closed in on the approaching sound source. When it came in sight, she fell back, clutching her spear. The vehicle, just a dark blob on the snowy thoroughfare, was driving without lights: without lights, at night, in a snowstorm.

That was deliberate, and it was sinister. Swallowing hard, she took one last look, then retreated to hide in an alley long before the occupants could see her.

She waited. The vehicle didn't go by. It stopped.

She cursed and hefted up the spear. There was no way she'd been spotted, but why had it stopped?

A figure suddenly appeared at the end of the alleyway, framed by the snow-light. It was a soldier, one of the raiders, one of the invaders. She weighed her choices. Stay back, and wait for it to come to her, so she could kill it quietly in the private darkness of the alley, or go to it and take it down fast before it got her cornered.

The figure took a step towards her, as if it knew she was there, as if it could see right into the shadows with its warpcraft. She couldn't just sit there.

She charged.

It recoiled in surprise as she flew out of hiding. She had the spear lowered to impale it through the gut. She let out an incoherent scream.

With a cry of its own, the figure jerked to one side, evading the thrust of the long Tanith blade. It grabbed the spear's haft with one hand, and tried to use Criid's momentum to bring her over. She wrenched back, refusing to lose control of the weapon. Her attacker was strong. He crashed her backwards into the alley wall, trying to pin her. She screamed and kicked out.

'For feth's sake, Tona,' Gaunt yelled. 'It's me!'

SEVENTEEN

Blood for the Blood God

'WHO IS HE?' Criid asked.

'He's the reason all this is happening,' Gaunt replied.

'He was on Gereon with us?'

'We never met him,' Gaunt said to her, 'but he was the one hunting us.'

Criid stared down at the sleeping face of the man on the stretcher. He wore his scars where anyone could see them. Gereon, probably more than anywhere else, had left the deepest scars inside her, invisible. Gereon was the chief reason she had a stress migraine behind her eyes and such an adrenaline spike that her sweat tasted of sour metal.

They had taken shelter in the refurb block where she had hidden earlier. The night air was still moving the heavy, soiled work curtains that partitioned the structure. The smell of cold, wet sawdust was intense. Maggs and Criid had pried open one of the boarded doorways, and Gaunt had driven the ambulance inside. Maggs was busy putting the panelling back in place so it looked as if it hadn't been disturbed.

'You saw me, in the dark,' Criid said to Gaunt.

He nodded.

'Those eyes of yours,' she remarked.

'You'd be amazed the things I'm seeing these days,' he replied.

'How far does this go?' Criid asked. 'Have they taken the city? Is it that big? Is he that important?'

'You know as much as we do,' said Gaunt.

Kolding was hovering beside the prisoner, checking the state of his dressings. They'd had to leave in a hurry. Kolding had protested, and his protests had all been on medical grounds. He didn't want the patient moved or disturbed. The patient needed post-operative rest and a chance to stabilise his vital signs. Gaunt had looked him in the face and told him how close the Blood Pact were and, rather more graphically, what would happen when they stormed the house.

'How is he?' Gaunt asked.

Kolding looked up at Gaunt. His eyes were unreadable behind his blue-tinted lenses.

'It's better now he's not being shaken and jolted. I don't want the wound reopening. His core temperature is low, however, and his pulse is thready. Can we risk a fire in here?'

'No,' said Criid.

Gaunt shook his head too.

'I'm sorry,' he said. 'With them hunting us, that's not an option.'

Kolding stood up. 'Then I'll get some more blankets out of the ambulance. I believe there are some old thermal packs in there too, which might still work.'

He walked away towards the battered old van.

'Where did you find him?' whispered Criid.

'Make sure you show him some respect,' Gaunt replied. 'Without him, the Blood Pact would have won already.'

Maggs returned. He looked exhausted, and the dried blood on his ear and neck made it look as if he'd been in a brawl.

'We're secure, as it goes,' he said.

'Unless things change, let's rest here for an hour or so. Anyone know where here is, by the way?'

'Moat Street,' replied Kolding as he came back from the ambulance with an armful of blankets. Criid moved to help him wrap the patient.

'Someone needs to stand watch,' said Maggs.

'I'll do it, Wes,' Criid called back. 'I'm way too jaggy to sleep.'

Maggs tossed her his laspistol. She caught it neatly, tucked it into her waistband, and crouched down beside Kolding.

'What's up?' Maggs asked Gaunt.

Gaunt shook his head, and said, 'Moat Street. It rings a bell. I think I may have been here before.'

'When?'

'Fifteen years ago.'

Maggs whistled.

'Really?' he asked.

'I can't be sure. We advanced down a lot of streets in Old Side to get at the Oligarchy. Most of them were rubble or burning or both. The name's familiar, that's all.'

'I thought you'd remember every last detail of a show like that,' said Maggs.

'I thought I had,' Gaunt replied. 'I've never thought much about it, actually. Never felt much need to reflect on it. But I've always assumed that my memories of that time were pretty complete, that they were there if I needed them. Now…'

He paused and shrugged. 'Now I come to look back, to search for the memories, I'm finding they're actually a bit of a blur. They've all run together.'

Maggs nodded.

'I get that,' he said. 'I get the same thing with Hinzerhaus, you know? I remember what happened, I remember what shade of hell it was. I just don't seem to have any of the details left.'

A strong gust of wind lifted the edges of the work curtains, and blew up a pile of wood shavings so that they scurried and drifted like thick snow.

'You know what's to blame, don't you?' Maggs said.

'Tell me,' said Gaunt.

'War,' said Maggs. 'It feths up your head. It feths it up in terrible ways. And the longer you're exposed to it, the worse it'll get.'

'I hear that,' said Criid as she walked off to take watch.

'Get some sleep,' Gaunt said to Maggs.

Maggs nodded, and went in search of some tarpaulin to curl up on.

Gaunt prowled around the site, pulling aside work curtains, and stepping into new spaces, blue darknesses that smelled of young wood and paint. *Moat Street, Moat Street…* Had he been here? Probably not in this very building, but outside on the street, moving from cover to cover with the Hyrkans as tracer-fire licked down out of the smoke-wash. Was that a genuine memory, or just a simulation his mind had amalgamated from driftwood pieces in his subconscious?

He heard a light tapping: the fleck of snowflakes being driven against the window-boarding by the wind. He parted another curtain and stepped through into the next area. Plastek sheeting crackled as the draught inhaled and exhaled it against the fibreboard panelling. He adjusted his eyes. Both the front and back walls of the chamber were being rebuilt. Cut stone was waiting to be laid, and the street walls were temporarily formed by wooden boards. Fifteen years ago, something had punched clean through this part of the building. On the interior walls that remained, he found ragged scratch marks running along the stone at about shoulder height. He traced them with his hand until he identified them. A tank, or similar armoured machine, had come through here, flattening the front and back walls under its treads, and raking both side walls with the skirts of its hull.

The strange thing was, it wasn't the first time he'd seen this. He'd been on Balhaut a year. He'd moved through its streets and gone about his business. How many times had he seen a street corner notched and ragged at shoulder height? Or a stretch of wall scratched with a long, ugly gouge? He'd seen it hundreds of times, and only now did he recognise it for what it was: the traces left by the iron shoulders of the predatory giants that had stalked Balhaut in its darkest days.

Even the things that survived a war, even the things left standing, came out of it with scars.

He went back to the chamber where the others were holed up. Maggs was asleep, and Kolding was sitting quietly beside the swaddled prisoner on the stretcher. Criid was watching the street from an unboarded side window.

'Anything?' he asked her.

'It's very quiet,' she replied. 'I think they've got the whole town bewitched.'

Gaunt shook his head.

'Don't think of it that way,' he said. 'Don't make them bigger monsters than they are. They're tough, and they've got unholy warpcraft, but there can't be that many of them. I'm pretty sure this is an insertion, not a full-scale invasion. The snowstorm is just bad timing, a coincidence.'

'Really?'

'We're not going to beat them unless we can beat them in our heads first. Don't hand them that advantage.'

Criid nodded, and flashed a grin, but she didn't look altogether convinced.

Gaunt went back to the ambulance and sat with his back against one of the wheel arches to rest. He was sore and bruised from the day's endeavours, especially from the feral brawl with the maniacal damogaur. Criid and Maggs were both jumpy, but only now did he realise how far back down he had had to come himself. The day had plunged him back into a life or death world that he hadn't visited in two years. It had been unpleasant: a shock, yet horribly familiar. His jaw muscles were clenched, his spine and the small of his back were damp, and there was a stale taste in his mouth. Just the day before, in the Mithredates with Blenner, he'd been complaining about how impatient he was to go out and re-acquaint himself with war.

He'd never expected it to come and find him.

He fished inside his coat for Eszrah's copybook, intending to steady his nerves by reading another of the nihtgane's painstakingly transcribed myths. They were fascinating. They contained old wisdoms about hunting and warcraft. He would, he resolved, when circumstances allowed, examine them carefully, and perhaps even learn from them. He had not, so far, been able to give them the attention they deserved.

When he pulled out the copybook, a folded sheet of paper fell out of its pages onto the ground between his legs. It was a letter, with a finely printed letterhead at the top of the sheet. It was a polite introduction from a Mr Jaume, a photographic portraitist.

Gaunt realised that he'd pulled out his own copybook. Eszrah's, virtually identical, was in the opposite side of his jacket. The letter, the one poor Beltayn had insisted Gaunt had seen and which he'd denied all knowledge of, had been tucked into the cover of his book, probably since the morning it had arrived at Aarlem.

He folded it up to put it away, and noticed the letterhead. The address of Jaume's studio was listed as '137 Carnation Street, off Moat Street'. *Moat Street*. That's where he'd seen it. It wasn't a memory of the Balhaut War at all, just a little speck of driftwood that had got jumbled up in his head.

EYL STOOD QUIETLY in the kitchen of Doctor Kolding's house on Kepeler Place. Though the middle of the night was not long past, a blue twilight was beginning to seep in through the windows. First light, and though the snowstorm had not eased off, the first hint of daylight was being magnified and reflected by the enfolding whiteness.

Apart from Kreeg, who was standing watch inside the front door, and Gnesh, who was minding the lower street access from the ambulance garage, the men of the philia were resting in the upper rooms of the house. Twenty-nine men; his force had been reduced to twenty-nine men. Kaylb Sirdar was gone, the first to die. Eyl had not witnessed the death to place it into any kind of definitive chronology, but he knew his sister couldn't lie.

Eyl had taken off his grotesk. He relished the pain in his hands, chest and face where the carbine had been exploded in his grasp and left him gashed and burned. The injuries reminded him he was alive, just as they reminded him who had to die.

Time was slipping away. With every passing minute, their mission became harder, the odds greater, the opposition more resolved. The philia had spent its weapon of surprise, and Eyl estimated they had only a few more hours left in which to exploit the enemy's shock. By morning, he thought, the Imperials will have gathered their wits and rallied. They will have closed the city down and begun the hunt for us.

Until then, Eyl meant to make the best use of his time. The city environs were still caught in an *un*-state, the sick half-light of the warpcraft that his sister had cast over the metropolis to numb, baffle and confuse. The storm continued unabated, and lent to them its gifts of concealment and mystery. The philia still had enough time to do its work. Once again, his sister was the key.

Eyl picked up one of the half-empty enamel mugs that was standing on the worn kitchen table. Out of curiosity, he sipped the cold, black liquid inside.

It tasted of blood. Everything tasted of blood.

He went downstairs to find his sister.

She was in the small surgical theatre that lay behind the swing doors at the bottom of the stone steps. Eyl pushed the doors open gently. He had no wish to make her jump or disturb her work.

And she was most certainly at work.

Eyl knew that the men of the philia had withdrawn into the house's upper rooms so that they did not have to linger too close to her witchery. Proximity to Ulrike's craft caused the skin to prickle and the heart to go frantic.

Eyl swallowed back the bile that had rushed up his throat.

'Sister?'

She had taken winding sheets of white cloth from a storage cupboard, and pinned them to the theatre's wood panelled walls using surgical blades, turning the sheets into stretched canvases. Then she'd made blood marks upon them.

She'd located the theatre's source of blood stock, a refrigerated unit beside the scrub sink, and raided its contents. Empty transfusion packets, torn open and discarded, were scattered across the tiled floor. She'd squirted, shaken and splashed the contents of the packets across the sheets.

As Eyl approached, she was gazing at the marks, her wet, red hands by her sides, dripping on her mourning skirts.

'What do you see?' he asked.

'Nothing. It's all broken. Disjointed. Incomplete.'

'Why?'

She shrugged. 'The future doesn't want me to see it.'

Eyl bent down and picked up one of the emptied blood packets. He read the label.

Synthetic blood supplement.

'This isn't real blood,' he said. 'It's artificial. Made in a vat.'

She nodded.

'I know,' she said. 'I can read. I thought it would work.'

She squinted again at the blood marks on the sheets, the blackberry darkness of the blood, the yellow-pink halo stains of the plasma.

'I'll have to use real blood. Bleed myself. Give me your rite knife, brother.'

'I lost it,' he admitted.

She turned to him. He could feel the heat of her gaze from behind the veil.

'Upon my soul,' she said, 'that is unfortunate.'

'It is what it is,' he replied, though he knew she was right. 'Tell me about the real blood.'

Striding like a headstrong child, she went over to the counter immediately. She'd emptied and washed a couple of the glass sterilising baths, and filled them with blood product. Suspended in the red liquid, Eyl could see the strips of bloodstained leather that Malstrom and Barc had cut from the upholstery of the limousine.

'Where did the blood come from?' he asked.

'From the synthetic store,' she replied. 'Don't worry, it's just a medium. It's not as reactive as blood, but it's better than water, and that's what I thought I'd be forced to use.'

'And?'

'I can sense him already,' she said.

Using a surgical tool, she'd scratched a grid and accompanying symbols into the worktop, and placed the glass baths at the centre. Arcane mechanisms were at work.

'You can?'

She nodded. 'I'll have his location soon. His heartbeat. There was a lot of blood on the leather. He bled all over the seats.'

She looked up at him.

'He might be dead already, Baltasar.'

'I suppose so.'

'The pheguth might be dead already,' she continued. She laced her arms around him, and rested the side of her veiled head against his chest. 'Our work might be done. We could slip away and–'

He pulled her arms off him.

'I must have a confirmed kill,' he said. 'Besides, you know we can't. We can't slip away from this. This world will end us. This mission will undo us. A day more, perhaps two, that's the measure of our lifetimes. We knew this when we accepted the burden upon our souls.'

'You did. Not me,' she replied.

'We were made for this, sister, we–'

'I was made. I was made for this. The gore mages wove me for this very purpose. You volunteered, Baltasar. Proud warrior, great damogaur, you volunteered for the glory of this mission. I was never offered a choice, and I wish I had been. That is one of my truths.'

He nodded sadly.

'If you'd had the choice, would you have chosen this?' he asked.

'I cannot lie,' she replied. 'Sometimes I wonder what life is like. I mean, what it is like to lead a life: to be born and grow up, and make choices and follow paths. I wish I could have done that. I wonder what choices I'd have made. But I know what I am, brother. A witched instrument. No childhood, no life, no choices. Bred for just one purpose. Even so–'

'Even so?'

'I would have chosen this. The pheguth must die.'

'And the Anarch?' Eyl asked. 'Will the Anarch die?'

'Brother, you know that's the one thing I can't see,' she said.

'WHAT'S THE MATTER?' Maggs asked.

He'd woken up suddenly, cold and stiff on the hard bed of the tarpaulin, with no idea of time or location. It had taken a panicky moment or two for him to remember.

His clipped ear hurt like a fether. The wound had begun to ache and throb, like any flesh wound after the initial sting and shock has worn off. Worse, the fear and stress that he'd accumulated the previous day was still flooding his system, the last thing he needed.

Gaunt was asleep. The bastard could sleep anywhere. Criid was undoubtedly prowling the perimeter. Doctor Death was kneeling beside the patient. Maggs could tell that something was up.

'What's the matter?' he repeated. It was bone cold in the blue darkness of the refurb, and Maggs saw his breath smoking out in front of his face. The patient, under the blankets on the stretcher, was trembling and murmuring.

'He's taken a fever,' Kolding replied.

'A fever?' asked Maggs.

'That's what I said.'

'What kind of fever?' Maggs asked.

Kolding looked up at him in the gloom.

'There is only one kind,' he replied.

'The bad kind?'

'Yes.'

'Uh huh. What do we do?'

Kolding laughed a little, odd laugh, and said, 'Why, sir, we take him at once to the Oligarchy Municipal Medicae Hospice on the Avenue Regnum Khulan, so they can begin intensive isolyte therapy... Except, oh, we can't do that, can we?'

Maggs shook his head.

'The fever came on suddenly,' said Kolding. 'I found rainwater caught in that sheeting over there. I'm trying to keep his face cool.'

'Is he going to die?' asked Maggs.

'We're all going to die, sir,' Kolding replied.

'I meant now,' Maggs snapped.

'Possibly. I think his wound has become infected. Hardly surprising, given the circumstances.'

'Look, Doc, I don't like this any more than you do,' Maggs said. He paused and then started suddenly.

Kolding stared at him.

'Are you all right, soldier?' he asked.

'Yes,' Maggs replied, shaking his head. 'Why?'

'You look pale, sweaty,' said Kolding.

Maggs didn't feel good at all, but he knew there wasn't time for any self-indulgence. Feeling like crap was his problem.

'I'm fine,' he said.

'I think you might be running a temperature too.'

'Just look after freak-face, all right, Doc?' Maggs said.

He realised that his hands were shaking. His knees felt soft. He watched the doctor in the half-light as Kolding mopped the prisoner's brow.

'Where's Criid?' Maggs asked.

'Who?'

'The girl, the woman,' Maggs said, frustrated.

'I think she went out to check the street,' Kolding replied.

Maggs reached for his weapon. Criid had his las. Doctor Death's automatic pistol was wedged in his pocket. He drew it.

'What's the matter?' Kolding asked, suddenly apprehensive as he saw the weapon come out.

'Nothing,' Maggs replied, but that wasn't the truth. The truth was he'd just remembered the dream that had woken him in the first place.

THE SIEGE OF Hinzerhaus, on the fortress world of Jago, had been an awful ordeal. It had also been the Ghosts' last major action before their retirement. Good men had died at Hinzerhaus, and one way or another Wes Maggs hadn't been one of them.

The place had haunted them during the siege. Ghosts had walked amongst the Ghosts. Everyone had fireside stories, stories about returning old friends or lost comrades, or pieces of childhood, or driftwood memories made flesh. According to the old Tanith, men like Mad Larkin and Shoggy Domor, the ghosts that had come to them on Jago had taken the form of actual lost souls like Bragg and Corbec, men who'd been dead and dust long before Maggs and the Belladon had joined the First. Maggs had little idea who Bragg and Corbec were, but the reappearance of their shades seemed to matter a feth of a lot to the Tanith-born troopers.

Maggs's personal ghost had been called the old dam. That was the name he'd given her. Some ancient, forgotten matron from Hinzerhaus's dust-erased past, she'd stepped down out of one of the old, time-ravaged oil paintings and followed Maggs around the gloomy, satin-brown halls. She had worn a long, black lace gown, which rustled as she moved. Her face… Feth, her face had been a meat wound, the kind of thing that even a professional soldier didn't care to look at for long.

When Hinzerhaus's spell had finally broken (and the rumour was, it had been psyker magic all along), the old dam had left Maggs alone, once and for all. A last hiss of her black dress against the satin brown floor, and she'd gone.

For the two years since then, every morning, Maggs had given quiet thanks that she wasn't stalking him any more.

Two years. *Two years.* For the first time since Hinzerhaus, Maggs realised he'd dreamed about the old dam. He'd dreamed about her long, black rustling dress and the face he did not want to behold.

Why had she come back? It wasn't fair! Why now?

Why had she come back?

Maggs's hands shook. The old gun felt slick in his grip. If the old dam had come back, he wasn't going to let her get him. He'd kill her. Ghost or no ghost, he'd fething kill her.

Droplets of sweat were beading his forehead. Maggs didn't feel good at all.

But he had a gun, and he wasn't afraid to use it.

EIGHTEEN

Zolunder's

Someone was knocking on the street door. The knocking was disturbing the cantor-finches, and they were banging and twittering around their delicate cages in dismay. Midnight had long passed. Elodie wasn't sure if that made it ridiculously late or ridiculously early.

She checked the security monitor covering the red door, but whoever was knocking was standing just out of pict-view. And why were they knocking when there was a perfectly good bell?

Elodie yawned. The night after the raid, Urbano had decided not to open. This had surprised Elodie, because Cyrus Urbano was normally such a get back on the frigging steed kind of man. There had been something funny in the air that day, though, and it wasn't just the sting of being taken for such a huge score, or the miserable snowstorm that had come in, out of season and unwelcome.

Urbano had told her to send everyone home for a day or two, and had then gone out to attend to some business.

Now someone was knocking on the street door.

Elodie had fallen asleep on the couch in her dress. Xomat, the member of parlour security who'd pulled premises watch that night, had long since drunk himself to sleep, and was snoring in the greeter lounge.

Elodie got up. The knocking came again. Then whoever it was found the bell-push at last, and started pressing it hard.

She took the las-snub out of the under-bar drawer, and tucked it into the back of her sash. She went to the street door and peered through the spyhole.

Outside, dawn was fighting a losing battle with the snowstorm. The court was a dim, lightless void, especially as the garmentfab had shut and no light was coming down from its windows. There was somebody out there. Elodie just couldn't see who.

She opened the door. The new lock they'd been obliged to fit following the raid was stiff.

'Oh, thank the Throne,' said the girl on the doorstep. 'I was starting to think no one was here.'

'Banda?'

Banda looked pinched and tearful. She was still dressed in the red silk gown she'd been wearing when the Commissariat had carted her away, and not much else. She was shivering, and leaning on the gryphon's beak of the black iron handrail for support.

'What are you doing here?' Elodie asked.

'They let me go,' Banda said. 'Hey, can I come in?'

'They let you go?'

'Yeah, yeah. No charges. They questioned me. Fething Commissariat. Then they slammed me in a cell overnight. But they had nothing on me, so they let me go.'

'What are you doing here?' Elodie repeated.

Banda gazed at her, a hurt expression on her face.

'Where else was I supposed to go?'

'Not here,' said Elodie. 'Go away.'

'What? Fething *what*? I took one for the team and you're brushing me off?'

'Not me,' said Elodie. 'I'm sorry, Tanith. Urbano doesn't want you around. He told me to let you go. He doesn't like hostesses who–'

'Who what?'

'Who get picked up. I know it wasn't you, although you should have known better. You should have pulled your head in. It doesn't matter. Urbano wants you gone. He's superstitious. He doesn't like the connection. Come back in a week or two, and maybe I'll be able to find you an opening at one of the other parlours.'

'I don't believe this,' Banda replied. Her voice sounded as if it had been crushed flat. She sat on the snow-crusted step and began to tear up.

'Oh, come on. Go home,' said Elodie.

'I've got no home,' Banda snivelled. 'Tanith burned, remember?'

'I didn't mean. Oh, Throne, this really isn't my problem. You must have friends in the city, family?'

Banda shrugged, and said, 'I don't know anybody.' She looked at Elodie. 'Maybe I can talk to Urbano? Make him see sense?' she asked.

'He's out,' Elodie replied. 'I'm sorry, Tanith. I've got nothing for you. Go and find a hostel or something.'

Banda sighed and shrugged. She breathed hard to control her sobs. She rose to her feet.

'Right. Fine. Thanks for feth all. I'll be seeing you.'

She turned and started to walk up the steps to street level.

'Tanith?'

'Yeah?'

Elodie held the door open.

'Come in,' she said. 'I can give you a drink and maybe some food, and some better clothes. But you've got to be gone before Urbano gets back. Understand?'

'Throne, yes! You won't regret this.'

Xomat was still snoring. Elodie went around behind the bar and fixed two stiff sacras.

'Were you expecting trouble?' Banda asked, gesturing at the las-snub tucked into Elodie's sash. It was visible now that Elodie had turned and bent to fetch shot glasses.

'This? No. I just like to be careful.'

Elodie pushed one of the brimming shots across the nalwood bar towards Banda.

'You should get out of those wet clothes,' she told the Tanith girl.

Banda knocked the sacra back and held the glass out for a refill.

'It was a rough night, wasn't it?' Elodie said, smiling and pouring again.

'Like you wouldn't believe,' Banda replied.

Elodie plonked a digital key on the bar-top. It was tied to a block of wood with a hank of twine.

'There's a box of cast-offs in the hallway behind the private rooms,' she said. 'It's just stuff girls have left behind over the years. You might find something more weather-appropriate in there. Take what you want. And use the staff toilet to get changed.'

'Thanks,' said Banda.

'I'll see what food I can knock up,' said Elodie, refilling their glasses.

* * *

HOLDING THE DIGITAL key in one hand and her glass in the other, Banda wandered back into the hallway. The lights were off, but she found the box, a ratty-looking hamper stuffed with stale clothing. She helped herself to the best of what was on offer: a pair of baggies, a singlet, and a combat jacket. No shoes, apart from some strappy things that were no better than the ones she was wearing.

She used the digital key to let herself into the staff toilet. With the door locked behind her, she pulled the red silk dress up and off over her head. Naked, she crossed to the toilet's small window and forced it open. Ancient overpainting had fused the seal shut, and she had to smack the frame with the heel of her hand.

Snow-cold air breathed into the dingy bathroom.

ELODIE HAD FOUND some eggs and some rashers of green-grox, and she'd slung them all in a pan while she sawed some thick slices off a loaf of spelt bread for frying.

'Cooking me breakfast?' asked Urbano.

Elodie turned, trapped. 'No, I was, I mean, I was just hungry.'

'What's going on?'

'Nothing, I swear.'

'There's enough in that pan for an army,' Urbano said, peering down into the sizzling skillet.

'Look, Banda came back, all right?'

'Banda?'

'The Tanith girl.'

'Ah,' Urbano said, nodding. 'And you felt sorry for her?'

'Yes, yes I did. She'll be gone in an hour. Just some food and a drink and some fresh clothes.'

'You're such a soft touch, Elodie,' Urbano chuckled.

'Yeah, well, I had it all covered,' she replied. 'I even had the snub in case–'

She paused.

'What's the matter?' asked Urbano.

Elodie ran her hands back and forth across the top of her sash and the small of her back.

There was no las-snub.

'Looking for this?' asked Banda. She was standing in the doorway of the parlour's small kitchen, wearing hand-me-down combats and baggies. Her feet were bare. She was aiming the las-snub at them.

'Is this some kind of joke?' asked Urbano.

'No,' replied Banda.

'Put that toy away,' Urbano laughed. 'Put that toy away or I'll kill you.'

'Oh, Banda, please–' Elodie began.

Urbano reached into his coat and calmly produced a massive double-celled laspistol. He raised it and aimed it at Banda.

'Is this some kind of frigging joke?' he repeated, over-carefully.

'Permission to take the shot,' Banda said.

'Who are you talking to?' Urbano asked.

'She's talking to me,' said Rawne. He appeared in the kitchen doorway beside Banda. Behind him, Varl was aiming a lasrifle at Urbano.

'Shit!' exclaimed Urbano, and lowered his pistol.

'Good boy,' said Rawne.

'You're Hark, right?' asked Urbano, looking at the commissar uniform Rawne was wearing. 'Listen to me, Hark, it doesn't have to go like this. We can do business. Didn't you get enough last time you were here? Why the frig are you on me like this?'

'Because we're pissed off,' said Rawne. 'Because we've been through hell. Because we need some serious kill-power, and you were the nearest outlet we could think of.'

Rawne paused and looked at Banda, who was still aiming the snub at Urbano's face.

'Thanks for leaving the toilet window open,' he said.

'No problem. You want me to take this shot?'

'Whoa, whoa!' said Urbano. 'Kill-power. I can get you kill-power. What do you need, Commissar Hark?'

'You still think I'm a commissar?' Rawne asked him.

'What are you, then?' Urbano asked.

'Serious bad news for Cyrus Urbano,' Rawne replied.

'Come on!' Urbano exclaimed. 'You want kill-power? I've got it. What do you want? Las? Hard-slug? Hell? I've got it all!'

'Good,' Rawne said.

'We just need to discuss price,' Urbano said.

'Price?' Rawne echoed. 'You're serious? In this situation?'

'Of course,' Urbano replied. 'I'm a businessman.'

'And I'm a bastard,' Rawne replied. He looked at Banda. 'Take the shot.'

'What?' Urbano managed.

Banda shot him through the forehead. The las-round made a scorched hole in Urbano's brow. He smashed backwards into the cooker, and brought the pan of frying eggs and rashers down on top of him as he folded onto the floor and lay still in a lake of his own spreading blood.

'Holy Throne!' Elodie cried.

'I guess we'll be negotiating with you now,' Rawne said to Elodie.

THEY OPENED UP what Elodie referred to as the 'gun room'. It was little more than a reinforced closet in one of the private rooms. Inside it, arranged on wooden racks, was the stock of side-arms kept to defend the premises. There were two combat shotguns, two lasrifles, and a lot of solid slug pieces, including a massive bolt-action rifle, and a crate of brand new, forge-fresh small pattern laspistols with their Munitorum tags still on them, a trophy of the lucrative crossover between under-world rackets and Guard quartermasters on the take.

'Nice,' said Leyr, lifting one of the pistols and arming it.

'Pull what you want,' Rawne told them. It seemed as if he was going to be staking personal claim to the Blood Pact lasrifle he'd taken in the cells at Section. The two lasrifles in the gun room went to Daur and Meryn, and Varl and Banda took combat shotguns. Cant, lower on the pecking order, armed himself with an old autogun and a bag of reloads. Leyr took the big bolt-action.

'Are you sure?' asked Varl.

'Used to hunt with a baby like this back home,' Leyr replied.

The gun room, due to its hefty locks, also held the club's stash of obscura and other narcotics, stored in tins and paper folds.

'Don't even think about it,' Daur said.

Varl and Meryn looked at him.

'Go feth yourself, Daur,' said Meryn.

Daur took a step forwards.

'Whoa, whoa!' interjected Varl, getting between them. 'We're all friends here!'

'We're really not,' said Daur, glaring at Meryn. 'We are deep in it, and I don't want the fether who's supposed to have my back to be anything less than wide awake.'

'Listen to yourself, Daur,' Meryn mocked, popping the lid off a tin of obscura leaf and sniffing it, 'it's like you're still in the fething Guard. You are so straighter-than-straight. Like I'm going to listen to you or even care what you say.'

Daur lunged at Meryn, but Varl held him back.

'Meryn?' said Rawne from behind them.

'Yes?'

'Throw it away.'

Mearyn turned to stare at Rawne.

'What?'

'Throw it away.'

'Why?'

'Because,' said Rawne, 'we are deep in it, and I don't want the fether who's supposed to have my back to be anything less than wide awake.'

Meryn glared.

'We're still fething Guard, Meryn,' said Rawne, 'we're just in a temporary bad place. So throw that shit away and start observing the chain of command, or I'll have Leyr shoot you with his ridiculously big rifle. No, no, worse than that. I'll have Cant mow you down with his stubber. Then there'd be shame involved.'

'You can mow Meryn down with that, can't you, Cant?' Varl asked.

Cant smiled.

'Yes,' he promised.

Meryn lowered his hands.

'Feth you all,' he said and tossed the tin away.

'I didn't hear you, soldier,' said Rawne.

'I said: feth you all, *sir*,' said Meryn.

'Better. Now perhaps you'd like to take yourself off and investigate what this place has to offer in the way of comms. Varl, assist him.'

Daur watched Varl and the glowering Meryn leave the room.

'Thanks for the support,' he said to Rawne.

'Please don't think I did it for your benefit,' Rawne replied.

'Perish the thought,' said Daur. He walked back into the main bar. Leyr, the big bolt-action resting across the crook of his arm, was watching Elodie, who had been left sitting on a sofa. The strong-arm, Xomat, was sitting in a chair by the back wall, tied up and gagged with adhesive tape. His eyes were wide.

Daur walked over to the bar and rested his lasrifle on the nalwood top. He sat on one of the stools, the same stool he'd sat on the night of the sting. He'd taken a pack of the club's hand-coloured cards from one of the gaming tables, and began to flip through them absently, placing them face-up on the counter.

'What size are your boots?' Banda asked. She had strode into the bar, barefoot, the shotgun lodged over her shoulder, and gone right up to Xomat.

Mmgggh! he replied.

Banda stripped the tape gag away from his mouth.

'What?'

'Nine!' Xomat stammered.

'Oh, you're no use!' Banda declared, and wedged the tape back into place.

'You're what, a six?' asked Elodie.

'Yes.'

'Upstairs, in my room. The blue door at the end. There's a pair of work boots under the bed. Size six.'

'Thanks,' said Banda. She turned to go, but paused. 'I never meant to feth your life up,' she said.

Elodie shrugged.

When Banda had gone, Elodie rose and walked over to Daur at the bar. Leyr watched her, but made no comment.

'I'd like you to do me a favour,' Elodie said to Daur as she sat on the stool beside him.

'And that would be what?'

'Kill me.'

Daur looked at her.

'What?'

'Kill me,' said Elodie. 'It would be a kindness.'

'How do you work that out?'

'Urbano has friends. Colleagues. Partners. They run all the serious clubs and bars in this part of town. If they come here and discover what's happened, and find me alive, they'll just assume I had some part in it all. So, please, kill me. Make it quick.'

'I'm not going to kill you,' he protested. He turned another card over.

'Please, Daur. Your name *is* Daur, isn't it?'

'Yes. My name is Daur.'

'So what is this? That Hark guy, he's no commissar. And Banda–'

'Banda is Banda. Hark, his name is actually Rawne, and no, he's no commissar. This was a scam. We're all Guard, and, Throne help us, we were bored. We decided to see just how much we could take the famous Zolunder's for. I think it was Varl's idea, originally. No, maybe Meryn's. I was the icing on the cake. What Varl calls the "beauty part".'

'Because you're straight and honest, and you don't do this sort of thing?'

'Precisely. You know what? Here and now, in this fix, I can't even begin to remember why I said yes.'

'The thrill of it,' said Elodie.

'What?'

'You're a soldier, a warrior.'

'So?'

'When did you last see action?' Elodie asked.

'Two years ago,' said Daur.

'You miss the risk,' she said.

Daur started to reply, and then nodded. He turned over a few more cards. He had a dynasty in front of him, capped by Blue Sejanus and the Queen of Mab.

'I like the cards too,' he confessed.

'Yeah?'

'I've never played,' he said, 'not much at all. I just like the cards themselves. Their permutations.'

'You're an undiagnosed gambler,' said Elodie.

Daur shook his head.

'No, no. I just like them,' he said.

'Can you see the future in them?' she asked.

'It's not like that.'

'Can you tell me what's going on?' she asked.

Daur sighed, and said, 'We ripped you off. The night before last, we ripped you off. Then we got caught and bad things happened to us. We were looking at serious charges, detention–'

'And?'

'Then the stakes changed again. Suddenly. The Archenemy is here, mamzel. Here on Balhaut. He's got his hands in the guts of this world, and he's going to keep twisting until it hurts.'

'Are you serious?' Elodie asked.

'Absolutely.'

'So if Urbano's partners don't get me, the Archenemy will?' Elodie asked.

'Not if I can help it,' Daur replied.

'Pretty standard vox,' said Meryn, sitting back with a shrug in the club's monitor room.

'Plus, we can watch all the approaches on these viewers,' Varl said. 'We're pretty secure.'

Rawne nodded, and asked, 'The vox is high gain?'

'It's a Guard-issue unit,' said Meryn. 'These idiots got it off the black market.'

'You know how to twin a signal, Meryn?' Rawne asked.

'Yeah, of course.'

'So twin one for me.'

Meryn adjusted the caster's dials.

'Who am I sending to?' he asked.

Rawne told him.

'Are you out of your mind?' Meryn cried.

'Uh, Meryn?'

'For feth's sake… are you out of your mind, *sir*?'

'Send exactly what I say, Meryn,' said Rawne. 'Right now, I need to trust someone, and he's the only bastard I can think of.'

NINETEEN

Traces and Results

THE INQUISITION'S BIRDS had set down in Viceroy Square and the courtyards of Section. Their fans were cycling on neutral and the snow fell
softly around them. The snowflakes perished fast when they landed on
the hot hoods of the turbo fan assemblies. Black smoke was still pluming from the HQ's damaged wings.

Kolea waited at the gate with a group of Tanith personnel that included
Baskevyl and Larkin. Edur prowled around nearby with some storm-
troopers from S Company, keeping his eye on Rime and the forces of the
ordos, who were searching the stands of trees in the square's gardens.

'Will we be expected to take shots?' Larkin asked Kolea.

'Of course not,' Kolea replied.

'But we'll be up and scoping?'

'Will you relax, Larks?' Kolea said.

'It feels wrong, Gol,' Larkin said. 'I shouldn't be going looking for
Gaunt through my scope.'

'So noted, Larkin,' said Baskevyl. He touched Kolea's arm. 'Here comes
Mkoll.'

Mkoll, Bonin and the other Tanith scouts came into view, walking out
through the gatehouse towards them. Behind them, Section smouldered
against the colourless sky.

'Talk to me,' said Kolea.

'Gaunt's alive,' said Mkoll, coming to a halt in front of the acting commander and pulling a small but respectful salute. 'The high-value prisoner too. We've seen monitor footage and track-back from the gate cameras, and pict-feed from guard-tower mounts.'

'Gaunt and Maggs busted out of here at the height of the attack,' said Caober. 'Hell of a thing. They were definitely the Blood Pact's main targets.'

'So they're alive,' said Kolea. 'Close by?'

'Give us ten minutes and we'll tell you,' said Bonin.

'Who's going aloft?' asked Baskevyl.

Bonin looked at Mkoll.

Mkoll said, 'You go up. Take Larks with you. Hwlan, get upstairs with Nessa.'

'On it!' Hwlan called back.

They ran to their waiting Valkyries. Turbo-fans began to wind up to speed. Mkoll gestured to Jajjo, Preed and the other scouts and they began to move forward. Eszrah ap Niht had been standing near Baskevyl. When the scouts moved off, so did he.

The trees in the square trembled and swished as the two Valkyries took off, and snow gusted out like dust.

'I didn't authorise any transport lifts!' Inquisitor Rime declared, striding over to them. 'Where are those Valkyries going?'

'We've got the scent,' Kolea told him.

'Really? And this scent? Who has it?'

'He does, sir,' said Kolea. He pointed across the snowy gardens.

'And he's your chief of scouts? Does he know what he's doing?'

'The Tanith know what they're doing, inquisitor,' said Edur.

Out in front, Mkoll was slowly following the tracks left in the snow. As if realising they were talking about him, he rose and looked back.

He beckoned them after him.

'Game on,' muttered Gol Kolea.

'It would have been nice to get out there with them,' remarked Nahum Ludd. He was gazing out of the command post's grubby windows at the snow falling onto Aarlem's parade ground.

'Too many chiefs,' replied Hark.

'How so, sir?'

Hark looked up at his junior from the stack of reports he was working through.

'The Inquisition's all over this. Did you not get the impression that the Edur fellow was doing everything he could to retain some control of the operation?'

'I suppose.'

'Thanks to him, we've got Tanith officers and scouts on the ground. I think if he'd tried to bring Commissariat personnel into the mix too, that creep Rime would have burst something aortic.'

'Do you know Edur?' Ludd asked.

'No,' replied Hark. 'I've met him a couple of times at Section. He seems a decent sort. I'm glad we've got him on our side.'

Hark fell silent and stared at the clock on the wall.

'What?' asked Ludd.

'Nothing, Ludd.'

'You were going to say something.'

'I was just thinking that I hope Edur's on the level. Whatever's going on here, it's messy and complicated, and everybody seems to want a piece of it. I hope Edur's the friend Gaunt needs. I hope Edur doesn't have an agenda of his own.'

'You think he might?' asked Ludd. 'He seemed a decent sort, like you said.'

Hark sighed. 'You develop a nose for these things, Ludd. Every commissar does, sooner or later. You get so you can detect what's behind the mask. Edur's keeping something back, though it may just be the nature of this high-value prisoner.'

'I'll develop this knack too, will I?' asked Ludd.

'Of course. And it will aid your work immeasurably. It will tell you, for instance, that Trooper Criid is not here simply to deliver his company day sheet.'

Ludd turned. Dalin Criid was standing in the office doorway, a fresh day sheet in his hands. He looked awkward.

'Sorry to interrupt, sir,' he began. 'I was told to bring this to you in Major Kolea's absence.'

'On the desk please,' said Hark. 'Then you can tell us what's really on your mind.'

Dalin wavered slightly.

'Come on, boy,' said Hark. 'It doesn't take two of you to deliver a day sheet, and if Merrt thinks I can't see him lurking out there in the corridor, his prosthetic face is not his biggest problem after all.'

Merrt loomed in the doorway. 'I didn't mean to cause any gn... gn... gn... trouble, sir,' he said, chewing the words out through his ugly augmetic jaw. 'I was just giving Dalin some moral support. He thinks he's found something.'

'Why do you need moral support, Criid?' asked Hark.

'Permission to speak openly, commissar?'

'Granted.'

'I knew I'd have to bring it to you, sir, and you scare the hell out of me.'

'Good answer,' said Ludd.

'I ought to scare the hell out of you too, Ludd,' growled Hark. 'All right, Criid, what have you got? Waiting around here for news from the city is driving me batty, so distract me with something interesting.'

'I'm E Company adjutant, and with Meryn, I mean *Captain* Meryn, off-base, that means I have to run all the dailies and keep on top of–'

'Funnily enough, I'm surprisingly conversant with day to day military business,' said Hark.

'Yes, commissar. Of course you are, commissar.'

'Let's have it, then.'

Dalin paused.

'I was running the daily tests on the company vox-sets, and I think I got a signal, sir,' he said.

Hark gestured towards the hall doorway behind Dalin. 'There are three nice men from the Inquisition in the vox office across the hall, Criid,' he said. 'I doubt you've picked up anything they haven't. They're monitoring all traffic.'

'Of course,' Dalin agreed. 'Except this is a twin, sir.'

Ludd looked at Hark.

Hark sat forward and gestured to Merrt.

'Would you mind closing the door please, Trooper Merrt?' he asked.

Merrt closed the door, and leaned against it for good measure.

'I don't get it,' said Ludd.

'Are you sure it's a twin?' Hark asked Dalin.

'Sure as I can be, sir,' Dalin replied. 'The sequence is buried, but it's clear enough. It's E Company signature, so that suggests to me it's Captain Meryn.'

'Because Meryn would use his company code to contact his own company's casters,' Hark ruminated.

'Exactly.'

'Excuse me,' said Ludd. 'I don't get it.'

'And there's a locator tag tacked on to the signature?' Hark asked.

Dalin nodded and said, 'I checked it back. It's your call sign code, sir. Captain Meryn… or whoever sent the signal, wants to talk to you.'

'Uhm…' said Ludd, and raised his hand.

Hark glanced at him in aggravation.

'What is it, Ludd?' he asked.

'I don't get it,' said Ludd.

'It's a sleight of hand thing,' Hark said. 'An old Guard trick. If you need to get a message through, and you can't guarantee that the receiving caster is secure, you send what's known in vox-officer vernacular as a *twin*.'

'How does it work?' asked Ludd.

'The sender broadcasts a signal on one of the standard operational Guard frequencies,' said Dalin. 'It sounds… I'm sorry, sir. I'm speaking out of turn.'

'Go on, Criid,' nodded Hark.

'Well,' said Dalin, 'the signal sounds like junk noise to anyone listening in. The Inquisition, for example. But it's not, in several ways. For starters, it's 'caster specific, coded for specific reception, in this case E Company vox units. And though it sounds like a random noise burst or static drizzle, it's got the company-signature vox-code buried in it. It took me a moment to recognise that.'

'So it's a message that sounds like vox-clutter?' asked Ludd.

Dalin nodded.

'And here's the clever bit,' he said. 'The junk signal contains the signature, plus another code called the locator. In this instance, someone has used Commissar Hark's call sign code. The locator tells you where you should really be looking.'

'For what?' asked Ludd.

'The actual message,' said Merrt from behind them.

'The locator is a code representing another frequency,' said Dalin. 'A non-standard channel, something out in the trash bandwidth. That's where the twin is hidden. It's called a twin, because it's a twin of the first message. It's usually passive-looped or non receptive, meaning that the receiver has to reach out, in vox terms, and capture the message. It's just floating out there in the aether, waiting, completely undetectable unless you know where to look for it.'

'And that's what the locator tells you?' asked Ludd.

Dalin nodded.

'How long ago was this, Criid?' Hark asked.

'About twenty minutes, sir. I asked Merrt to check my findings on the quiet before I came to you.'

'I think it's authentic, sir,' Merrt said, 'but maybe you'd better gn… gn… gn… get Beltayn to look at it.'

'Did you look at the message itself?' Hark asked Dalin.

'No, sir.'

'All right then, that's what we'll do first. Ludd, go and find Beltayn. And Rerval. Let's get some vox expertise on this. Criid, grab one of the E Company casters and bring it to the temple house. We'll work in there, out of the way. Merrt can get a weapon and watch the doors. This is strictly between us until I say otherwise, gentlemen. Right, let's move.'

THEY WENT OUT into the hallway. Ludd and Merrt sped off in one direction, and Hark and Dalin strode the other way. There was the usual mid-morning activity, and a braised bean-and-cabbage smell wafting in from the canteen.

Hark and Dalin passed Curth, coming the other way with her arms full of medical reports.

'Everything all right, Viktor?' she asked as they passed.

'Everything's fine, Ana.'

'Are you sure? You look–'

'I look what, doctor?'

Curth turned and considered him.

'You look like something's up,' she said. 'Like something's happened. Has something happened, Viktor?'

Hark shook his head, and said, 'Nothing at all, Ana. Just a few discipline issues I have to take care of. You know how these things are. Perhaps I look flushed because I'm relishing the prospect of shooting someone who deserves to be shot.'

'As long as that's all it is,' Curth replied, and went on her way towards the medicae.

'Something's afoot,' she said to Dorden as she came into the medicae office.

'Anatomically?' he asked, glancing up from his work.

Curth smiled.

'Hark's covering,' she said. 'I saw him just now in the hall. Something's going on.'

She dumped the stack of reports on Dorden's desk and began to work through them.

'What's this?' asked Dorden.

'Everything we sent to the pharmacon yesterday has come back.'

'You're joking! It usually takes a week.'

Curth shook her head.

'Nope,' she said. 'Everything. Every single test, every single sample, every single blood. Praise be the Emperor for lock-down.'

'What?'

'The pharmacon staff couldn't leave base last night, so, for want of anything more interesting to do, they worked through the entire case-load. I think we should remind them how fast they can work next time we have a rush on and they tell us they're pushed.'

'Agreed,' said Dorden. He began to help her sort the file packets, breaking the seals on confidential examination reports.

'Costin's hep is confirmed,' she read. 'I'll get him in to discuss remedial care.'

'Have you got Twenzet's bloods there?'

'Yes, and they look all right. Which is more than can be said for Neskon's augmetics. It looks like he's rejecting again.'

'If Neskon can't keep that leg, it could see him out of the Guard on a 4-F.'

'I know,' said Curth. 'I'm exploring other options.'

'What were you saying about Hark?'

'He's hiding something,' Curth said. 'Something's going on.'

'How could you tell, Ana?' Dorden asked.

'You develop a nose for these things,' she replied. 'Something is afoot.'

She opened another packet.

'Oh, this one's yours,' she said, handing it to him.

Dorden read the tag strip.

'Aha, Zweil,' he said. 'Thank you.' He pulled the envelope open and slid out the contents.

'Viktor just had this look on his face, you know?' Curth said, sorting through the remainder of the reports for priority. 'You know that look he gets? Dorden?'

She turned and looked across the desk at the Ghosts' elderly doctor.

'What's the matter?' she asked.

'Oh, Throne,' Dorden whispered, turning the pages of the pharmacon report and reading quickly.

'Dorden? What's the matter?'

'Oh, feth,' said Dorden. He closed his eyes, shut the report, and handed it to her. Curth took it from him and started to read.

'Shit,' she murmured.

'The old dog must've known,' Dorden said, taking off his spectacles and massaging the bridge of his nose. 'That's why he was dodging the medicals.'

'Oh, this is just awful,' said Curth. She sniffed hard and rubbed her eyes. 'It's unfair, that's what it is.'

Dorden nodded.

'So who gets to tell him?' Curth asked.

TWENTY

Old Ghosts

GAUNT FOUND CRIID watching the refurb's road access entrance.

'You need to rest,' he told her.

She shook her head.

'You're no good to me tired,' he said.

'I've been resting for months,' she told him quietly. 'Standing still. This is what I need.'

'The prospect of a bloody death at the hands of the Archenemy?' he asked, raising an eyebrow.

She snorted.

'A purpose,' she said.

Gaunt looked out onto the snow-heavy street. His wrist chron appeared to have stopped at some point during the night, and he could not shake or wind life back into it. His best guess was that it was approaching mid-morning. They'd been holed up in the refurb for about six hours.

It didn't look like mid-morning. The Old Side street was silent and empty. Snow was still fleecing down out of the cloud cover, and icing every surface. It had drifted deeply across the pavements and around parked vehicles. There was no sign of life: no traffic, no civilians, no pedestrians, no municipal street workmen or ploughs, no gritting trucks. The sky was as grey as slate, and visibility was severely restricted. The Old Side skyline was a faint black phantom in the flurrying snow. The more

201

he looked at the snow against the sky, the more it looked like static flooding a jammed pict-feed.

The city's haunted emptiness could be explained by the bad weather, and it could also be put down to a security lock-down following the attack. Either of those explanations suited Gaunt fine.

The third one, at the back of his mind, the idea that it was entirely unnatural, did not. He set it aside, even though there was a yellowish quality to the snow-light, and an odd sensation of brooding in the air, and his wrist chron had stopped dead and refused to work.

'A purpose is good,' he said, belatedly.

'A plan would be better,' said Criid.

He nodded.

'Doctor Kolding says the etogaur's too sick to be moved. He's running a serious fever. Kolding didn't want us to move him from his practice in the first place, although our hand was forced. As this place seems a little more secure, I'm loathe to ignore his professional advice.'

Criid shrugged and pouted.

'What?' he asked.

'This man is really that important? Do we really care if he dies?'

'You've seen what the Archenemy has put into motion to silence him,' Gaunt replied. 'There's your answer.'

'I suppose,' she replied. 'It just feels wrong. I mean, we've spent most of our careers trying to kill men like him.'

Gaunt sat down on a pile of fibreboard.

'If we can't move him, we need to bring help here,' he said. 'One of us… you, me, Maggs… could go out and try to raise some help. But just one of us, in case trouble comes calling.'

'I'll go,' said Criid. 'I've been running a lot recently. I can cover some ground. Question is, who do I go to? Who do you trust?'

'I trust the regiment. But we don't know how deep the infiltration runs, so I don't trust any of the standard lines of communication. We need an unimpeachable point of contact. If I could speak directly to Hark or Gol.'

'We could find a vox.'

Gaunt shrugged.

'We also need food if we're going to stay here any length of time,' she said. 'Let me scout the area, and see what I can scrounge up. I'll see if there's anything moving around out there, while I'm at it.'

Gaunt nodded.

'Let's start with that. But be careful.'

* * *

CRIID SLIPPED OUT through one of the refurb's side windows, and ran down to the eerily empty main street. Snowflakes caught in her hair.

She was already spiking again, but it felt good this time, it felt right.

She turned left, and ran along the centre of the road, ignoring the pavements where the snow had drifted into deep banks. She followed the half-buried glitter of the tram rails, and splashed across stretches of meltwater where the snow cover had been heated by pipe-work or power sources under the street's surface.

She went two junctions east, and then turned south around the church of Saint Sark, where the green iron railings looked as if they'd been dipped in icing sugar. There was a baker's shop she knew on Londolph Square where she'd be able to get some bread and perhaps some cold meat or cheese. Gaunt had given her all the money he had on him.

That was presuming the baker's shop was open. If it wasn't, she'd impose Martial Provisioning Rules and help herself.

Something made her stop running. Afterwards, Tona couldn't account for it. Something had just clicked in her head. It was intuitive. It was as if Caff had been at her side, and had just reached out and touched her arm.

She stopped running, and found cover behind the snow-caked tombs that filled Saint Sark's little graveyard. She kept low. Her pulse was beating like a drum.

Three figures appeared a hundred metres away. That was a shock in itself, because the streets were so devoid of life.

They were soldiers. They were carrying weapons. They were hunting.

Fighting to control her breathing, Criid kept down, her hand on the grip of her laspistol. The three soldiers spread out, moving down the broad thoroughfare towards the church in a classic covering pattern. She could see the steam of their breath. She could see the glint as the snow-light caught their iron battle-masks.

The Blood Pact was this close. They were just streets away from Gaunt's bolthole, and they were closing in, as if they had some scent! How could they know? How could they have the city at their mercy like this?

How many of them could she take, she wondered? Two, probably, then the third would drop her. If she was lucky and accurate, all three, but a hand-braced laspistol, rapid fire, at that range? And what if there was another team, beyond the street corner?

She heard a noise, over in the east. It was the rattling drone of turbo-fan engines. She adjusted her position, and looked up in time to see two Valkyrie gunships track past, heading west in a paired formation. They went behind the double spires of Saint Sabbat the Martyr, so that put them at least a kilometre away. They vanished into the blowing snow.

The Blood Pact soldiers heard the Valkyries too. They looked up, then scattered off the street, running fast. Criid wasn't sure where they went, but they broke quickly.

Hunters, and hunters hunting hunters.

Rival forces were closing on Balopolis, and when they finally met, the result wasn't going to be pretty at all.

Worse still, it reduced her and Gaunt to one thing: prey.

Bread and cold meat and cheese be damned. Criid knew she had to get back to the refurb fast.

'MAGGS?'

A voice had called his name, but Maggs wasn't sure where from. He'd wandered into part of the refurb that he hadn't been in before, and discovered, to his bafflement, that it somehow linked to Hinzerhaus. He stepped through an archway, pushing a work curtain aside, and went from the cold grey shadows of the refurb on Balhaut to the warm brown shadows of the house at the end of the world on Jago. On the Jago side, the wind blew the eternal dust like drifting snow.

Or was it snow drifting like dust in a dry valley with–

'Maggs?'

Dust or snow, it hardly mattered. Either would make a deep, insulating blanket that he could lie beneath, lie beneath and be buried by. Snow or dust, it would protect his bones against the heat. It would prevent his blood from boiling.

There was a heat in his blood that would not go away. It made a hissing, rustling sound as it squirted around his body, like lace dragging on–

'Maggs?'

Who the feth kept calling his name?

'Maggs? Your name is Maggs, isn't it?'

Maggs opened his eyes and looked up. The albino freak in the blue-tinted glasses was crouching over him.

'I think you're sick, Maggs,' the albino said. 'I think you're running a fever. I need to help you–'

'What time is it?' Maggs mumbled, trying to sit up.

'I don't know,' Kolding replied. 'My wrist chron has stopped. It's day. It's morning. Mid-morning. It's light out, but it's still snowing.'

'Your chron has stopped?' asked Maggs.

'Yes. Why does that matter?'

'Mine's stopped too. It's really hot in here, isn't it?'

Kolding shook his head.

'It's cold as hell,' he said. 'It's like midwinter, and there's a draught coming through the window holes.'

Maggs shook his head and sat up.

'It's really hot. I'm running with sweat.'

'This is what I'm trying to tell you. I think you're sick. I think you have a fever too.'

'Why? Who else has a fever?'

Kolding blinked.

'Well, your precious prisoner, obviously.'

Maggs got to his feet off the tarpaulin. He was unsteady. Droplets of perspiration splashed off his forehead as he rose. He had a sick feeling in his gut, but it was nothing compared to the burning turmoil in his head. He couldn't even remember going to sleep.

'I think you should sit down,' said Kolding.

Maggs waved a hand at him.

'I think you should sit down now and let me give you a shot.' Kolding reached out a hand to steady Maggs.

Maggs shook it off.

'I don't want anything,' he snapped.

The breeze picked up. The refurb's work curtains swayed in the cold exhalation of the snowstorm. Was that the archway that led through to Jago?

Dry skulls in a dusty valley with all the—

The words made a rustling sound in his head.

Maggs snatched the old gun out of his pocket.

'Oh, Throne!' he hissed. 'How long has she been here?'

'Who?' Kolding asked.

'The old dam! The old bitch!' Maggs whispered, circling, and aiming the weapon at random shadows. 'Can't you hear her? Can't you smell the stink of her?'

'There's no one here,' Kolding said, rising to his feet. 'Please. Please. Put the gun down.'

'She's right here!' Maggs insisted. 'It's like she's so close she's inside my head. That fething black lace gown. The hiss of it!'

'There's no one here,' Kolding insisted.

Except there was.

The snowstorm gusted again, and the work curtains billowed. The woman stepped quietly through one of the swaying curtains to face them.

Maggs couldn't see her face. She was wearing a veil. He was glad about the veil. He really, really didn't want to see her face. Just the idea of it made him shudder. His hands were slick-wet and shaking. Her dress was very long, black lace, and it made a rustling noise as it dragged across the ground.

'How long has it taken you to find me?' Maggs asked her. 'How long has it taken you to follow me here?'

'Who are you talking to?' Kolding asked.

'Her. *Her*!'

'Please, Maggs, there's no one there.'

Kolding pointed at the empty work curtain swaying in the breeze. The train of it rustled against the rough flooring.

Maggs aimed the old gun at the veiled woman in the black dress.

The pistol that had been left behind banged hard on auto, slamming out its spent cases. Kolding cried out and flinched, covering his ears. The rounds ripped through the work curtain, punching holes in the fabric.

The bullets struck her in the face and the chest. They went through her veil and her torso as if she wasn't really there.

BALTASAR EYL STEPPED back as his sister suddenly gasped.

'What is it?' he asked.

The witch's hands and arms were drenched in blood to the elbows. She had plunged them into the glass sterilising baths to retrieve the strips of leather cut from the limousine's seats. She was clutching the lank, dripping strips in her scarlet fists like fronds of wet seaweed.

'The blood,' she said. Her words seemed to etch into the unnaturally chilly air of the theatre as if they'd been drawn in acid.

'What about it?'

'It wasn't all his.'

'What do you mean?'

'Some of it was the pheguth's, but some of it came from one of the men with him. One of them must also have been injured.'

Eyl remembered clinging to the side of the car as it sped towards the gate. He remembered, like a snap-shot, his half view of the driver's head and neck, running with blood.

'The driver,' he said.

'Yes. He's the one I've got,' said Ulrike. 'I am upon his soul. And he's fighting back.'

'Can you dispose of him?'

The witch smiled at her brother. Her veil was down, but he could feel the smile, like the hot leak of lethal radiation.

'I can do better than dispose of him,' she replied. 'I can use him.'

'WHAT ARE YOU doing?' Kolding cried.

Maggs turned and struck the doctor across the temple with the old gun. Kolding barked out a cry and fell hard. He tried to get up. Maggs kicked him, and then clubbed him across the back of the head with the butt of the gun.

Kolding dropped and lay still.

Still shaking, and sweating hard, his body stricken with the furnace of his fever, Maggs staggered over to the prisoner.

The etogaur was trembling beneath his heaped blankets. Sweat pasted his face. His eyes had rolled back, showing just whites.

Maggs poked the muzzle of the old gun against the etogaur's head and pulled the trigger.

TWENTY-ONE

Bleed

MKOLL PAUSED. HE turned in a slow circle, reading the snow-covered ground.

He shook his head.

On the empty, winter street behind him, Preed and Jajjo were checking side turnings for traces. The chief scout was pretty sure they wouldn't find anything either.

The signs had been there. From the gatehouse at Section, out into the streets, they'd been easy to track, as clear as day. It was snowing, for Throne's sake! An absolute gift to any tracker. Gaunt might as well have left a trail of taper flares, or blood.

Something had begun to outfox the acute senses of the Tanith scouts. Something was deceiving Mkoll's eyes and wits, and it was deceiving his best men too.

This snow was different. It wasn't like any snow he'd ever read. It teased and it flirted, and promised to reveal all manner of secrets, but it was uncooperative. It blurred and it blended. It covered and it erased. It forgot more than it remembered.

It didn't behave like snow.

Mkoll was certain, stone-cold certain, that there was *something* in the storm, some ugly influence in the bad weather that was deliberately blinding them and confounding them.

Silent as any ghost, Eszrah came up beside him.

Mkoll looked at the nihtgane and shrugged.

Eszrah narrowed his eyes.

'Close, he ys,' he said.

Mkoll nodded. 'Except it's just so… you must have noticed it too, Ez. The trail's wrong. The snow's lying to me.'

Mkoll looked up. The distant, thudding shapes of the Valkyries were swinging around for another pass.

'Jago,' Eszrah replied.

Mkoll shrugged. 'You're right. You and me, we followed him across the dust of Jago and found him. We can find him again.'

COMMISSAR EDUR WATCHED the progress of the search teams.

'I hate to sound remotely impatient,' he said to the Tanith officers, Kolea and Baskevyl, 'but I expected a little more from the vaunted Ghost scouts.'

'You're not the only one,' replied Kolea bluntly. 'It's not like Mkoll to be this much off his game.'

'Explanation?'

Baskevyl shrugged. 'Colonel-Commissar Gaunt has gone to ground. He's an intelligent man, and he may have covered his tracks well. He knows how Mkoll and the scouts operate. He knows how to hide the signs they would look for.'

Edur pursed his lips. 'Which begs the question: is he hiding to stay alive, or hiding because he's guilty of something?'

He noted the expressions on the faces of Kolea and Baskevyl.

'Just thinking aloud,' he assured them. 'The problem being that the inquisitor's capacity for patience is going to be far less than mine.'

The three of them turned to look together. Further down the street, Rime and his circle of henchmen were grouped in quiet discussion. The displeasure on Rime's face was readable even at a distance.

'If he orders us out,' said Edur, 'we lose all control. Then, I'm afraid, Gaunt's going to wind up dead, whether he's guilty or not.'

MAGGS FIRED. HE fired and fired again. Nothing was coming out of the albino's old gun. He'd used up everything in the gun's clip shooting at the old dam.

Maggs tossed the empty pistol aside and bent down. He clamped his hands around the etogaur's throat and twisted.

Gaunt slammed into him from the side, and tore him off the etogaur. Locked together in a tangle of limbs, Gaunt and Maggs rolled heavily across the partly boarded floor of the refurb, and collided painfully with a stack of fibreboard.

'What are you trying to do?' Gaunt yelled at the Belladon as he attempted to pin him and subdue him. The gunshots had brought Gaunt running.

Maggs didn't reply in any properly articulate way. He shrugged his shoulders backwards violently, breaking Gaunt's grip. The back of his skull butted into Gaunt's cheek.

'Maggs! Stop it,' Gaunt warned, rolling clear.

Maggs made a gurgling, inhuman noise. He was back on his feet, hunched low, like an ape or an ursid. He drove at Gaunt. His teeth were bared in a snarling grimace: an animal's threat display.

Gaunt couldn't do much other than try to absorb the feral charge. Maggs ran into him, bear-hugging him, and they struck the pile of fibreboard together, again, this time on their feet. Gaunt had seen Maggs's eyes. He knew the man had lost his mind. He could feel the grease of sweat on Maggs's skin, the fever-heat throbbing out of him.

Maggs wrestled Gaunt into the fibreboards a third time, and tried to crush him into them. Gaunt jabbed his elbow down onto the back of Maggs's neck. He had to repeat the ruthless blow several times before Maggs flinched away from the source of pain and released his grip.

As Maggs sprang away, Gaunt threw a punch that caught the Belladon's jaw, and lurched him sideways into a pile of paint pails, buckets and loose timbers. Metal containers clattered as they fell. Trying to keep his feet, Maggs ploughed through the wood and the buckets with his arms milling and clawing, scattering the obstacles out of his way.

Gaunt moved forward to restrain him. He called out the Belladon's name again, in the hope that it might snap some sense or recognition into the man.

Maggs came up, out of his stumbling collision with the paint pails, clutching a fat plank of timber. He hefted it like a bat or a club, and swung it. Gaunt had to jerk back to avoid being hit.

'For Throne's sake, Maggs.'

Maggs advanced on him, swinging the timber hard. Maggs was making a whining, sobbing noise.

'Maggs!'

Gaunt tried to dodge around Maggs, but Maggs caught him across the shoulder with the makeshift club, and Gaunt fell sideways into one of the work curtains. He clutched at it for support, and the top edge tore away from its iron fixings with a sharp, rending sound. Maggs came at him again, the plank raised over his head in both hands, ready to slam across Gaunt's skull.

Gaunt tried to shield himself. He twisted hard, wrapping the heavy curtain tarp around him and over his head. He felt the blow, but the lethal force of it was soaked up by the taut curtaining.

Gaunt scrambled free of the curtain, and stumbled into the adjoining chamber of the refurb. The curtain's thick, waxy seams caught on the buttons of his uniform, tangling him, and he was forced to pull free of his coat to get clear. The contents of his pockets, upended, scattered onto the floor.

Maggs wrenched his way through the work curtain after Gaunt. He was still clutching the plank, and he was still whining and sobbing, the thick, wet sounds mixing with rapid panting noises. His eyes were pink and bloodshot. He blinked, trying to focus, trying to see where Gaunt had gone.

Gaunt had ducked to the right, just inside the doorway. Maggs only saw him at the very last moment. Gaunt had found a workman's mop, and swung it like a bat of his own. It caught Maggs across the shoulder blades, and the old handle snapped in half, but the force of the blow was sufficient to knock Maggs sprawling onto his hands and knees. The fat plank of wood clattered out of his grip. Maggs tried to grab for it, but Gaunt struck it out of reach with the splintered end of his mop handle. Gaunt brought the mop handle around as a baton, aiming it at Maggs's head, but Maggs, still on his knees, intercepted it with his right hand, and stopped it dead.

The fever had bred an astonishing power inside Wes Maggs. He only had one hand on the broken handle compared to Gaunt's two, and he was kneeling where Gaunt was better braced on both feet. With a grunt of exertion, he tore the handle out of Gaunt's hands.

He rose. Gaunt backed away.

Gaunt expected Maggs to attack him with the mop handle, but Maggs threw the broken shaft aside.

Gaunt saw why. On his hands and knees, Maggs had found a better weapon. He had found the damogaur's soot-caked rite knife. It had fallen out of Gaunt's coat pocket.

Maggs took a step forwards, holding the jagged knife low and ready. His breathing had become really laboured. He lunged, and Gaunt jumped back. Maggs lunged again, sweeping the knife around. Gaunt barely avoided the second blow.

The third blow – a vicious, front-on stab – came closest of all. Gaunt had almost run out of space to back up. There was a wall close behind him. Maggs was boxing him in. The ground was uneven. There was no space in which to turn. Gaunt wondered if he could feint left or right. He was fairly certain that the panting, sweating, blood-shot Belladon would be too quick.

He had run out of choices. The only option remaining was the one he wanted to avoid most of all.

He drew his bolt pistol and aimed it at Maggs.

'Stop it,' he warned. 'Stop it, Maggs. Drop the blade and stop this.'

Maggs growled.

'Don't make me finish it this way, Wes,' Gaunt whispered. His finger tensed on the hard curve of the trigger. He wasn't getting through. He could feel another lunge about to come his way.

There was a loud and dull metallic impact. Maggs swayed, and then collapsed sideways. He hit the ground bonelessly and lay still.

There was an ugly bruise on Doctor Kolding's temple. He lowered the dented metal bucket he'd swung into the back of Maggs's head.

'Are you all right?' Gaunt asked him.

Kolding didn't answer.

Gaunt ducked forward and plucked the rite knife out of Maggs's limp fingers. Maggs was deeply unconscious.

'We need to tie him up,' said Gaunt. 'Throw me that bolt of twine. Over there, doctor.'

As if slightly dazed, Kolding put the dented bucket down, and fetched the twine. Gaunt quickly began to bind Maggs's wrists together.

'I thought he'd killed you,' Gaunt said.

'He hit me,' said Kolding. 'He hit me hard. I'm not a soldier. I don't know how to fight. Once I went down I decided to stay down for my own good.'

'That was probably very wise,' said Gaunt.

'It doesn't feel very courageous,' said Kolding. 'Not now, and not when I was sixteen.'

'You saved my life,' said Gaunt, 'and for that, and more besides, you have my thanks.'

Kolding pointed at Maggs. 'He is running an awful fever. I think that may have driven him to this. He was seeing things. They were things that he was evidently scared of.'

'It's more than that,' said Mabbon Etogaur.

* * *

THE PRISONER LOOKED like an upright corpse. The fever was still upon him, and his breathing was as laboured as Maggs's. He was leaning in the doorway behind them, holding onto both the torn work curtain and the doorpost for support.

'You should not be on your feet,' said Kolding, striding towards him. 'Help me get him settled again,' he added, over his shoulder, to Gaunt.

They supported the prisoner and walked him back to the bed that Kolding had set up for him in the adjoining room. The prisoner was leaden and unsteady. There was a sort of diseased smell coming off him that Gaunt did not like at all.

'He woke me,' said Mabbon. 'He woke me from my fever dream, tearing at my throat. He was trying to break my neck.'

'Don't waste your strength,' said Gaunt.

They settled him back. 'I tried to move. To call out.'

He looked at Kolding, who was preparing another shot from his case. 'Are you a doctor?' he asked.

'You were wounded. We found a doctor to help us,' said Gaunt.

'I would have died,' Mabbon said to Kolding.

'You may still die,' Kolding replied tersely. 'I've treated your wound, but you have developed a secondary infection, probably due to the less than ideal circumstances of your post-operative recovery. The fever—'

'My wound isn't causing the fever,' said Mabbon quietly. 'It's them.'

Gaunt looked at him.

'It's the work of the ones who have been sent to silence me,' said Mabbon. The spaces between his words were getting longer. 'They've got warpcraft into my blood. Into your man's blood too, I think.'

'How?' Gaunt asked.

'They have a witch with them,' Mabbon wheezed, 'a strong one. She is upon my soul, and she's calling out to me in my dreams, commanding me to die. I can hear her. She'll have been in your friend's dreams too, urging him to kill.'

'How do we fight this witch?' Gaunt asked. 'Do you know?'

'You must let him rest,' Kolding insisted.

'Do you know how to fight the witch?' Gaunt demanded.

Mabbon Etogaur's eyes closed, and then flicked back open.

'She's wickedly strong,' he breathed, 'but I know a trick or two. I was an etogaur in the Pact. Give me that rite knife.'

'Now wait a minute!' Kolding exclaimed.

'Listen to me,' Mabbon hissed. 'She's in my blood. She's upon my soul. That means this game is close to being over. They know where we are. All the while she's in my blood, they'll be able to find us. I need to break that tie, and then we must move to another place.'

'How do we break the tie?' Gaunt asked.

'I cannot believe you're even listening to this,' Kolding exclaimed. 'The man's feverish. He's delusional. What's more, he–'

'How do we break the tie?' Gaunt snapped.

Mabbon held out his hand. 'I have to bleed her out of me, and then I have to bleed her out of your friend.'

'I'm NOT GOING to be part of any barbaric ritual,' Kolding said, but he handed Gaunt a small medicine basin.

Gaunt took the stainless steel bowl from the doctor and walked back to the prisoner. He'd carried Maggs's bound body through from the other side of the curtain and laid him down beside the etogaur. Maggs was still unconscious, and twitching deliriously in the embrace of a dream that Gaunt had no desire to share.

Gaunt put the basin down and, after a final, thoughtful pause, handed Mabbon the rite knife, handle first.

'Keep the basin ready,' said Mabbon, his breath rasping in and out. 'We mustn't spill a drop, or leave any they can use.'

Gaunt nodded.

'Hurry up,' he said. 'I don't like this at all.'

Gaunt held the basin close. Mabbon opened one of Maggs's bound hands, held it firmly, and sliced the rite knife's blade across the palm. Maggs shook.

'It won't take much,' said Mabbon. 'The witch, she's monstrously powerful, but to bind into our blood, she has to make a link, you see? For us to be tied to her, she has to be tied to us.'

He squeezed Maggs's hand, and the blood welled and ran.

A FIT CAME upon her. It came without warning. Eyl was so shocked by it that he recoiled.

His sister screamed. She had her hands in the sterilising baths, elbow-deep in red liquid, and as she screamed, the right-hand jar shattered. Over six litres of blood product vomited out of the exploded cylinder and gushed across the theatre bench.

Ulrike staggered backwards, pulling her hand out of the intact bath. Blood splashed out across the tiled floor in long, drizzled sprays from her hands. She cried out again, a squeal of rage and pain.

She turned to Eyl.

'Sister? What is it, sister?'

She was breathing so hard that the front of her veil was sucking in and out. Droplets of blood had caught in the lace net and glittered like cabochon rubies. She raised her right hand and opened the palm towards him. The whole hand and arm was dripping with blood, but he could see the wound across her palm. He supposed she had been cut by broken glass from the exploding bath.

'Your knife!' she wailed.

'What?'

'He's got your knife, and he's bleeding me out of them!'

'The pheguth? You mean the pheguth?' Eyl demanded.

She screamed at him again, but this time it was a petulant scream of frustration and anger. She sank to the floor.

'It hurts!' she complained. 'He's hurt me. He's cutting the tie!'

Eyl knelt down beside her, and held her tight, rocking her. She sobbed. Her clutching hands made bloody imprints on the tan leather of his coat sleeves.

He heard his men at the theatre door. Her screams had drawn them downstairs in concern.

'Magir?' Karhunan called out, unwilling to cross the threshold.

'It's all right!' Eyl shouted back. 'It's all right. Leave us. Go back upstairs, and get the men ready to move.'

Eyl felt her wince again in his arms. She opened her left palm and held it out for him to see.

He watched as an invisible edge sliced the palm open.

MABBON GRUNTED OUT a breath and clenched his left hand over the basin. His blood spattered out of his fist and collected with the measure they'd already taken from Maggs.

'Are we done?' Gaunt asked.

Mabbon nodded.

'Doctor?' Gaunt called.

Kolding was just finishing the compression dressing on Maggs's palm. He got up and came over.

Gaunt handed him the basin. 'Get a lid sealed on that, then bind the prisoner's hand.'

Kolding took the basin. He looked scornful and disapproving.

'Quickly, please,' Gaunt said. He wasn't in the mood for the man's disdain. Gaunt had crossed a few lines in his life, always out of necessity. Some heathen blood-magic ritual felt like one of the worst.

It had better damn-well work.

There was a noise from the refurb's outer entrance.

Gaunt signalled to Kolding to keep quiet, drew his pistol and hurried towards the entrance.

It was Criid, squeezing back in through the boarded window from the street. Her hair was wet with snow, and she'd obviously been running hard.

'You're back sooner than I expected,' said Gaunt, holstering his pistol.

She shook her head.

'They're close,' she said. 'We have to move.'

'No argument,' Gaunt replied. He bent to pick up his cap. It had been on his lap when he'd been sitting watch, and heard the gunshots.

'Get any food?' he asked.

'There wasn't time.'

She followed him into the chamber where Kolding was tending Maggs and the prisoner.

'What the feth happened here?' she asked.

'They got to Maggs somehow,' Gaunt said.

'What?'

Gaunt stepped through the work curtain he'd half-torn down, and began to retrieve his coat and the items that had scattered from his pocket. Criid followed him.

'It doesn't really matter,' said Gaunt. 'The simple truth is, they know exactly where we are, so we need to switch locations. Gather your things and help the doctor.'

'We need to run,' said Criid.

'Maggs is sick, and the prisoner is sick and wounded,' said Gaunt. 'The purpose of this entire exercise is keeping him alive, and moving him any distance is going to be contrary to that aim. We've moved him too much already. I have to trust the doctor on this.'

'So where do we go?' she asked.

Gaunt stopped to pick up his pen and his copybook.

'I have an idea,' he replied.

TWENTY-TWO

Contact

'WILL IT WORK?' asked Ludd, dubiously.

Trooper Brostin looked insulted.

'Of course it'll work,' he insisted. 'I cooked it up, didn't I? Just like you asked. I know this stuff.'

'He does know this stuff,' said Beltayn.

'See?' said Brostin.

Ludd took the small paper twist from Brostin's permanently grimy paw. It was about four centimetres long, and no thicker than a pencil. The end had been folded down and sealed with what looked like treacle.

'This isn't going to be in any way...' he began.

'What?' asked Brostin.

'Excessive?' Ludd replied.

The wounded look returned to Brostin's face.

'I did it just like you asked,' he said.

'All right, all right,' said Ludd. 'It's just that I know your stuff too, Brostin, and for you there's no such thing as *too big*.'

Brostin grinned and shook his shaggy head.

'This is small. It's cute. It'll be pretty.'

'All right,' said Hark. The small huddle of troopers turned to look at him. 'You all know what to do. Let's get on with it.'

* * *

LUDD TOOK A deep, calming breath, and walked into the company vox office. It was late afternoon, and it was already twilight outside. Driving snow tapped against the grubby windows.

The room was gloomy and over-warm. The electric filament heater units on the wall were kicking out a dull blast of dry heat, regulated by Aarlem's automated thermostats. It was stuffy.

There were six large vox-caster units set up in the office; three were active and in use. Signal strength indicators flickered and glowed, and Ludd could hear the background murmur of a thousand voices, as dry and parched as the heat.

The Ghosts' regular vox-operators had been turfed out when the Inquisition arrived. Three Inquisitorial vox specialists were on station, each manning one of the active casters. They were attentive and diligent men in sober black suits, their ears cushioned in large headphones. They were carefully monitoring all traffic in and out of Aarlem Fortress. Portable memory recorders had been plugged into the three casters to assist with any later transcription work, and the operators were making regular, abbreviated notes on the data tablets that rested beside their right hands.

Their supervisor was a haughty-looking ordo agent called Sirkle. He too was dressed in black, though part of his attire was body armour. He was pacing behind the operators, hands clasped behind his back, occasionally pausing to lean over and read one of the noted comments.

When Ludd walked in, Sirkle glanced at him dubiously. Ludd had only seen Inquisitor Rime at a distance during his visit, but he was struck by the marked facial similarity between Rime and his henchman.

'Can I help you?' Sirkle asked.

'Sorry to intrude,' said Ludd with what he hoped was a relaxed grin. 'I was just wondering if there was any news.'

'News?'

'Of the colonel-commissar,' said Ludd.

'Why do you want to know?'

Ludd laughed. 'You're kidding? The men want to know, friend. The Ghosts are a very loyal bunch. Feelings are running quite high in the barracks. They want to know what's going on.'

'This facility is the subject of an investigation by the holy ordos. There are strict–'

'I understand that, friend,' said Ludd. 'I was just hoping, you know, off the record, just between us...'

Sirkle stared at him.

'You must know what it's like to feel loyalty to a senior commander.'
Sirkle paused thoughtfully.

'There's nothing yet,' he said. 'No trace of Gaunt's whereabouts at this time, although the signs are that he did exit Section alive.'

Ludd nodded. 'All right. Thanks. Thanks for that, I appreciate it.'

There was a tap at the outer door, and Beltayn entered, carrying a tray.

'Sorry to interrupt, sir,' he said to Sirkle. 'Commissar Hark suggested I brought some caffeine in.'

'I'm sure that would be very welcome,' said Ludd. He stepped back as Beltayn moved in so that Sirkle and his operators could help themselves to the mugs on the tray.

The tiny window of opportunity opened. Ludd had his back to the half-open door into the inner office. He took Brostin's paper slip out of the palm of his glove, keeping his hands behind his back. Then he leant backwards quickly, reached around the office door, and dropped the slip into the grille of the nearest wall heater.

'Well, we'll leave you to your work,' Ludd said, heading towards the outer door. 'Thanks again,' he added, looking at Sirkle.

The ordo agent nodded back, sipping his caffeine.

'Sir?' said Beltayn, looking at Ludd.

'What?'

'Something's awry,' said Beltayn, and pointed towards the inner office door.

'Oh feth!' Ludd cried.

Through the half open door, they could all see fierce bright flames licking up out of the wall heater. Sparks were boiling out across the inner office carpet, igniting smaller fires, and a thick, acrid smoke was already pouring into the main vox office area.

Beltayn hit the fire alarm and bells began to jangle.

'What the hell is this?' Sirkle demanded.

They all began coughing as the smoke hit their throats.

'Feth!' Ludd cried. 'Bel, grab an extinguisher from the hall! Feth it all. This is the third time this week!'

He looked at Sirkle. 'Dust gets caught in these old heaters and catches fire. You'd better move out while we get this under control.'

'It's a bad one this time, sir,' Beltayn coughed as he ran back in with a cylinder extinguisher.

The foul smoke was stinging their eyes and scorching their throats, and the height of the flames in the adjoining room was alarming.

Sirkle got his operators up and out of the room quickly, all of them covering their mouths, and hacking out coughs as they went.

Beltayn looked at Ludd, and Ludd looked back. Beltayn tossed the extinguisher to the young commissar, then sat down at the nearest active caster station. Both of them pulled folded, moistened squares of vizzy cloth out of their pockets, and bit down on them, breathing through their mouths to take the burn out of the smoke.

Shielding his face from the heat of the flames, Ludd pushed the inner office door open and began to blast the ferocious heater fire with the extinguisher.

At the caster station, Beltayn worked as fast as he was able. He quickly scanned and noted the frequency batches that the operator had been listening to; then he used a small screwdriver to remove the caster's front inspection panel. Ludd gave the fire another couple of blasts and glanced back.

Come on! his eyes pleaded.

Beltayn ignored him. He paused the portable memory recorder then he reached into the inspection panel, selected one of the fat main cable trunks, and unscrewed it at the connector. He took the bypass – a small, metal unit – out of his pocket, screwed one end to the connector, and the other to the loose cable. A small green 'active' light lit up on the side of the bypass.

Beltayn began to screw the inspection panel back into place.

Ludd finally vanquished the fire with the extinguisher. He closed the inner office door, took the wadding out of his mouth, and started to open the vox office windows to vent the smoke. Snowflakes whirled in on the cold air.

He looked over at the caster stations. Beltayn had two of the panel's screws back in place and was starting on the third. Someone killed the fire alarm.

'Did you get it under control?' Sirkle demanded, appearing in the doorway.

'Yes,' Ludd replied. 'I'll get a work crew in to clean it up.'

Sirkle stared at Ludd and Beltayn. They were opening the last of the windows to clear the smoke.

'This happens a lot?' he asked.

'Too often,' replied Ludd. 'I don't know where the maintenance budget goes.'

'Back to your stations,' Sirkle told his operators, and they filed back in. Beltayn and Ludd glanced at one another. In Beltayn's pocket was the small screwdriver and the fourth and final panel screw. There had been no time to fit it. He prayed no one would notice the fact that it was missing.

The operators resumed their seats.

Beltayn suddenly froze. He'd forgotten to turn the portable memory recorder back on.

He moved forward quickly, scooping his tray off the side desk where he'd left it.

'Let me get you some fresh drinks,' he said, busily, 'these will taste foul now.'

He picked up Sirkle's, then leant in over each station in turn to collect the mugs. At the third station, he shielded his hand from the operator using the tray, and turned the recorder back on as he reached for the mug.

Ludd and Beltayn headed for the door. In the hallway, Beltayn flashed three fingers to Merrt as he hurried towards the mess with the tray. Merrt was one of several Ghosts who'd gathered in the hallway to see what the commotion was about.

Merrt walked to the hall's swing doors, pushed through them and showed three fingers to Dalin, who was waiting at the far end.

Dalin nodded, and turned to run towards the temple house. Arms folded, Brostin was watching the door.

'Everything all right, lad?' Brostin asked.

Dalin nodded.

'Mister Yellow all fine and dandy?'

'He sends his regards,' said Dalin, and went into the temple.

Hark was waiting inside, standing beside Gol Kolea's adjutant, Rerval, and a battered E Company caster unit.

'Three,' said Dalin. 'It's three. Go ahead.'

Rerval adjusted the channel setting, raised the vox-mic and began.

'Nalwood, Nalwood, this is Stronghold, this is Stronghold, please respond.'

SNOOZING, HIS FEET up on the edge of the monitor room desk, Meryn started awake as the vox lit up, and nearly fell out of his seat. He scrambled for the mic, scattering an ash tray, some pens and an empty beer glass.

'It's live!' he shouted.

His hand was moments from the mic when Varl reached in and picked it up.

'Stronghold, Stronghold, this is Nalwood, this is Nalwood acknowledging,' Varl said calmly into the mic.

'Give me that,' Meryn hissed, trying to snatch the mic out of Varl's hand. Varl slapped Meryn's hands away repeatedly.

'Uh uh uh,' Varl warned, listening hard.

'Give me that!' Meryn repeated, his voice a corrosive whisper that would have eaten through lead.

'Hello, Nalwood, hello, Nalwood,' the vox crackled. 'Good to hear your voice.'

'You too, Rerval,' Varl responded with a grin.

Meryn reached for the mic again, and Varl knuckle-slapped him so hard he leapt back with a bark of pain.

'I've got Commissar Hark standing by,' the vox said. 'Is this a good time?'

'It's fabulous, Stronghold,' Varl replied.

Daur, Banda and Rawne had entered the club's monitor room. Varl held the mic out to Rawne.

Rawne took it. Meryn glared at Varl.

'Stronghold, this is Rawne.'

'Stand by, major.'

The vox crackled.

'Rawne, this is Hark.'

'Reading you, sir. I take it we're secure?'

'As far as we can be sure. We've slipped a bypass into the Inquisition's listening watch that we're hoping they won't notice. What's your situation?'

'We're holed up in an establishment in the vicinity of Selwire Street.'

'That's the Oligarchy?'

'It's pretty central,' said Rawne.

'All right, I'll find it on a chart. So you all got out of Section alive?'

'That's right,' Rawne replied. 'I can confirm seven alive, no injuries.'

'Rawne, are you armed?'

Rawne glanced at the others. Even Varl was looking serious.

'I can confirm seven armed,' Rawne replied. 'Why the question, Hark?'

'It won't come as a staggering surprise to you, but we're looking at a bad situation, major.'

'Is this planet-wide?'

'I can't confirm or deny, Rawne, but from the intelligence I've got, it looks like it's confined to the Balopolis-Oligarchy region, which means you're smack in the middle of it. Confirmed Archenemy hazard.'

'Strength?'

'Unknown, but we're thinking no bigger than an incursive or expeditionary force. Watch yourselves.'

'Understood,' said Rawne.

'It's more complicated than that, Rawne,' said Hark over the link. 'Gaunt's in trouble, and you might be the only real help the Ghosts are able to offer him.'

'I read you, Hark,' said Rawne. 'Tell me everything you know.'

BY THE TIME the call transmit was finished, Ludd, Beltayn, Dalin and Merrt had joined Hark and Rerval in the temple house. Hark signed off and handed the mic back to Rerval.

'Rawne's gang is alive, and we know their position,' Hark said.

'Gang?' Ludd echoed.

'Got a better term for them?' Hark asked. 'Bunch of criminal idiots, perhaps? Recidivist morons?'

'Gang's fine,' said Ludd.

'We can stay in touch with them as long as the bypass goes unnoticed,' said Beltayn.

'And how long will that be?' asked Dalin.

'If we've got any luck on our side, young man,' said Hark, 'long enough for us to learn Gaunt's whereabouts, and pass that intelligence on to Rawne.'

'Let's hope, in the meantime,' said Ludd, 'that Major Rawne doesn't take it upon himself to do anything else.'

'Such as?' asked Hark.

'Well, you told him to stay put. You told him to stay with that vox-set, where we could contact him,' said Ludd. 'What if he decides to… go somewhere?'

Hark let out an exasperated sigh. 'Even Rawne wouldn't be that stupid, would he?'

'Of course not, sir,' said Beltayn.

'So long as it's up to him,' said Dalin.

DAUR WALKED BACK into the parlour's main area. Elodie was sitting at the bar, nursing a small amasec. The muscle, Xomat, was still taped to the chair by the back wall. He looked entirely unhappy about his predicament. Leyr was catnapping on one of the parlour couches.

'Drink?' Elodie asked Daur.

He shook his head.

'What's the story?'

Daur began to flip through the pack of cards he'd left on the bar top.

'We've managed to contact our regiment, on the sly. There's stuff happening, but the full picture's not clear. Orders are to sit tight, and wait for further instructions.'

'And are you going to do that?' Elodie asked.

'Yeah,' said Daur.

'All of you?'

'Yeah.'

'I only ask, because following orders doesn't appear to be your lot's strongest suit.'

Varl walked into the parlour.

'Is there any danger of food in this place?' he asked.

'You know where the kitchen is,' Daur told him.

Varl sighed, and left the room again. From the bar, they heard him shout, 'Cant? Can you cook or can't you?'

Elodie smiled and got down off her bar stool. She went around the bar to find the amasec for a refill.

Daur suddenly looked up. Urgent voices had begun to issue from the monitor room. Daur looked at Elodie and they hurried out of the bar together.

'What's going on?' Daur asked as he strode into the monitor room. Banda, Meryn and Rawne were studying the pict-feeds coming from the club's various security viewers.

'Company,' said Rawne. He pointed at one of the screens. 'Which door is that?'

'Service,' said Banda. 'Freight access, at the back.'

'Do we know these handsome gentlemen?' Rawne asked.

Elodie slipped into the room alongside Daur and peered at the viewer. The exterior lighting was bad. There were perhaps six or seven men approaching the club's service door from the loading dock on Conaut Row.

'I don't recognise them,' she said. 'Wait. Run it back and freeze on their faces as they pass under the light.'

Rawne played with the viewer's control toggle, and the feed ran backwards jerkily.

'There?'

'Yes,' Elodie said, and studied the fuzzy image more closely.

'Oh shit,' she said. 'I think that's Csoni.'

'Who?' asked Meryn.

'One of Urbano's infamous partners?' asked Rawne.

'I wish,' Elodie replied. 'Lev Csoni is part of a business cartel in direct competition with Urbano's crowd. We've had trouble with them before. They've been looking for an excuse or opportunity to knock this club out.'

'And with the city shut down by a freak snowstorm–' Daur began.

'Safeties off, everyone,' said Rawne.

HE WENT UP the snow-laced steps and knocked on the front door of the mouldering old tenement.

Half a minute passed. He was about to knock again when the door opened. A young, slightly scruffy man in a black, buttoned suit and a cravat peered out at him. He looked rather confused.

'Can I help you?' the young man began to ask, and then stopped, and instead said, 'Wait, wait aren't you Colonel-Commissar Gaunt?

'Hello, Mr Jaume,' said Gaunt.

TWENTY-THREE

Headshots

'I don't understand,' Jaume said. 'Was our appointment rearranged, or…?'

'No, Mr Jaume,' said Gaunt, 'this is a rather more improvised visit.' He stepped into the hall, past the mystified young man, and looked around. Like the building's front door and entrance, the hall had an air of impressive, sober dignity. The floors were varnished and blacked, the walls were painted in dark, subdued colours, and the hall chairs and drapery were silky blacks, purples and maroons. It felt like the foyer of an upmarket bordello.

But there was an underlying scruffiness. Gaunt noticed immediately the odd chip in the paintwork, the hasty way the drapery had been gathered and pinned, the faint smell of musty dampness that scents of lilac and lavender could not quite disguise.

'I wonder if you could enlighten me,' said Jaume. He was staring at Gaunt. It seemed likely that, just as Gaunt had seen through the initial impression of Jaume's premises, so Jaume was seeing past the initial impression of Gaunt. He was seeing the dirty, scuffed clothes, the two-day stubble, the various bruises.

'I find myself in an unfortunate situation,' said Gaunt. 'I need help, and there are very few people I can turn to. Just now, Mr Jaume, you are the closest. Are you a loyal servant of the Imperial Throne?'

'Am I what?' Jaume began. 'Of course!'

'You would, therefore, have no objections to assisting an officer of the Throne in the pursuit of his duties?'

'What is this?' asked Jaume.

Gaunt looked at the doorway behind Jaume, and gave a brief nod. Suddenly, other people were coming in out of the snow and the gathering darkness.

'What is this?' Jaume repeated as they pushed past him.

Criid was escorting Maggs, who was dazed and bleary, his hands still bound. Kolding, weighed down by his medical kit, was supporting the prisoner.

'Through there,' Gaunt said, gesturing, and then closed and bolted the front door behind them.

Criid had led the way into the reception room off the hall. It was similarly appointed in dark romantic shades of maroon, red and black. There were couches and armchairs, side tables decorated with arrangements of dried flowers, and a great deal of gathered drapery dressing the walls.

Criid left Maggs slumped on one of the couches, and Kolding settled the prisoner on the other.

'Check the place, please,' Gaunt said to Criid. 'Entrances and exits. Is there anyone else here, Mr Jaume?'

'No,' Jaume replied. 'I'm here alone. There were appointments booked for today, but they were all cancelled due to the snow.'

Gaunt nodded to Criid. She drew the laspistol and slipped out of the room.

'Why is she armed?' Jaume asked.

Gaunt ignored the question.

'You work here?' he asked, looking around.

'Yes,' said Jaume.

'This is your studio?'

'Yes,' said Jaume.

'And you're a portraitist? You make picts?'

'Photographic exposures,' said Jaume, 'and also some hololithic work.'

The reception room was as discreetely shabby as the hall. Gaunt could see that boot-black had been used to cover scuff marks on the floorboards and the legs of the furniture. The drapery had been gathered so as to hide old watermarks, and the flower vases had been painted over to disguise chips.

Several large, black albums with embossed felt covers were arranged on one of the side tables for casual inspection. Gaunt opened one, and began to turn the oversized card pages. The picts inside were large, and mounted in elegantly muted paper frames. They were portraits of men in uniforms: Guard, Navy, PDF, militia. The men's uniforms were all dress formal, and their faces were uniformly solemn. They stood stiffly, facing the camera, looking into the lens with vacant or preoccupied eyes, and expressions that would never alter. There were chin straps and moustaches, dress swords and bugles, standards and drums. There were shakos perched on heads, and gilded chase helmets cupped under arms. There were bearskin capes, breastplates, and frogged button loops. To his surprise, Gaunt found he couldn't identify many of the uniforms.

'I make commemorative portraits,' said Jaume, watching Gaunt go through the album, eager for approval. 'There is a great demand for it here on Balhaut, because of the Famous Victory, of course. A great demand.'

Most of the portraits showed the skyline of Balopolis or the Oligarchy in the background. The same views, over and over. In most, Gaunt could read a skyline that had not existed for fifteen years. Some portraits included proud families in their formal best, gathered around the son or husband, brother or father in uniform.

'Families come here, or send commission orders,' Jaume went on, 'from all across the sector, actually. There is dignity in a commemorative portrait. And consolation.'

Gaunt realised that it wasn't a bordello that Jaume's premises reminded him of. Rather, it was a funeral parlour. Jaume's business was part of the mourning industry. The men he was looking at were dead, surely. He was reviewing images of men who no longer existed, which had been skilfully combined with images of a city that no longer existed either.

Gaunt closed the album.

'What's through here?' he asked, and walked through the draped arch before Jaume could answer.

The main studio lay beyond the arch. Powerful lights and pict-imagers on tripods were arranged in front of a scenic area. To one side were racks of clothes, and boxes of props, like a messy backstage dressing room. Gaunt turned on one of the lamps, and its powerful filament lit with a *ftoom!*

Balopolis lay before him, noble and magnificent. Above, the Oligarchy; below, the bending river. There, the Tower of the Plutocrat, the Monastery, the High Palace, the Sirene Palace, the Emancipatory, the Oligarchy Gate.

The Oligarchy Gate. The afternoon of the ninth day, at Slaydo's left hand. Ahead, the famous Gate, defended by the woe machines of Heritor Asphodel. Mud lakes. Freak weather. The chemical deluge triggered by the orbital bombardment and the Heritor's toxins. Molten pitch in the air like torrential rain–

Gaunt walked towards the bright vista. It was untouched. War-clean. It was Balopolis as it had been.

Wire barbs skinning the air. The thuk *of impacts, so many impacts. Clouds of pink mist to his left and right as men were hit. Ahead, below the Gate, the machines whirring again–*

'Stop it,' Gaunt said.

'Sir?' Jaume asked.

'I was talking to myself,' said Gaunt.

Balopolis was one of a number of theatrical backdrop flats arranged behind the posing area.

'There is a selection,' said Jaume, moving *Balopolis* aside on its running wheels. 'The Oligarchy is especially popular. But also Ascension Valley, Zaebes City... I can do Khulan too. Terra itself, at a pinch.'

'But your subjects are dead men,' said Gaunt.

'Not all of them,' said Jaume.

'But most of them. You take their images from old stock, and superimpose them. Why do you need a set?'

'It depends upon the commission,' said Jaume. 'If the family wants to be included, I have them sit here, arranged in front of their chosen scene. Then I dress an assistant appropriately to stand with them.'

Jaume moved to the heaped racks of clothes, and picked up, at random, a hussar's jacket and a sabre.

'You see? Something appropriate. I have a great deal to choose from. War surplus. Stuff that was left behind.'

'The gun that was left behind,' Gaunt murmured.

'Pardon?'

'Nothing.'

Jaume brandished his props. 'The assistant stands in a pose that matches the pose of the family's loved one in an old pict, and then I match the face in later. It's most satisfactory. The families are always delighted to be reunited in that way, one last time.'

'How do you get the uniform details right?' Gaunt asked.

'To be honest,' said Jaume, 'many of the old picts I'm given to work from are not in formal dress, or sometimes the uniforms just aren't very... compelling. Heroic, if you like. The families are always keen to make their loved one look as dashing and martial as possible.'

'So you make it up?' asked Gaunt.

'I manufacture commemoration, sir,' said Jaume. 'I give my clients a memento of the way things should have been.'

Criid entered. She looked around and whistled.

'Clear?' Gaunt asked.

She nodded, and recounted the basic layout of the premises. As she spoke, she picked along the clothes rail, and tried on a plumed dragoon's cap.

'How do I look?' she asked.

'Astonishingly authentic,' Gaunt replied sourly. 'Did you find a kitchen?'

He glanced at Jaume. 'Do you have any food?'

'Yes, of course. Not much, but–'

'When this is over,' said Gaunt, 'the Munitorum will reimburse you for all costs.'

'Sir, may I ask,' said Jaume, 'exactly what "this" is?'

GAUNT WENT TO the kitchen with Criid. He was in a foul mood. He wasn't sure if it was a response to Jaume's tawdry fantasies, or to the memories of the ninth day that had been summoned so unexpectedly by the shabby set.

Away from the public areas, Jaume's premises were sordid and neglected. The kitchen was a festering horror. The milk and eggs they found were off, though Gaunt had a suspicion that all the milk and all the eggs in the city were off, in the same way that all the clocks had stopped.

There was, at least, some bread, some cured sausage, some pickled cabbage, and the makings of decent soup and caffeine.

'He lives in these back rooms like a slob,' said Criid as they prepared the food together.

'I think the death industry of Balhaut is itself dying,' Gaunt replied, chopping onions for the broth. 'Mr Jaume insists otherwise, but I don't think there's much money in it anymore. Grief only lasts so long. When it's done, there's only emptiness, and emptiness doesn't want or need a gravestone or a commemorative portrait.'

'Grief lasts a long time,' she said. There were tears in her eyes.

'Tona?'

She laughed.

'It's the onions,' she said.

'I know it's not,' said Gaunt, and scraped the onions off his board and into the pot with his kitchen knife.

* * *

M<small>AGGS WAS AWAKE</small>. The fever in him had subsided somewhat.

'Why are my hands tied?' he asked. 'Why does my head hurt like a bastard? Hey, who cut up my hand? It's sore!'

Criid held out a bowl of hot soup. 'Eat this. Don't ask questions.'

'But my hands are tied, Tona. Come on.'

'So are mine, in a much more metaphorical sense. You want to eat? Be inventive.'

'H<small>OW IS HE</small>?' Gaunt asked Kolding.

Kolding was so busy devouring his soup and bread that he'd steamed up his glasses.

'The prisoner?' he asked, between mouthfuls.

'Yes, doctor.'

Kolding lowered his bowl, swallowing. He looked over at the prisoner, asleep on the nearby couch. Mabbon had managed a little soup and bread before sleeping.

'He's surprisingly… *well*. The fever's broken. It's a turnaround, I confess.'

'And nothing to do with any mumbo jumbo ritual, obviously.'

'Well, *obviously*,' said Kolding, picking up his spoon.

G<small>AUNT AND CRIID</small> ate their soup and bread sitting under the lights in front of *Balopolis*.

'You were here, weren't you?' she asked, mouth full, nodding at the backdrop.

'In another life.'

'Was it as bad as they say?'

'I don't know,' Gaunt replied. 'What do they say?'

'That it was bad,' replied Criid, spooning more soup into her mouth as if there was a race to finish first.

'Then that's what it must have been,' he said.

He sat back on the couch, and stared at the backdrop for a long time.

'It was something,' he said at length.

'Worse than we've seen?' she asked.

'Of course not. With the Ghosts, I've walked through bad, and worse, and worse still. Balhaut was just an action. They're all just actions. Balhaut was a major action. A *major* action. Of *course* it sticks in my memory. But it doesn't define me.'

Criid stared at him. 'Oh, I think it does.'

'What?'

'I think Balhaut was hell on a stick, and I think it matters to you because Slaydo mattered to you more than you'd like to admit. I think Balhaut is an old wound for you.'

Gaunt laughed.

'I'm serious,' she went on. 'You won a massive victory for the Warmaster here on Balhaut. You and the Hyrkans? The Oligarchy Gate and then the Tower of the Plutocrat? Hello? And what did he do for you? Eh? He died, that's what he did.'

'That's not how it happened,' said Gaunt.

'But that's *effectively* what happened,' Criid replied, putting down her empty bowl. 'You and the Hyrkans fought like furies for Slaydo, but when the dust settled, he was dead, and there was another Warmaster on the ascendant. You got overlooked. A pat on the back and a sideline to some backwater forest world where–'

'It wasn't like that.'

'Wasn't it?' she asked.

'The Hyrkans were honoured and rewarded. I was rewarded. My own command.'

Criid smiled sadly. 'You were Slaydo's best. His favourite. You should have been his heir. His anointed one.'

Gaunt laughed again. 'You have no idea what you're talking about, Tona.'

'I may not have much in the way of book learning or formal schooling,' she replied, 'but when you became my commanding officer, I made a point of reading up on you. I studied. You excelled at the Gate and excelled at the Tower. How much older than you is Macaroth?'

'The Warmaster?' Gaunt asked. 'He has seven years on me, I think.'

'Not much to split. Two young men. Two young protégés. Little to choose between them. Like brothers, inheriting. Slaydo died. And in death, only in death, Macaroth succeeded him.'

'It wasn't like that at all,' he scoffed. 'Macaroth was a high order commander. I was just a commissar.'

'Slaydo loved you,' she replied. 'Think how he favoured you. He gave you the left flank, into the Gate. Yes, I've read the accounts. Memorised them. He favoured you into the Gate from the left, not because that was the easy path but because he trusted your ability. You took two impossible obstacles. Bang, bang! Macaroth had taken command of the Balopolis assault simply because everyone above him in rank was dead.'

'He still won it,' said Gaunt.

'And you would have won it too, in his place. Have you ever met him?'

Gaunt looked at her.

'Macaroth?'

'Yes, Macaroth, our beloved Warmaster.'

'No.'

'No, never?'

'Never.'

'So he didn't get you sidelined to some backwater forest world where–'

'No!' Gaunt snapped.

'Just asking,' Tona smiled.

'Don't,' said Gaunt.

'For an hour or two there,' she said, turning to point at the cityscape backcloth, 'for an hour or two right *there*, you were on the verge of becoming Warmaster.'

'That's not true.'

'Yes, you were.'

'No.'

'You really were.'

'Criid. Enough!'

'Listen,' she said, rising from the couch, 'who were Slaydo's obvious successors? Cybon? Dravere? Blackwood? They were all old, senior men. He gave it to Macaroth. Slaydo was absolutely ready to give the warmastery to someone younger and less qualified than the usual chain of command suggested. Macaroth proves the precedent. You could have been Warmaster! You *should* have been!'

Gaunt looked away.

'You weren't there,' he said.

She watched him. He stared at the floor for a moment, and then looked up into her eyes.

'You weren't there,' he repeated. 'I applaud your imagination, but it wasn't like that. Believe what you like, the only thing you really need to know is this: I would never have missed the chance of becoming the Ghosts' commander. Tanith, Verghast, Belladon, it's been an honour to serve alongside them all.'

They both looked around as Maggs screamed out from the other room.

'He's got a knife!' Maggs was yelling.

Gaunt and Criid ran through to the reception room. The etogaur was on his feet, holding the rite knife. Both Kolding and Jaume had leapt up, and were backing away. Maggs was sitting bolt upright on his sofa, his bound hands in front of him as though he were praying.

'He's got a knife!' Maggs yelled as soon as he saw Gaunt. 'Where did he get a knife from?'

Gaunt stared at Mabbon. He wasn't sure how the prisoner had ended up with the rite knife. Gaunt had probably simply forgotten to take it back from him in the refurb. It was an oversight, a simple oversight.

All that mattered was what the prisoner intended to do with it.

'Give it to me,' Gaunt said. 'Give it to me or drop it.'

The prisoner did neither of those things. Criid swept the laspistol out of her waistband, and aimed it at the prisoner in a two-handed grip.

'Do what he told you to do,' she said.

Gaunt raised his hand to ease Criid back.

'Give me the knife,' he said again.

'I'm not going to hurt anybody,' Mabbon replied. 'Did you think I was intending to hurt anybody? We simply have to make ourselves safe here.'

'With a knife?'

'The witch will be looking for us,' said the etogaur, looking directly at Gaunt. All signs of fever seemed to have left him. There was a healthy flush in the scarred pink tissue of his face. 'This isn't far, is it?'

'What?'

'This isn't far from the place we were hiding in before, is it? I don't really remember. I was still delirious when we moved. I don't remember how long it took.'

'No, it's not far. A couple of streets away, if that,' said Gaunt.

'The witch will be looking for us. We shook her off, made her lose the scent, but she will renew her efforts. I was intending to cloak us. Where is the blood?'

'The blood?' Gaunt asked.

'The blood you took out of me and your man there.'

Gaunt looked over at Kolding. 'You've still got it, haven't you, doctor?'

'Yes,' said Kolding.

The doctor produced the basin. Mabbon took it, and walked to the front door of the studio. Criid shot a questioning look at Gaunt, but Gaunt shook his head.

At the door, Mabbon used the rite knife to scrape an intricate symbol in the wood of the doorstep, a symbol that Gaunt didn't care to look at too closely. Then Mabbon filled the scratches with blood from the basin.

Methodically, he repeated the process on the sills of the building's main windows, and the steps of the back and side doors.

'That'll keep her blind to us, for a few hours at least,' he said. He handed the basin back to Kolding, who had followed to watch the work warily, and then offered the knife back to Gaunt.

Gaunt took it, and returned it to his coat pocket.

'Heretic magic,' muttered Kolding, and went to put the basin away in his bag.

'Exactly,' said Mabbon.

GAUNT GAZED OUT into the last hours of the night. The sky above Old Side had gone an odd, pale colour, and the snow had eased off for the first time in two days. Gaunt had, against his better nature, begun to associate the snowstorm with the force of the witch set in opposition to them. The easing of the snow suggested, perhaps quite wrongly, a waning of her power and her influence.

'What do you think?' he asked Criid.

They were sitting by the window in the reception room, sipping caffeine. Mabbon had gone back to sleep, and both Kolding and Jaume had withdrawn into some semblance of slumber. Maggs lay on the sofa, his eyes wide open.

Gaunt had spent the last few minutes outlining an idea to Criid.

'It's not a great plan,' he admitted.

'It's not,' she agreed.

'It's the best I've got.'

'You trust him?'

'With my life. I'm just sorry you'll have to go instead of me. I need to stay with the prisoner, and we can't trust Maggs.'

She nodded. 'Makes sense. I can get there fast.'

'We'll need to get you some clothes from Mr Jaume's racks.'

'Really?' she asked.

He nodded. 'You won't get in without them. And you know what to say?'

'I know what to say. What happens if I don't come back for... for whatever reason?'

'I'll still be there.'

Criid looked at him. 'That's way too much of a risk.'

'It's too much of a risk not to be. We need this to be over and done. There could be all sorts of factors preventing you from coming back. I will be there.'

'And if it's a total fething mess?'

'I'll fight my way out of it,' said Gaunt.

* * *

WITH A SMALL bag of Mr Jaume's dressing up clothes over her shoulder, Criid left the studio on Carnation Street just before dawn. Gaunt watched her run off into silent, empty streets where the snow had stopped falling.

He hoped that the cessation of snowfall was a good omen.

He hope that he'd see her again.

He wasn't confident about either of those things.

TWENTY-FOUR

Repulse

First, it went dark, then there was a crackle of hot, white noise as Csoni's men compromised the club's security countermeasures and crippled the comms.

'The work of an EM charge, and a couple of seconds with a pair of needle-nosed pliers,' Leyr said with grudging admiration. 'Nothing too fancy, but they know what they're doing.'

A red gloom flooded the club premises and, with the power out, the air-circulation systems died. It got stale and warm very rapidly. They could smell the beer-soaked carpets and the cantor-finch shit. In the monitor room, the screens, running on a battery circuit, boiled with static like a snowstorm.

As it had, by then, stopped snowing outside, Rawne considered this to be ironic.

In the red gloom, they waited for sounds of the doors being forced. The loading dock was a given, because they'd seen the men approaching on the monitors. If they were approaching the loading dock, they also had access to the east side of the building.

'Roof,' said Leyr.

Meryn looked at the scout. 'You reckon?'

Leyr glanced at Elodie.

'Where's the main junction box of your comms and cameras, miss?' he asked.

'Behind the main chimney stack on the main roof slope,' she replied.

'Well, that's where they went to work with the needle-nosed pliers, so someone's on the roof too,' said Leyr.

'Skylights? Roof access?' Varl asked.

'I can show you,' Elodie said.

'Just tell him,' Daur said firmly.

Elodie explained the upper floor layout, and Varl moved out with Cant.

'What now?' asked Elodie.

'Just stay real fething quiet,' Meryn told her.

'Why?'

'Because he's listening,' replied Meryn, pointing through the gloom at Rawne.

A silhouette in the red darkness, Rawne had his head cocked.

'Metal saw,' he said at last, 'portable. That's the back door. You want to cover that for me, Meryn? I'm sure Leyr will assist.'

Meryn nodded, and got up. Leyr followed him out, the big bolt-action rifle over his shoulder.

'Captain?' asked Rawne.

'Yes, sir?' Daur answered.

'Perhaps you and Banda could cover the front?'

'On it,' Daur said.

'Are you just going to sit here and let us do all the work?' Banda asked.

'No,' Rawne replied.

IN PREPARATION FOR his initially effective, but ultimately disastrous, move on Zolunder's, Rawne had studied every schematic of the site that he could get his hands on. He'd had Meryn, Varl and Cant visit the Munitorum archive on the Avenue Regnum Khan, and the Oligarchic Library of Architects on Salpeder Square, to procure and request public records and make cheap grease-paper copies. Cant had shown a peculiar propensity for trace copying schematics with forensic precision. Rawne had even pulled a couple of things off the city's datasheaf.

He'd mixed and matched. He'd overlaid. He superimposed, working to develop the most recent and current plan of the club premises.

He had planned it, and his little circle had executed it, with the same eye for detail that he planned any known target operation. He'd used precisely the same skill set that made him a decorated major in the

Imperial Guard, the same skill set that had got him in and out of particular places like the Hagian Doctrinopolis, and Gereon, and trouble in general. He'd assessed the best way in and the best way out, and how to procure transport and dud uniforms.

He hadn't done any of it because he was that fussed about getting rich. Rawne had done it because he was getting terminally bored.

The most useful schematics had come from the Balopolis Archive of Reconstruction, which itemised all post-war refurb, rebuild and reclaim. The knot of sub-street buildings, now known as Zolunder's, had once been a vaguely successful dining hall. It had taken two anti-tank rounds through its eastern wall during the war, and the bulk of it had burned out or been looted.

Rawne knew how the refurb had gone. He knew that Zolunder's had kept the dining hall's old freight access and front access, and added a service gate in the east during the rebuild.

Urbano, or one of his low-life business chums, had sealed off and locked out the service gate when they'd taken the place over, and turned it into a club that they could rinse for a couple of years before selling on. They'd wanted to minimise the number of entry points, which made good sense from a security point of view. It was what Rawne would have done if he'd been running the place.

It was, however, a dormant vulnerability. It wasn't as if Urbano and his ilk had actually bricked the service gate up. It was still there.

Studying the schematics before running his boredom-banishing operation, Rawne had noticed the service gate, and seriously considered it as an option. In the end, he'd gone another route, the 'Ban Daur is so innocent that doves nest in his hat' route.

Rawne knew it never paid to underestimate an opponent. He was quite sure that Lev Csoni, a man he'd never met, let alone heard of, was a bastard piece of work, and smart with it. If Rawne knew about the service gate, then Lev Csoni knew about the service gate, supposing he had the common dog sense he was born with.

For safety's sake, Rawne simply presumed Lev Csoni was approaching the problem of Zolunder's the way he had done.

That is why he took up his weapon and went to cover the service gate.

Up on the top floor, Varl hushed Cant. He could hear men moving around on the roof, making furtive rat-sounds, scuffles and scrapes. It reminded Varl unpleasantly of the high galleries of Hinzerhaus, where the Blood Pact had climbed up out of the dust of the mountains, onto the ramparts, to prise open the metal casemates. He held his shotgun ready, staring upwards. It was stifling in the dark. He'd have given a great deal for a pair of no-light goggles or a scope like Mad Larkin's.

Light appeared before him. A pale blue band of light had begun to slant down from the ceiling, as broad and thin as a sheet of paper. It was like a holy vision, a shaft of ghostly, ethereal light spearing down from on high into the infernal gloom of the airless building.

Someone was opening a skylight, and soft, cold snow-light was penetrating the darkness.

Cant had seen it too. He took cover across the walkway from Varl, crouching behind a jardinière that supported a dead fern in a glazed pot.

The ladder of blue light broadened. Varl caught the first, wet-raw whiff of snow on the air, just a hint in the breathless warmth. There was a muffled thump, and the light increased dramatically.

They just lifted the skylight too far, thought Varl, and all the snow-weight on the top of it slumped off onto the roof. The panes of the skylight had been blocked, and now they aren't.

Varl heard the first man about to drop in. He caught Cant's attention with a gesture, and signalled to him to hold his fire until they had at least two targets.

Framed in the pale, chill shaft of snow-light, a dark figure began to lower himself through the skylight frame. The intruder was trying to be stealthy, but it was a terribly clumsy effort. Somebody was evidently on the roof above, playing out a line or lowering him in a hand lock. It was the most feth-awful manoeuvre Varl had seen in a long time. He realised that, though they might well be dealing with violent, vicious men, the Ghosts weren't dealing with competent, professional soldiers. Any decent Guardsman or ex-Guardsman would have known that the quickest and quietest mode of entry through the skylight would have been to simply jump down to a hand-arrest, and then drop the rest of the way. The skylight wasn't especially high. Jump down, brace, drop: quick and simple. Forget this dangling and grunting with your legs waving around, trying to brace a foot hold.

'Oh, for feth's sake,' said Varl, 'this is just too painful to watch.'

He raised his shotgun, and blasted the intruder with a single shell. The noise was deafening, and the acrid fyceline fumes stung his nostrils. The intruder was thrown backwards through the air with such force that it snatched down the man playing out his line too. The second man smashed in through the skylight, yanked by the rope, and struck his face against the skylight rim with such a tremendous impact that Varl winced.

Both men landed on the walkway floor under the skylight in a tangled, unmoving heap.

Varl racked the pump of his weapon to chamber a fresh shell.

Then somebody, a third man that neither he nor Cant had yet identified, began to shoot down through the roof with a heavy stubber.

MERYN AND LEYR, at the freight access, heard the shooting begin upstairs. They knew that neither Varl nor Cant was packing a stubber heavy enough to make that distinctive chugging snort, but there wasn't much they could do about it.

The small metal saw had just finished with the lock on the loading dock hatch.

The heavy door swung in, slack on its hinges, and somebody sprayed las-fire through the opening as an aperitif. Meryn and Leyr had already planted themselves behind heavy supporting walls, and the las-shots spanked off masonry.

A second spray came in, to wash down the first, and then the first intruder charged.

Leyr had no angle on the hatchway so he shot the hatch instead. At short range, the huge round from the bolt-action rifle dented the metal hatch, and slammed it with considerable force into the men coming through the entrance. Meryn heard yelps of pain and cursing. One of the intruders kicked the door back open on its hinges, but before he could get off a shot, Meryn had dropped him with two sure body hits from his las.

Somebody outside raked another, much longer spray of las-fire in through the door, forcing Meryn back into hiding. The bolts scorched the air beside his flinching face, grazing close.

Leyr tried to repeat his trick of slamming the hatch with a rifle round, but the body of the man Meryn had dropped was blocking the frame and wedging it ajar.

Another long spray of las-fire hosed in. Leyr made the *play dead* gesture to Meryn. They were swaddled by a ruddy, close darkness and the flowing fumes of gunfire and brick dust sucking out into the cold night. The hatchway had the soft, natural light of the outside world behind it, a seeping grey radiance that seemed to Meryn and Leyr to be as bright as a full moon's light. Instinctively, they'd clamped their eyes shut every time the las started to hose, in order to minimise flash-shock, and retain their night vision.

The hatch, probably steered by the muzzle of a las weapon, began to swing open provocatively. It moved slowly, suggesting a tantalising target about to be revealed. It was an old trick, and both Ghosts knew it, a tease to coax them into taking a shot and revealing themselves. A young or inexperienced gunman would be tempted to take a pop, even though there was no real target to hit. He'd take the pop, and give himself away.

The men outside weren't sure if their liberal bursts of las had killed off any defenders inside the hatchway, and they wanted to be reasonably certain they had, before committing.

In the circumstances, it was simply a case of resisting the temptation of that early pop. You had to stay down and quiet about ten or twenty times longer than felt right. You had to wait what felt like an eternity, the blood banging through your temples like water through a sluice. You had to have the patience of a statue, the patience of a steel-and-velvet card player, who could hold his nerve long past the point where anyone else would fold or call.

Meryn and Leyr were part of Rawne's inner circle for two principal reasons. One was that neither of them had the most crashing respect for rules and regulations. The other was that they were both excellent card players.

After what seemed like an eternity, an eternity in which suns could have been born and gone out again, and dynasties of saurians and mammals could have arisen and receded, a silhouette slowly edged in through the open hatch, black against the grey. Meryn and Leyr didn't move.

They didn't move when the second silhouette appeared either. It stepped over the body in the doorway.

A third silhouette appeared.

An excellent card player knows you can only raise so far.

Leyr's bolt-action rifle boomed like a howitzer in the quiet darkness, and ejected the third figure from the hatchway and out onto the dock. The man simply disappeared, as if violent decompression had sucked him out of the doorway.

Meryn didn't waste shots. The first and second men were in line with him, and closely spaced. Meryn knew that at this kind of range, a las-round from a rifle could go through two torsos as easily as it could go through one. There was no need for a burst of full auto. He fired, and dropped the men together, as one, tumbling them down in a tangle of limbs as they clawed in vain at each other for support.

There was silence. Nothing stirred beyond the hatch. Leyr drew his rifle open slowly and quietly, and chambered another massive round.

He and Meryn would wait once again, just to be sure.

* * *

THE RED STREET door at the front of Zolunder's got its locks kicked out for the second time in three days. Banda and Daur let the three men who entered come all the way inside, and then filled the lower hall with a house-clearing crossfire of shotgun rounds and las. The whole thing was done in less than ten seconds.

Letting Daur cover her with the las, Banda slid down the corridor to the front door with her back to the cold wall, her shotgun low at her side. She edged around the three dead men on the corridor floor, one of whom was still twitching out the last of his nerve memories in a horizontal chorea.

She felt the cold night air against her face, and checked the street. There was no one left outside at the front, just some scuff marks in the snow on the steps.

The stubber fire from the top floor was chattering furiously, the way the stitching machines in the garment-fab over the yard had been, the night she'd arrived for her job interview.

It sounded bad.

Behind her, in the chilly corridor, Daur heard something else that sounded worse.

Elodie had screamed.

VARL THREW HIMSELF back to avoid the cannon fire tearing down through the roof. Clouds of tile dust and splintered lathe were exploding out of the ceiling; the stub rounds were punching huge, frayed holes in the carpet. He fired his shotgun at the roof, and made a large hole of his own, with all the spalling, debris and force trauma poking out through the roof rather than in through the ceiling. Varl tried to judge the angles and work out where the man had to be if he was firing the weapon that was making the holes.

Cant opened up with his old autogun, and simply raked the stuffing out of the ceiling with the contents of an entire clip.

There was silence when he was done: silence, except for a lot of dust, and the rattle of particle debris spattering down out of the lathework. Cant anxiously changed his clip, not realising that he'd already made the kill.

The man with the stubber, along with a considerable quantity of snow, and a lot of broken roof tiles, came through the ceiling as the rotting and frail old joists that Cant had sawn through with his gunfire gave out. The landing shook with the weight of the fall, and the slam of cold air rushed dust into their faces.

Varl coughed and spat, and put two shots through the body twisted up in the roof debris. The fether was probably dead, but he had inconvenienced Varl, and Varl liked to take these things personally.

Varl looked at Cant, and spat out some more dust-thick phlegm.

'You see?' he asked. 'Sometimes you can, can't you?'

Cant grinned. 'Yeah, I really can,' he said.

RAWNE REACHED THE service gate, but it was shut. There was no sign of anyone trying to force it from outside.

He paused, puzzled. Gunfire was bursting off through the club around him, especially on the top floor. He was confused. He had been sure the main thrust would have come from the gate. It's what he would have done.

Maybe Lev Csoni just didn't have the smarts that Rawne had credited him with.

The service gate was a big, reinforced hatch in the club's east wall, secured by heavy bolts that padlocked in place. As it wasn't in use, the area in front of it was used for storage, and crates of drink had been stacked there.

Rawne narrowed his eyes and looked again. The stacks of crates had been partially pushed back, pulled aside so that the hatch had clearance to open.

They'd been pulled aside ready. The keys to the padlocks had been left on the top of one of the crates.

Now he understood. He got it, as clear as day.

Csoni had been expecting someone to let him in.

Rawne picked up the keys. He decided it may as well be him.

XOMAT, THE MUSCLE, had the las-snub pressed to Elodie's throat. The cantor-finches were going wild in their cages, fluttering apoplectically like overwound clockwork toys. Some had flown into the bars so hard that they'd stunned themselves, and dropped onto the floors of their cages.

'What are you doing?' Elodie yelled, feeling the gun against her throat. 'What are you doing?'

She'd freed Xomat so that he could help them. If Lev Csoni was coming down on their heads, they were going to need all the guns they could muster. She'd ripped off the tape wrapping him to the chair. He'd spat out the gag.

She'd actually said, 'We're all in this together.'

Xomat evidently saw it quite differently.

He'd grabbed her, and held her in an armlock while he fished a las-snub out of a magnetic holster under the bar till. Elodie hadn't known that Urbano kept a back-up there.

'Shut up,' Xomat told her. He had his arm around her neck, and his weapon was poking into the side of her head. He began to manhandle her in the direction of the hallway that led to the service gate.

'What are you doing?' she yelled again, struggling. Despite the very real threat of the weapon, she was refusing to cooperate.

'For Throne's sake, Xomat! I know they tied you up, but Csoni's sent a strike team against us!'

'I know,' said Xomat.

Elodie went limp, and stopped fighting. Now she understood.

'Oh, you worthless son of a–' she began.

Daur appeared in the parlour doorway opposite them. He threw his lasrifle onto the floor, and drew his laspistol. They faced each other in the dark red gloom of the unpowered parlour.

Xomat yanked Elodie close, so tight that she gasped for breath. He made a shield out of her, the gun planted against her head.

'Back off!' he offered.

Daur took a step forward, and aimed the pistol, straight-armed.

'Let her go,' he told the muscle.

Xomat graphically outlined something that Daur might like to do, provided he could find a number of specialist agricultural items, some livestock, and a means of contacting an elderly female relative at short notice.

'He's in on it!' Elodie squealed.

'Shut up,' Xomat barked, vicing her neck with his forearm.

'You're in on it?' Daur asked. 'You're what, the inside man? Feth, you must have been gakked off when we turned up and taped you to a fething chair.'

'It was a setback,' Xomat admitted. 'But since I didn't open the door, Lev's coming in the old-fashioned way, and that means you'll be leaving in a zip-up carry bag.'

'If Lev's coming in hard,' Daur said, 'he's made the worst mistake of his life. So let her go. Now.'

Xomat shook his head, and pulled Elodie closer.

'You're going to let me past, or I swear I'll put one through her head.'

Daur half-shrugged.

'Actually, she doesn't mean that much to me, so that's not much of a threat. Do what you like.'

Elodie's eyes widened.

'I'm not joking!' exclaimed Xomat.

'Me neither,' said Daur, focusing his aim. 'In fact, she matters so little, I may just shoot you through her and have done with it. We're trained to do that, did you know? Specialist marksman stuff. I know where the soft targets are, you know, the places where a body isn't bone dense. I can hit an area like that, and the round punches clean through into you. You might as well be hiding behind a curtain.'

'You let me pass!' Xomat yelled.

'Gut, for instance,' Daur said, lining up his weapon.

'Holy Throne!' Elodie wailed.

Xomat roared, and aimed the las-snub at Daur instead.

Daur fired once.

The las-bolt blew out Xomat's forehead, and toppled him onto his back. He still had his arm halfway around Elodie's neck, and she went over with him.

Daur rushed to her, and pulled her up.

'Are you all right?'

'What the hell was that?' she yelled. 'Soft targets?'

'Take it easy!'

'I don't mean anything to you?' Her eyes were staring in angry disbelief. The shock was still a few seconds off. Elodie had spats of blood on the side of her face from Xomat's explosive demise.

'Listen!' Daur urged, trying to wipe the spats away, 'I had a good head shot. Right over your shoulder. I just had to get him to take the weapon away from your head in case he pulled the trigger with a muscle twitch when I took him down. I had to get him to change his aim.'

'You were going to shoot me too!'

'I wasn't!' Daur yelled back.

'You said you were!'

Ban Daur realised that she was a little too flustered to grasp any of his explanations and calm down.

So he kissed her instead.

RAWNE DREW BACK the last of the bolts and opened the service gate. The three men waiting outside started to move towards him, but then stopped in surprise.

Rawne had them casually, but securely, covered with his battered Blood Pact lasrifle. The three of them were armed, but they instantly recognised that raising any of their weapons was going to constitute a terminal decision.

'Which one of you is Lev Csoni?' Rawne asked. He knew full well it was the slightly balding, ruddy-faced man in the middle, because he recognised him as the one the girl Elodie had picked out on the pict-feed. He was, however, feeling sportive.

'Uh… I am,' Csoni said.

'You picked a really, really bad night to do this, Csoni,' said Rawne, and shot the other two men.

Csoni turned white and began to quiver.

'Toss your weapon outside,' Rawne told him. Csoni obeyed.

'Now drag those two inside the gate, and bolt it shut.'

Csoni did as he was told. When he had finished, he looked at Rawne.

'Who are you?' he asked.

'Let's go,' Rawne replied, and ushered with his gun.

RAWNE WALKED CSONI into the parlour. On the roof, Varl had just reconnected the power and the lights were flickering back on. Rawne heard the air-circulation cycling up too, and felt it starting to skim off the smells of fear and sweat, gunsmoke, blood and birdshit. The air began to cool.

Banda was watching the front door. Daur was comforting Elodie at the bar. Rawne raised an eyebrow. He knew precisely where comforting like that could lead a man.

Leyr came in from the back.

'Rear's secure,' he said. 'We've got the hatch blocked again.'

'And no one's lying around dead outside?' Rawne asked.

'Who the Throne are you people?' Csoni muttered.

'We dragged all the stiffs in before we shut the hatch,' said Leyr.

Rawne nodded.

'And no one got perforated?'

'Varl and the lad report they're intact so, no,' said Leyr.

'Which outfit are you working for?' Csoni pleaded. 'You're not Urbano's regulars. Look, I can pay you. Pay you good!'

'You're keeping him alive, why?' Banda called from the front access, nodding at Rawne's prisoner.

'Collateral,' replied Rawne.

'Please, which outfit are you with?' Csoni implored.

'The Tanith First and Only,' said Rawne.

Csoni blinked. 'Who?'

'What do you mean, "collateral"?' asked Daur.

Rawne shrugged.

'Csoni's… what was the word again?'

'Outfit?' asked Leyr.

Rawne sat down at the bar and poured himself a sacra.

'Csoni's outfit decided that tonight was the night they'd take down Zolunder's. Now, I'm only guessing, because I have no idea of their resources, but I figure if they don't come back, then maybe the outfit will send another strike team, and another, and maybe even another and, frankly, by that stage, I will have become pissed off with the whole thing. So, we're keeping Mister Csoni alive in case we need a negotiating chip. Leyr, tape his sorry arse to that chair. Mamzel?'

Rawne was looking at Elodie.

'What?'

'Don't unwrap this one, all right?'

Elodie nodded.

Rawne sipped his sacra. A slight smile whispered across his lips.

'What?' asked Banda.

Rawne sighed.

'In hindsight,' he said quietly, holding his glass up to the light, 'this entire fething thing was a bad idea. I know. I recognise the fact. I admit my mistake. The op, the scam, the getting arrested, the whole thing, was a wrong-headed feth-up from the very start. We are still, all of us, in a very bad, dark place, and the only glimmer of hope in the distance is the sunlight shining out of Viktor Hark's backside. That, you'll agree, is a dismal prospect.'

He took another sip.

'But, you know what?' he asked. 'If you think about why we all did this, what drove us to it, I'll tell you this… feth, I'm not bored any more.'

No one spoke.

'In fact,' said Rawne, 'this is the most fun I've had in ages.'

He began to chuckle. Leyr began to chuckle too.

After a moment, the chuckling had become proper laughter, and Banda had joined in.

Even Daur couldn't suppress the grin on his face.

Meryn entered the parlour.

'And then Meryn walks in and spoils it all,' said Rawne. The laughter died away.

'What?' asked Meryn.

'Give us the bad news,' said Rawne. 'I can tell it's going to be bad news from the look on your face.'

Meryn pointed at Csoni.

'That chump's EM bomb screwed everything,' he said.

'How?' asked Rawne.

'The vox is down and dead. We've lost contact with Aarlem, and I think it's permanent.'

HARK WAS SNORING. Ludd tugged his sleeve.

'What?' Hark asked. 'I'm not asleep, Ludd.'

'Of course not, sir,' said Ludd.

'What time is it?' Hark asked, sitting up. It was gloomy in the temple house, with just the glow of the vox-caster dials and the snow-light coming in through the windows.

'Early,' said Ludd, 'and late. Beltayn's taken over from Rerval.'

'And something's awry?' asked Hark.

'Beltayn tried to make the scheduled check in,' said Ludd. 'He's tried six times in the last half an hour. No joy. Major Rawne's signal has gone dark.'

ANA CURTH WOKE up in the middle of utter darkness with a gasp.

She steadied herself. She was in her cot in Aarlem.

She'd been dreaming about Zweil and how she'd break the news to him. In her dream, he wouldn't listen to reason. She understood denial. It was one of the recognised stages.

She got out of bed in her single billet, a luxury reserved for only the most senior officers. Gaunt had secured her room for her. The deck was cold under her bare feet. Outside, it seemed to have stopped snowing at last. The night sky was oddly grey, flowing with departing clouds.

She'd talked to Dorden, and they'd decided that the news would be better coming from her. Zweil liked Curth, he treated her with affection and concern. Better from her.

But how to do it?

Ana Curth knew all about denial, because she'd denied herself everything, including the hope of salvation, in the time she'd spent on Gereon. She knew what a death sentence felt like, too, because Gereon had all but killed her.

How could she break it to the dear old ayatani and make him understand? She got dressed, and let herself out of her room.

She needed guidance. She decided she'd sit herself down in the temple house and reflect. The calm darkness would soothe her, and allow her mind to rally. No one would be in the temple house at this hour.

* * *

SHE PUSHED OPEN the door into the temple, but was stopped in her tracks.

Hark, Beltayn and Ludd looked around at her with guilty faces from the glow of a vox-caster propped up on a pew.

'What the–?' she asked.

'Ah,' said Hark, rising to his feet. 'Ana, this is going to be a little awkward.'

THE SNOWSTORM HAD died off, and left in its vacuum a deadness of thick darkness, a stagnant hollow of night that had swallowed the whole city.

The sky had cleared, and the stars came out like static snowflakes, but the air temperature had dropped so sharply that engine fluids began to freeze. Spotter Valkyries and search birds were called down to wait for dawn. The Tanith hunt elements were recalled, unwillingly, to Section, to wait for first light.

IN THE EMPTY streets of Old Side, the philia kept hunting. Eyl's men threaded corners and side turnings in the vicinity of the refurb, their breath wisping into the glassy air from the mouth slits of their masks. Like the night, the trail had gone cold.

Eyl and the witch sheltered nearby.

'Find him,' he told his sister.

She shrugged. She was sitting on the floor in a heap of her folded skirts.

'I can't!' she hissed through her veil.

They'd broken into the house together. It was a *nothing special* place, just a residence on the by-road, a home to six members of the same family and two servants, shuttered in because of the snowstorm.

Ulrike had killed them all. Like a daemon, like a fury, she had cut them down. The image of her frenzy made Eyl shudder, and he had done his share of things in his time. What disturbed him was the mania of it, and the fact that Ulrike had been able to make cuts like sword wounds with the merest flicks of her fingers.

So much blood had been spilled, with sufficient frenzy, that the walls had become pressure-painted, and the air was still dewed with aspirated molecules of blood. There was a blood mist in the house.

Ulrike was trying to read the blood. She had eviscerated all the corpses, so as to read their prognostications.

She flung the clotted ropes of meat aside, and stamped her feet furiously in the growing lake of blood.

'I can't see him!' she shrilled. 'I can't see him. He's hiding from me!'

'How can he do that?' Eyl asked her, holding her hands to calm her down. 'Is he a witch too?'

'No,' she breathed, 'he's just a man. No witchery, no witchery. He just seems to know a few tricks.'

'You can get through tricks,' Eyl said, stroking the back of her veil as he held her close. 'You can get to him. You can do anything.'

'I can,' she nodded. 'I know I can.'

TWENTY-FIVE

The Net Closes

THE NIGHT WAS nearly done. The first grey stains of day had begun to soak into the sky. The cold, glass-clear night that had followed the snowstorm had bred, by morning a translucent fog that hung upon the silent, snow-bound city like the breath of a winter daemon. From the windows of Jaume's studio, the street was a smoky ghost.

Ghosts hiding in a ghost town.

After Criid's departure, Gaunt had been unable to rest. He'd paced the studio, and the grim rooms adjoining it, while the others slept. He flicked through more of Jaume's albums, and studied the eyes of faces that would never come home, as if they might offer him some advice or wisdom.

He thought about what Criid had said, and the foolishness of it made him smile again, but it also made him think about Slaydo, and Hyrkans, and the Gate, and so the smile quickly vanished.

Jaume had a large old desk in the room next to his studio. Like every-thing else beyond the public rooms of his premises, it was cluttered and untidy. Gaunt sat at it, and picked through the stacks of yellowing paper for the sake of distraction. There were bundles of letters tied with ribbon, sheaves of communications, and orders and requests, miserable, grief-strangled messages from widows and bereaved families. These were the fuel of Jaume's business. Gaunt wasn't sure how he felt about it any

257

more. He wasn't sure if he thought Jaume was some kind of ghoul making money out of other people's loss, or if he was actually, in some counter-intuitive way, offering them some real comfort. The comfort wasn't authentic, but perhaps the effect was.

On one side of Jaume's desk was a battered old manual rubricator. Beside it was a deep pile of papers that Gaunt, at first, presumed to be invoices, or perhaps handbill brochures.

They were something else entirely. They were epitaphs. They were short, descriptive obituary notices, recording the heroic deeds of dead men. Each one was addressed, and Jaume had clearly composed each account individually. Gaunt began to read them.

'Those are private papers,' said Jaume. He wandered into the room, and found Gaunt at the desk.

Gaunt nodded, but kept reading.

'How much do you get for each one?' he asked.

'The cost isn't the issue,' said Jaume.

'It's a price, not a cost,' said Gaunt. 'How much? A crown? Two crowns? Five crowns for a particularly lurid exploit or a mention in dispatches?'

'I charge a standard rate of two crowns,' Jaume admitted.

'And how many can you churn out in a sitting?' Gaunt asked, leafing through the stack. 'A dozen? Twenty?'

'I don't churn them out,' said Jaume.

'Maybe, but it's not what you'd call hard work, is it?' asked Gaunt. 'I mean, two crowns a letter, that's good money, considering there's no research to do.'

Jaume didn't reply.

Gaunt held up one letter.

'There was no Cantical Gate. Good name, though.' He gestured with another. 'In the zone you mention here, there was no "valiant fighting on the sixth day", because the action was over in four. In this one? The commanding officer is an invention. In this one, you've actually awarded a medal that doesn't exist.'

He looked over at Jaume.

'You just make it all up, at two crowns a notice. It's just like the portraits. You just make it all up.'

'The content doesn't matter,' Jaume answered quietly. 'Who's going to care? Who's going to know? Who's ever going to spot the contrivance or point out an error?'

'Well, me?' Gaunt suggested.

'With respect,' Jaume replied, 'in fifteen years, you're the first person to set foot in here, who was actually on Balhaut at the time. No, sir, the details don't matter. To the bereaved and the grieving, to the heartbroken and the inconsolable, the details aren't remotely important. All that matters is a handsome portrait of the soul they've lost and, if it helps, a few lines that speak to good character, sound duty, and a minimum of suffering. Two crowns, sir, is a small price to pay for that kind of easement and solace.'

Gaunt shook his head, and dropped the sheaf of notices back onto the desk.

'I must remember,' he said, 'to remind my men the next time we go into battle that the details don't matter.'

Jaume snorted.

'I think you're being rather naive, sir,' he said. 'Why do you suppose I was so eager to secure the commission to make your portrait?'

'I would imagine there was two crowns in it for you,' Gaunt replied.

Jaume laughed humourlessly.

'This is my living, colonel-commissar, this is my trade. I stalk a city that almost died on a world that almost died memorialising those who were lost. I never get to meet the living. I never get to meet the men who won the war and came through that fire alive.'

Gaunt didn't reply.

'You think I trivialise it,' said Jaume. 'Perhaps I do. I manufacture heroes. I've never met a real one before.'

'I'm no hero, Jaume,' said Gaunt.

Jaume laughed.

'If you're not, then God-Emperor help us all.'

'I APPRECIATE YOUR understanding in this,' said Hark to Curth quietly. They stood in the temple house, watching Beltayn and Rerval work the caster. Nothing had come through from Rawne in a very long time. Dawn was on them, and impatience was beginning to turn into irritation.

'I'm surprised you would even question my response, Viktor,' Curth replied. 'I was on Gereon with Gaunt. I was on Gereon for longer than anyone. I appreciate the grey areas of this more than anyone, and my loyalty to Gaunt is absolute. You could have trusted me earlier.'

'It wasn't a question of trust,' said Hark. 'I didn't want to put anybody in a difficult position unless it was necessary.'

'How long are you going to give it?' Curth asked, nodding to the vox-caster.

Hark shrugged.

'And if you can't raise Rawne, what else can we do to reach out to Gaunt and help him?'

'Short of taking on the agents of the Inquisition, disobeying direct orders and bursting out of Aarlem Fortress by force if necessary you mean?'

'Those would certainly be less favourable options,' she replied.

'Then I really have no idea,' he replied.

THE IMPERIAL HUNTERS set out again from Section, at daybreak, into a city hazed white with thick winter fog. The fog blurred but magnified the sun, creating a strange, luminous glare in the air.

Less than four kilometres from the Imperials, within the projected sweep radius, the philia circled and re-circled the small patch of city turf in the vicinity of the refurb, worrying like a pack of blood hounds at a scent trail that had been strong and was suddenly gone.

In his bolt hole, Eyl knew that time was draining away. They needed success fast before their luck ran out altogether. Every time Karhunan or one of the other men checked back to the house with a negative report, Eyl's agony increased.

His sister was at work in the back room of the house. She'd been labouring all night, weaving ugly witchcraft in a corpse room rank with blood. He kept hearing her squeal and moan as frustration followed frustration.

Just after dawn, she called out to him. He went into the corpse room. She had laid out the chart of Inner Balopolis and the Oligarchy, the chart that Valdyke had provided, and which she'd used to pinpoint Section. She had spread it on the floor, and it was soaked with blood.

'Have you found him?' he asked.

'No,' she whispered, and shook her head under her veil. 'I cannot see him at all.'

She pointed to one tiny part of the map that the spattered blood had curiously not blemished.

'But I can see where I *can't* see,' she said.

CRIID APPROACHED HER destination well before dawn, on the cusp of the change from frost-glass cold to phantom fog. Gaunt had told her there wasn't much point making a direct approach before mid-morning.

The snow-thick streets were quiet, though at this end of town, there was more activity than in the unnaturally still thoroughfares of Old Side, beneath the Blood Pact's warp-crafted spell.

She circled the target twice, assessed it, and then looked for somewhere to rest. A small public chapel, dedicated to the beati herself, occupied a street corner close by, and Criid found that it was the sort of place left unlocked at all hours of the day or night.

She clunked open the heavy wooden door and let herself in out of the bitter cold of the empty night. The place was old and uneven, stone built with heavy wooden beams, and a fading painted ceiling. Glow-globes had been left lit up in the vault, casting a soft yellow light, and the last flames of votive candles lit the day before were sputtering out in the metal rack in front of the beati's effigy.

Criid curled up in one of the choir stalls, and used the pack containing her change of clothes as a pillow. She got a couple of hours of uneasy sleep.

When she woke, the chapel was bathed in a soft, white luminescence. The sun had come up, and brought the fog up with it, and strange, diffuse white light was glowing in through the chapel's windows.

She picked up her pack and went through into the small rooms at the rear of the chapel where the ayatani priests kept their sacraments and some of the holy codices. It was a drab, cobwebby place that was obviously seldom visited. She lit a glow-globe, and began to get changed into the clothes in the bag. The clothes had all come from Jaume's dressing up racks, as had the small, battered case of make-up. Criid couldn't remember the last time she'd had to apply any face paint that wasn't camo or black-out. It wasn't a talent she'd ever developed, growing up, and she was concerned that she might overdo it and end up looking like one of those frightful transvestite castrati at the Circe du Khulan. She set the make-up case to one side, unopened.

Jaume had helped her pick out the clothes. He had shown some interest in her choices. Apparently, a widow's dress was called weeds, and the best were made of bombazine, crepe and fine lace. Criid had run her hands across the jet silk of one of the dresses that Jaume was showing her, and thought how ironic it was that she was selecting clothes to allow her to play the part of a widow, when, inside, she'd been a widow since the Gereon Liberation.

Jaume had suggested a particular dress in purple, which, he said, was slighted mourning. The colour change from black to purple denoted that the mourning period had lasted more than three years. The widow was no longer obliged to wear her veil all the time, and she could make sparing use of marginally more decorative keepsake jewellery. A further slighting, to mauve, followed after another year, and signalled the eventual return to the world.

Criid put on the slighted mourning, and the shoes and gloves that Jaume had selected, and then the veil. She decided that the widow she had become was so anguished that she had no time for fripperies like make-up, so she went without.

COMMISSAR BLENNER HAD only just been seated at his regular table when the visitor was announced.

It was a dreadful morning, with the snow still thick, and a hellish fog like artillery smoke, and that on top of a couple of days when the city had been quite turned upside down. He'd heard the most appalling stories about some business up at Section that had sealed the centre of the city off.

At least the snowstorm had stopped. Blenner had a zero tolerance approach to barracks food, so he slipped his driver the usual bonus to convey him through the elemental murk to the Mithredates for a late breakfast of tanzato pastry and thick, sludgy caffeine.

There was hardly anyone there. The staff, in their liveries of crimson, black and gold, seemed glad of something to do, and his breakfast arrived in record time.

'There is a visitor to see you,' the majordomo said as he was tucking in.

'Really?'

'A lady, sir.'

'Good show.'

'She's asking for you by name.'

'Twas ever thus.' Blenner dabbed his mouth with a napkin. 'Did she say who she was, by any chance?'

The major domo nodded.

'She says you knew her husband, sir. His name was Vergule.'

Blenner frowned. 'Vergule? I never even knew the man was married. Well I never. All right, you'd better bring her over.'

'I'm sorry to have to remind you, sir, that ladies are not permitted in the main rooms of the Mithredates,' said the major domo, 'but if sir so desires, I can arrange for her to be conducted to the day room so you can greet her there?'

Blenner glanced down at the breakfast he had barely touched.

'Oh, all right,' he said, scraping his chair back, 'but can you have some caffeine brought through to the day room? And, maybe, the dessert trolley?'

* * *

'MAMZEL,' SAID BLENNER. 'I'm Vaynom Blenner. I am honoured by your visit.'

The widow was veiled. She stood waiting for Blenner by the windows of the day room, beyond which the phantom white morning was uncurling. Waiters brought in a tray of caffeine and a large trolley of cakes and desserts.

'Commissar Blenner, it's good of you to see me.'

'Not at all. I knew your husband well, and was damned sorry to hear of his passing. I take it that his memorial is what brings you to Balhaut?'

'Yes, but it's not what brings me here today,' she replied.

Blenner offered her a seat.

'Drink, perhaps?'

'No, thank you.' She waited until the club staff had left the room.

'Something to eat, then?' Blenner gestured towards the trolley. 'The crustuko is especially good.'

Forget the crustuko, Criid thought. Look at the almond sepis. What a glorious thing.

'Thank you, no,' she said, with great reluctance.

'How can I help you, then?' he asked.

'I don't need your help, but a mutual friend does.'

'Indeed. Who?'

'Ibram Gaunt.'

Blenner stared at her. 'Ibram?'

'That's who I said.'

'I say, what's going on?'

'Gaunt's in a difficult position,' Criid said. 'You're the only person he can call on for help. I'm the only means of contacting you.'

'You're not Vergule's widow at all, are you?' asked Blenner.

'My name's Criid. I'm one of his Ghosts.'

'Tanith?'

'No, Verghast,' she replied.

Blenner leaned back. 'Look this is all rather silly. Is Ibram playing some sort of practical joke? Because I tell you now it doesn't suit him.'

'No joke,' said Criid. 'There is some necessary subterfuge involved, and for that you have my apologies. I had to get in here to find you.'

'How do I know this isn't some trick?' asked Blenner. He was looking decidedly uneasy.

'Gaunt sent me,' she replied. 'He said to say that the day you first met, you lied to him about your father.'

Blenner snorted. It was true enough. A life time ago in the schola prog-enium on Ignacius Cardinal, two little boys in a draughty corridor.

'Very well. What's going on?' Blenner asked.

'I'll explain it as simply as I can,' said Criid. She paused. 'I've just got to do this first.'

She got up, and helped herself to a large wedge of sepis from the trol-ley, yanked back her veil, and began to eat. Blenner watched her with wry amusement.

'What's Ibram got himself into now?' he asked.

She told him, between bites, and detailed the events of the last two days as clearly and simply as she could. Blenner's amusement turned to concern, and then to something that Criid was alarmed to see looked like fear.

'On Balhaut?' Blenner asked. 'The Archenemy is active on Balhaut?'

She nodded. Blenner turned pale. He'd cut himself a slice of sepis while she'd been talking, but he now showed no interest in touching it.

'This is serious,' he said. 'We have to take it to Section.'

'No.'

'For Throne's sake!'

'Haven't you been listening to me?' Criid asked. 'Nothing's safe. We don't know how deeply the enemy has infiltrated. Gaunt can only trust people he knows personally. He needs you to meet him.'

'Me?'

'Yes. You, sir. You and perhaps a small group of Guard that you trust from your regiment. He needs a bodyguard, fire-team strength.'

'Oh, this just isn't on!'

'And transport,' said Criid.

Blenner rubbed his forehead and punched the bridge of his nose. 'He's going to be the death of me. This is typical of his nonsense. I have a good mind to go straight to the commissar general–'

'If that's your decision, sir,' she told him, 'you won't get out of this room.'

Blenner was silent for a moment.

'When does he want this meeting?'

'Four o'clock,' she said.

'And where?'

'He said you'd know where,' she replied. 'He said you'd know the place that he'd made sure isn't there.'

'What? Riddles on top of everything else?'

'That's exactly what he told me to say.'

Blenner rose with a long sigh.

'You'd better come with me to my barracks. I'll get things in motion.'

SIDE BY SIDE, they hurried from the day room down the stairs and out towards the club's main entrance. In the foyer, Blenner looked around for a staffer to order up his car.

A man approached them. He was not wearing club livery.

'Commissar Blenner,' he said, more of a statement than a question.

'What about it?'

'Your association with Ibram Gaunt is a matter of record. We've had you under surveillance since yesterday.'

Criid began to back away. She'd lowered her veil before leaving the day room. She reached down to where her straight silver was taped to her thigh under her bombazine skirts.

'Who the hell are you?' Blenner asked the man.

'I think it's time you came in for questioning,' the man replied. He looked at Criid. 'Your friend too.'

Two more men had closed in behind them from the direction of the cloakroom. To Criid's horror, they had precisely the same face as the first man.

'My name is Sirkle,' the man said, showing them his rosette. 'Do not try to resist.'

TWENTY-SIX

A Place That isn't There

THE INQUISITION'S VALKYRIES had been grounded by the bright fog, which capped the summit of Balopolis and the Oligarchy like an arctic ice-shelf half a kilometre thick.

With the Tanith scouts along its leading edge, the main Imperial sweep had switched its attentions from the central routes of the city, along the main east-west avenues, to the maze of streets and narrow lanes of Northern Old Side. In slow, meticulous fashion, they threaded the lines of the tenements and hab stacks, and searched the under-barns, the lower sinks, and the long, semi-derelict municipal allotments on their suspended irrigation platforms above the highways. The ground was dead-white with almost undisturbed snow, and the air was bright white with pearl fog. Visibility was down to twenty metres in places.

Kolea and Baskevyl moved with the main force behind the scout line, keeping close to the vox truck that was rolling with the search formation at walking pace, and snorting regular blurts of yellow exhaust from its upright stacks into the smoke-white air.

The cold made their eyes water and their cheeks flush. Kolea's nose had turned red, a fact that Baskevyl had seen fit to mention several times. For his part, Kolea kept going on about a particularly good caffeine that was served in a dining hall that he had taken to frequenting on the Aarlem side of the river. They both knew they were talking about nothing, that this idle chat between two men, who had become good friends and comrades in the five years since their regiments had been amalgamated, was all that stood between them and screaming frustration.

The tension had become unbearable. The progress had become so slow. Every hour or so, they took it in turns to go up to the scouting line and walk with Mkoll or Bonin or Jajjo for a while, just to see how things were going. The frustration there was palpable too. Neither Kolea nor Baskevyl had ever known the famous Tanith scouts to be so adrift. They had both read what amounted to a helpless fury in Mkoll's eyes.

'The snow's lying to us,' he had told them both, separately, and the words had made both of them shiver. The Tanith scout master's ability to track was legendary. It was almost regarded as preternatural. If something was outfoxing him, if something was deluding his wits and his honed senses, then it had to be seriously unnatural.

The toxic curse of warpcraft lay heavily across this ancient street.

Due to their proximity to the search areas, squads of troopers from the Kapaj First had been drafted in from Oligarchy Fortress to assist with canvassing. The men, all young lads with the typical stocky frames and olive skin-tone of the Kapaj, were dutifully and seriously moving from house to house along the search perimeter, knocking on doors and asking the residents if they recognised holo-picts of Gaunt's face or had seen anything untoward.

Baskevyl and Kolea chatted about the way the area's residents seemed to be behaving so oddly. It often took the Kapaj canvassers two or three knocks to get a reply, and the residents were wary and unforthcoming. Scared, pale faces could regularly be spotted looking down on the passing Imperial search party from upper windows. Families had holed up in cellars and vaults as they had done in wartime. Merchants and shop owners had pulled down their shutters, and hidden in their back rooms. Nobody, it seemed, had seen or heard anything since the snows began.

'Snow's not rare here, is it?' Baskevyl asked.

Kolea shook his head. 'It's normal. Seasonal. I think it's snowed at least once already since we shipped planetside.'

'So why is everybody treating it like the end of the world?' asked Baskevyl. 'Why's everybody hiding? Why are the streets empty?'

Kolea didn't have an answer.

One thing that Baskevyl and Kolea didn't chat about was the Kapaj regiment itself. The Kapaj First was a new founding, nothing exceptional, reasonably promising. Gaunt had been appointed to the regiment as visiting instructor as part of his retirement duties on Balhaut. He'd taken quite a shine to them, and took his mentoring responsibilities seriously, visiting them upwards of two or three times a week. Sometimes, he'd even taken his senior officers with him to brief the young men, none of whom had seen any combat, about the actual niceties of war. Baskevyl had been up to Oligarchy Fortress with Gaunt twice, Kolea three times.

There had been rumours that Gaunt was going to get the Kapaj command permanently. The Kapaj First, all told, was nearly fifteen thousand strong. Someone had started the gossip that the Kapaj was going to be Gaunt's ticket to the rank of general or general marshal, a significant step on the ladder to a full high-staff position, such as an appointment militant or a marshallcy of guard. The Kapaj First would be his new First and Only. The gossip also suggested that if Gaunt were to be elevated in this way, the Tanith First would be broken up, and rendered into discrete specialist teams to supervise training or operate as special advisors. This, the gossip declared, was why the Ghosts had been retired to Balhaut in the first place: a slow and thorough dismantling, the assets of the regiment stripped.

Gaunt had heard the gossip. At a senior staff dinner, just a week earlier, he'd torpedoed the rumours with such phlegmatic humour and outrageous disrespect for the system that all the officers around the long tables, Baskevyl and Kolea included, had been quite crippled by mirth.

Baskevyl and Kolea didn't chat about the Kapaj simply because the Kapaj reminded them of Gaunt. The Kapaj weren't an idle-enough subject for chat. They were too heavily freighted with notions of their missing commander and future possibilities. In the friendless, foggy streets of Old Side, where they could taste the ice crystals in the air, and the cold bladed around them, there were no possible futures anymore, except for a grim resolution in some mouldering tenement.

Kolea tapped Baskevyl on the arm, and Baskevyl turned. A black, unmarked cargo-8 with armoured bodywork had driven up out of the surrounding fog to join the tail-end of the search formation. It had flashed its headlights as it rumbled in behind the vox truck.

'Look,' said Baskevyl.

Up ahead, one of the apparently numerous men called Sirkle had alerted his master to the vehicle's approach. Inquisitor Handro Rime turned and began striding back towards the black truck.

Kolea and Baskevyl changed course to intercept him. Commissar Edur got there first.

'News?' he asked Rime, walking backwards to match Rime's stride and remain face to face.

'Maybe,' Rime replied.

'Who's in the truck, inquisitor?' asked Edur.

'Persons of interest to this investigation,' Rime replied curtly.

'Going to reveal any identities?' Edur asked.

'We'll see,' said Rime.

'Please get out of the inquisitor's way,' said one of the Sirkles.

'Oh, now,' said Edur, 'the inquisitor and I have an understanding, don't we, sir?'

Rime stopped in his tracks and glared at Edur.

'When this is done, Edur–' he began.

'What?' asked Edur, with a wink. 'Are you talking dinner? I don't know, I'm not that sort.'

Rime let out a quiet curse of rage. One of the Sirkles stepped towards Edur.

Edur put his hand quickly on the butt of his pistol.

'Uh uh,' he warned. 'An understanding, remember?'

'What's in the big black truck, inquisitor?' Kolea asked as he and Baskevyl arrived.

'Yes, inquisitor,' said Edur, 'what's in the big, black truck?'

'I'll tell you as soon as I've completed the questioning process,' said Rime, and pushed past them.

'He's a friendly soul,' said Kolea.

'Lovely manners,' said Baskevyl.

Edur watched Rime stride away. A Sirkle unlocked the rear of the cargo-8, and Rime hoisted himself into the back.

'It's quite possible this is all going to get very ugly indeed,' Edur remarked.

'That's fine,' said Kolea.

'Just say when,' said Baskevyl.

'Ugly is what we do best,' said Kolea.

'My name is Rime,' said Rime as he climbed into the back of the armoured truck and sat down on one of the grille seats.

'A rhyme for what?' asked Blenner.

'What?'

'A rhyme for what?' Blenner repeated.

'You mis-heard me, sir,' said Rime. 'My name is Rime. Handro Rime, of the Inquisition.'

He opened his heavy leather wallet and displayed his rosette.

'Oh, my mistake,' said Blenner.

It was airless in the back of the truck. The portly commissar, who thought himself so amusing, was sweating, and the veiled widow beside him was resolutely saying nothing.

The datasheaf link had already told Rime more about Vaynom Blenner than Blenner would ever care to divulge. A Sirkle in the Balopolis Administratum had pulled Blenner's dossier and sent it to the Sirkle surveying the Mithredates.

'You know why you're here?' Rime asked.

'I don't even know where here is, frankly, so "why" is a whole separate enigma,' Blenner replied.

Rime tried to assess if Blenner was just an idiot, or if he was playing some kind of clever game. On the grille bench beside Blenner, Criid was wondering precisely the same thing.

'You're a person of interest to us,' Rime said, 'a long-time associate of Ibram Gaunt. You met at school, I believe?'

'I try to forget that part of my life, to be honest,' said Blenner. 'I was hopeless at games, and the other boys used to bully me. Wait though... I think one of them might have been named Gaunt. Basher Gaunt we used to call him, and he–'

'Shut up,' said Rime. 'We know you know Gaunt. Our records are fairly detailed. Schola progenium, Ignatius Cardinal, and then several periods of contact, the last and longest since school being here on Balhaut during the last eighteen months or so. You meet regularly. You are both members of the Mithredates Club. He paid off your club dues last month because you were financially embarrassed.'

'Wait... Is he a short, fat man with a beard?' Blenner asked.

'You last ate together three days ago,' Rime said. 'Gaunt signed the tab. He's fond of you, evidently. You're a childhood friend. Very few people in the service or the Guard have childhood friends anymore. He looks after you when your gambling problems get out of hand.'

'I don't have any gambling problems,' said Blenner.

'Do you want me to send for an audit of your fiscal affairs?' Rime asked. 'There's one available, fresh off the sheaf. I hear it's a shameful mess.'

Blenner fell silent.

'You know Gaunt,' said Rime. 'The fact is well-documented. That's why we put a watch on you, as a person of interest. Less than twelve hours before Ibram Gaunt went missing with a high-value asset, and Section was attacked, you had lunch with him. What did you talk about, Vaynom?'

'Oh, you know,' said Blenner, 'the usual chit-chat. How to recruit reliable Archenemy troopers this far into Imperial territory, the best way to
storm the gatehouse, etcetera. All that blather–'

Rime's fist caught him across the face, and smashed him off the grille
seat into the side wall of the truck. Blenner's head and shoulder met the
metal wall, and he fell down hard.

Criid rose to her feet.

'Leave him alone,' she said.

'You bastard,' Blenner was moaning from the deck.

Rime rose to face Criid. 'What did you say?'

'Leave him alone,' Criid repeated slowly.

'Protective, are you?' asked Rime. 'Protective? Sergeant Criid? Oh, yes,
we know who you are too. Palm-scans don't lie. Conveying a message to
Gaunt's good friend, were you?'

Criid pulled off her veil, and glared at Rime.

'Interesting,' Rime said, not breaking eye contact. 'You're not what I
imagined from the first female officer of the Tanith Ghosts.'

'What did you imagine?' she asked.

'Something rather more masculine,' he said.

Criid kicked him in the face. Despite the heavy trains of her slighted
mourning, she rotated enough to smash her foot into his mouth. He
crashed backwards into the truck's wall. Criid raked up her hopelessly
stupid skirts to get at her straight silver.

Rime came back at her. He was laughing. It was a nasty laugh, the sort
of laugh a man would utter if he were playing games and liked a little
rough stuff. He punched Criid in the shoulder, hard enough to make her
cry out, then slammed a rising forearm into her mouth so hard that it
tumbled her into the cab wall of the truck's back space.

Rime was on her in a second, before she could rise, before she could
stop her head spinning. Somehow, the bastard had got her knife.

He put it against her throat.

'No more fighting from you,' he said. He looked over at Blenner.

Blenner had crawled into a corner of the cabin space on his arse, dab-
bing the blood that was weeping from his nose.

'Last chance, Vaynom,' Rime called. He had Criid's own straight silver
pressed against her exposed throat. The blade was already welling blood.

'Last chance. What did he tell you? What message did he have this
bitch bring to you?'

'I think the message ran, "Screw you, inquisitor",' said Blenner,
'although I can't be sure.'

Criid laughed out loud. Rime drew the knife deeper.

A long rivulet of blood streamed down Criid's neck, and began to soak into the collar of her dress. She made no sound.

'Really, Vaynom, the very last chance. What did he say?'

'He wants to meet me,' Blenner cried.

'When?'

'Today at four! Please stop cutting her!'

'Where?' asked Inquisitor Rime.

'That's the thing, I don't know!' cried Blenner. 'He said I'd know the place, but I can't make head nor tail of it. Please, stop it!'

'What did he say?' asked Rime, very slowly and precisely.

'He said I'd know the place that... that he'd made sure isn't there.'

RIME JUMPED DOWN out of the truck, and the nearest Sirkle secured the door.

The other two Sirkles closed with their master.

'Blenner's an idiot,' Rime told them quietly. 'He really hasn't the wit for subterfuge, so Gaunt must be desperate to try to use him. Gaunt's tried to arrange a meet, but Blenner is confused by the coded nature of the location.'

'Perhaps he's acting dumb?' a Sirkle suggested.

Rime shook his head.

'If that's the case, he deserves an award from the Theatrum Imperialis.'

'What about the female?' asked the other Sirkle.

'I believe Gaunt didn't tell her the meaning so she couldn't betray it. But she's smart. She may have figured it out.'

'Should we submit her for deep purpose interrogation?'

'We've only got until four o'clock,' Rime replied. 'The female is extremely resilient. You can tell that just by looking at her. She would most likely hold out until the time frame had passed. We have to cut through the marrow of this, and we can't afford to be fussy.'

Rime took out a data-slate and quickly copied down the key phrase. He handed the slate to one of the Sirkles.

'Run this against Gaunt's file. See what comes up.'

The Sirkle nodded.

'We were using the Tanith to find their commander,' said Rime. 'I suggest we continue with that policy. Contact our agents at the Tanith HQ and see if the phrase means anything to them. Have them quiz the Tanith especially. The Tanith core of the regiment has been with him longest, and knows him best.'

'Oh, and get rid of this,' Rime added, and passed Criid's straight silver to his agent. The Sirkle hurried away.

The other agents waited for their master's next decision. Rime looked over his shoulder, and spotted the Tanith officers standing with Edur, watching him from a distance.

'What is your will?' one of the Sirkles asked.

Rime began to talk towards them.

'Let's ask them the question too,' he said.

'HERE HE COMES again,' muttered Kolea to Baskevyl.

'You saw what he had?' Baskevyl whispered back.

'Oh, yes.'

'What?' asked Edur quietly. 'What did he have?'

'He brought a Tanith warknife out of the truck,' said Kolea, 'and there was blood on it. I want to know who's in there and what he's done to them.'

MABBON, THE PRISONER, the pheguth, was awake.

Gaunt found him standing in front of one of the studio's windows. He'd opened the shutter a little to peer at the luminous white nothingness of the foggy daylight outside.

'Your woman, she's gone?' Mabbon asked.

'She's not my woman,' Gaunt replied, sipping a cup of caffeine he'd made for himself.

'I wasn't suggesting you were sexually involved,' said Mabbon. 'She's your woman. She serves you. She's one of your Ghosts, isn't she?'

'Yes.'

'She was on Gereon, wasn't she?'

Gaunt nodded.

'It's funny,' Mabbon murmured.

'What is?'

'On Gereon, if I'd won, if I'd been successful in my mission, you'd be dead, and so would she. Yet here you are, risking your lives to protect me.'

Gaunt scowled.

'Yes,' he said. 'Ironic, isn't it?'

'Is there any more of that?' Mabbon asked, pointing at Gaunt's cup.

Gaunt nodded, and Mabbon followed him into Jaume's rancid cubicle of a kitchen. Gaunt poured another cup.

'Can I trust Maggs?' Gaunt asked. 'I could really do with an extra pair of hands.'

'You're asking me?'

'Yes.'

Mabbon shrugged, and sipped from his cup. 'I'd trust him.'

'I'm not you,' Gaunt said.

'Well, if I was you, I'd never trust him again,' said Mabbon. 'I'd probably kill him, to be sure.'

'Throne,' Gaunt breathed.

Mabbon suddenly put down his cup, and scratched at the back of his head.

'They're closing in,' he said.

'The Blood Pact?'

Mabbon nodded.

'You can feel them?'

Mabbon looked at Gaunt.

'You ever serve on a tropic world so wet-hot the dust flies tap at your eyeballs faster than you can blink?'

'Yes, I've been there.'

Mabbon took up his cup and breathed deeply before sipping again.

'That's what it feels like. Micro-contact in my arms, at the base of my spine, deep down. Something touching my eyes.'

'And this tells you they're close?'

'Close and closing,' said Mabbon Etogaur.

Gaunt blinked. Once again, he could see it, as clear as day: the Blood Pact, dripping in wet gore, stepping over the threshold into Jaume's premises.

His new eyes had been showing him an awful lot in the last couple of days.

Every step of the way, he'd dismissed the images as system errors, as glitches, as imaging artifacts, as optical reconciliations, as patterns of accustomisation.

But he'd seen such things through his new eyes. He'd seen his driver's bad attitude. He'd seen the attack on Section before it had come. If truth be told, he'd seen Maggs trying to kill the etogaur. It hadn't been the wild shots of the gun that had been left behind that had alerted him.

He'd already been running before the gun had started firing.

'How close are they?' he asked.

'Very close,' Mabbon replied.

Gaunt looked at his pocket chron. It had stopped.

'We have to move anyway,' he said. 'We've got an appointment.'

* * *

'THE PHRASE DOESN'T mean anything in particular to me,' Hark told Sirkle. 'But I'll give it some careful consideration. It may be more obvious than it sounds.'

Sirkle nodded.

'Of course,' Hark went on, 'if the message was intended for Commissar Blenner as you suggest, it might be very specific to his relationship with Gaunt. They've known each other for a long time. It might reference something that none of us have any knowledge of.'

With a sour look that suggested he thought Hark was being less than entirely helpful, Sirkle walked away to continue his questioning. Ordo agents were already moving through the main barrack-rooms, quizzing the rank and file.

'You know what it is, don't you, sir?' Ludd asked Hark quietly.

'Remind me never to play cards with you, Ludd,' Hark murmured. With Dalin and Merrt in tow, they turned and began to walk briskly in the direction of the temple house.

'You *do* know what it is,' said Ludd.

'Of course I do, Ludd. It's hardly vermillion-level cryptography. A place that Gaunt has *made sure isn't there?* Anyone?'

'The Tower of the Plutocrat,' said Dalin.

Hark stopped in his tracks and looked at the young adjutant.

'Give the boy a medal! Well done, Criid.'

Dalin coloured up. 'My mother– I mean, Sergeant Criid, she has studied the colonel-commissar's career in some detail. I grew up on the stories.'

Hark clapped Dalin on the shoulder, and then resumed his stride towards the temple.

They entered the temple. Rerval, his arms folded, was standing beside the vox-caster while Beltayn worked at it.

'Anything?' Hark asked.

Rerval shook his head.

'It's still dead. It's like Major Rawne has just dropped out of existence.'

'Shame,' Hark replied, 'because we've now got something to tell him. Keep trying. Where did Doctor Curth go?'

'She took a break, sir,' said Beltayn. 'I don't think she could stand the tension. She said she'd be back. She said she had something important to do.'

'YOU LOOK FUNNY,' said Zweil.

'Charming,' Curth replied. She sat down opposite him. The closed folder lay on the desk in front of her.

'I mean, there's a funny look on your face,' Zweil said. 'Get on with it, will you? I don't like doctors' offices. They don't agree with me. Besides, I've got things to do. Urgent things. I've got hymnals to re-cover. In hessian, which is the best I could come up with. And there's half a bottle of altar wine that won't just drink itself.'

'The results of your medical examination have come back,' she said.

'Really?' he mocked. 'I didn't think you'd called me in here to tell me I'd been promoted to general.'

She opened the folder.

'This is very difficult, father. Difficult for me to say and difficult for you to hear.'

Zweil didn't reply. He stared at her.

'The pharmacon report has revealed a concern.'

'I said it would,' Zweil snapped. 'No good ever came of tests. No good at all. Ignorance, you see? It's better not to know. People generally underestimate the power of ignorance.'

'I'm sure they do, father,' she said gently. 'However, in the circumstances, we need to discuss this.'

'Has it got a long name?'

'Yes, father.'

'Don't tell me what it is!' Zweil cried, holding up a hand. 'I don't want to know. I don't want to make friends with it. We will refer to it only as The Concern.'

'If that's what you want.'

He nodded. 'I'm assuming the length of The Concern's real name is inversely proportional to the length of time it's going to leave me with?'

'Sort of,' she replied. She swallowed. It was very hard to stay professional.

'So where's it lurking? In my head? My liver? My lungs?'

'It's in your blood, actually. It's a haematological c—'

'Bup-bup-bub!' Zweil interrupted, making an urgent shushing gesture. 'I don't want long words. I don't want to have a conversation with it!' He dropped his voice to a hiss. 'In fact, we should whisper. I don't want it to hear us. I don't want it to know I know about it.'

He looked her in the eyes.

'I don't want the fething thing to know I'm scared,' he whispered.

Curth opened her desk drawer to find a tissue.

'And crying is a complete giveaway,' he scolded her.

Curth nodded and blew her nose.

'So,' Zweil whispered, 'how long?'

'We can administer palliative treatment to retard the progress of–'

'I don't want drugs. I don't want nurses and tests and monitors. I'll just keep going on the way I am, if you don't mind, for as long as I can, for as long as it will let me. How long?'

'Without treatment,' she said, 'no more than three months.'

Zweil blew a raspberry.

'That's absolutely shitty,' he said. 'I assume there's no possibility that the test results are wrong?'

She shook her head. 'I'm so sorry.'

The old priest sat back, deflated. Then a new expression crossed his face. Since the start of their conversation, he'd shown little more than anger. Now he wore an expression of shock.

'Oh, crap,' he murmured.

'What?'

'I've just thought of something,' he said. 'I've just thought of one tiny detail that makes this business a thousand times worse.'

THE PHILIA SLIPPED through the mist. The city was still veiled in luminous swathes of white, like high-altitude cloud, but the sun was beginning to burn it off. A hard, bright, clear day threatened to become a reality.

Karhunan Sirdar was confident their holy business would be done and finished by the time the fog departed. They had faced a canny foe, who had thrown them off the trail more than once. But they were Blood Pact, and they were sworn and driven. They had the resolution of the Consanguinity behind them, and they had sworn to perform this duty upon their souls.

They were tired, and they were hungry, and the approaching prospect of their collective, violent doom, though a glorious destiny, touched many of them with fear. However, none of them, not a single one, harboured even the slightest thought of giving up. They all loved the damogaur and, as the warp was their witness, they would not fail him, not in this life.

The witch had done her work. The damogaur had told the men that the pheguth had concealed himself. The witch was unable to read him. However, after a lengthy process of arcane elimination and prayer, the damogaur's infernal sister had identified the one part of the Imperial city that she could not see into. One small location had been made blank to her. The logic was simple. The target was hiding in the place she couldn't see into.

The witch swore to this fact, and Karhunan Sirdar had no reason to doubt her. She could not lie. Only truth ever passed her lips.

Up ahead, Imrie came to a halt at a street corner. He pointed up at the black metal sign on the wet brick wall.

Carnation Street.

This was the place.

'TAKE ME WITH you,' Maggs insisted.

Gaunt shook his head.

'No.'

'Look, I don't know what happened,' Maggs protested. 'Untie me and let me help.'

'I don't really know what happened either, Maggs,' said Gaunt, 'and that's why I can't untie you or bring you along. You're staying here with Mr Jaume. When this is all done, I'll come back for you.'

Maggs stared at him. There was a great deal unspoken in the stare.

Gaunt looked at Jaume, who was standing nearby.

'Thanks for your hospitality, Mr Jaume. We'll try not to inconvenience you much longer.'

Jaume shrugged.

'Can I come with you? Help you in anyway?'

'Thank you, no. I'd like to keep you out of danger.'

Over in the corner, Kolding was finishing re-packing his medical bag. He was ready to go. Gaunt was already risking the life of one civilian, and that was one too many.

'Hey,' Mabbon called out. He was at the front window, looking out at the street through a gap in the shutters. 'I think our plans just altered.'

Gaunt went over to join him.

Outside, the fog was thick. Slowly and silently, dark figures were emerging from its brilliant depths. Gaunt counted three, four…

They approached slowly, spaced out a distance from each other. They were coming straight for the house.

Gaunt could see that they were armed. Their weapons were held low but ready.

They stopped on the snowy pavement and looked up at the house's shuttered windows.

Now, he could see their masks too.

TWENTY-SEVEN

Famous Battlefields of the Balhaut War

'MOVE!' GAUNT ORDERED. 'The back way, all of us. No one can stay here.'

Everybody began to move out into the hall and up the short, rickety flight of steps into the rear of the house. Gaunt saw fear on Jaume's face. He was swept up in it now, the real thing.

'Undo my hands,' Maggs hissed.

'Be quiet,' Gaunt told him.

OUTSIDE IN THE luminous fog, Karhunan nodded. Gnesh stepped up, facing the front door of the old tenement. He flexed his broad shoulders to settle the strap of his heavy lasgun, and opened fire. He hosed the doorway from the hip, pumping fat bolts of las into the door, the frame and the brick surround. The door shredded, puncturing like a desiccated autumn leaf. The frame ripped and burst in spiking clumps of splinters and wood pulp. The brickwork fractured and cratered, vomiting clouds of brick dust. Some shots tore through into the reception hall behind the door, and detonated furniture or dug up floorboards.

His burst finished, Gnesh stepped back, and Kreeg ran in past him to lead the assault. Kreeg barely needed to kick to take down the ruins of the door. Lasrifle up and aiming, he came in over the threshold, hunting for a target.

He got less than a metre into the hallway when he began to tremble. The sensation was mystifying. Kreeg was almost more troubled by the sudden onset of the ailment than by the discomfort it brought him. He swayed, and his gunsight dropped.

It took ten seconds for the effects to amplify, boiling through his body like a chemical toxin, or like the burn of a class six hot virus, the sort of monster pathogen a man might contract on a deathworld, and which would kill him in three days.

This took ten seconds. Kreeg began to convulse. He dropped his rifle and staggered, his balance gone. He felt as if he had caught fire inside. Fluid was filling his lungs, choking him. He started to cough, and blood sprayed from his mouth. He hit the wall and collapsed, dragging down one of Mr Jaume's artful mauve drapes, tearing off its stud pins to reveal a scabbed, unfinished wall surface. Kreeg was bleeding out. Unclotting blood was gushing from his nose, his eyes and his mouth, from his fingertips, from his pores, from every opening of his body. He shuddered one last time, slumped further, and died.

Outside the front door, Gnesh looked on in disbelief as his comrade died in the hall in front of him. He took a step forward to try and help him, but Karhunan Sirdar held him back.

Karhunan pointed down at the doorstep, and Gnesh saw the sigil that had been scratched in the wood and inked with blood: a blood ward, and a lethal booby-trap. Kreeg had stepped right over it.

'The house is blocked,' said Gnesh. 'Can we go around? Is there a side way?'

'No time,' said the sirdar. He waved Malstrom up.

They backed away as Malstrom rolled a grenade onto the step, and ducked aside. The blast blew out the rest of the doorframe, dug up the step, and hurled Kreeg's corpse several metres further down the hall.

It also erased the blood ward, and broke its craft.

'In!' Karhunan ordered. 'Watch for more wards like that. In. In!'

GAUNT AND HIS companions heard the *crump* of the grenade behind them as they came out through the back of Jaume's house into the dingy rear yards and dark alleys behind the premises. Undisturbed snow lay thick on the wall-tops and in the yard spaces. Through the slow fog, Gaunt could see lank, frost-stiff laundry hanging from washing lines in neighbouring yards.

'Do you have a vehicle?' Gaunt asked Jaume as they ran through the snow to the end of the yard.

Jaume shook his head.

Gaunt had a single clip left in his bolt pistol. He drew the laspistol Criid had left with him, and toggled it to 'armed'.

'For Throne's sake!' Maggs cried. 'Let me go and give me the other weapon.'

Gaunt ignored him, and drove them down the high-walled spinal alleyway that connected the back gates of the tenement row. Piles of garbage and junk half-filled the space, smoothed out and shrouded by the recent snow.

They ran as hard as they could, Gaunt bringing up the rear with the weapon in his hand. Twice, he stopped and aimed it at what appeared to be movement behind them.

Then they heard another dull, gritty blast as their pursuers mined out the ward that Mabbon had left on the back step. It was very quickly followed by bursts of las-fire that stripped through the fog, making it swirl and coil.

Gaunt raised his weapon again, but the shooting was just loose and haphazard. He wasn't going to waste precious shots on a target he couldn't see.

They had nearly reached a major street adjacent to the one on which Jaume's house stood.

'Doctor,' said Gaunt as they ran, 'would you please cut Maggs's bonds? Quickly, please.'

Kolding fumbled a scalpel out of his kit, and ripped through the twine that was securing Maggs's wrists.

Maggs looked at Gaunt.

'A weapon?'

'Wheels,' Gaunt replied.

Maggs nodded, and ran on ahead of them into the broad avenue and the fog beyond.

Gaunt herded the others out towards the street, moving backwards with his gun braced for any movement in the fog-choked alley behind them.

Maggs came out into the open. In the broader space of the main thoroughfare, the fog was beginning to thin. He could see the roofs of the buildings on the far side of the street, as well as patches of milky blue sky. The sun was burning through the fog like a halogen lamp.

There was some light traffic, and a few pedestrians, wrapped up in coats and scarves against the cold. The shop juniors of nearby merchant houses were clearing snow from the pavements outside their display windows. A little way ahead, two cargo-6 trucks had pulled up to let a municipal work-gang unload sacks of salt for road gritting.

Maggs ran up to the rear truck, and began to climb into the cab.

'Hey. Hey, you!' the gang boss yelled out, throwing down his spade and hurrying towards the truck.

'Imperial Guard!' Maggs shouted back, fumbling with the ignition. 'I'm commandeering this vehicle.'

'Oh, right. Like there's a war on,' the boss retorted.

'There's always a war on,' Maggs told him. He started the truck's engine.

'Get down from there, now!' the boss yelled.

Maggs stared out of the driver's door window.

'Back off, friend. Don't make me get out and hurt you.'

The boss saw something in Wes Maggs's expression that he clearly didn't like. He backed away sharply, and so did the members of his crew. They watched in bemused wonder as Maggs threw the truck's transmission into reverse, and jerked the vehicle backwards. Its tyres slipped and scuffed in the snow, and its knifing tail-end knocked down several of the salt sacks unloaded on the curb.

'Whoa! Whoa! Whoa!' the boss yelled.

Maggs ignored him, and continued to reverse along the kerb, the cargo-6's fat tyres spraying up slush as they whipped and churned. He backed up ten metres to meet Gaunt and the others, who were running along the pavement from the alley mouth.

Several loose shots sang out of the alley into the street. Most went wide. One clipped a lamp post, and another blew out the headlight of a passing car. The pedestrians in the street froze, and then scattered in terror. More blind shots sliced out of the alley. The display window of a merchant house opposite fractured, and exploded in a billion slivers of plate glass. The two juniors shovelling snow in front of it ducked and ran.

Gaunt bundled the prisoner up into the back of the truck, and then helped Kolding and Jaume to hoist themselves in. He ran for the passenger door of the cab.

Pedestrians nearby were shouting and screaming as they ran. The work crew had fled. Gaunt turned, and saw the first of their pursuers emerge into the foggy street from the alley, lasrifle raised.

Gaunt lifted his laspistol in a two-handed brace and pinched off two quick shots. Both of them hit the Blood Pact warrior, knocking him back into the shadows of the alley.

Gaunt threw himself into the cab.

'Go!' he yelled.

Maggs put his foot down.

The cargo-6 slalomed away across the snow into the main lanes of the street. A flurry of las-fire and hard rounds lit the air around it, and spattered against the bodywork.

'Keep down!' Gaunt shouted through the cab's fanlight.

It was hard to control the heavy truck with any finesse in the snow. Maggs oversteered, and crunched the front end off a stationary car that its owner had abandoned at the first sign of gunfire. Then the truck sideswiped a small cargo van, shunting it into another vehicle. Bodywork buckled, and windows and headlamps smashed.

They were gaining speed. One last clip that bashed a car into the flank of a tram, and they were clear, and turning out at the junction into the next street.

'Which way?' Maggs demanded.

'The Oligarchy.' Gaunt shouted back. 'Make for the Oligarchy!'

EYL LED HIS sister through the fog at a run. He was leading her by the hand, and she was holding up the hem of her long dress. Several members of the philia moved with them.

The witch began laughing.

'What?' Eyl asked.

'We've made contact!' she cried, pulling her hand out of his so she could clap delightedly. 'Karhunan sirdar's element has made contact. The pheguth is running, but we have the trail again, strong and fresh!'

She turned her veiled face to look at her brother.

'He's out in the open again,' she said. 'We have his trail. Upon my soul, he is finished.'

INQUISITOR RIME SNAPPED the dossier shut and slapped it back into Sirkle's hands.

'It's so obvious,' he said, shaking his head and chuckling. 'So damn obvious. I was over-thinking it.'

'Sir?'

'I was assuming that Gaunt's message was an oblique reference to some private matter. It's far less sophisticated than that.'

Rime began to pace up through the search group towards the front of the line, calling for the senior Tanith officers and the commanders of the S Company brigade. The Sirkles hurried after him.

'Re-disposition!' he shouted. 'We're moving towards the Oligarchy.'

'The Oligarchy?' asked Edur. 'But there's no evidence to suggest–'

'That's where he's going,' Rime snapped. 'The Tower of the Plutocrat. Look it up on Gaunt's record. I was an idiot not to make the connection before. How's the fog looking?'

'Clearing fast, sir,' reported one of the Sirkles.

'Put the birds back up. I want marksmen covering us overhead. Only the best.'

One of the Sirkles hurried off to do Rime's bidding. Another two escorted Blenner and Criid over from the armoured truck.

'Feth!' Kolea whispered. 'He's got Tona. And isn't that Gaunt's commissar buddy?'

Baskevyl nodded. 'When we get moving, we'd better stay near the front. We don't want Rime getting there first.'

'Agreed,' said Kolea. He shouldered through the gathering press of men, and tried to get to Criid.

'Tona. Tona!' he called. She heard him, and saw him. She looked pale. She gave a little wave with cuffed hands.

'That's far enough,' said one of the Sirkles, blocking Kolea's path.

'I want to talk to my sergeant,' said Kolea.

'She's in Inquisition custody, so that's not possible just now.'

'But–'

'Get back to your duty, major,' Sirkle told him.

As THE SEARCH group got ready to switch its focus, Edur caught a moment with Captain Tawil, one of the S Company officers.

'Rime does not make a kill on Gaunt or the asset, all the while we can do anything to prevent it. Are we clear, captain?'

'As glass, sir,' said Tawil. He snapped his hellgun up across his shoulder, and ran towards his waiting men to give them instructions.

Edur watched him go. The commissar drew his bolt pistol, and checked the load. Then he holstered it and checked the charge of the short-frame laspistol that he kept in a shoulder rig under his coat as a back-up piece. Given the sledgehammer effect of the bolt pistol, Edur reasoned that he might soon have need of the laspistol's finesse.

He looked up at the sky. The fog was lifting rapidly now, and the sky was a bowl of clear, glassy blue.

Out of the east, Edur heard the rising whine of gunship engines as the Valkyries swung in to join the hunt.

* * *

PRETENDING TO BE rearranging the latest crop of notices on the bulletin board, Nahum Ludd executed an expert bit of loitering around the doorway of the vox room.

The afternoon had cleared, and turned bright and sharp, and outside, he could hear men whooping and shouting as they played bat-and-ball out on the snowy quad.

Something caught Ludd's attention. He peered through the half-open door, and watched the activity going on between Sirkle and the vox-operators. He tried to lip-read.

Sirkle suddenly strode out of the vox room, and Ludd quickly started to pin up the week's duty roster. Ludd waited until Sirkle had disappeared. Then he hurried to Hark's office.

'What's the matter, Ludd?' Hark asked, looking up from his desk.

'Something's going on,' Ludd said. 'Sirkle just got very excited. I think I overheard him saying something about leaving Aarlem to rejoin his master. Sir, I think they're onto something. I think they've figured out it's the Tower, too.'

Hark swore and threw down his stylus.

'We're getting perilously close to the point where I end up doing something I know I'm going to regret,' he said. He got to his feet. 'Let's check in on the temple.'

They went out into the hallway. Sirkle had reappeared, and was talking to one of the vox-operators near the door to the vox room. At the far end of the hallway, Dalin Criid suddenly ran into view. He skidded down to a walk in a hurry as soon as he spotted the ordo agent in the hallway.

He saw Hark and Ludd, made eye contact with them, and flicked a tiny gesture that they should follow him with a minute tilt of his head.

Hark walked up to Sirkle.

'Developments?' he asked.

'You'll be informed in due course, should they concern you,' said Sirkle.

'Well, you know where to find me,' replied Hark and walked on down the hallway.

HE AND LUDD entered the temple house. Beltayn was manning the set with Dalin and Rerval, with Merrt left to watch the door.

'Well?' asked Hark.

Beltayn had the phones pressed to his ear.

'It just woke up,' he replied. 'It's coming from a different source, and the codes are wrong, but I think it's genuine. I'm just waiting for the handshake.'

No one said anything for a minute. Then the vox-caster crackled into life.

'Stronghold, Stronghold, this is Nalwood, this is Nalwood, please respond.'

Hark took the mic-horn from Beltayn.

'Nalwood, Nalwood, this is Hark. Where the feth have you been?'

'NICE TO SPEAK to you too, Hark,' said Rawne, sitting back in the comfortable leather armchair. 'We ran into a few difficulties at our previous location, so we've been forced to reposition, over.'

He glanced up at Meryn and Daur standing behind him in the small office. The vox-caster, a compact model, was set up on a sideboard in the corner of the room. They could smell obscura smoke drifting up from the parlour below.

'Do I want to know what sort of difficulties, Rawne? Over,' Hark asked over the line.

'Probably not. Our comms went down. We've managed to locate an alternate resource, thanks to our bestest new friend, Mr Csoni.'

Lev Csoni was sitting in the outer office under the watchful eyes of Varl. Taking them over to his own gaming club, *The Eight of Wands*, on Brigantes Street, and allowing them free use of his vox had seemed like a small price to pay for his continued existence. Csoni had even let them use one of the big maroon limos that had brought his strike squad to Zolunder's. The rest of the team was waiting with the car.

'Tell me all about it later, Rawne,' Hark said. 'Things are moving fast. Gaunt's surfaced.'

'Where?'

'As far as we can be sure, he's due to show at the Tower of the Plutocrat, at four.'

Rawne looked at the long case clock in Csoni's office. It was a quarter to, gone.

'That's cutting it fine,' he replied. 'The Tower's long since fallen, hasn't it?'

'Correct.'

'But it used to be by the Oligarchy Gate on the way into the High Palace?'

'Correct again.'

'The place we're at is further north than Zolunder's. It's a twenty-five-minute trip from here, especially with snow on the ground.'

'Then shake your arses, major.'

'I was about to,' Rawne said, already rising to his feet. 'Anything else I should know before I hang this up? Last chance.'

'Be advised, there's likely to be Inquisitorial interest in this, as well as forces from Section, and maybe even the PDF. If the balloon goes up, you could be looking at a five- or six-way free-for-all.'

'Got it. Anything else?'

'The Emperor protects, Eli.'

'Thanks, Viktor. See you on the honour roll.'

'Good fortune, major.'

'Nalwood out.'

Rawne threw the switch that killed the vox, and tossed the mic-horn onto the desk.

'Let's move,' he said, picking up his weapon.

'If we've got to get there quickly, let me drive this time,' said Meryn.

'Oh feth off,' said Daur. 'There's nothing wrong with my driving.'

'You drive like an old woman,' said Meryn.

'And you will cry like a little girl if I have to shoot you somewhere semi-vital below the waist,' said Rawne, 'so do as Daur says and shut the feth up, Meryn.'

They entered the outer office. Varl and Csoni looked up.

'Are you done?' asked Csoni.

'It pains me to say it, Mr Csoni,' said Rawne, 'but we must now bid you farewell, and cut you loose.'

Rawne looked down at the seated man, and sighed.

'Mr Csoni, for you, I'm going to break the habit of a lifetime and keep my word. I'm not going to pop you to guarantee your silence. Throne, it would be so much neater and simpler if I could, but I made a promise. You get to live.'

'Thank you, thank you!' Csoni exclaimed, and then started to cry.

'One thing, Csoni,' said Rawne, bending down to look the man in the face, 'you do not want to be the man who makes me regret a decision.'

'I don't?' sobbed Csoni, looking up.

'You don't,' nodded Rawne.

'Oh, you really fething don't,' laughed Varl. 'You screw him over, he will hunt you down like a rabid larisel, and feth you up so bad, you won't be able to–'

'Thanks, Varl,' said Daur. 'I think Csoni gets the picture.'

'I do. I do!' said Csoni.

THE FOUR OF them thundered down the club's back stairs to the rear yard, where they'd stowed the limo. Rawne brought Varl up to speed on what Hark had said.

'Feth,' said Varl. 'Did he say anything else?'

'He said, "The Emperor protects",' Daur said.

They came out into the snowy rear yard. The big maroon limo with its chrome furniture was parked beside the access gate. The figures standing around it jumped to attention as they saw the four men come into view.

'You know the full version of that blessing is "The Emperor protects the virtuous", don't you?' asked Varl as they ran for the car.

'Yeah?' said Meryn. 'Well, we're screwed then.'

THE PRECINCTS OF the High Palace, as its name suggested, sat at the summit of the gigantic, gently sloping peak, above the river on which Balopolis was built. The Oligarchy, a vast acreage of governmental structures and ancient colleges and chapels, formed the mantle, with the palace itself as the crown.

The fog had fled from the high places more quickly than it had from the deep, steep streets of Balopolis below. Up at the High Palace, the air was blue and as sharp as crystal. Snow iced the reconstructed battlements and rooflines of the noble palace, and frost skinned the lawns of the ornamental gardens inside the palisades. Windlarks, so high up they were invisible, sang clear, trilling notes in the cold air. Sentries of the PDF, in formal furs, stood watch, blowing on their hands.

The Oligarchy, and the High Palace that lay at its heart, were key destinations for any visit to Balhaut. The planet boasted some of the most infamous battle-sites in the sector, and had become a magnet for scholars, theorists, enthusiasts, tourists and, of course, those mourning the fallen and grieving old losses. The High Palace was the culmination of any mourning pilgrimage, an act that had become an industry of its own. The High Palace was where the war had been decided. It was where Slaydo had fallen. It was where they had raised the memorial chapels, especially the Honorarium, where Slaydo's bones were interred.

They called it, perhaps harshly, the Widow Tour, for it was most often taken by wealthy widows from the scattered outworlds of the Khulan Group, travelling to Balhaut with long-suffering servant-staff and squabbling children, who had never known the deceased personally. Expert guides and escorts offered their services; the elaboration of the tour was usually decided by wealth and status. Various theatres and battlefields could be included, depending on the deceased's career. One could attend the Raising of the Aquila ceremony at Zaebes City, or walk the elegant rows of simple white posts in the cemeteries overlooking Ascension Valley.

There were even authoritative books one could consult. Some were extensive, others could be obtained from any corner merchant for a few coins: encyclopaedias and tatty chapbooks, learned tomes and flimsy pamphlets. One of the most ubiquitous and affordable was a sixty-page booklet now in its forty-seventh impression, entitled *Famous Battlefields of the Balhaut War*. It was published by the Munitorum, and approved by the Society of Balhaut Veterans. It was a cheap and slightly worthy account of the war's key phases and conflicts, complete with some astonishingly bad maps and pictprints.

Gaunt took a copy off the shelf outside the docent's booth, and skimmed through it.

'What's that?' asked Jaume.

'A memento,' Gaunt replied. He had a page open, and was reading.

'What does it say?' asked Jaume.

'It says that on the ninth day of fighting, Slaydo drove his left flank against the Oligarchy Gate. The attack was nominally commanded by Captain Allentis of the Silver Guard, but his charge was devastated by the Heritor's murderous machines. Thus, the first unit to reach the Gate was the Hyrkan Eighth, which famously managed to blow wide the Archenemy's defences, and breach a position that had resisted nine days of assault.'

'Is that correct?' Jaume asked.

Gaunt looked over his shoulder. In the shadows of the colonnade, he could see Kolding and Maggs with the prisoner. The day was quiet. The fierce snowstorm had kept most tourist parties and widow tours out of the High Palace for a couple of days. The guards and the docents, the latter mostly history students from the Collegio Balopolis, were wandering about bored, or snoozing in their wooden booths.

'Come with me,' Gaunt said to Jaume.

He led the younger man out into the middle of the new stone quad. Some of the original stones from the Gate, mauled and smashed, had been placed on display in armour-glass boxes around the edge of the space, like trophies.

'This is where the Gate stood,' Gaunt said, extending his arms. 'Right here. They've been good enough to mark its footprint on the new paving.'

Jaume looked down. The new quad had been laid with black stone, matt and flush-fitting. He saw that the outline of a vast structure had been marked out in thick silver wire, inlaid into the stone.

'That's where the Gate stood,' said Gaunt.

'And you brought it down,' said Jaume. 'Throne. It was huge.'

'Allentis had done most of the work,' said Gaunt. 'He broke the back, not us. Throne, I was sorry when they told me he was gone.'

'He was Silver Guard, this Allentis?'

'Yes.'

'So, an Astartes?'

'Yes.'

'I was told that the Astartes are not like normal men. That they are other. More than human and still less too.'

'I've known Astartes who were more like animals than men,' Gaunt shrugged. 'Allentis was a man. A human soul. One of the bravest and tenacious I've ever had the privilege to serve with.'

Jaume pursed his lips, and nodded.

'So is this where Slaydo died?' he asked.

'No, not here. About a kilometre to the west.'

Jaume nodded.

'Is it odd being back here?' he asked.

'Strangest thing I've ever done,' Gaunt smiled. 'What's the time?'

'Ten minutes to four,' said Jaume. He had a good sight of the palace clock tower. None of their watches had worked since the night of the snowstorm.

'We'd better move,' said Gaunt.

'My good sirs, can I help you?' a docent asked, approaching and bowing. He was a tall young man, skinny with long hair that hung down around the neckline of his red docent robes. He smiled a friendly smile.

'A tour, perhaps?' he suggested. 'A crown per person, and you see all the sights. It's very thorough. I can walk you through the High Palace fighting zones, the Gate, the Tower and, of course, the death of Slaydo. I am fully versed. Did you lose a loved one here?'

'Plenty,' said Gaunt.

'Yes,' said Jaume. 'My father. He was PDF. He assisted in the assault of the Gate, or so I'm told.'

'Well, that was a valiant endeavour indeed,' the docent agreed. 'I'd be delighted to show you the key sites.'

'Yes. Do that,' Gaunt said. He fished into his pocket for coins. 'We want to see it all, but we especially want to see the Tower of the Plutocrat.'

'One of the highlights, sir,' said the docent.

'Take us there first,' said Gaunt.

The docent nodded. 'How many in your party, sir?'

'Five,' said Gaunt. He had found three crowns. 'Help me out here, Jaume.'

Jaume hurriedly produced another two crowns, and Gaunt paid the guide. He beckoned to Maggs, and Maggs and the doctor led Mabbon out of the shadows to join them.

'Oh, the poor man!' the docent exclaimed, indicating Mabbon. 'Is he a veteran?'

'Yes,' said Gaunt.

The docent set off. Three or four other parties were threading the rebuilt ruins with them. Docents in their trademark red robes were leading family parties along the walkways, reciting the narratives of war, parrot-fashion. Gaunt saw parties of weeded widows in veils, parties of earnest young soldiers, and family groups that mixed both together. Small children attached to family groups toddled free across the quads and open spaces, their aunts and mothers cooing after them. Gaunt watched each party in turn, hearing the soft echoes of the docents' narrations.

Their own docent was in full-flow as he led the way across quads and along cloisters.

'Here, on the ninth day! The death of Captain Ollark! At this very site! Two rounds, as he tried to crest the bank of bodies!'

'Ollark shot himself on the fifth day,' Gaunt whispered to Jaume. 'He couldn't take it any more. This man is as bad as you.'

'It must be contagious,' said Jaume.

'Was your father really here?' Gaunt whispered as the docent banged on.

'Yes. I wouldn't make a thing like that up,' said Jaume.

'I don't recall a Jaume,' Gaunt whispered. 'There were PDF units right in it with us, but I don't recall a Jaume.'

'I hardly expect you to,' Jaume replied as the docent babbled on. 'He was a junior man in a minor unit, and it was fifteen years ago. You probably never even saw him. Besides, are you telling me you can remember the name of everyone on every battlefield you've ever been on?'

'Of course not,' Gaunt said, looking at him.

'Well then,' said Jaume. 'You wouldn't remember him. He wasn't important.'

Gaunt frowned. 'The PDF were right with us, every step of the way. Their contribution is often overlooked. Jaume, if your father was here, he was a brave man. You say he died here?'

'We never knew where,' said Jaume. 'He died at the Gate, that's what we were told.'

'You said to me you'd never met a hero,' said Gaunt as the docent went on and on, 'but you have. Your father was a hero.'

Jaume looked at him, and smiled.

'Thank you,' he said.

'What for?'

'For being kind enough to tell the same white lie to me that I tell to others.'

'It's not a lie,' said Gaunt.

'Perhaps,' said Jaume. 'I bless you for it, anyway. Perhaps now you better appreciate the merits of my occupation.'

'You know Kolding's father died in the war too?'

'The doctor?' Jaume asked.

'His father died trying to defend the wounded. It seems I have the sons of heroes watching my back today.'

Jaume laughed.

'I never expected such sentiment from you,' he said. 'I should put you on retainer. Shall we say half a crown per epitaph?'

The docent, still gabbling, had brought them to the entrance of the eastern palisade. He became operatic.

'And here! Here it was that great Slaydo fell in his mortal combat with the foul Archon! See how his falling place is marked by an aquila of inlaid silver and rubies.'

They looked down at the holy site. It was lit up by spotlights and atmosphere globes.

'I think we should all take a solemn moment here,' said the docent.

'This isn't where Slaydo fell,' Gaunt whispered.

'No?' Maggs whispered back.

'He went down about sixty metres that way on the western palisades. Then they dragged his corpse another hundred metres, and ritually dismembered it. I bet that isn't on the tour.'

'It's not,' whispered Jaume.

'I can't believe they've got so much of this stuff wrong,' murmured Gaunt.

'Unlike you, they weren't here,' said Mabbon quietly.

The docent began walking again.

'What's the time?' Gaunt asked.

'Five minutes to four,' said Kolding. 'At least, it was the last time I saw the palace clock.'

Gaunt looked to the docent. 'We'd like to see the Tower of the Plutocrat now,' he said.

'But of course,' the docent exclaimed. 'And I'm sure you'd like to view the death venues of the key fallen there!'

'The... death venues?' asked Kolding.

The docent nodded.

'As with Slaydo, the places where the heroes fell. Captain Menhort of the Kolstec "Hammers", Gaunt of the Hyrkans and, of course, Allentis.'

'What?' asked Gaunt.

'Did you say Gaunt?' asked Jaume.

'Gaunt, the Commissar of the Hyrkans,' said the docent. 'He died taking down the Tower.'

Gaunt looked back at his companions.

'Honestly, I didn't,' he whispered. Maggs and Jaume snorted. The hint of a smile even found its way onto Kolding's lips.

'Let's look at the death venue of Gaunt,' Maggs said to the docent.

'Yes. Why don't we?' Gaunt laughed.

'This way,' the docent declared. 'It was the ninth day. The Heritor was resisting. Gaunt, Throne rest him, led the Hyrkans through the obliterated Gate, and dug down in the yards under the Tower...'

It was just two minutes to four.

TWENTY-EIGHT

The Death Venue of Ibram Gaunt (visitors welcome)

THE EAGER DOCENT led them towards the great quad where the footprint of the Tower of the Plutocrat was outlined in silver and gold.

Gaunt felt the air chill.

He reached for the reassuring grip of his bolt pistol. It felt comfortable in his hand. He kept the group close to him, and picked up his visual checking. He noticed that both Mabbon and Maggs were scanning the area too. They'd felt it as well, and whatever they were, both of them were soldiers first. They had keen skills that could never erode.

Gaunt kept his hand on his bolter as he let the docent guide his party through the cloister shadows towards the Tower site. Maggs sidled close to Gaunt.

'Give me a gun,' he whispered.

Gaunt shook his head.

The sky above the High Palace had become an aching blue, unblemished by any clouds. The sun, beginning its afternoon track down the sky, was still bright. The shadows of the cloisters and the memorial chapels around the great quad were hard-edged and black.

Gaunt could hear a general murmur of voices: other docents, leading their parties; conversations between visitors; an ayatani priest performing a simple service of remembrance in front of a memorial plaque, a family grouped around him with their heads bent. The light wind ruffled long skirts of black silk.

Gaunt heard a clock tower down in the Oligarchy chiming four. He turned to the docent.

'Can you keep my group here for a few minutes?' he requested. 'Tell them about the Tower. Tell them about the extraordinary noise it made when it fell, like the world splitting in half. Tell them about the dust-cloud that blotted out the sunlight. Tell them about the piles of bodies steeper than the piles of rubble.'

'Sir?' the docent asked, looking puzzled.

'Tell them all about Commissar Gaunt and what an amazing soldier he was.'

Gaunt turned and walked out of the shadows into the sunlight of the great quad. He saw tour groups in the distance on the far side of the area, and several more closer to, grouped around the memorial statues in the centre of the quad.

It was nothing like he remembered it, though he had begun to seriously doubt the quality of his memories. The terrain was different, flatter. The topography of the buildings surrounding the area had changed, which was hardly surprising, given the collateral of the Tower's demise. He remembered being holed up for hours under fire, staring at a small gatehouse with distinctive finials in the shape of aquilas. He wondered what had happened to the place. It had still been standing when he and the Hyrkans had finally been able to storm a path past it. Had it fallen later? Had it been demolished much later on to make way for these memorial vaults?

Even the sky was different.

He turned in a slow circle. He could see the High Palace, hazed by the blue distance. He could see a wheeling flock of birds. He could see the huge, dark drum-shaped monolith of the Honorarium rising behind the great quad like a battlement.

He walked towards the centre of the great quad. Though it was long gone, he could feel the presence of the Tower above him, clinging like a ghost. His orders had brought it down: his sweat, his effort. The Tower had added almost half a kilometre to the Oligarchy's overall height. Falling, the roar it had made…

He saw a figure in the distance, standing at the edge of the cloisters. He recognised it instantly. The sight almost brought a spontaneous tear to his eyes: not a tear of sadness or weakness, but a sudden upwelling of emotion. To be here, so many years later, and to see his oldest friend coming to his aid, on this very spot…

Gaunt did not cry. It was one design feature his new eyes did not possess.

He began to walk towards Blenner. Blenner was smiling his shit-eating smile, his 'Let's blow the rest of the day off and go to this little bar I know' smile. His cap was on at its trademark, almost jaunty, entirely nonconformist angle.

Everything was going to be all right.

As he got closer, Gaunt noticed Blenner's hands. Blenner's arms were down at his sides. The index and middle fingers of each hand were, quietly and subtly, making 'walking' motions.

It was one of the old codes, one of the scholam codes that they'd used so long ago on Ignatius Cardinal. *Fellow pupil, friend, I can see trouble that you can't see; I can see the master or the prefect waiting to pounce, waiting to catch us out for running or singing or chatting, so walk away while you still can. I'm done for already, but you can still save yourself. Walk, walk, walk, for Throne's sake, walk...*

Gaunt stopped in his tracks, and began to back away. A big grin crossed Blenner's face. *Yes, you've got it, Bram...*

Two men suddenly shoved past Blenner, and burst out of the cloisters into the sunlight. They both had laspistols. They both had the same face: two of Rime's agents.

They aimed their weapons at him.

'Ibram Gaunt!' one yelled. 'By order of the holy Inquisition, we demand your immediate surrender! Do not resist. Get on the ground, face down, with your arms spread!'

'Why?' asked Gaunt.

'Do as I say!'

'I don't recognise your authority.'

'You are consorting with a known warp cultist. Guilt by association. Get on the damn ground!'

Eye-blink fast, Gaunt drew his bolt pistol, and aimed it at the Sirkles.

'All right,' he said. 'Let's do this.'

The Sirkles baulked slightly.

'Take him,' one said to the other.

There was a bone crack. Vaynom Blenner had wrapped his fists together and smacked them across the back of one of the Sirkle's skulls.

'Run, for Throne's sake, Bram!' Blenner yelled as the Sirkle he had struck went down onto his knees.

The other Sirkle looked at his twin, distracted.

Gaunt put a bolt-round into the quad paving at the Sirkle's feet. The *boom* was gigantic, and echoed around the vast area. Flocks of startled birds exploded up into the blue from cloister roofs. Visitors looked around, wondering what the hollow thunderclap meant, not recognising the sound of gunfire.

Who on Balhaut recognised the sound of gunfire anymore?

Hit by paving debris, the other Sirkle staggered backwards. Gaunt started to sprint across the sunlit open ground, his stormcoat flying out behind him like ragged wings.

'Run!' he yelled at the group waiting for him in the cloister shadows. Maggs was already getting them moving.

'I think you should stay here,' Mabbon said gently to the bewildered docent. 'This is probably the point at which you'll want to disassociate yourself from this group.'

'If you think that's best, sir,' the docent stammered. 'Uhm, the Emperor protects.'

'So I keep hearing,' said Mabbon, as he turned to follow Maggs, Jaume and Kolding along the cloister.

'It's a trap! Move,' Gaunt yelled, catching up with them.

Squads of troopers, some of them S Company, but many of them ordo fire-teams, rushed out onto the great quad from the eastern cloisters where Blenner had been waiting.

Rime was with them, yelling orders to his agents.

'Spread out. Flush the cloisters! Is the area locked?'

'Yes, sir! Strike teams at all the gates. They can't leave the Oligarchy precincts.'

'We can't let him run!' Rime declared. 'Bring the birds in. Marksmen. *Now*, Throne damn it!'

'Yes, sir,' a Sirkle replied, waving up a vox-officer.

'This Gaunt's shown his true colours!' snarled Rime. 'If he'd surrendered when he'd had the chance, I would have had some measure of pity. But it's clear where he's cast his lot. Old habits die hard, and he learned all of his on Gereon. Tell the birds to take any shot they can get! They're *all* viable targets, do you understand?'

'Yes, sir!' the Sirkle replied.

EDUR EMERGED INTO the sunlight of the great quad with the first wave. He shouted his S Company men forward, hoping to secure Gaunt in the confusion that followed Rime's fumbled play.

'Go. Go!' he yelled.

'Targets have gone into the cloisters, west side, sir,' Tawil voxed back via micro-bead.

'Dammit!' Edur cried.

'We think the targets are heading east towards the Honorarium and the memorial enclave, sir.'

'Follow them!'

'Sir, there are an appreciable number of civilians in our path!'

Edur cursed again, and turned in a frustrated circle in the sunlight.

He saw Kolea and Baskevyl, and the Tanith scout squads, running towards him.

'Back off. Back off, now!' he yelled, raising his hands. 'Stand down. You're only going to make this worse!'

'Well, great job you're doing,' Baskevyl yelled as he ran past.

'Throne damn it,' Edur screamed.

'We look after our own!' Kolea yelled back at him.

'That's exactly why this is a bad idea,' Edur replied.

Mkoll was the first of the Tanith party to reach the western cloisters. Eszrah was close behind him.

Mkoll suddenly skidded to a halt, and looked up at the sky.

'Something's coming,' he said.

'You mean the air cover?' Jajjo asked, running up behind them.

'No,' Mkoll growled. 'Something bad, I think.'

He raised his rifle and rushed on into the cloisters.

'SHOULDN'T WE JUST surrender to them?' Jaume asked as they ran.

'No,' said Gaunt.

'But they were Throne agents, weren't they? Officers of the Inquisition?'

'The answer's still no,' said Gaunt.

He skidded to a halt. He could hear the uproar of the fire-teams chasing them, the screams of the visitor parties scrambling out of their way.

It all seemed very distant, suddenly.

Gaunt looked up. A scatter of snowflakes, no more than three or four, was falling towards them out of the cloudless air. They fell until they were a few metres above their heads.

Then they froze in the air. They hung, impossibly, in nothingness, as if time had been suspended.

'Now we're really in trouble,' murmured Gaunt.

'She's here,' whispered Mabbon. 'The witch is here.'

Heavy gunfire suddenly raked at them. They flew for cover behind the pillars of the colonnade. The throaty las-fire punched holes in the stone flags, and sent paving stones spinning into the air.

Closing in behind Gaunt's group, the ordo fire-teams turned to blast at the sudden source of fire. They got off a few shots before the heavy gun-fire turned on them, cutting many of them down. Men crumpled or jerked back, smashed off their feet. Some of them got to cover. Some of them fell, hideously wounded.

'Into them!' Baltasar Eyl commanded.

Gnesh moved forward along the cloisters, hosing with his heavy las-gun. Las-bolts squealed and spat from the massive, oil-black weapon slung over his shoulder. His shots were chewing the corners off the colonnade's stone pillars. Facing stone cracked and shattered. Brick dust bloomed like shocks of pollen. Ordo agents toppled and fell. A Sirkle, hit twice, smashed back into a pillar, and slid down, dead.

Around Gnesh, elements of the philia laid in support. Their gunfire greeted the S Company formations arriving behind the ordo units. The Commissariat storm-troopers took cover, and began to return fire with their hellguns. In less than a minute, the western cloisters of the great quad had turned into a furious, howling nightmare of a firefight.

This is the Tower of the Plutocrat I remember, Gaunt thought.

He looked around, gauging the best exit route. Las-rounds smacked into the wall above him. Somewhere, a grenade went off. Above the gun-fire roar, he could hear turbofans whining.

Gaunt rose, blew a Blood Pact warrior off his feet with a single bolt, ran, and tried to reach the next archway, hoping to duck in, and provide cover for the men following him.

Imrie of the philia swung out of the archway shadows, and rammed the muzzle of his weapon against Gaunt's forehead.

'On your knees,' he said in broken Low Gothic. 'On your knees. Where is the pheguth?'

'Tar shet fethak!' Gaunt replied, cursing the Blood Pact warrior in his own tongue.

Imrie took a step back in surprise, and then aimed the gun to shoot.

A chunk of paving stone smacked him in the face, cracking his grotesk.

Imrie fell on his back, his weapon discharging uselessly into the ceiling of the colonnade.

Maggs appeared at Gaunt's side.

'Don't give me a bloody gun then,' Maggs said, and helped himself to Imrie's weapon. Gaunt didn't stop him.

Maggs checked the weapon. On the ground, Imrie began to stir. Maggs put the rifle to his head, and fired.

'One less to worry about,' he said.

'We've got to find a way out of here,' Gaunt told him.

Two more Blood Pact shooters opened up on them from the cloister end. Las-bolts chopped and stripped through the air. Gaunt and Maggs ducked down, and fired back.

'Oh holy Throne!' Gaunt heard Jaume cry out. 'Oh holy Throne, this is insanity!'

Maggs adjusted his angle, and took out one of the Archenemy shooters. The other tried to reposition to get Maggs into his sweep of fire, and Gaunt put two bolt-rounds through him and the wall behind him.

'Run!' Maggs told the others. 'Now!'

They all ran.

THE VALKYRIES SWUNG in low over the High Palace. Smoke was pluming up off the cloisters near to the great quad.

Strapped into the open doorway of the leading bird, Larkin looked up at Bonin, who was holding on to the door's overhead rail.

'It's a fething mess down there,' he yelled over the wind rush.

Bonin nodded. He pulled out a scope, and started spotting.

'Get your eye in, Larks,' he said.

'I don't even know what I'm looking for anymore,' muttered Larkin, settling up to his long-las's scope.

'Bad guys,' Bonin said.

'Ah, gotcha,' replied Larkin.

RIME AND THREE Sirkles ran down the western colonnade, past the bodies of dead agents and at least two other Sirkles. Rime could hear the strip and slap of fierce gunfire exchanges in the precincts directly ahead of him.

'Close in, close in!' he yelled over his link. 'Condition red! All forces close in and subdue. Kill shots approved, all targets!'

Crossfire ripped through the colonnade, killing both of the Sirkles, outright. Rime stumbled with a flesh wound to his left thigh. The philia warrior known as Naeme ploughed out of hiding behind the inquisitor with his weapon raised to finish his attack.

'Then it is Golguulest,' he was saying, 'then it is Nyurtaloth.' Naeme was ebullient. He knew in his heart that the mission his philia had been sent on was almost done, and he knew his rite was nearly done too. There were only a few of death's names left to be recited.

'Then there is Djastah,' he said.

'Then there is Rime,' said Rime.

Naeme hesitated, and stared at the inquisitor in amazement. There was no denying it. *Rime* was certainly one of the last names of death.

'You,' Naeme breathed. 'You are–'

Rime raised his hand and caught Naeme by the throat. He snapped the Blood Pact warrior's neck with an effortless flick.

'Yes,' said Rime, allowing the body to fall. 'I am.'

KARHUNAN SIRDAR KNEW that the philia was losing bodies fast. The running gun battle through the High Palace was costing both sides dearly. He'd just seen his brother Barc fall, his brains splashed up the wall. The area ahead of the sirdar was littered with Imperial dead.

Ever the strategist, Karhunan reckoned he had enough men left to cut across the line of Imperial assault, and hold it long enough for his beloved damogaur to make the kill.

Yelling the *Gaur Magir!* war cry of the Pact, he ordered what was left of the philia forward. It had begun to snow quite heavily. The light had gone, the blue of the sky turned to zinc. Karhunan could smell blood and snow.

They had reached the end of their last mission.

He sprayed fire, and cut down three Commissariat storm-troopers, who were trying to advance along the contested colonnade. From cover, Captain Tawil took a shot that hit Karhunan in the gut. The sirdar fired back, instinctively on auto, and shot Tawil to pieces.

Karhunan could smell his own blood.

He winced, and tried to remain upright. He waved his men forward.

The last of his men: Gnesh, Samus and Lusk.

Gnesh led the way, hosing the colonnade with fire. S Company troopers, screaming for want of cover, burst like meat sacks. Gnesh was laughing. There was blood aplenty for all the thirsty gods of the Consanguinity.

Gnesh fell.

Karhunan didn't see what hit him, but the big man fell with an awful and final certainty, a death fall.

Karhunan screamed in rage. He saw several figures in black fatigues flanking his line along the outside of the colonnade's wall. He fired at them, chipping stonework.

Mkoll swung up, and fired back. His first burst slew Lusk, and his second winged Samus. Jajjo, at his left-hand side, aimed over the colonnade wall, and nailed Samus with a squirt of full auto.

Howling, Karhunan ran for them.

A tall figure in nightmarish war paint stepped out of the shadows of a pillar in front of him, and fired some kind of powered bow.

The bolt hit Karhunan Sirdar in the forehead, and crashed him over onto his back, dead.

'Clear,' Eszrah ap Niht yelled to the Tanith fire-teams.

'Advance!' Mkoll bellowed.

'IT'S A DEAD end!' Gaunt yelled.

'No, this way,' Jaume cried. 'This leads through to the Honorarium.'

'Are you sure?' Gaunt asked.

'Of course I am. I've been coming up here every Friday for the last six months.' Jaume yelled.

Gaunt didn't even think to ask the portraitist why.

'Maggs!' he yelled. 'Move Jaume and the doctor into cover in the Honorarium!'

Mabbon had fallen behind. His strength had held up well, but he was flagging now, slowed by the returning pain of his wound. Snow was swirling around them.

'But–' Maggs protested.

'That's an order!' Gaunt yelled.

Maggs turned, and scooted Kolding and the terrified Jaume away in the direction of the vast Honorarium.

Gaunt got his arm around Mabbon, and supported him.

'Not far now, magir,' he said.

'You're a good man, Gaunt,' wheezed the etogaur.

'If they take us, please don't say that to anyone. Tell them I'm your sworn enemy.'

An RPG shrieked down the colonnade, and blew out the roof. The concussion dropped Gaunt and Mabbon hard.

Malstrom stalked forward through the coiling smoke and the random snow, slamming another fat shell into the launcher. Dust from the blast had given the air a gritty, grainy quality.

Up ahead, the two bodies lay amongst the rubble, swathed in stone dust. Both looked dead. One of them was the pheguth. Malstrom tossed his launcher away, and drew an autopistol. They had done it. The philia had won. All he had to do was confirm the kill.

Coated in stone dust, and looking like a statue come to life, Gaunt sat up abruptly. His bolt pistol was in his hand.

'Not today,' he said, and fired.

The bolt blew Malstrom in half, and painted the cloister wall with a terrible quantity of blood. There were no gore mages of the Consanguinity present to read the blood mark, but the prognostications were nothing but violent death.

Mabbon was dazed and woozy. His wound had started to bleed again. Gaunt hoisted him upright, and got his arm under the enemy officer's armpits. Both of them were covered in stone dust and blood, and both of them were a little deaf from the concussion.

'Come on. Stay with me!' Gaunt yelled. He stared up into Mabbon's face, and slapped his scarred cheek. 'Stay with me!'

He could hear whining. He thought it was just his ears. Snowflakes touched his face.

The muzzle of a pistol rammed against Gaunt's temple.

'I will give you credit,' Baltasar Eyl said, panting hard. 'You have been a worthy adversary. You have led my philia a proper dance. But now, we end this.'

His voice was full of accent, of outworld accent. In the extremity of the moment, it had become hard for Eyl to maintain his civilised veneer.

'One last thing you might want to consider, damogaur,' Mabbon said in the Archenemy tongue. 'When you've got the bastard, kill the bastard. Don't *talk* about it.'

Gaunt threw a savage elbow that smacked Eyl away. The damogaur reeled, his teeth broken, and his mouth bloody, but he still had the gun. Gaunt kicked him in the belly.

Eyl still had the gun.

'WE'VE GOT TARGETS! Out in the open!' Bonin yelled.

'Take them! Take them all!' Rime was shouting over the static heavy line.

'Feth that, there's smoke and snow all over the place!' Larkin replied, snuggling up his aim as the Valkyrie bucked and wallowed.

'Big boss says take the shot, Larks,' said Bonin.

'Wait...' Larkin advised. 'Wait... get the pilot to level us out! All right, I have three targets. Repeat, three hot. What's the advice?'

'Instruction is take the shot,' Bonin repeated over the roar of the cycling turbofans.

'I aim to please,' Larkin replied, the long-las banging in his hands.

THERE WAS A crunch of overpressure and punctured vacuum. Blood vapour drenched Gaunt and Mabbon, caking their dust-covered faces.

Eyl's skull had just detonated. His headless body fell against Gaunt. A gunship wailed in overhead, tossing and pluming the rising smoke and the billowing snow. A second later, its shadow went over them,

'Holy Throne,' Gaunt stammered.

'HIT! HIT!' LARKIN yelled.

'Yeah, but what did you hit?' Bonin demanded, leaning down over Larkin in the doorway.

'I only ever see what's real and true through my scope,' Larkin replied. 'I got the bad guy, of course. Didn't I?'

GAUNT AND MABBON ran towards the Honorarium. Leaking blood, Mabbon was getting slower all the time.

Behind them, vicious fighting was ripping through the great quad's cloisters as the last of the Blood Pact philia made their stand.

The Honorarium was huge, a massive, gloomy dome of cold, echoing air and silence. Lights illuminated displays at floor level around the vast rim of the building. The skirts of the huge temple housed individual chapels, dedicated to certain heroes or campaigns. In the centre of the floor space was the giant basalt crypt housing Warmaster Slaydo's remains.

Halfway across the immense open floor space of the Honorarium, Mabbon's legs gave out, and he fell. Gaunt turned back to scoop him up.

Jaume, Maggs and Kolding had been hiding behind the front rank of pews. They ran out to help Gaunt.

'We need to get him into cover,' Gaunt said.

'He's bleeding pretty badly,' Kolding said, opening his kit.

'Pack the wound. Pack the wound, then!' Maggs urged.

'Let's carry him somewhere quiet and out of the way,' Gaunt said. 'Come on. These side chapels look good to me.'

'Your chapel is just over there,' said Jaume, pointing.

'My what?'

'Your chapel,' Jaume repeated.

'What the hell are you talking about?' Gaunt snapped. 'What chapel?'

'For Throne's sake,' Jaume replied. 'It's why I was commissioned! Didn't you even read the letter? I was commissioned to make your portrait for the dedicated chapel here!'

'I don't believe Ibram Gaunt is going to be commemorated anywhere in Imperial circles after this,' said Handro Rime.

He walked towards the group across the broad, sunlit floor space. Snowflakes were tapping against the skylights far above their heads. Rime had his weapon aimed at them, a laspistol.

'A heretical monster and his enablers. You have fallen a long way from the greatness you once achieved here, Gaunt.'

Gaunt stood up, and faced Rime.

'And you're the worst kind of fanatic, Rime. You've got this so wrong. You should be thanking me.'

Rime grinned a smile that all of his Sirkles could copy.

'I don't think so, you despicable traitor.'

Gaunt shook his head. 'Whatever I say, you'll just reply "That's what a heretic would say", won't you?'

'Of course he will,' coughed Mabbon.

Gaunt turned. Jaume and Kolding were helping Mabbon to rise. The etogaur was clearly determined to get up and face his adversary.

'I don't even want to look at you,' sneered Rime. 'Archenemy scum.'

'It isn't just Gaur's Blood Pact that wants me dead,' Mabbon said to Gaunt, swaying against Kolding's support. 'The Anarch's forces want me silenced too. They're rather more subtle.'

He looked at Rime.

'You've changed your face a thousand times, but I still know you, Syko Magir.'

'This animal is talking nonsense!' Rime declared.

'Is he?' asked Maggs.

Rime raised his weapon to shoot the etogaur. The split second he did so, Gaunt realised it was snowing.

Indoors.

The blood-scream knocked them all flat, and blew out the huge skylights of the Honorarium. Howling, the witch came for them, surrounded by a coruscating ball of warp-lightning. She was demented and raving. She was screaming vengeance for the death of her beloved brother. She came at them across the floor of the Honorarium like a typhoon, driving an arctic blizzard before her. Dry lightning tore the air.

All Wes Maggs saw was the old dam who had haunted his mind since Hinzerhaus. All Wes Maggs wanted was to be free of her phantom torment.

He opened fire, screaming, on full auto, and discharged the lasrifle's entire energy reservoir.

His shots exploded the witch's cocoon of warp-energy, and shredded her. She took nearly two hundred hits, and by the time her body struck the paving stones, it was pulped beyond any semblance of articulacy. The last few shots lifted her veil for a second as she fell back.

Maggs saw her face, a face he would never forget.

His weapon misfired, and began to chime repeatedly on *charge out*.

He killed the alert, and lowered the gun.

'Feth me,' he stammered. 'Did I do that?'

Gaunt slapped Maggs on the back. 'Yes, you did. Makes me glad I didn't kill you.'

Maggs smiled a half-surprised smile.

'Wake up, trooper, and help us carry the prisoner to cover,' said Gaunt. Beyond the walls of the Honorarium, they could hear sirens wailing and gunships thundering in.

'Oh, shit,' said Kolding.

Gaunt turned.

Rime was back on his feet. He had a gash across his scalp, and what lay beneath looked more like augmetic artifice than flesh and blood. His face was half hanging off.

He was aiming his pistol at them.

'You're not going anywhere,' he announced.

Gaunt heard footsteps running out across the echo-space of the vast temple. Troops were deploying into position around the confrontation, weapons trained.

He realised they were his.

'Glad you could join us, Major Rawne,' Gaunt said, his eyes never leaving Rime's.

'Apologies, sir. Got a little waylaid.'

'Who's with you?' Gaunt called.

'Varl, Meryn, Daur, Banda, Leyr and Cant, sir.'

'All aimed at this lunatic as opposed to me?'

'Oh, yes, sir.'

'Even Cant?'

'Locked and blocked, sir,' Cant called out.

'See?' said Rawne, 'Sometimes even he can.'

'Well,' Gaunt said to Rime. 'This is a proper stand-off, isn't it? Toss down your weapon.'

Rime smiled. 'Don't be ridiculous. Tell your people to surrender. This facility will be overwhelmed in another five minutes.'

'My people don't work like that, inquisitor, especially not when the man they're facing has been identified as an agent of the Anarch.'

'That's preposterous! The ravings of a heretic who'd do anything to save himself!'

Gaunt shook his head. 'Mabbon was certain. He identified you, *Syko Magir.*'

'The man is insane,' Rime scoffed. 'Put up your weapons. Come on, Gaunt. I know how straight-laced you are at heart.'

The bolt pistol was still in Gaunt's hand. There was one round left in its clip.

He raised it, and aimed directly at Rime.

'No,' he said, 'I have reason to believe that you are an agent of the Archenemy, and I demand that you drop your weapon, now.'

'Or what, Gaunt?' Rime grinned. 'You'll shoot me? I know you. I've studied your dossier. Without unequivocal proof, you'd never act against the Throne. *Ever.*'

Gaunt hesitated, and lowered his weapon.

Rime glanced over as Rawne stepped forward.

'We're done, thank you, trooper,' Rime said. 'Step back.'

'My boss doesn't trust you,' said Rawne.

'He's got no actual proof,' said Rime. 'And he won't act. I've read his dossier.'

'Yeah,' said Rawne, 'but you've never read *mine.*'

Rime brought his pistol up, firing, screaming.

Rawne took him down with two kill-shots to the chest.

TWENTY-NINE

Exit Wounds

'TAKE A SEAT, Ibram,' said Isiah Mercure. They were meeting in a room in Section, one of the wings that hadn't suffered smoke damage.

So, I'm Ibram now suddenly, am I?

'Full marks for this, sir,' Mercure said. He was busy at three things at once: a data-slate, a letter, and some reports. 'Seriously, man, good work. We're going to run with this. Edur tells me your regiment is prepared to lead the way with the operation? Is that right?'

'The Tanith First is happy to serve, sir,' Gaunt replied.

'Well, I can tell you,' said Mercure, flashing a quick grin as he finished and closed the data-slate report, 'that's good news. It's great to get good people on your side. You think you can handle it?'

'My regiment is mobilised, sir. We'll be heading towards Salvation's Reach within the week.'

'A lot depends on this, Ibram,' said Mercure, 'and I won't be there to hold your hand all the way.'

'I understand, sir,' said Gaunt. 'I have just one question. The Inquisition, what has it been told?'

'Just that the valiant Inquisitor Rime was lost in action during a Chaos uprising,' replied Mercure.

'I see. I'd rather not have the holy ordos on my back, on top of every-thing else.'

'Understood.'

'And I want Blenner and Criid released to my jurisdiction.'

'Agreed.'

'You can fix that?'

'You have friends in high places, Ibram,' Mercure mocked. 'And you have friends in very low places too. How's the etogaur?'

'Stable. Eager to help. He's–'

'What?' asked Mercure.

'A good man,' said Gaunt.

'I had a horrible feeling you were going to say that,' said Mercure. He stood, and walked to the side table. 'A drink? A toast?'

'Why not?' replied Gaunt.

Mercure poured two sacras and handed one of them to Gaunt.

'You do realise that you won't be coming back from this one alive, don't you?' Mercure asked.

'That's what they tell me every time I ship out,' Gaunt replied.

'Really? Damn,' said Mercure, and chinked glasses. 'Cheers anyway.'

'WE'RE SHIPPING OUT in a week,' said Ban Daur. 'I think you should come with us.'

'Oh, right, yeah. Why?' asked Elodie.

'Because I can't kiss you like this if you're light years away,' he replied.

'Like what?' she asked.

He showed her.

'Right,' she nodded, 'I'd better come with you then.'

THE VAST SPACE of the Honorarium was full of faint echoes and a sense of eternity. On their last day on Balhaut, the Tanith First marched into the temple for a special service of benediction. It was a warm, bright day, the snow long gone, and most of the damage done to the building during the final battle had been repaired. They wore their number one uniforms, and their marching was impeccable, even though they had been stagnating in turnaround for two years.

Once the service was done, and the platoons had filed out, Gaunt walked with Dorden around the rim of the great temple, pausing to look into the side chapels. The bandsmen of the ceremonial brigades were packing up. Drums were being muffled and rolled into their boxes. Buglers and horn blowers were cleaning their instruments, the chin straps of their caps still hooked up over their noses.

Gaunt hadn't realised how old Dorden had got. The walk was slow.

'There's something I need to tell you,' Dorden said.

'Yes?'

'It's not an easy thing, and you won't like it,' Dorden added.

'Let me show you this first,' Gaunt said.

He led the way into one of the side chapels.

'Oh, great Throne,' Dorden gasped.

'All the satellite chapels have been dedicated to the worlds lost in the first years of the crusade,' Gaunt said. They sat down together on one of the pews in the side chapel. 'This is the memorial chapel dedicated to Tanith. This is what Jaume wanted me for, to make a portrait of me to sit on display in here. Can you imagine?'

'I can't,' Dorden replied. He had tears in his eyes.

'I know. Look, I wanted you to see this, Tol. Of all people, you needed to know this place existed.'

'Thank the Throne you did,' Dorden replied.

They sat back, side by side, on the new, waxed pews, and gazed up at the hololithic projection of Tanith.

'It was a pretty world, wasn't it?' Dorden asked.

'It was,' Gaunt agreed. 'Oh, something else. It seems, I'm dead.'

'What?'

'According to the guides who work around here, I died during the Famous Victory. You can pay to visit my death venue.'

'That's funny,' Dorden chuckled.

'No one remembers anything properly,' said Gaunt. 'Everything gets twisted and forgotten.'

Dorden nodded. 'Except the things we care to remember ourselves.'

Gaunt sighed. 'When they told me about it, I wondered for a moment if I had died here. I wondered if I had died at the Gate and become a ghost, and had been a ghost for all the time I had been with the Tanith.'

'I can see how you might have arrived at that conclusion,' replied Dorden. 'Who am I to deny it?'

Gaunt smiled, and nodded.

'I need to tell you something,' Dorden said, turning to look at Gaunt.

'A bad something?' Gaunt asked.

'I said you won't like it.'

'All right,' said Gaunt.

Dorden sat back.

'I did the examination. I tested that old bastard.'

'Zweil?'

'Yes. I did all the tests.'

'Something's come back, hasn't it?' asked Gaunt.

Dorden nodded. 'Leukaemia. Blood cancer. It's all through him.'

'Oh, Throne. How long?'

'Zweil? That old bastard will live forever.'

'But–'

Dorden sighed. 'He doesn't like the blood tests, does he? Old Zweil doesn't like needles. I had to show him how to do it.'

'So?'

'When my back was turned, he switched the samples.'

'So… oh no. No. *No!*'

'Hush,' said Dorden.

'My eyes won't let me cry,' Gaunt said, looking at his old friend.

'It's probably best that way.'

'How long?'

'Six months, if I'm lucky. But I want to keep going. You know, and Ana knows. Don't tell anyone else. I want to fight to the end. I want to serve to the end.'

Gaunt nodded.

'And I'd like to rest here when I'm done,' said Dorden.

Gaunt looked up at the roof of the Tanith chapel. The dead had a knack of finding their way back to Balhaut.

'I'll make sure of it,' he said.

EPILOGUE

The Ninth Day

THE OLIGARCHY GATE, on the afternoon of the ninth day, at Slaydo's left hand. Ahead, the famous Gate, defended by the woe machines of Heritor Asphodel. Mud lakes. Freak weather. The chemical deluge triggered by the orbital bombardment and the Heritor's toxins. Molten pitch in the air like torrential rain.

Gaunt kept his head down as the shells rained in.

Wire barbs skinned the air. The *thuk* of impacts, so many impacts. Clouds of pink mist to his left and right as men were hit. Ahead, below the Gate, the machines whirring again.

They were dug in opposite a small gatehouse with distinctive finials shaped like aquilas. The bombardment was so severe that Gaunt doubted the building would be standing in another day, or even another hour. It would be erased from the world and from his memory.

His sergeant, beloved Tanhause, yelled out over the onslaught. *Formation moving up!*

Gaunt looked back. PDF units were advancing to the front, scurrying, heads down. He had to admire their resolution. Often, they had little more than bolt-action rifles and bayonets, but still they threw themselves into the front line.

'How are we doing?' the young PDF officer yelled over the roar of the bombardment as he ducked into cover.

315

'Pretty decently,' Gaunt yelled back. 'If we can rally here and press on, we may have a good day yet!'

He looked up. The Tower of the Plutocrat was the most massive structure he'd ever seen. Nothing in the universe could topple it.

'Ah, who knows what we can do,' the young PDF officer returned. 'We might even bring that terrible big bastard down!'

'I like the sound of that,' Gaunt grinned. He held out his hand.

'I'm Gaunt,' he said.

The young PDFer grasped Gaunt's hand and shook it.

'Jaume.'

Gaunt smiled.

'Good to know you,' he said. 'Let's finish this.'

ABOUT THE AUTHOR

Dan Abnett is a novelist and award-winning comic book writer. He has written numerous novels for the Black Library, including the acclaimed Gaunt's Ghosts series and the Eisenhorn and Ravenor trilogies, and, with Mike Lee, the Darkblade cycle. His Black Library novel *Horus Rising* and his Torchwood novel *Border Princes* (for the BBC) were both bestsellers. His Black Library novels have sold over one million copies worldwide. He lives and works in Maidstone, Kent.

Dan's website can be found at *www.DanAbnett.com*

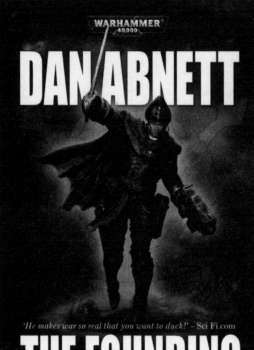

WARHAMMER 40,000

DAN ABNETT

'He makes war so real that you want to duck!' – Sci Fi.com

THE FOUNDING

A GAUNT'S GHOSTS OMNIBUS

ISBN 978-1-84416-369-4

Includes
the novels
First & Only,
Ghostmaker and
Necropolis

Includes
the novels
Honour Guard,
The Guns of Tanith,
Straight Silver
and *Sabbat Martyr*

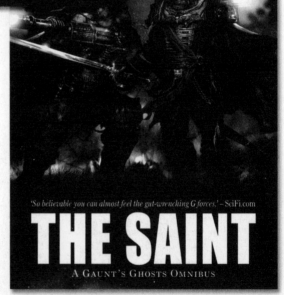

RHAMMER 40,000

ABNETT

'So believable you can almost feel the gut-wrenching G forces.' – SciFi.com

THE SAINT

A GAUNT'S GHOSTS OMNIBUS

ISBN 978-1-84416-479-0

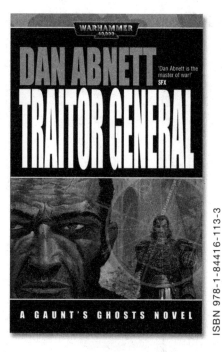

ISBN 978-1-84416-113-3

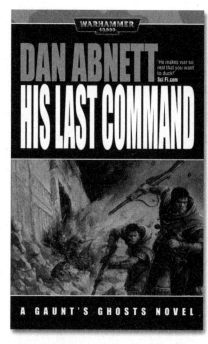

ISBN 978-1-84416-239-0

Buy the whole series or read free extracts at
www.blacklibrary.com

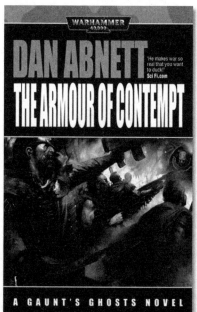

ISBN 978-1-84416-402-8

UK ISBN 978-1-84416-662-6 US ISBN 978-1-84416-583-4